RUMOR HAS IT

CATERINA CAMPBELL

Rumor Has It
Caterina Campbell

ISBN: 978-1-7365301-0-8 (print copy)

Publisher: Hope Chest Press, LLC

http://caterinacampbell.com

Collaborators:

Developmental, copy and line edit – Angela Houle
Proofreader – Rebecca Kimmell
Cover Designer – Sarah Kil Creative studio/www.sarahkilcreativestudio.com
Formatting – Shanna Swenson
Beta Readers: Grahame Claire, Miranda Grant, Shanna Swenson, Tiana Campbell, Kayla Zaldivar, and Sara Firth

For my mom, Lee, who fostered my love of books and writing.

and

For my husband, Ron, and my children, Tiana, Cameron, Chaney, and Brielle, who never wavered in their support of my dreams.

CHAPTER ONE

The contents of my mom's purse, tossed from her Jeep Cherokee's window, are strewn all over the beach parking lot like the tail-end of a trailer park yard sale. And not a nice trailer park like the one my grandma lived in before she moved to a "home," but the kind that has toilet bowls for flower pots and crack pipes for wind chimes.

Joe, the perpetrator of the toss and dash and the longest-running relationship my mom has had since my absentee father left eleven years ago, is long gone in said Jeep Cherokee. My mom is probably still running after him. It'll take a second for her to figure out the Jeep can burn a lot more ground than her scrawny legs. Not inclined to chase after anyone, I'm left wondering why my mom had a Downy ball in her purse. Bristol, my twin sister, older than me by fifteen minutes, is off to find someone who will help us get our cooler off the beach since the man with the muscles split in a blaze of douchery.

I look down at the smorgasbord of shit that only Teresa Sloan would pack in a purse and hesitate over a tampon, wondering if I shouldn't do her a favor and throw it all away. I'm burnt red, my bathing suit is crawling up my ass, my hair, holding a sandcastle's worth of sand, has dried into a nice crusty, blonde nest, and I'm supposed to care about a tampon with road rash? After a few curse words, none of which are a true representation of my vast four-letter vocabulary, I pull my bikini bottoms out of my ass one more time before picking through the lot sale. I'm God-given, not man-made, and what God gave me is more expansive than a bean pole. I need a damn suit that fits my curves, one I don't have to search for every time I bend over.

With the stuff I can salvage back in my mom's purse and the stuff I can't tossed, I head back to the sand where my unseasoned feet can have some relief. The sand has cooled, the early May evening making for a much easier walk back to our stuff after an unseasonably hot day. I cram as much of our stuff as I can into the cooler knowing the car barely has room even for that and slip into my sandy coverup. Packed to the gills, the cooler is too heavy, and dragging it across sand is damn near impossible for my five-foot-four-inch frame now ten pounds heavier than it used to be. College has made my average body soft, but once I've unpacked for summer and recouped the sleep I lost on parties, finals, and Bristol's unexpected meeting with the Dean of Students, I'll be able to surf and run off the weight gain.

"Brenna! I told you I was getting someone for that." Bristol's voice, extra sugary, sneaks up behind me.

Spinning around, I look up with a sweat trail running from forehead to cheek like a socially awkward geek at a pep rally to find Bristol with a tattooed Adonis straight out of *Magic Mike's* hunky gene pool. I could lose a lot of time staring at his well-defined muscles, eight of which are abs. I look like something that slept under a bridge in my grandma's pajamas and he, wearing only a pair of shorts and a scowl, looks like he stepped right out of *Jock* magazine.

"God, she never listens." Even Bristol's shitty version of an introduction sounds flirtatious.

I wonder briefly if his irritable, tight-lipped facial expressions are a product of Bristol's incessant talking or just his version of resting bitch face. Honestly, as good looking as he is, even the scowl is attractive. Rather than waste his time, I drop the handle while Bristol drivels on about how no one stuck around to help us. If by anyone, she means Joe and his two worthless friends, one of which kept hitting on Bristol because he heard college had improved her blow job skills, then we're better off.

"Thank you." I'm not nearly as honeyed as Bristol, but I'm pleasant.

He ignores us both and hefts the cooler up to his abdomen where he shifts it until he can get a better handle on it. I let him. I don't even try and pretend I'm a headstrong, independent, almost-twenty-one-year-old female. Right now, I'm as weak as I look and have no inclination toward changing that perception. He's not here to find a date, though that may have slipped past Bristol, who continues to push her small Bs at him like she's got a crick in her back. If we're ever going to live down our reputation, she's going to have to start putting those things away.

Like Bigfoot on a mission, I scoop up the rest of our day into my arms and walk behind Bristol, who is empty-handed and mercilessly chatting to Adonis. We may be identical twins, but our looks, right down to the red splotchy birthmark on our scalps, is where the similarities end.

Bristol has always been the more flamboyant one. While I'm not opposed to standing out, I typically stand out in a way that embarrasses us both. She's a lot more in tune with her looks and can make even the worst outfit look trendy. Like today, for instance. We both started out looking hot enough to land a Magic Mike of our own, but at the end of this sweltering day, the only one taking a second look at me is Miss Gladys, the Rec Center's resident swim instructor since 1952.

I reach the parking lot as the hot guy is putting our cooler into the trunk of the Ford Mustang we nicknamed the Silver Stallion the second we bought it out of an impound auction. The decade-old horse is rusted around the wheel wells and shimmies like an epileptic seizure once it hits sixty, but it's reliable and doesn't ask questions or gossip. I value that kind of loyalty. It's a rare commodity in small-town Milagro Beach, where our reputation was built off a lot of loose lips and a few honest indiscretions.

I shove the stuff in my arms around the cooler, using up what's left of the trunk space as well as my four-letter vocabulary, because it's not exactly an easy feat. It's a landfill in there, and listening to Bristol flirt her way into a one-night-stand is making me gag. If she worked this hard at school, she wouldn't be in danger of losing her scholarship.

"Fuck me! Why can't you live out of a dresser and a medicine cabinet like the rest of us? And is this *my* shirt? I've been looking for this for a month." Lunatic-pissed, I spin around and hold up the dehydrated white top that's shriveled into a small ball of cotton and barely refrain from nailing her in the face with it. She already looks horrified by my language, which isn't any worse than hers. It's the company I'm using it in that bothers her. She usually waits until she has the date before she drops the F-bomb, just in case he's religious or a mama's boy. I let it go for now, erring on the side of diplomacy for the sake of our Adonis.

The dark-haired, chiseled hot guy, tattooed from wrists to collarbone, is looking back and forth at us, probably just now figuring out we're twins. I don't know where my eyes should land, but I know where they want to. He has abs that should come with a warning, like distractions on the roadway, and his chest, though covered in some sort of baseball crest tattoo, is so defined and sculpted nothing on it moves unless commanded by him to do so. When I finally make it to his face, it too is worthy of more than one look, but I can't afford more than one if I'm ever going to figure out the logistics of getting the car packed.

With our college belongings packed in suitcases and two U-Haul boxes taking up the back seat, there is absolutely no room in the

Silver Stallion for Mom too, assuming she ever figures out she can't outrun a Jeep and comes back to find us. Had we unpacked before Mom's family barbecue beach-play fun-day, we'd have room for the hot guy too, but that would have required forethought.

Instead of wishing Bristol had found some compost-making survivalist to help us rather than People's future Sexiest Man Alive, I continue to ignore him and spin back around to face the trunk, heart beating faster than it should for a girl just trying to make room for her spiraling mother.

"So, you girls good then?" His voice is a buttery, deep tone that sounds less irritated than I expected it to.

Focus, Brenna.

"We're good. Thank you for your help," I offer, with my face in the trunk. I move a bottle of moisturizer and toss it toward the back seat with a box of tampons, a cereal bar, and two hair clips.

"It's no problem," he replies, assisting me with a loose Frisbee before stepping back to give me more room.

I open the passenger side door and flip the seat forward, checking to see if I can find a way to fit me back there. There's no way unless I want to leave a suitcase behind. I pop my head back out and look over the top of the car. "Where's Mom?"

Bristol, pulling her hair back into a ponytail, throws her hands up once it's confined. "I don't know. Probably still running after Joe. Wait. We're talking about Mom. She's somewhere holding her knees and gasping for air while she checks her eHarmony account in case Joe doesn't take her back."

Despite my irritation, I smile, because it's scary accurate. "You lost Mom, didn't you?"

"I didn't *lose*-lose her. She's around here somewhere." She half-heartedly scans the parking lot, biting on her bottom lip, but otherwise looks unconcerned. Bristol has no tolerance for my mom's breakups, makeups, or move-ons.

As if she knew we were looking for her, Mom, in between heavy tears and run-on sentences about why men are the Devil, shows up carrying her flip-flops.

"Is it too much to ask your boyfriend to keep his eyeballs in his head and his hands to himself when he's taking selfies with some random chick in a thong?" "Random chick" is accompanied by strong finger quotes beside her cheeks. She sniffs, "Am I being unreasonable?"

Bristol looks at me, our matching green eyes locking, her face a tad more dramatized than mine, and then she speaks.

"Crazy unreasonable." Each word is clearly enunciated and dripping in sarcasm. "What wouldn't be unreasonable is asking him not to take the fucking selfies in the first place. Jesus Christ!"

Hot Guy sees his opportunity to bail and takes it, leaving me to fend for myself and Bristol to regret not paying more attention to his exit strategy.

Forcing a smile, I thank him again, garnering a dismissive wave and a quickly uttered, "Good luck," before he's on the bike path, hopefully heading someplace where he won't witness any more of our crazy.

Back on track, I look between the two women ready to do battle over their differences. "Okay, let's calm down."

"NO!" My mom shouts, fat tears rolling down her cheeks. "You two have never been in love. So you don't know what it's like to lose it." Bristol's sunburn reddens, and the shouting begins.

"I know what it's like to lose a dad and multiple other men you tried to make my dad after two days! So, don't tell me I haven't loved and lost. I'm just not falling for every guy who winks, smiles or sticks his di—"

I cut her off, grabbing her wrist. "We're not doing this here." We have an audience on both sides of us, and we've had enough dirty laundry aired in public and at several contentious court hearings to last a lifetime. There is nothing this town doesn't know about us and I don't particularly want to add more, though Grundy Beach hasn't had a really good Sloan Show since my dad failed to observe the reservation system at the Picnic Pavilion and was arrested for squatting at some kid's birthday party.

"Calm down," I repeat, rejecting the pavilion memory like every other pockmark in my life left by my family's indiscretions.

"You calm down!" she yells at me, eyes harsh. "You're just like her. The only difference is you're actually waiting for the right one to break your heart. And that's not meant as a compliment."

I grind my teeth, nostrils flared like bat caves. "I'm going to ignore you because we don't need more rumors," I say, glaring at her. "And it's not a freebie. I'm going to punch you in the face at home."

Bristol smirks. "I've seen you fight. I'm not scared."

My mom moves between us. "I've had enough for one day." She shifts her glassy gaze to Bristol, oblivious to my discomfort and the audience forming. "Do you think you could take me home, or is there not enough room for me and your judgmental attitude?"

I laugh at my mom's spontaneous dig, "There's never enough room for her attitude. They're both going to have to stay behind."

"Hell no!" Bristol snaps. "You're staying. I'll take her."

"Uh-uh," I shake my head vehemently. "Something bad always happens when you're in charge."

"I won't let her crack the headlights or dent the hood," she says, referring to my mom's trip to jail four years ago for taking a bat to her cheating boyfriend's car. That night, and subsequent others, landed us both with Uncle Rodney for a week while the courts decided whether Mom was fit to care for us. Turns out, fits of passion aren't necessarily dealbreakers for parenting. I question that ruling from time to time, usually during moments like these or like when my mom's request to chaperone school dances was denied— indefinitely, by a unanimous decision at a school board meeting. The Sloans don't get a simple shake of the head and a softly spoken "no." We get board meetings and court proceedings.

I glare, measuring Bristol for sincerity.

She smiles. "I got this. I promise."

I give in. "I need panties, and then you can go."

She nods and relays the plans to my mom while I dig through a suitcase and grab the first thong I can find. I slip out of my bikini bottoms, still wet from swimming and being trapped between my thighs, and shimmy into the thong without showing anything more than upper thigh and the bottom curve of my butt cheek.

I snap the passenger seat back into place, clear out the bag of fast-food trash from our trip home, grab my phone from the front seat, and admonish Bristol, "Home. Dab at a few tears. Put her in the shower. Come get me. Can you do that?"

"Dude, I've got this."

CHAPTER TWO

W ith a motorcycle on my left and a Prius on my right, I
sit on the curb, legs out in front of me in an empty
space with freshly painted white lines over chip-sealed
pavement. The lot hasn't had visible lines since my dad walked one
as a sobriety test. I don't know how true the rumor is about his face-
plant, but if it's anything like the rest, it's an embellished half-truth.

I bitch about the rumors spread about us all the time, sometimes
to the point that Bristol has to point out that without them we never
would have seen the inside of Tucker Blossom's house. She also
wouldn't have been counseled on the teen pregnancy crisis or interviewed by countless parents before being allowed to spend the night.
I'm hoping that today's incident with Joe isn't going to be added to
the long list of Sloan misdeeds.

"Hey, is this yours?"

Startled out of my boredom and the mind-fuck known as
memory lane, I look up and the tattooed hot guy from earlier is
holding out a piece of silver jewelry. I look around for takers but see
only an oblivious older man walking a dog and two dudes standing
around a Hibachi singing Post Malone.

I stand up, giving him the full frontal of my old lady beach sheath and hopelessly lost expression. Why he didn't run as far from us as possible baffles me.

"Can I see it?" It's possibly an item from my mom's exploded purse. She wears a charmed anklet and a toe ring from nineteen eighty-three.

"Yeah," he says rather flatly. His abs tighten, drawing my eyes downward to those speed bumps and a tiny trail of dark hair just beneath his belly button.

As much as I'd like to keep objectifying him, I return my gaze to his face and the nice bone structure, strong and prominent, with a little bit of stubble along his jawline. Blue eyes flicker over me but probably with a whole other narrative than the one going on in my head. Damn, the man is beautiful, the kind of beautiful you stare at until he clears his throat to remind you he is breathing and I'm supposed to be looking at jewelry.

"Uh," I blink several times trying to fix the universe, "yeah, this is my mom's." I touch the small turtle charm. "Thank you," I offer as I take it from him. I look it over, not that I need to, but I need time to think. It's not every day I'm in the presence of a guy hot enough to be a model. "You're the guy from earlier, right? You carried our cooler. I'm Brenna, by the way." I offer a wide smile and a hand, neither of which he reciprocates.

"I know who you are." His curbside manner could use some work, though his deep, smooth tone is on point.

My eyebrows shoot toward my hairline. "Please don't believe everything you read on bathroom walls." I grin, testing to see if I can pull him out of dick mode.

Coughing an exhale to disguise what I suspect is a well-hidden sense of humor, he adjusts his expression from indifferent to curious. "Is that usually a problem?"

I shift my weight, which, in front of this god, feels like a lot more tonnage than it did when I stood up. "It's been known to happen," I admit. "Tends to make for awkward dates."

His face softens considerably. "I only know you from your sister."

I can't think of one person outside of my mom and Uncle Rodney who can tell us apart without hearing us talk. "How can you be sure which one I am?"

He shifts, his posture less tense. "There are differences. Maybe not at first sight, but there are some."

What differences could there be that a guy I've known for point-five seconds can see that people who've known us our entire twenty years can't? Just as I'm about to ask, it dawns on me. When you compare the Brenna and Bristol he met today, of course we're distinguishable.

If I didn't have on the millennial equivalent of a muumuu, he'd be able to see Bristol and I have identical assets, we just use them differently.

"Was it the muumuu or the hair that gave me away?"

His humor surfaces and he stumbles over a laugh. "It was your vocabulary, actually."

I smile, maybe even blush a little, though it would be hard to tell through the sunburn dominating my winter white. "I've been told I have a way with words."

He pulls the T-shirt in his hand over his head and shoves his hands through the sleeves, adjusting the way it sits before he replies, "That you do." He brushes a palm over the top of his hair, smoothing down the brown spikes left from pushing his head through a small hole. According to his lip-twitch, I'm growing on him.

I should probably call good good enough and start walking before he hates me again. Bristol isn't returning, and my dead phone ensures I can't call Tori or Tracy, and Toolbag Carl doesn't get home until tomorrow. They're my staples when Bristol forgets she has a sister. "Well, hey, thanks for the saves today." I dangle the anklet in front of me, turtle swinging, and I point at it. "Save number two."

Instead of making fun of my nerves, he nods. "All in a day's work."

I smile, sigh, and edge past him, turning back for one last look.

THE BLOCKS BETWEEN GRUNDY BEACH AND THE FAR END OF MILAGRO Beach's mile-long boardwalk fronting Ocean Avenue are a mixture of familiarity and unfocused oblivion as I begin my trek north. On my left: sand right up to the boardwalk with palm trees breaking up the flat, brown terrain. On my right: Ocean Avenue and the businesses that keep Milagro Beach's tourists supplied. Shops like Griffin's Collectibles and the touristy shop, Mutton's Tees. Beyond that and closer to the northern end of the street are Stricker Bait, your one-stop fishing supply, and Beachwiches Sandwich Shop. Between all of that are The Seam, a sports bar my Uncle Rodney owns, a bookstore, and a small café where the locals like to sip coffee on Sunday mornings.

The roar of a motorcycle approaches from behind me, sending ripples of its rumble through my chest. *Sons of Anarchy* crosses my mind, but I'm pretty sure I'm not the motorcycle club type. I've got no tattoos, my boobs—still perky because I haven't used my womb as a hostel yet—are downright unimpressive, and my criminal record is nonexistent.

As the motorcycle rolls up beside me, I keep my eyes straight ahead and count the palm trees between me and the next intersection.

"Did your car break down?" Looking at me from behind mirrored aviators is my beach Adonis, though he doesn't know he's mine yet.

"No. Bristol didn't come back, and I'm too shy to put out."

"Did you just say, 'put out'?"

I nod, trying not to laugh, but his horrified expression doesn't make it easy. "Cash, grass, or ass, right?"

"Doesn't Uber take credit?" It's hard to tell if he's being serious or playing along. I laugh anyway.

"I have ass, a McDonald's gift card, and two bucks." Of those, I really only have ass on me. I left everything but my dead phone in the Silver Stallion.

He laughs, shaking his head like he doesn't know how to take me. "I can give you a ride."

I stop abruptly and face him as he brings the bike to a stop with his feet. He peers at me expecting an answer. "I was kidding about putting out."

"Wasn't even on my radar." He offers a lopsided grin that under any other circumstances would probably have me dropping my panties, but I'm thinking it's best not to do that on the busiest thoroughfare in Milagro Beach. "No offense, but I can get my own ass without having to pick it up off the street."

"Yeah, I can see how that might not be a problem for you."

He sets his sunglasses on the top of his head and eyes me as I cringe through the aftermath of my unfiltered honesty.

I bite the inside of my cheek. "I'm in a dress."

"Tuck it between your legs."

"I take it you've done this before?"

"Not me personally, but yeah, it's come up a time or two for others."

"Did they survive?"

"I didn't kill them, if that's what you're asking."

"Wasn't even on my radar."

He unstraps a helmet from the seat behind him, and holds it out to me. "Yes or no?" He revs the bike and it roars, rumbling everything in the vicinity.

In my family, I'm the sensible one. Sensible, meaning if the stove is hot, I leave it alone. In my family of knee-jerk reactions and blatant disregard, it's not hard to be more responsible. I know my options, and I choose between them. This time, I don't want to be sensible. I want to throw caution to the wind and take the ride with the hottest potential serial killer the central California coast has ever seen. Bristol would. My mom would. So I go with my heart instead of my head, top my head with the helmet, climb on the bike, and clutch him like we're flying down the highway at speeds greater than eighty. Just in case he is a serial killer, it's best for him not to know where I sleep, so I give him directions to The Seam.

He smells of heat and cologne, and not the kind you buy at Walmart, but the good kind that comes from Nordstrom's. I sniff his T-shirt right where his collar touches his neck and decide right then and there that if he is a serial killer, there are worse ways to go.

Two-and-a-half minutes later we're coasting into a parallel spot in front of The Seam. At this time of day Ocean Avenue isn't congested and parking is a breeze, which means my time wrapped around him comes to a close much too soon for a girl just discovering her vagina has more than one emotion.

The breath I take is flavored with the remnants of kettle corn from a street vendor nearby, and the sigh I release is tinged with something akin to remorse. I'll most likely never get to do this again. I'm either going to be a single cat lady or married to an asshole who cheats on me. My upbringing doesn't allow for much else, though I'd hoped for one really good romantic tale to tell before I'm settled in with an audience of orange bobtailed cats.

I climb off the bike with embarrassing difficulty and face him, nerves buzzing as I hand him back his helmet. "Thank you." My grin defies my nerves. "I would offer you my McDonald's card, but with your body, it's unlikely you'll use it." His eyebrows settle high, and his lips sample a curvature but fall short of an actual smile.

"I was kind of hoping you'd change your mind and put out."

"Will you settle for a beer? You're sure to get head that way."

He laughs, a reaction I should probably bask in as I don't think it happens often. "I wouldn't be a guy if I refused that."

CHAPTER THREE

My Uncle Rodney, who is actually my mom's uncle and the only father figure in my life, greets me with a half-hearted wave while he sets a mug in front of Mr. Davidson, a Seam regular. I would usually take a seat in one of the empty booths with the fruit leather-red vinyl, but tonight, I hit the bar.

"Hi, Uncle Rodney." I sound a bit more solemn than intended, but before I can correct it, his light green eyes collide with the beach Adonis beside me and I'm forced to switch gears.

Uncle Rodney's face lights up like it does when he's watching baseball. He's a smiley guy anyway, but he seems downright giddy looking across the bar at us. I can't tell if he's checking him out because he thinks he's my date or if he's flirting. It's a bit odd for a guy who didn't bat an eyelash at Diane Sawyer when she popped in two years ago. "Are you going to introduce me to your friend, or should I ask him for his I.D.?"

"Oh, shit, sorry," I offer, thinking maybe he was just sizing him up instead of flirting. Everyone looks young to Uncle Rodney, so he cards everybody unless they look like him, which is to say mostly gray with smile wrinkles around the mouth, a beer gut he calls a small paunch, and an occasional ear hair he announces like it's bingo. "This is, uh…" I can't finish my sentence because I don't have the info.

"Vance." Hot Guy from the beach saves me from looking like a careless idiot and reaches across the bar to shake Uncle Rodney's hand.

Upon hearing his name for the first time, I feel like I need to say it out loud, let it roll off my tongue once. "Vance, meet my Uncle Rodney."

Uncle Rodney smiles and shakes his hand vigorously. I worry he's going to kiss him, but he pulls his hand back and spreads his arms wide. "Welcome to The Seam," he says proudly, lips locked in a prideful perma-grin.

Vance smiles, eyes alight with the same genuine emotion. "Great place you have here." He looks around, seeming to admire the décor as much, if not more so, than Uncle Rodney who eats, breathes, and shits Renegades baseball. "Awesome name, too."

"Yeah," Uncle Rodney says all breathy. "It's all about the balls in sports," he laughs. "I breathe that red seam."

It takes a few good seconds to register what they're talking about, and even then, I'm not sure we're not talking about testicles. "Wait! What?" I'm totally confused and stare between the two of them for a quick explanation. "The Seam's name is about a baseball?"

"Oh, for the love of Pete, Brenna. What did you think 'The Seam' meant?"

"Uh, a seam, but not like a seam on a baseball."

"What can I get you?" Uncle Rodney, still shaking his head, looks proud to ask, like he's offering him something of value.

"Something on tap would be great." Vance takes a seat on the barstool in front of him and looks at me to follow suit, but I'm too anxious to sit, so I remain standing beside him, arms propped on the bar.

It takes Uncle Rodney less than two seconds to get Vance his beer and run off again to assist a couple at a table.

Without Uncle Rodney to keep his interest, Vance sips his beer while looking around the bar. The baseball theme throughout is comprehensive and extends back to when the San Jose Renegades were known as the Sacramento Renegades. I don't know when they switched, but it was before I was born.

I point to the mirror behind the bar with "The Seam" etched in red lettering across the middle of its glass. "That makes so much more sense now."

"I bet. Probably just looked like a sign before tonight." He sips and looks at me. "I take it you're not a fan?"

"I'm a fan of Uncle Rodney, which makes me a fan of the SJRs."

"The SJRs?"

"San Jose Renegades."

A half-smile forms before he sips, and I ponder his discretionary silence.

"They don't call them that, do they?"

"No."

"Huh, maybe they should. It's a lot shorter."

"Do you call the Dodgers the LADs or the Giants the SFGs?"

I laugh and put my finger up to my lips. "Shh, those names are banned in here."

The door to the bar flies open, and Bristol's voice precedes her. "Uncle Rodney, I'm going to need those mob contacts of yours." She barrels through the door a second after her voice, and proceeds, arms swaying at her sides, to the bar.

She goes straight for the bat beneath the bar where Uncle Rodney has always kept it and stands upright, bat in hand, eyes full of mad determination that changes on a dime when she notices me. "Oh, hey, what are you doing here?" She should be surprised seeing as she was supposed to pick me up at the beach. But her eyes dart back and forth between me and Vance before settling on him while she processes. "Hey! You're that guy from the beach."

"And you're putting that back where you got it from." Uncle Rodney yanks the bat from Bristol's grasp while she's happily distracted by Vance. "What the hell do you need it for anyway?" Bat in hand, he's behind the bar staring at Bristol and waiting on her explanation, though he hasn't yet denied mob affiliation.

I stare at her too, waiting on details she's too distracted by Vance to give. "What happened between the time you left me stranded at the beach and now?"

Tearing her eyes away from Vance to look at me, she replies. "Mom is staying with him."

I don't know if I should be celebrating another day when the revolving door of men isn't circulating, or shaking my mom for settling for a man she should have sent back through it. After all these years she's still looking for love in all the wrong people, but at least unlike Bristol, she still believes in it.

"That doesn't explain the bat."

"I'm going to bust her knees. Maybe if she can't get on them, she'll stop begging shitty men to stay." Bristol, always dramatic, doesn't see men in any capacity other than monetary and sexual convenience, so she doesn't understand why mom can't let go, or for that matter, continues trying.

"And Uncle Rodney's mob contacts?"

"I don't have mob contacts." It's a denial delivered with a shake of his head and a mirthful grin.

Bristol pointedly looks at him. "You said you had mob contacts."

His eyebrows sink, pinching in real close. "Which should have been a deterrent, not a resource."

The three of us look at him, each expecting a different explanation from him. Uncle Rodney growls, wipes down the counter in front of him and, losing his battle, smiles. "I told her that when she was thirteen to keep her from running away with Ol' What's-His-Name, Barry's kid."

Bristol looks horrified. "Edward Ball?"

18

Uncle Rodney snaps his fingers. "That's it! Shitty kid, if I recall. Had that homemade tattoo on his bicep."

"At thirteen?" Vance pipes in, looking equal parts horrified and curious.

"He was fifteen," Bristol adds, like that makes it better. "Why didn't you just tell me no like a normal parent?"

Uncle Rodney shrugs. "You didn't run away with him, did you?"

She looks up, huffs, and replies, "No. But that doesn't excuse lying to me."

He pats her hand. "It was an embellishment. I do know a guy from New York."

"Is he in the mob?" I ask.

He shrugs again, pinching his lips. "Probably."

It's my turn to shake my head and get this conversation back on track. "Why would you need mob contacts anyhow? Sounds like you were gonna do the dirty work."

"For Joe!" Bristol barks. "I can't make people disappear. Believe me, if I could, it wouldn't be an underutilized skill."

"Put that out of your head right now, doll," Uncle Rodney says, tapping her on the shoulder with one hand while he hangs onto the bat with the other. "Your mother will see the light eventually."

"Yeah, you know mom lives for her happy endings." I add, "And you'd never survive a prison gang bang."

She rolls her eyes and looks at Vance with a smugly sweet smile. "Betcha wish now you'd left her at the beach."

"Nope. No regrets." Expressionless, he sips from his beer.

I sit up a little straighter, feeling for the first time like I outshine Bristol in a room. A quick look in the mirror would fix that delusion, but for now, my improved posture at least eliminates a stomach roll.

Bristol's face, taut with irritation, loosens a fraction as Uncle Rodney touches her hand with the bat. "How about you focus all that energy on something useful like, say, finding a good man of your own."

She scoffs loudly. "They're unicorns, Uncle Rodney." She smiles, batting eyelashes that still look impeccably made-up. "And you'd be the last one if they weren't." She kisses his cheek and I wait for her to snatch the bat, but instead she turns her attention to Vance, who is looking at each one of us like we're glue sniffers. "Although, I wouldn't mind seeing how you measure up."

Uncle Rodney saves Vance from a salivating Bristol. "What did I tell you about pestering my guests?"

"It's only pestering, Uncle Rodney, if they object."

"He wouldn't be here if you hadn't left me at the beach. He objects," I snap too harshly, and Bristol, usually oblivious, catches my tone, and using her wide eyes to convey I'm out of line, snaps right back.

"Oh, excuse me for taking too long while the queen of gullibility made excuses for her ass-grabbing boyfriend. Look at him." She throws her chin up in Vance's direction. "I think you got the better end of the deal."

"I don't think that's the question here." Uncle Rodney tosses a wink to Vance, and I wonder if Uncle Rodney treats all his customers to wide, cheesy grins and winks. "Look," he says, directing his words to Bristol, "you're not getting the bat, so take a seat."

"Yeah, no. Time to get creative. That bastard isn't staying the night." With renewed focus and Vance off her radar, Bristol heads toward the entrance. "I have an idea. Wish me luck." She waves over her head and leaves the way she came in.

Uncle Rodney sighs heavily. "That girl is going to do some major damage someday." He puts the bat back under the bar, shaking his head as he does so. "Lord, I hope I'm dead when that happens." He swipes his cloth beside Vance's beer and looks up at him. "Another beer?" He points at the beer Vance is currently nursing his way through. If Uncle Rodney was in love with him earlier, I doubt he is now. According to Uncle Rodney, beer shouldn't be left long enough to sweat, and Vance's beer has soaked the napkin beneath it.

"Uh, no, thanks. I should probably get going." He stands as he tosses a twenty-dollar bill on the bar.

I grab the twenty and hold it out to him, but he just tightens his gaze on me and ignores the gesture. "My treat," I say, waving the bill in front of him.

"And if it's not hers, it's mine," Uncle Rodney adds, and I shake the bill harder until Vance snatches it from me with a quick hand and a grimace.

"Can I give you a ride home?"

"It's only a few blocks. I'll be fine, but thank you."

"If it's only a few blocks, let me take you."

THE RIDE TO MY HOUSE TAKES THREE MINUTES, BUT IT'S ENOUGH TO feel how tight his abs are and to smell him again. How is this guy not taken? And if he is, why would she leave him alone? As much as I want to linger on the bike behind him, I climb off, set the helmet on the seat, adjust my old lady beach sheath, and cross my feet at the ankles, facing him.

Mr. Jones' dog, Goldie, has made herself at home beneath the tree in our front yard despite having one of her own next door. Between Mr. Jones, who has been our neighbor since I can remember, and his dog, we don't need a security system because one of them is always watching out for us. They must approve, because she hasn't moved toward Vance yet and Mr. Jones hasn't cracked his door.

Vance kills the bike, and in the silence, watches me, observing my nervous twitches with a keen eye. "Thanks for the beer."

"Thank you for the rides." I finger comb the tousled hair around my face and pick out a strand or two from my mouth. "And for bearing witness to my family dysfunction."

"I hardly noticed."

"Liar." I grin, trying one more time to get my fingers through my hair. "I better get going." I throw a thumb over my shoulder and gesture to my house. "I may be saving more than one person tonight."

He starts up the bike and adjusts the handlebars to pull away while I make my way through the opened gate. "Hey, uh, Brenna?" His voice draws me up short, and before the gate closes, I look over my shoulder at him.

"Um . . ." He looks utterly amused and close to laughter. "Uh . . ." He points at my backside and rubs his upper lip like he's making a finger mustache.

"What?" I look, craning my head to look at my backside.

"Um, you might want to fix your dress."

The proverbial light bulb flips on, and I am suddenly draped in its recognizable fiery glow. I smooth a hand down my backside and feel nothing but bare butt cheek. How is it fucking possible I can feel a single loose hair on my shoulder but not the salty breeze on my bared-to-the-world ass?

The deep breath I inhale tastes like exhaust as I lower the clinging fabric wrapped around my waist to the proper place. "I'm usually not this pathetic." Unconsciously, I smooth my dress again and groan under my breath.

"Pathetic isn't how I'd describe you."

"I'm afraid to ask," I say, neurotically smoothing the fabric down again.

"You shouldn't be."

I grin, laughing as I speak. "Stop looking at me like that."

"Like what?"

"That." I shake a finger at his face where he's mastered stoicism.

"Like I'm trying to figure you out? Because that's what I'm doing."

"There isn't much to me. What you see is what you get, and unfortunately for you, what you've seen tonight is the worst."

He tilts his head to the side, eyes pointed directly at mine, "At least you can say it's real. I prefer that."

"Real can be a mess." I point at my backside as an example, eyes wide for effect.

"Not from here."

My sunburn heats with his seeming acceptance of me. It's a rarity, and I wish for once that words were a tangible thing I could pull out and handle from time to time. Maybe feeling them in my palm or brushing them against my cheek would make them easier to believe.

CHAPTER FOUR

T he roar of Vance's motorcycle ebbs as I close the front door behind me. The house is dark and muggy, Mom having opted to leave the windows open instead of running the air conditioner. It's the one thing she has always scrimped on to save her tight budget. I flip the first light switch I come to, and the foyer light illuminates two pairs of flip-flops, my mom's road-rash purse (none the worse for wear, really, despite being tossed today), and a bag of Cheetos folded over and clipped with a clothespin.

"Hello?" I holler, flipping on the next light as I step into the extended darkness. It's the middle of May and I haven't been inside the house that raised me just as much as my mom did since spring break, and Mom has moved the furniture around so the sofa faces the two front windows and the television hangs on the wall between them. I like it, but I can be inattentive, which makes lighting a requirement until I get used to the new placement.

"We're in Mom's room." The strain in Bristol's voice draws a cringe, and though I know I'm already too late to make a difference, I hope it's at least something I can fix.

My mom is sitting on the floor, knees bent, head in her hands with her fingers threaded through her hair, which is much blonder than it was in March. I look at Bristol, who looks guiltier than ever with eyes betraying the tiniest bit of regret.

I don't have to ask; Mom volunteers it the second she hears my footsteps. "I don't get it," she says, looking down into her thighs. "I talked to him a little bit ago. He said he was coming home."

"I told you," Bristol says, sounding too harsh for Mom's fragile state, "he needs tonight to think. That's what he said."

"Think about what? I told him I'm not mad."

Bristol's eyes and nostrils flare, and she pinches her lips together in frustration, a look I've seen a thousand times where my mother is concerned. She calms, drawing on some inner *chi* she relies upon a lot. "He did grab a girl's ass. It would be okay if you were mad."

"I was. I'm not now. I know he loves me. And it's not like he cheated. He just had his hand somewhere he shouldn't."

"Mm hmm," Bristol mumbles condescendingly. "How 'bout you lay down. We'll unpack while you get some sleep. And maybe tomorrow things will be clearer . . . for the both of you."

Bristol actually sounds like she knows what the hell she's doing, and I marvel briefly because consoling my mom is usually my job.

AFTER TAKING QUICK SHOWERS AND SETTLING FOR OLD PAJAMAS THAT smell like twelve months of abandonment, Bristol and I are alone in the room we've shared since we were born. Standing in front of the soft yellow curtains we picked after we were too old for Hannah Montana, Bristol confesses her sin to me. "I pretended to be Mom on the phone when Joe called. I told him I didn't want to see him again. I told him he was a womanizing pig and I deserved better. Well, 'I' being Mom. I also told him to bring back my fucking Jeep. Well, Mom's Jeep."

My mouth drops and nothing comes out of it, shocking us both with the unusual silence.

"I know what you're thinking. She won't do it for herself, Brenna. I had to make the first move."

"No. No, you really didn't."

"If you had seen the way she was groveling and apologizing, you would have done it too."

I lock the door, a habit formed since Mom started bringing men home who didn't stay past daylight. It only took the one time – Mr. No Name with the UFO boxers mistaking our room for the bathroom – for Uncle Rodney to exchange our doorknob for one that locked from the inside.

I sit on my bed, plopping down without restraint. "You can't control people that way. You can't run their lives because they aren't doing what you want. She's going to be pissed."

She lifts a single shoulder, moves toward my bed, and plops down, bouncing us both. "Someone has to adult."

I laugh because we're all in trouble if Bristol is the one playing the adult. "At some point they're going to talk, Bristol."

With an indifferent pinch of her lips, she drops back, laying on her back with her hands on her tummy. "I'll worry about that then." It's just like her. Do now. Pay later.

I pick a red thread off of her nightshirt and drop it on the carpet. "And you need to take it easy on her. Stop being so critical."

"She hasn't made a good choice since she told Dad to fuck off. And we know how long that took her. God, how many times did she take him back? I'm tired of being her second choice, Brenna. I'm sick of watching her spiral into a spineless, meek, co-dependent, twat who forgets she has kids when she's happy."

"We're almost twenty-one. We're not kids. What's wrong with her being so blissfully in love she can't see outside of her own heartbeat? Isn't that what being in love looks like?"

She coughs a laugh and backhands my arm. "You are doomed to repeat our mother's mistakes. Listen to you. 'Outside of her own heartbeat.'" She mimics my words in a slow, dumb voice. "Where were you for our entire life? If there is such a thing as true love, why hasn't she found it? She's been searching for that shit since the eighties."

"You can have more than one true love. Dad loved her. Tom loved her. Louis, he kinda loved her. He just hated us. I think once you get a taste of love, even if it does fail for one reason or another, it's a lot harder to live without it. So sometimes Mom settles for close."

I can't see it, but I feel her eyes roll. "I said *true* love. Dad loved her when they were in high school. No one in high school knows what love is, so it doesn't count."

"He loved her when we were little."

"No, he loved alcohol and Peggy Barnes. I also heard through the grapevine he loved Alisha Cortes, Dina Sayer, and Donna D., too. And don't forget Anna Johnson, who blew our world up with paternity papers and financial requirements. He didn't love Mom. He stated that in court, remember? My point is, if it's not true love, why work so hard for it?"

I shake my head, staring straight ahead at the curtains. Despite my dad's example, I still believe there are good men. I'm just leery of the packaging, and my mom has to unwrap them all with the hope of finding something worthwhile. Bristol, on the other hand, unwraps them all without a single expectation.

"Screw it," Bristol finally says. "It's not worth fighting over. I'll ease up on her, but I can't promise I'll stand by and watch her delude herself into believing Joe's her soulmate." She rolls onto her side. "Will you sleep with me tonight?"

"Yeah, scoot over." I shut off the light and climb in beside her, our feet touching. We learned long ago that close proximity brought us comfort when so much around us was in turmoil. Being twins, we've always had a built-in friend, confidante, and comfort zone. It's gotten us through a lot of shit. Being Sloans, God must've known we'd need all three, so he made us twins. Sadly, being a twin still wasn't always enough, and we had to make up mottos, sacred vows, and pinky promises just to ensure our own reliability, too afraid to take chances, even with each other. After being let down by not one, but both parents time and again, you start to wonder if flakiness isn't somewhere in your genetic makeup too. "We have to work the early shift, so try not to hog the bed so I can sleep too." The mundane actions of a regular work day sound exquisite, and after Joe's drama-filled departure today, I'm ready for it.

Bristol groans softly, pushing her butt toward the wall to allow more room on the twin bed we've shared on way too many occasions. Her eyes droop, and in the trail of moonlight peering in through the crack of the curtains, they are dark instead of the vibrant green we share. They glass over in the space between two heartbeats and swell with unshed tears. "Do you think Dad is happy?"

My throat constricts and then aches as I hold back the tears spawned from hers. "I don't give him much thought anymore, but no. I think karma has seen to that."

Tears absorbed, Bristol sighs. "I hope so. I hope karma has seen to a lot of people." She blows a piece of hair off of her lips. "How many more bad guys is Mom going to go through before she gives up?"

"I hope she never gives up," I whisper, my voice barely audible. "I love that she still believes in love. I worry about the day when she stops."

"How can we be so different?"

"You got an extra cynical gene."

She chuckles sadly, wiping her nose with the back of her wrist. "Maybe I did."

Seeing Bristol exposed saddens me as much as it relieves me. She's usually an anchor, an unmoving, headstrong force that breaks even the strongest tide at its peak, but the bravado that has kept her upright through so much of our lives is also what stunts her. I want to save her from herself and show her there are men outside of Uncle Rodney who can love us, and that she can rely on more people than just me. I don't know if either is true, but sometimes just having faith that it's possible is enough to push you through.

"I love you, Brenna. I honestly don't know what I would do without you. Sometimes, I think you're the only one I truly believe in anymore."

Tears struggle against my restraint. Her hurt runs deep. Mom's fluctuating affection following Dad's abandonment has disconnected something in her that only our sisterly rituals seem to reconnect. It's times like these I'm ever so grateful we have them. "I love you, too. Pinky swear that no matter what happens, no matter who steals, breaks, or runs away with our hearts, they'll always have to contend with the two of us."

"You're hopeless. You know that?"

"Hopeless and cynical, yin and yang. Thank God there's balance. Now promise."

We kiss our own pinkies, hook them together, and together we recite the vow we know by heart. "My word is my bond, your trust is key, no matter what, you can count on me."

The slamming of a car door draws us both from the bed and over to our bedroom window. Outside, the street light splashes Joe with its unforgiving yellow glow as he slides into the passenger seat of his fat friend's blue pickup. Mom's Jeep is parked at the curb with one tire on the sidewalk.

"Coward," Bristol spits out before climbing back into bed. I let her comment be the final word as I'm not really in the mood to rehash Joe's many flaws, and then I climb in beside her.

Bristol falls asleep, and I wait for her breathing to even out before I leave her for my mom, whose crying can no longer be heard through the thin walls. When I was a kid the quiet used to soothe me to sleep knowing she was at least, for the time being, cried out. As a teenager, it signaled something much darker, and I would lay awake praying for sound so I would know she was okay. Now, as an adult, I worry that one heartbreak too many will finally break her.

My bare feet make a tacky noise against the hardwood floors, and in the quiet, it may as well be thunderclaps. I cringe with each step, hoping I don't disturb the sleeping beauty behind the cracked bedroom door. I peer in, seeing my mom's prone figure lying on top of her bed covers. She's changed into shorts and a tank top, and her beach hair is pulled up into a messy bun on the top of her head. All signs that she's not completely wrecked.

Sneaking in on tiptoes, I turn off the lamp on the bedside table where her romance book lies with her place marked by an old book-mark Bristol made when she was in second or third grade. It's ancient and peeling apart, but she refuses to use anything else. For all her faults, not loving us enough isn't one of them. Even if sometimes I wonder, all of her simple treasures reassure me.

Mom's room isn't big and is made smaller by the clutter she calls mementos. She must have at least six homemade necklaces on her dresser along with the Popsicle stick picture frame that features two toothless girls in pigtails. Her jewelry is in a shoebox covered in scrapbook paper and seashells we formed into a heart on the lid. This is what I choose to focus on when her focus is on the next relationship or the one she's trying to salvage. This is the real her.

I cover her with a blanket and take a moment to look at her peaceful face before leaving her to find some sleep of my own.

AFTER TWO HOURS OF SLEEP IN A TANGLE OF FEET, KNEES, ARMS, AND hair, the coffee I picked up to help with my disposition sits on the counter inside Stray Charlie's Pedal Pushers, with two sips and a spill missing from it.

Stray Charlie's, located at the north end of Milagro Beach's boardwalk, sits just off the sand beside the wooden pier that hosts fishing, an ice cream parlor, boat rentals, and sweeping views of the Pacific and the lighthouse that guided in Milagro Beach's savior.

We've only ever had two steady jobs in our entire lives. One at the Fractured Bean, a coffee shop a half-mile from our apartment in

L.A. we leave every summer as sales decline to head up to our summer job in Milagro Beach at Stray Charlies, where sales pick up.

Bristol and I have been renting out beach cruisers, tandem and Surrey bikes, paddleboards, and the occasional beach skimmer for four summers now. It pays a few bills and keeps us afloat through summer. And bonus, it's not far from The Seam.

Halfway through our four-hour shift, it feels like a Black Friday at Walmart. I think every cheerleader within a fifty-mile radius rented something with wheels today. During a break forced upon us due to lack of inventory, Bristol and I sit on a bench outside of Stray Charlie's to steal some sun.

Normally, I'd watch the foot traffic on the boardwalk, but today I can't find any curiosity for it. Eyes closed, chin pointed at the sun, I sigh, relaxing for the first time since we arrived back home. Knowing that it may be the last uncomplicated moment of summer, I bask in it. Toolbag Carl, Bristol's only sexual experience to mean something and the only guy I know who works out more than he shits, got home this morning, the last of our close friends to arrive from college. It won't be long—two days, tops—before the gang is back together and summer kicks into full gear.

Just as they were rented out, the bikes return in back-to-back transactions, and we're soon busting our asses again. I'm sweating through my shirt and my hair has slipped loose of its ponytail when Bristol shouts for me.

She sounds grouchy, but I chalk that up to lack of sleep, work abuse, and her sandals rubbing the inside of her arch raw. I finish filing the last of the waivers and slip the file box beneath the counter.

I step outside the small office, more like a shack or kiosk than an office building, and stand beneath its flapping orange and white striped awning. Bristol, eyes shaded by her hand, is standing beside the boardwalk talking to someone I don't immediately recognize until I hear the distinguishable witch cackle.

My heart stops, and it's not from the two sips of coffee, lack of sleep, or from thinking about Vance, which has stirred more than a few skipped heartbeats. Tiffany Langley, the carrier monkey of the gossip that made our life hell throughout the last half of high school, stands front and center before Bristol. She is the quintessential Barbie doll, if Barbie were a brunette. She even has the itty-bitty waist of Barbie, and also the plastic boobs and useless vagina. She's nothing more than a showpiece, dressed in designer clothes with a Gucci handbag hanging off her arm and a pair of bug-eyed Snooki sunglasses. She auditioned two years in a row for *American Idol* and has since crowned herself "the biggest celebrity to come out of Milagro Beach."

I can't stand her. After she blabbed Bristol's deepest, darkest secret to everyone, Bristol was the topic of every major conversation at school. You can't tell a two-faced bitch that you lost your virginity to a college guy and not have it make the rounds throughout high school. Never mind that it wasn't completely consensual. That portion of the truth never quite made it to the cafeteria conversations, but it defined Bristol nonetheless, to the point she believes the rumors herself.

I stand a bit longer beneath the flapping awning and mess with my hair, too far gone to really make a presentable change, but I have to do something while I decide how to handle this. I want to approach with guns blazing, but Tiffany rarely makes it fun.

I inhale a deep, bitchy breath, and I'm not quite sure yet if it's to fuel me or to save Tiffany, but we'll soon find out as I head her way. Before I come to a stop at Bristol's side, just shy of Tiffany's Jimmy Choos, I let loose. "Daddy's going to be pissed if you parked your broom in his city council spot again."

She pinches her orange lips together, smirks, and tilts her head to the side, "It's nice to see you too, Brenna." She digs in her purse, and considering it's the size of a suitcase, she's quick about retrieving the piece of paper.

"Made your way through the college guys already, huh?" She looks around, dramatizing the neck cranes since her emotionless eyes are hidden. "I guess you had to come back to Milagro Beach to see if there was fresh meat."

I seethe beneath a calm exterior, too proud to let her see me rattled. I've lived too long with the effects of Tiffany Langley's tactics to break beneath them now.

"Well, I haven't had your boyfriend yet." Bristol's quick response makes me laugh, and while I'm still giggling, she's just getting started. She shrugs, smirks, and finishes strong. "But since he's been with you, I wouldn't necessarily call him 'fresh.'"

Tiffany's demeanor changes. Her more-arrogant-than-confident stature goes rigid, and she stiffens her back to a righteous level of bitchiness. "I'm not worried. He doesn't take out the trash."

We could insult each other all day, but I don't want to, so I jump in. "Why are you here, Tiffany? Plastic melts in the sun."

She sneers, flexes attitude, and replies, "Mrs. Dixon said you're going to be doing the Miracle Days fliers." She addresses this comment to me, leaving Bristol out completely. She's even maneuvered her body to face mine, giving Bristol the cold, detached shoulder that in high school was reserved for the Robotics Team, and now that we're older, anyone with a blue collar. I worry for a second she's going to pull her family's weight and yank the job out from under me. I need the money more than ever with Bristol's scholarship under review, but I won't beg Tiffany Langley for it no matter the stakes, and I don't think Tracy's mom would fire me anyway. "Personally, I think she's crazy," she adds, flipping her dark hair over her shoulder, "but let's see if college has taught you something other than swallowing." I feel the degrading humiliation that came with each rumor she spread about us all over again. As much as I'd like to say it didn't affect me, the red creeping up my neck says differently. "Oh, relax Brenna. I came to give you the check to have them printed. Langley Law is sponsoring the fliers amongst other things this year, like, oh, your meager fee. You're not going to have to blow anything for it this time." She preens, her jab meant to be insulting, but I just roll my eyes. I hate to admit the relief I feel at the offering presenting itself from Tiffany's hand, but it's there for the world to see in the exhaled breath I release.

I take the check, not as a grateful girl should, but as a cornered girl does. Actually, I snatch it before she can change her mind, but she isn't paying me for the last word. "Bristol, be sure to tell her daddy thank you when you're with him tonight."

CHAPTER FIVE

Done with our first workday of summer, Bristol drops me off at The Seam, honking the horn of the Silver Stallion as she drives away. I don't bother waving. She's already looking ahead, and anything in her rearview mirror is history. I find The Seam virtually empty. The muted television above the bar is tuned to ESPN, and the ancient stereo sitting on a shelf is playing something from the sixties.

Eating a burger in one of the fruit leather booths, Uncle Rodney waves, trying to choke down his bite so he can say hello. I head right for him, slipping easily onto the bench across the table from him. I steal a fry off of the Burger Baron's wrapper he's laid his food on and take a bite, and then another before the first is finished.

"Eat as many as you want, love. I'm done," he tells me between bites. "And your mom's laptop is in the storage room."

It's the whole reason I'm here. I need some pictures off of it, and for reasons known only to her, she keeps it here at the bar. I steal another fry as he finishes his burger. "It'll just take me a sec to email the pics to myself. I'll be out of your hair in no time."

"You're never in my hair. There's no rush."

Two more fries disappear from his paper wrapper, and I grin at him, unapologetic.

He rolls his eyes at me and says, "Finish them. I'll get the laptop."

He produces the laptop minutes later along with a glass of soda for me, to go with his fries. It takes me thirty minutes to find the pictures I need for the fliers and not the hours Bristol predicted when she refused to wait for me.

In that time, Uncle Rodney has muted the sixties music in favor of baseball on the television, while the seats around the bar have filled in with some locals who take their beers in bottles and their baseball loud.

I hand off the laptop and wash my glass. "Thanks for the meal," I say, kissing him on the cheek, and just before I get to the door to leave, I wave over my head to the regulars. "Shalom."

My mom, entering just as I reach for the handle, already has her standard response to my farewell. "You're not Jewish, Brenna. That's offensive."

I roll my eyes, kiss her on the cheek, and whisper, "Only if you take it that way." I'm out the door with plenty of sunshine left to walk home in.

I'm half a block away from The Seam when my phone whistles a text.

Bristol: *I'm on my way. Be there in 10.*

Me: *I'll wait out front.*

With me waiting at a table out in front of The Seam, Bristol surpasses her ten minutes by another ten, so when the motorcycle pulls into a space in front of me, I'm there to offer a smile to the hot guy straddling it.

Vance lifts his sunglasses to the top of his ball cap; his eyes are striking blue and full of mischief. "They kick you out?"

"Waiting on Bristol," I offer, standing to move closer to him.

"Seems to be a pattern with you two."

I shrug a shoulder, agreeing more or less. "What are you doing here?"

"Came for a beer." His strong legs maneuver to set the bike solid.

"Careful, or you're going to end up a regular, and the only thing you should ever want to be a regular in is a Ferrari dealership."

He crinkles his face, lifting his chin. "So save me from myself and show me around Milagro Beach instead."

I point at my chest with four fingers. "Me? Even after the whole dress thing and all the drama?"

"Especially because of the dress thing and drama."

My cheeks heat, a rarity until I met him. He has no idea what he's in for with me. I come with a lot of baggage, one piece of which weighs one hundred fifteen pounds and is ten minutes late. With that thought, I decide Bristol can wait on me for a change and agree to show him Milagro Beach.

"Take me to your favorite place." It's a suggestion he offers after I inform him that Milagro Beach, for all its beauty, is boring.

I climb on the back of his bike, and the familiar scent of his cologne draws a smile. My phone won't fit into the shallow pockets of my khaki work shorts, so I clutch it and him before he pulls away from the curb.

On Ocean Avenue, I have him make a U-turn and we head south toward Grundy Beach where we met. Down a side street, past Grundy, a small parking lot covered in sand and suitable for maybe five cars brings the street to an end. Opposite two other cars, Vance parks the bike with the front tire in a hedgerow of bright pink Indian hawthorn.

Weathered wooden stairs with two small platforms surrounded by a hand railing zigzag down to the beach, and I lead us down to the first platform. The front half of the hand railing facing the ocean is gone and only a battered center post remains. I plop down, dangling my feet over the edge, and gesture for Vance to join me. He sits beside me, the center post pressed against his left shoulder, feet dangling over like mine.

"Snuggle in. It's the best place to watch the sunset." I have no doubt he'll agree when he sees the unobstructed view of the fading sun. Oil rigs, piers, and harbors are all out there as eyesores in either direction, but from here, none of them are visible.

"Do you spend a lot of time here?"

"Not as much as I'd like. I spend more time at Grundy."

"Where's that?"

"It's the beach where we met. It's technically part of Milagro Beach, but some time ago the locals dubbed that section Grundy because of the return of the grunion."

"Return? Don't they have some sort of predictable cycle?"

"Short version, yes."

"Long version? I sense a story."

"Long version is they quit spawning here a hundred years ago, and then the fishing industry tanked, or so the story goes. They returned years later along with all the other fish after a ship with two priests and thirteen religious refugees landed on the beach on the heels of a storm. It's said they left a blessing on the beach as payment for their safe arrival as well as the kindness of the remaining townspeople. The grunion returned on the next full moon, two days after the priests' departure. The beach, and then the town, where they landed became Milagro Beach, meaning Miracle Beach. The wooden pier by Stray Charlie's on the boardwalk is supposed to be the best fishing pier between L.A. and San Francisco, but we keep that pretty close to the vest."

"Wow. That's a lot of knowledge for one girl."

I laugh, "Sorry, I've had to brush up on my Milagro Beach history for Miracle Days. And I've just spared you five bucks and an evening at the museum."

"Frugal. I like that. What's Miracle Days?"

"It's an annual festival held at the end of June to celebrate our good fortune. You should come. It's usually a good time. There are vendors galore, religious ceremonies that may or may not include consummations on the beach, bake-offs, beach volleyball tournaments, paddle boarding. Lots of things."

"Hmm, sounds fun." He looks out across the sand where there are a few straggling surfers heading in from the surf. They'll strip off their wetsuits, dig their boards in, and watch the sun sink in the waves before leaving for the night.

"I promise I won't let my reputation rub off on you."

"You seriously have a reputation?" He seems genuinely surprised, a refreshing change of pace for me.

This could take a while, and he clearly didn't think it through when he questioned me on it. "It happens when you lose your virginity in the back seat of a Volvo. Well, I think I lost my virginity. The jury is still out." I sweep some sand off the platform with the tips of my finger while Vance absorbs what makes me me.

"Are you being for real right now?"

I snort with embarrassing proficiency. "I wish I were making it up. I think girls have had better experiences with their vibrator."

"Ouch!" He cranks his head to the side and scrunches up an eye as if trying to ward off pain. "Poor guy."

"Poor guy? I'm the one who doesn't know if I'm a virgin. His virginity is wrapped in a sweaty gym shirt he found under the front seat."

"So, is that all it takes to get a reputation and your own bio on a bathroom wall?"

"No." I snort-giggle again. "Bristol exploring half the high school with her mouth did that."

His eyes widen, and he does that head-shake thing again. "Wow! Wasn't expecting that. How does Bristol's mouth get you a reputation?"

"One of the hazards of being an identical twin."

He shakes his head, and I shove him in the shoulder, pushing his athletically muscular body away from me. "What?"

Without looking at me, he replies, "Nothing." He takes on a more serious look. "I just think we're in similar boats, and I'm fascinated by how differently you row yours."

"Similar, how? You mean you lost your virginity in the back seat, or you gave a lot of blow jobs?"

He choke-laughs. "Neither. Damn." And it takes him a minute to regain his train of thought, which, if I'm not mistaken, has shifted. "So, what do you do when you're not defending yourself, waiting on Bristol, or taking rides with strangers?"

"I told you where I lost my virginity. That makes us friends, not strangers." Technically inaccurate since the confession came after I took a ride, but no one but God is keeping track. "I'm studying graphic design in L.A.," I answer, prouder of that than anything else in my life, other than successfully mastering a childproof lighter. "But right now, I'm working at Stray Charlie's down on the board-walk for the summer, hence this lovely tank." I pinch my Stray Char-lie's tank top and tug, watching his eyes drop to my chest and then move back up to my face.

"Is that the place down by the pier?"

I nod, grabbing hold of my hair as the wind blows it across my face.

"What are your plans for after college? What do you do with a graphic design degree?"

"Well, there are lots of options, but I plan on designing book covers and print logos for entrepreneurs starting their own busi-nesses or established ones trying to rebrand. Bristol planned on designing websites for those same businesses so we could combine our efforts, but shit happens and her plans had to change, so now I don't know what we're doing. How about you?"

"Well, I lost my virginity in my girlfriend's bedroom."

I laugh, touching his arm. "I was asking about what you do for a living, but I'll let you run with virginity."

"I know. I just figured it was a lot more fun to talk about."

"Are you certain you're not a virgin? It happens, you know?" I point at myself for emphasis.

"Definitely not a virgin. She had to talk me into it though."

My eyes expand. I'm envisioning an ugly girl with cash, because I thought all guys wanted sex. Well, maybe he's so hot he has to turn them down on occasion for sleep. "She had to convince you? You gotta tell me how that worked."

"We were at her house, parents in the living room, brother next room over. I kind of liked my balls where they were. You know what I mean?"

"Those are pretty high stakes. How'd she convince you?"

"She dropped her skirt." He covers a rare grin as he looks down into his lap and back up at me as I laugh with him. "Didn't take much. How 'bout you? What gets a girl in the back seat?"

"As if you don't know."

"I don't know what it takes to get a girl like you in the back seat."

"Two beers and a Big Mac." For that, I get a fleeting smile, which I return.

"Shit. That was funny. But I don't believe that for a second."

I smile, appreciating his confidence that I valued my virginity more than that. "Thanks."

My phone whistles and I ignore it, but Vance tells me to get it before someone calls beach patrol over my disappearance. He's probably right so I check, groaning as I see Bristol's name:

Bristol: *Where are you?*

Me: *With Vance. Be back in a bit.*

Bristol: *Hot guy Vance?*

Me: *Yep. Gotta go.*

Bristol: *I was coming to meet you and you ditched me for him?*

Me: *Ditching would imply you didn't make me wait forever. Gotta go.*

My phone rings and I silence it quickly, shoving it into my back pocket where it sticks halfway out.

"Everything okay?"

"Perfect." With him, every second of this night has been perfect. But I'll be lucky if Bristol doesn't bring this up in the eulogy at my funeral, so it's also a loaded answer.

"Do you need to go?"

"After the sunset." I nod in the direction of the setting sun, still a few minutes away from perfection.

Minutes later, the sky is on fire and the ocean looks like the trail of gasoline igniting it. Vance puts his hand in mine and squeezes. No words. No sounds other than the ocean. And I breathe in, content.

On the drive back to The Seam, we're both quiet. There is no talking at stoplights. No idle chatter between my directions or laughter when I grip him tighter around a corner. Once, and only once, he drops his hand to mine on his abdomen and squeezes, but no words narrate his thoughts, leaving mine to question the gesture.

Vance pulls into a spot a few spaces down from The Seam. It's Saturday night, so premium spots are harder to come by. I pull away from him, hands on my thighs. A twilight chill present in my skin heats up beneath his hand as he attempts to assist me off the bike.

"Do you want a beer?" I ask, forking fingers through my hair to relax it. "That and a shot of Jameson are a part of the Milagro Beach tour."

Probably trying to read something in my invitation, he doesn't drop his eyes. "I was hoping it would be." He climbs off the bike, adjusts his T-shirt, and grabs my arm before I step up the curb.

I look up at him as he brushes my hair off of my shoulder so that it falls down my back and then brushes a light knuckle over my cheek. "Thank you."

"For what?"

"The tour. The laughs. You. This."

I swallow, shift on feet that shake, and lean toward him, rising on tiptoes before hesitating briefly to stare at the lips I'm about to press mine against. They're full, with a perfectly dipped cupid's bow that fills me with anticipation.

When I finally touch my lips to his, my heart races ahead to embrace the feel of his breath on my face and his lips on mine. It's a tender kiss. One I might get practicing on my own mirror, but then his hand curves around my neck and he kisses me back, losing himself briefly before pulling away.

I open my eyes to see him looking at me, and I cover my lips with a few fingers. "I'm sorry. I—"

"Don't be sorry." It's whispered, meant to ease my embarrassment no doubt, but falls terribly short.

"Are you coming in?" Bristol shouts from the open door of The Seam, and I look at her, questioning her timing and feeling confident it's not a coincidence.

CHAPTER SIX

Using Bristol's untimely interference as an exit strategy, I walk ahead of Vance, leading with a fast pace he's not trying to thwart. He either senses my urgency to get inside, or he is content with moving forward like nothing major just happened.

The Seam is full, baseball on every available television except one, and that one is broadcasting MMA. Vance lowers his ball cap, the brim tilting low over his eyes as Uncle Rodney greets us both with a smile. It's a far more pleasurable welcome than the scowl from Bristol four feet away. Mom is behind the bar tending to Mr. Davidson and oblivious to our arrival.

"Have a good time?" Bristol's tone is deliberately snotty.

I don't reply, but Vance clears his throat to respond in my place.

"Yeah. Sorry if I messed up your plans. It was spur of the moment."

"Yeah, I'll bet it was." Bristol's pissiness is meritless. If she'd been on time, I wouldn't have been around when Vance showed up.

Uncle Rodney's glare hits Bristol before he addresses Vance. "Grab a stool. I'll get ya a beer."

Vance looks at me first, gesturing with his head for me to join him. Reluctantly, I follow, taking the stool on his right since Bristol occupies the one on his left. Uncle Rodney sets a beer and a soda in front of us, not realizing that our family staple of Jameson whiskey is the only thing that has a chance of sneaking past the cluster of butterflies in my stomach. But he's a stickler and won't part with the 80 proof until I'm twenty-one.

"Where'd you go?" Bristol questions Vance.

"The Lookout," I tell her, looking past Vance and into her accusatory eyes, daring her to say what she's really thinking.

"Can he not speak for himself? Or are you two already finishing one another's sentences?"

"Oh, for fuck's—"

My mom's shriek cuts off my reply and draws unwanted attention toward us. "Brenna Frank! Bristol Charles! Backroom! NOW!"

The backroom is filled with boxes of liquor, supplies, and a brownish, hairy couch I've spent hours doing homework on over the years. I take a seat beside Bristol at my mom's insistence.

She prattles on about the comings and goings of boys, and sisterhood, and all I can do is think about how many times she has chosen a man over our objections. And now she wants to preach the importance of our bond over the temporary pleasure of a man? What the honest fuck? "You're young," she continues. "There are going to be many young men interested in you. You can't fight over them all."

I pinch my lips together so I don't bite through my tongue as I'm sure Bristol already has. As quiet as she's been through this spiel, she's probably choking on tongue blood right now.

Obviously, she didn't bite hard enough, because she finally interjects, "You can have him. I don't want him now. But if you're expecting love from that guy out there, think again little sister. He's probably already cheating on you with his girlfriend."

"You don't know shit about him and obviously not enough about me if you think I'm already in love with him. It was one drive. One."

"A drive? Is that all it was? Looked to me like he was sucking the lipstick right off your face."

"Look at you two." My mom paces in front of us in short strides no longer than the length of one cushion. She stops, bends at the waist so she's eye level with us, and looks first at Bristol and then at me. "What happened to that silly vow of not letting a boy come between you?"

"We were ten," I snap. And we also promised to live with one another forever. What the hell did we know?

"And tired of having men chosen over us," Bristol adds.

I backhand her thigh, thinking her comment too cruel, but my mom glosses right over it like it wasn't aimed directly at her guilt sensor.

"Well, anyway, until you know it's forever, I wouldn't start a precedent of fighting over men. It will become easier and easier to forget the pact."

"Didn't you just say it was silly?" I ask it, but Bristol and I both look up in solidarity.

"I called it silly because it's unrealistic, not because it isn't a good idea."

"Unrealistic, how? It seems pretty simple to me."

"Bristol, baby, at some point a man is going to sweep you off your feet and he'll be all you want and need. You're going to need Brenna less and less, and vice versa when Brenna finds someone. I don't know if it's this guy or not, but there will be someone someday."

"Bullshit!" Bristol gets to her feet. "I'm not you!" "You" is spoken bitterly, like she can't stomach the taste of it in her mouth, and I swallow, getting to my feet to stand united with her but also to spare my mom if I need to. "I will never be you!" She glares hard. Every moment my mom disappointed her is fueling her argument and cementing her stance. "She will always come first. No guy will ever be more important than her." Bristol's anger is pointed and delivered with as much bitter sincerity as I've ever seen from her. "Maybe if you'd chosen us one time other than at birth, you'd get that."

Bristol turns to me, leaving our stunned mother with her mouth agape and her eyes brimming with tears. I don't know what is bringing this out. I didn't accept a marriage proposal, for fuck's sake. It was a kiss. "The second you start turning into her and choosing him over me, I will make sure you remember our 'silly pact.' I'm tired of being chosen last or not at all. You're supposed to be different." She brushes past me, shoulder-checking me as she does so, and storms out of the storage room, leaving a wake unlike anything I've ever had to wade through.

I stare blankly for a second. For me, it was one ride with a boy. For Bristol, apparently a whole lot more. In her defense, it's easy to feel overlooked when your parents continually choose other people and other things over you. Even the boys she's dated chose her reputation and not necessarily her. But none of that means I don't get to have a life. Does it?

My mom waves me off, shooing me away as I try to give her a hug. "I'm okay. Go. Just be careful."

Reluctantly, and with too many reservations to name, I rejoin The Seam crowd. Uncle Rodney is cheering on the Renegades much louder than anyone else, and Vance watches quietly, beer between his hands.

Bristol, barely concealing her hostility, takes off, and I stand by myself hoping I look better than I feel. After a minute, I return to the stool beside Vance, to find my soda mostly clear and bleeding all over my napkin.

"You good?" Vance asks it in such a way that I believe it encompasses the kiss, Bristol's behavior, my response, and my mom's intervention. Holy fuck, when I said he wasn't ready for my baggage, I didn't know how much weight I was actually carrying.

I nod, sip from my watered-down soda, and reply, "Perfect. You?"

"Perfect."

My mom reappears looking more put together than I feel and takes her place behind the bar like nothing happened. She's a damn chameleon, far more acclimated to fights with us than with her boyfriends.

"Mom?" I speak up to get her attention and she looks at me, smiling like she's on painkillers. "I meant to do this earlier. This is Vance. Vance this is my mom, Teresa."

Vance directs a brilliant smile toward her, stopping my heart with its intensity as he reaches across the bar to offer her his hand. "Nice to meet you."

She takes his hand with the same look Uncle Rodney got the first time he met Vance. "You too. Sorry about the scene."

He adjusts his hat, grinning with so much charisma I may need a cold shower. "Didn't even notice."

Uncle Rodney delivers two shots of Jameson like he read my mind and lost his. I grab hold of one, ever thankful for his timely understanding . . . that I've apparently misread, because he stops me with an even timelier two-finger smack to my wrist.

"That's mine," he states with authority and a grin I'm partially convinced is boastful satisfaction.

I glare, no words necessary.

"One week, love," he whispers with a wink. "One week, and I'll proudly serve you your first shot."

Holding his beer with two hands, Vance watches our exchange but doesn't intervene until we appear done with our disagreement. "So, Brenna Frank, you going to tell me that story?"

I nod at their glasses. "Take the shot first. It's the last stop on the Milagro Beach tour, and who better to take it with than Uncle Rodney." I manage to minimize my grumble, which dissipates anyway when Uncle Rodney looks so satisfied draining his alongside Vance.

I answer Vance while he recovers from a shot he doesn't look used to taking. "It's my Pop's name. Charles, Bristol's middle name, is my other grandpa's, on my dad's side."

"Do you not have grandmothers?"

Full of chuckles, despite my argument with Bristol and my mom,

I answer him in the middle of one. "Brenda and Crystal. My mom was groggy from the drugs I guess, and my dad signed the birth certificates thinking my mom had said Brenna and Bristol. Thus, our names were born." He winces with a whistle.

I shrug. "Eh, it makes for a funny story."

He grins, looking too lost in his own thoughts to care about the origin of my name. "So, she left you again?" He looks around for Bristol.

"High and dry," I reply, without inflection but quick enough to be funny.

"Is she coming back?"

I feel like we've had this conversation before. "No. I'm on my own. She's probably at home changing for the party at Toolbag Carl's."

"Toolbag Carl? Honestly, Toolbag?"

"A friend. He's five-eleven with more brawn than brain."

He nods knowingly. Everyone has a friend with more gym hours than sense.

"Can I give you a ride home so you can get out of your work clothes and still make it to your party? I am the one that kept you."

I just want fresh air that he isn't trying to breathe too. I need to focus. I need to regroup and get my heart flutters under control. "I can manage, but thank you."

Vance waits on me to lift my attention from my hands, and looking as serious as I've seen him yet, responds to my rejection. "I want to."

Fuck. How do I refuse that?

Outside, ahead of Vance, I breathe deeply and blow it out as he speaks my name and the door to The Seam closes behind him.

I close my eyes and turn to face him, my embarrassment tucked shrewdly beneath my Sloan confidence. I've endured worse. I've survived worse. I can certainly survive the hottest guy I've ever seen, let alone kissed, telling me it's him not me.

"Can we talk?"

"Yeah, of course."

"Somewhere other than here, I mean?"

Bristol suddenly pulls up beside two cars, the passenger window visible between the hood of one and the bumper of another, a break in Ocean Avenue traffic giving her a minute to yell at me through the passenger window. "Get in if you're going. I grabbed you a change of clothes. You can change at Toolbag's."

I groan, holding up a finger to gain a minute, and she pulls forward to park behind Vance's bike.

"I'm sorry. I already pissed her off once—"

"It's okay. I get it. Maybe tomorrow? If you're free?"

I groan again because my plans are already set in stone with Bristol, Tori, and Tracy. "I have plans, but I'm free on Monday."

He smiles. "I'll see you Monday. Okay if I meet you here?"

I nod, struggle with my next action, and go for broke, kissing him on the cheek. "See you Monday."

CHAPTER SEVEN

Hungover from Toolbag's party and sporting the anti-glow of having slept on his pull-out sofa, I pray the two Advil and Red Bull I downed for brunch will appease the empty stomach screaming at me. I skipped feeding it so I wouldn't be late to the semi-torturous but beloved tradition I wouldn't give up even for Vance.

Bristol and I don't have traditions. Christmas and Thanksgiving have been a distorted version, I suppose, given that we always celebrate them on the day the calendar says we should, but no two have ever been alike. So, after being butthurt about not having what everyone else had, Bristol and I, with our two best friends, Tori and Tracy, started an annual Thrift Store Dressing Room Swap. When we started it six years ago, we had no idea it would morph into the can't-miss tradition it's become.

At our first Dressing Room Swap, the concoctions we made from all the rejected clothing were supposed to be for our eyes only and maybe a few lucky shoppers, but of course that changed the second Bristol stopped laughing and started plotting. On her dare, that very first year, we ended up at a volleyball game looking like a flamboyant cruise director, a seventies bridesmaid, and two colorblind housewives. It turned out to be one of the best nights of our lives. Tori, sheltered from life by two doting parents, grew up on a short leash and needed clothing approval before leaving the house. It was a miracle her parents allowed us to be friends. Tracy shops on Rodeo Drive with an assistant and until meeting us didn't know thrift stores had dressing rooms. But thanks to the Swap, despite our vastly different backgrounds, for a few hours a year we are all judged equally by the rest of the world. We are all unified under one umbrella of crazy, and we love it.

We arrive at Belvedere's Attic thrift store seven hours after they've opened to ensure the dressing rooms will be full of discarded clothes. I thought this wonderfully bizarre tradition would be made slightly less humiliating by the wide array of choices I'd have until I see what's waiting for me in my dressing room, and then I'm thinking I'd rather sleep on nails.

"Bristol?"

Her voice carries over the stall beside mine. "Yep?"

"Do you have any clothes over there that aren't for seven-year-olds?" Groaning inwardly, I hold up a pair of pink cotton shorts covered entirely with orange, white, yellow, and fuchsia flowers. They are a girl's size ten, but they're spandex stretchy, which is about the only thing worthwhile about them.

"That's against the rules," she says, snickering. "You chose your own room. Live with it." That's easy to say if you picked the room with Quiksilver and Roxy clothes.

I have no right to complain, but I'm not that gracious and do so with a fevered pitch. "There is nothing in here for someone over seven."

"Good thing you have little boobs." Her optimism pisses me off, but the grunting that follows eases it slightly as I envision her trying to fit into size two jeans.

Fifteen minutes later and after several angry curses about me taking too long, I emerge from my dressing room dressed like a seven-year-old hooker-in-training. My pink, floral print, stretchy shorts ride so far up my ass they have ripped my crack to my shoulder blades, and my itty-bitty tank top is obscenely deficient. Fortunately, the rules do not deny me the right to wear my own underclothes, so my bra covers what the paisley tank does not. Over the tank, I wear a white down vest with a fur-lined hood, sized children's small, the bottom of which only comes to the top of my navel. It zips up maybe an inch before the teeth strain and it's forced to stop. My midriff, between shorts and vest and stuck zipper and tank, is bare.

Accessorized with a gold turban on her head, Bristol collapses forward, gripping her knees, which incidentally are hidden beneath a pair of high-water red and blue diamond-patterned pants. A pair of raspberry-colored slacks is wrapped around her chest, and with no straps visible, it's anyone's guess where her bra went. Her midriff plays peek-a-boo between the tied pant legs dangling over her belly. Bristol had to improvise a fucking shirt and still looks better than me. She laughs hysterically, tears forming but not falling. Fighting for composure, she turns away to catch her breath.

Tori is speechless with her mouth gaped open like she is waiting to be fed a worm. Her cheeks are red, and she slowly dissolves into laughter as the full calamity of my outfit hits her. She looks like a rich snob with a lack of color coordination and apparent ignorance of her recent weight loss. Her wool pantsuit is, at minimum, a size fourteen, and she is, at best, a size six. As she laughs, she hoists the deep Barney-purple slacks up to her chest. The shirt, which I think might be a pajama top, is orange with an owl saying "hoot" across the midsection, and the brown wool coat has arms long enough for a gorilla.

Tracy wears a pink flannel nightgown that is so tight around her neck she had to leave it unbuttoned to breathe. It's sleeveless, which makes the whole flannel thing even weirder, and her short black hair makes her look like Snow White, and no one wants to think of Snow White meeting her prince in granny's jammies.

With literally no shame and the added accessories of knee-length socks shoved into lime green Crocs, me and my big set of balls walk into public ridicule. Lucky for me, it's a short walk to Tori's car and an even shorter walk into Watson's to eat chicken wings with Toolbag Carl.

For the most part, we're ignored as we walk to our table, and the few snickers and insults we hear are mild compared to Toolbag Carl's reaction, which garners the attention we dodged walking in. The high-pitched squeal-laugh thing he does is embarrassing on days we're not dressed like hookers and country club rejects. He scoots out of the booth, and his squeal, blocked by his fist, still pierces.

"This is awesome!" He's practically in tears, slapping his leg as a way to release his blooming amusement. "Holy shit," he cries out, "this is the best year yet." His cackle escalates as he absorbs the scene, and his face, usually the color of an enhanced salon tan, is rosy red, and his veins, thick and protruding, pulse. "Jeezus, Brenna. I-I-I can't look at you." His squeal sounds like something out of an aquarium, and the girls begin laughing all over again. Bristol's turban accessory bobs with her laughter.

"You're an ass," I snap, scooting into the booth so I'll be at least partly hidden behind the table when someone decides to hit record on their cell phone.

"I'm an ass?" He's a bit more contained now that he's in defense mode. "You're the one who showed up in your third-grade clothes."

The girls take turns hugging him before they scoot into the booth and squish me into the wall. Toolbag takes the outside, sitting next to Bristol, and faces me with a grin and a wink, letting me know in his own way that it's all in good fun.

Our waitress arrives. Her blonde hair is several shades darker than mine and Bristol's, but her blue eyes are duplicates of our dad's. My body stiffens involuntarily, my unease visible as I search for something to say. Saving me from a tumble over a stiff tongue prone to cursing under stressful situations, Colette, my half-sister, greets us. "Welcome to Watson's." Four years younger than us, she drew the long straw when our dad denied her existence until eleven years ago when a court said he had to recognize her, at least monetarily, after a DNA test confirmed her to be a Sloan.

She smiles uncomfortably, placing a glass of water in front of each of us without so much as a lift of her eyelashes to peek at the sisters she's usually much better at avoiding. Outside of local gossip and the court proceedings that brought us together, she knows nothing substantial about us. Distant and without an ounce of acknowledgment, Colette pulls out a notepad. "What can I start you out with tonight?"

Bristol stiffens across from me, her bitterness a physical presence and her distaste for being snubbed noted prominently in her scowl. We don't talk about Colette. She is the sordid secret that prompted Mom's drinking binges, the loss of friends, openly hostile public confrontations, and our dad's departure from our lives. It's no more Colette's fault than it is ours, but she is a living, breathing reminder of those rough early days and the years that followed. "Really? That's all you're going to say to us. Not hello, or hi, long lost family, how have you been?"

Colette's cool blue eyes, narrowed slightly at the corners, meet the focused, gritty green of Bristol's. "The only thing that makes us family is sperm." She snaps her eyes to me, but they pinball back to Bristol when my tongue seizes in shock.

"Well, I've lost my appetite," Toolbag chimes in. "I can't eat after that word."

"Sperm *and* that check you cash each month make you a Sloan, like it or not." Bristol's brash tone matches her stern expression while her fingers relieve a straw of its paper.

"I'm not a Sloan, and I don't associate with Sloans." Colette's all-business front collapses, and the real Colette, bitter and defensive, takes center stage. "That filthy name and its legacy can die with you, as far as I'm concerned. Your dad is trash and so are you."

She looks us over, eyes dropping and lifting like she's just realizing how we're dressed. The outfits do nothing to change her opinion of us, of that I'm well aware, but even I know there is more to her than the controversial circumstance of her conception. The stigma of being a Sloan has cost us all a lot. That said, it's easy to brush off the judgment when it's people like Tiffany Langley belittling you, but when your own DNA dismisses you, it chips away some of your tolerance.

Bristol's intolerance has sharpened her tongue, and she lashes out. Words, like bullets, can leave a good-sized hole in weakened flesh, and Bristol barrels for Colette's thin skin. "Trust it's true when I say I don't want you to be a Sloan any more than you want to be one. But you are, and your bloodline is every bit as tainted as ours, more so if you ask me. We're not dirty little secrets."

With her pulse throbbing in her crimson neck, Colette scurries off, leaving our table speechless for all of ten seconds.

Toolbag clears his throat, fingers scratching at his napkin. "After that exchange, I'm pretty sure wings aren't in our future tonight."

"Watson's wings are overrated anyway. Water's fine with me." Tori says softly, then she looks at us sympathetically. "I wouldn't give her a second more. She doesn't know what she's missing." With two fingers on each hand she pinches her shirt, showcasing the owl. "Who, who, who wants to have fun?"

We laugh and manage to put aside the reminder that our dad's misdeeds can still burn us even years later. Tori's spot-on timing with her dumb interpretation of an owl brings us back into the circle that matters.

Sliding an arm over the back of the booth behind Bristol, Toolbag eyes me, his pearly smile so Crest-white it's blinding. We've always had a great friendship, and though it was strained during a small period of time when he and Bristol were on the outs, we've maintained it for well over ten years, even when it wasn't the popular thing for him to do. His grin spreads, cheesy as ever. "So, ladies." He makes it a point to look at each one of us, and as an added effort, touches Bristol's shoulder. "All joking and stupid people aside,

I did a solid for a guy my dad works with, and he took care of me in return."

"Um, is this your way of coming out?" I ask, kidding, but trying to remain stoic. "I always suspected, but I thought it would be more spectacular than that."

He cocks a brow. "Uh, no!" He points a finger at me, pops his tongue off the roof of his mouth and continues. "As I was saying, he hooked me up with Renegades tickets to next Saturday's game. You girls interested? I picked up the tickets on the way over." I hadn't noticed the envelope before now, but he drops it on the table like he's dropping the mic at a rap battle.

"How many tickets did he give you?" Tori, always concerned with the details, is the first to ask, though I can confidently say the rest of us don't care as long as we all get to go.

"In addition to mine, six. I asked Jerry and Mike to go too. And since Saturday is a certain set of twins' twenty-first birthday, I thought, what better way to celebrate?"

We all nod our heads quietly affirming our interest. We're certain a celebration in San Jose will be better than one in Milagro Beach, but Tracy, scratching her neck where the lace collar has left a nice red irritation spot, pipes in as enthusiastically as I've ever seen her. "I would kill to meet Corky Alvarez. Kill!" She stretches the collar of her nightgown out. "Did you guys know I asked him to prom?" She is positively glowing for a girl who just admitted to being a fangirl of epic proportions.

Tori is brimming with questions she can't fire out fast enough. "Did he come? Wait, of course he didn't. Oh my God, did he respond? Were you devastated? Why didn't you tell us?"

Bristol flicks water from her glass at Tori. "Easy, Oprah," she teases. "First, let's find out who the hell Corky is?"

Toolbag Carl pulls away from Bristol and stares at her like she's grown a second head. "You're not allowed to have one of the tickets." He sips from his glass of water, pretending to be appalled by Bristol's ignorance. "I can't take a girl who doesn't know the first baseman for the Renegades. It's like not knowing the President of the United States."

"Not even." Bristol spouts back. "The president is everywhere. What else has this Corky dude done? Is that even his real name?"

Tracy has the same look as Toolbag, but I'm not sure which one wants to wring her neck more. I feel the need to save her, so I butt in. "Okay, so we'll go check out this Corky guy, find out why he stood up my girl for prom two years ago, and maybe if we're lucky, catch a ball. I've always wanted to do that." I haven't, but I'm trying to show some enthusiasm.

Toolbag jumps in with an objection the second I stop talking. "This isn't Tinder. I'm not inviting you so you can act like groupies. I need real enthusiasm for the game. You're going to eat hot dogs, drink beer, and dance to organ music. No, and I mean, NO showing the tatas on the Jumbotron."

Bristol tosses a napkin onto the table. "You're no fun."

"I'm a lot of fun. I just like to be the center of your world, baby." He laughs and squeezes her shoulder acting as though he's kidding, but he's carried a torch for her since I can remember. Tracy snatches up the envelope and pulls the tickets out, fanning them out so she can see them all. "Can I have mine? I swear I won't lose it." She glows with hope. Toolbag nods, his eyes gleaming with pride to have at least one of us in the vicinity of excited. "Yeah, of course. Damn, I can't wait."

CHAPTER EIGHT

Minus Toolbag Carl, who is meeting up with his meathead friends, the four of us head toward The Seam. It's the only place where judgment feels like friendship, and after Colette, I think we need a circle bigger than the four of us.

In the spirit of tradition, and because we haven't been through enough embarrassment, we walk into the bar to share our outfits with the ones who know and love us best. As we get past the entrance, but not by much, Uncle Rodney adopts the same method of coping with my outfit as Tori—mouth open wide, taking it all in slowly—while Mom, a bit more horrified, shrivels a tad as she absorbs what she's seeing.

"Dear God," she says behind her cupped hand used to mask her gasps. "Is that outfit legal?" This from a woman who once accidentally wore a see-through swimming suit.

I roll my eyes, still pissed at my unfortunate pick of dressing rooms, but committed now. "I'm not sure," I reply snidely, "but the bicycle cop on the corner didn't arrest me."

"He was too busy taking your picture," Tori says, because Bristol and Tracy are faltering over their own laughter. Uncle Rodney, whose one claim to fame is two lines in Arnold Schwarzenegger's *Terminator,* is abnormally speechless. My mom continues to stare in disbelief and what I'm pretty sure is self-inflicted guilt. I am, after all, half from her, and what isn't in my DNA is pure nurture, which is all her.

"Take the picture," I grind out through gritted teeth, though normally I'm a bit more jovial about mom documenting our twisted tradition. "No social media," I insist, pointing a threatening finger at my mother as Bristol pushes me closer to the bar and Tracy and Tori detour to the restroom.

My mom puts her hand on my arm, halting our forward progress. "I think someone came in to see you. If there had been time, I would have warned you." Stuck somewhere between finally tapping out and honoring an age-old tradition, I spot Vance, standing at the bar, eyes missing no part of the spectacle I make.

Trapped by insecurity and mortification, I stand there as his eyes look me over, tripping several times over my chest and pelvic region. I can see the exact moment he registers my identity and processes my attire for the unexplainable train wreck that it is.

"What the hell are you wearing?" Vance asks while his eyes once again travel over my crazy train evening attire.

I can barely look at him, and to cover for it, I pull absently on the white down vest, trying to make two inches of fabric cover a twelve-inch gap.

"That isn't going to help," he chuckles, using a closed fist to stifle another laugh.

"Yeah, I know. I'm afraid my kid is going to be born in these." I try to look down at my shorts, but I can't see past the poof of the down vest.

"Real possibility. You'll definitely have to be cut out of the vest."

I try to act natural in this otherwise unnatural moment, but it's not happening. "I—I wasn't expecting you to be here."

"I stopped for a beer," he starts, covering another chuckle with his hand before he continues. "So, is this the 'plans' you mentioned?"

I nod slowly. "Is this Monday?"

"No," he laughs. "I thought you had plans. I came for a beer."

"We do have plans." Bristol, finding an oxygen level she can function with, pipes in with an air of irritation she's starting to perfect.

We move as a group to the right as another couple tries to get to the bar. They whisper something about a costume party and then wonder what size my balls must be to wear this in public. If they'd look a bit harder, they could probably see them poking out the bottom of my shorts.

"Are you going out like this?" Vance asks, wearing his surprise openly.

"Is that a problem?" I respond with a bravado I don't feel.

"You have a camel toe," he says flatly.

I am slow to comprehend, but when I do, my head shoots forward as I suck my stomach in and smash the vest into my gut so that I can see a full set of vagina lips—*my* vagina lips—eating my shorts. Not one single supposed friend or member of my family told me my vagina was gobbling up flowers faster than my ass.

After the initial shock wears off, I turn to glare at my partners in fashion crime. Bristol is laughing so hard she's wheezing, and Tori is staring at Vance, looking a little shell-shocked. Tracy is nowhere to be found and therefore doesn't have to dodge my pointed anger.

"They didn't tell me," I mumble accusingly before turning back to Vance, "but, yes. Me and my camel toe have made a few appearances this evening."

Vance looks at me with curiosity, and I feel like he's observing more than my attire. He takes a step toward me, his eyes never leaving mine. "On anyone else, it would never look this good." He is matter-of-fact and direct rather than amused, and this somehow erases the lingering effects of the encounter with Colette, leaving her and all sources of humiliation a footnote in what is now a quickly improving night. "Are you sticking around?"

Before he asked, I wasn't sure, but now I don't care what the plans are. "For a bit."

"I've got to take this call." He holds out his buzzing phone. "Don't go. I want to talk to you."

I nod wordlessly, and he heads toward the front door to take his call outside.

"So, I needed a camel toe to get noticed by him?" Bristol's ill-timed quip draws my claws.

"Less desperation might have helped you too." She doesn't laugh.

"He looks familiar." Tori, ignoring us both, is staring at the door, her mind exploring the hot guy data bank she has stored up there. "I think he's famous. Is he? What's his name?"

Tori will be working on how she knows him all night long unless we distract her. She's probably already turned fifteen virtual pages of the last *Candid* magazine in her head, and she'll dissect the last six if we leave her unattended.

"He's not famous." Bristol's reply is brittle.

"Who's famous?" Tracy pipes in, returning from the bathroom where she apparently spent the last five minutes reapplying her lipstick.

"No one." Bristol barks at her then redirects to Tori. "He's the guy that helped us at the beach and then helped himself to Brenna."

I sneer at her, and she dishes it right back. It's like we're ten again, fighting over who got to sit next to our dad in the front seat of his pickup the last time he bothered to show up for us.

"Oh my God!" Tracy's exclamation and whatever might have come after is cut off by her hand flying up to her mouth, air whistling through her fingers as she depletes the room of excess oxygen.

I look to find a source for her surprise, but with Tracy it could be a Kate Spade purse, so I'm really not all that concerned until she points at Vance, who is reentering The Seam with a grin he's slowly losing track of.

"Ya-You're Van Hatfield." Tracy's voice trips over her tongue in a whisper, the extreme opposite of her original attention-getter.

"He's who?" Bristol is the one to ask, because I'm still looking between Tracy and Vance to see what the hell I've missed.

Tori clamps her hand over her mouth, eyes bulging over the top of her fingers. "She's right!" It's muffled, but you'd have to be deaf to miss it. "I totally called it." She looks at me, "Brenna," she grabs my arm, holding back a squeal I can see forming, "your hot guy is Van Hatfield, pitcher for the San Jose Renegades."

I jerk my head away from Tori and stare straight into blue eyes that don't look at all amused at the mistaken identity. They drop along with his chin until he picks them both back up and releases a sigh, exhaustion written all over his face. Is he going to speak up? Is he going to blow off their accusations with an "I get that all the time" spiel we can all laugh at? Is he going to fucking deny it?

Everyone is looking at me, wanting answers to questions that I'm shouting in my head. No, I didn't fucking know the guy I've been crushing on for the last several days was a pitcher for the San Jose Renegades. No, I didn't know Vance is Van or Van is Vance. No, I didn't know that for the last three days, I've been sharing intimate parts of my past and present with someone who was lying to me. Jesus Christ, I showed him my ass and stood through the embarrassment of being told I had a camel toe without even knowing it was Van Hatfield telling me. And then it hits me with the weight of a thousand bricks to the chest—not only was my guard down with him, but so was everyone else's. He got to see the huge complexities of my functioning dysfunctional family like we'd known him for years. I've spent the last two years trying to keep my name off of bathroom walls and wagging tongues but didn't think twice about sharing my family with someone who couldn't even give me his real name.

Vance moves forward, his body confident in its strides. His face, however, looks stricken.

"Is this a fucking joke?" Bristol's tone matches my own emotions, and I wait for Vance to respond to her, but instead, he walks past her to stand in front of me.

"Can we talk outside?"

"Is it true?" I ask softly, looking up at him, trying to find any resemblance of the celebrity in his features. It's there. It's always been there. I'm just an unobservant cow who saw dark hair, abs, and striking blue eyes. I see it now. I've seen him on the cover of *Jock* magazine while standing in line at Walgreens. I've flipped through countless copies of *Candid* at Tori's, and he's probably been in half of them, but I don't pay attention to who's "hot" according to tabloid trolls. I have a hard enough time keeping track of the not-so-hot guys my mom brings traipsing through our house.

"Can we step outside, please?"

As I've been processing all of this, Bristol, too, has come to her own conclusion. "It's true, isn't it? Holy shit. Van Hatfield."

I look to my mom for help. She looks a little starstruck, totally oblivious to my racing heart and inescapable embarrassment. What she doesn't look is surprised. Oh my god. She knew. And of course Uncle Rodney knew. They won't hesitate to tell me I have a bat in the cave when it's just us, but they couldn't even give me a hint when I looked like a bridge troll in front of a baseball god? Sonofabitch. They both fucking knew.

"I knew I'd seen him somewhere!" Tori rails on as if I'm not standing beside her shocked stupid. "He was just in *Candid* for dating a stripper. He's also been linked to Nikki Kline and Juniper Jones, but I think Juniper was a load of crap. She's hopelessly in love with Grant Crandall." Her eyes glaze over while mine wish for their ignorance back.

I shut out her commentary and lower my eyes from my hands to my Crocs, mortification setting in deep. Couldn't this celebrity reveal have happened when I looked less like Honey Boo Boo and more like me? I mean, I'm short, and ten of my one hundred fifteen pounds is ass, and Victoria's Secret probably wouldn't snatch me up out of a mall like they did Nikki Kline, but I'm not Go Fund Me ugly. I'm certain, even staring down at my Crocs, he could do worse.

Motherfucker!

Why do I care? He lied.

A whiff of Irish Spring soap fills my nose. It's the smell of strength and stability that has come to symbolize every good thing in my life that I can recall. The source of its power slips an arm around me, drawing me into his side. "Okay girls, let's keep our voices down, or I'll have to ask more than one of you to leave."

"Seriously, Uncle Rodney. You're going to choose his celebrity over us? Me?"

"No, Bristol, I'm choosing calm over chaos, and in this bar, everyone, including him, is entitled to their privacy. Now zip it or hit it."

She grumbles but doesn't argue, which only means I'll get an earful of opinions and unwanted advice later.

"I need air." I maneuver past all of them, unable to get out of there fast enough.

Outside, the night air is thick with salt and eucalyptus, and the light breeze is just enough to take the edge off the warm summer night. I don't want to go home, but I don't want to go inside and answer questions either, or for that matter, face the one guy who's ever made me feel more than just a passing attraction. It would be nice to get into a pair of shorts that don't touch my asshole, but walking home alone like this is a no-go.

Compromising, I sit in one of the metal chairs and watch cars pass by, the occupants oblivious to my heart's curiosities and subsequent disappointment.

Across the street, the boardwalk is quiet, the waves off in the distance a phantom sound from memory. Stray Charlie's, across the street and a few blocks north of The Seam, is shut for the night as are all the other vendors that line the boardwalk. Traffic in front of me is light, the weekend coming to a close for most.

"Can I explain?"

I jump at the voice and look back over my shoulder to see Vance standing outside the bar's entrance. The sight of him hasn't yet lost its appeal, but I'm expecting it to soon. He takes a few steps toward me, looks out at traffic, sighs, and does the opposite of everything I anticipated. "I'm sorry."

Having survived countless apologies that have only deepened my disappointments, I don't respond. I've learned to cut my losses and move on rather than let it eat away at me.

"I wasn't planning on—"

"Doesn't matter now, does it?" I cut his explanation off and get to my feet, abstaining from pulling my shorts out of my ass as I start walking toward home, willing to risk it rather than stay in this conversation.

"Brenna?"

I keep walking, but he doesn't stop talking.

"If you had known who I was, would you have treated me differently?"

I spin, the Crocs gripping sand for an easier pivot. "No!" I am firm in that belief, and based upon his expression, he believes me.

"Would you have been different?" He takes the opportunity my pause creates and jumps in with more. "Would you have dressed in that ridiculous outfit had you known I was Van Hatfield?"

I wouldn't have. "I don't know," I say softly, the lie absent of conviction.

"And that's what I was trying to preserve." He steps closer to me until he is inches away. "I loved that you were uncensored and completely you around me. I liked that you didn't know about me from the tabloids or baseball. I liked getting to be Vance again. I liked you. It wasn't until you kissed me that I realized you were more than just a peaceful retreat."

"Jesus Christ, you let me kiss you, knowing I had no fucking clue who you were."

He blows out a breath. "I didn't know you were going to do that."

"Doesn't change the fact that it happened or that you lied to me."

"You're right, and I'm sorry. It got away from me. What do you need to hear from me?"

"Anything I would have wanted to hear should have been said upfront."

"I realize that now. At first, keeping my life a secret was intentional. I'll admit that. But once I got to know you, I wanted you to know me."

I swallow the dry knot of disappointment in my throat. "Sadly, I don't know Van Hatfield."

"You know him better than you think."

I shake my head voluntarily while the rest of my body shakes of its own accord. "I don't trust him or his motives, and that, Van Hatfield, is our problem."

"Brenna?" He uses the voice that so often had me wishing I was capable of landing a guy like him. He touches my hand as he crouches down to look into my eyes. His touch is fire against my cooling skin.

I lift my lashes and look him in the eyes. "Save it," I say before he can say anything else. "I'm not interested."

He adjusts his stance so it is powerful again and not accommodating of my height.

With a heavy heart, I walk away, knowing it's the last time I will ever see him. I've witnessed too many men break my mom's heart because she overlooked things and made them a priority when she wasn't theirs. I won't be her. I won't settle for less than I deserve.

I make it a few paces away before his voice interrupts my thoughts, my reservations, and my resolve. "I won't keep you tonight, Brenna. But this isn't done. Not by a long shot."

Steadfast, I continue walking. "Your celebrity and smooth talk do not make you irresistible."

"No, but my tenacity will. When you change your mind, Tori will have my number."

CHAPTER NINE

After two days of feeling sorry for myself, I finally manage to take my board out on the waves. When running doesn't help, surfing almost always clears my head. Not today. Probably because all I can see is that damn lookout where I watched the sunset with Vance. I should have gone somewhere else, but it didn't click until I parked my mom's Jeep in the small, sandy lot.

Tired, I strain against the surf as I traipse through the whitewater to get to shore. In the parking lot, I peel off my wetsuit and toss it in the back of the Jeep. I throw on a dry T-shirt and pull my bikini top through an armhole, discarding it with the wetsuit, and then jump behind the wheel.

I've taken this whole thing with Vance, Van, whatever his fucking name is, way too personally and have probably made more out of it than I should. He didn't say it, and I didn't accuse him of it, but I feel like if I had been platinum blonde with size F tits and a modeling contract, he would have introduced himself as Van. Instead, he lied and let me look like a fool on multiple occasions. But then I get real with myself, because the truth is, I walk around like an idiot all the time. Case in point, my run-in with Colette wearing my thrift store getup. Channing Tatum could've been in the bar, and I still would have walked in with my camel toe preceding me. It's who I am. It's who I've always been, and Van Hatfield isn't going to change that about me.

I am summoned to the bar two minutes into my drive home and given no opportunity to refuse unless I want to be dragged in by my hair, as Uncle Rodney so eloquently put it in a text. So, sandy and dressed in my inherited Dairy Queen T-shirt and bikini bottoms, I head on over.

The bar is empty when I arrive and, except for the Renegades game being broadcast on ESPN from Arizona, it's silent.

"Uncle Rodney?" I yell it because he could be anywhere, and I don't have the energy to look.

The loud thunk that rattles the bar is Uncle Rodney's head colliding with the underside as he rises to answer my call. He rubs his thick head of graying hair and mouths a cuss word. "I heard you, doll." He winces, checks his fingers for blood, and the absence of any seems to appease him enough to focus.

"Oh-kay." I take a stool two spots away from where Vance usually parked his ass when he came in to nurse a beer.

It's ten minutes at least before I have Uncle Rodney's undivided attention, and then only after I lean over the bar top to grab a napkin. He stares at me, mouth open, brow knit tightly. "Where are your friends?"

"I don't know, why? Did you call them? Are they supposed to be here?" I'm looking around, expecting Tori and Tracy to appear out of nowhere.

"No. I want to know why one of them hasn't told you you're not wearing a bra?"

It's painfully obvious, even beneath the capital D and double E in Dairy Queen, that I am unsupported, but I hadn't planned on going anywhere but home. I sigh. "Why am I here, Uncle Rodney?"

He sets a Diet Coke in front of me, napkin beneath. "Because you need to snap out of this, doll."

I take a slow sip. "I'm fine." The fizz tickles my lying throat.

The door to the bar opens, and my mom runs in. "Sorry I'm late," she wheezes through rib-splitting breaths.

"Why are you running? And what are you late for?" I hop off the stool, fearing her inevitable collapse and need for a spotter.

She holds up a finger, indicating she needs a minute. It takes a full five before she can control her breathing, and sweat has drenched the armpits of her gray T-shirt, but other than a lingering wheeze or two, she finally seems okay. I repeat my earlier questioning of the whys and whats of her running, and she answers, "For you. I ran from Margie's. Did I miss anything?" she asks, looking at Rodney. Then she moves behind the bar in slow motion because her legs are Jell-O from the two-block run at what I imagine was the speed of a racing tortoise.

"All we've talked about is her girls hanging loose."

My mom instantly looks at my chest, and her down-turned mouth strengthens into a deeper frown. "Brenna."

I roll my eyes and hunker beneath the lip of the bar. "Why am I here?"

"Show her, Uncle Rodney."

Uncle Rodney reaches beneath the bar and pulls out a manila envelope that he holds up with great theatrics before tossing it on the bar top. "That's for me, so don't do anything crazy like Bristol it. Understood?" I find it mildly amusing that Bristol is now a verb.

Wondering what is so important he would defend it so fiercely, I stare briefly at the envelope before opening it. Inside the envelope are four tickets to Saturday's game at Renegade Stadium as well as information on the meet and greet beforehand. I rifle through the information with my mouth agape. My hands begin to shake when I come to a folded white card. I open it slowly and stare at the carefully handwritten print.

Rodney and Family,
Please accept the tickets and the gift package for you and your

family, with my sincere gratitude for your kindness while I was in town.
Sincerely,
Van

I read the card fifty times before I look even once at the rest of the enclosed papers. Vance has arranged for hotel rooms, car service to and from the stadium, room service vouchers, and a VIP pass to Red Hooligans, whatever that is. The package is an incredible opportunity for anyone, but more so for someone who would sell their soul to see the Renegades up close and personal—Uncle Rodney.

"Wow!" I say, sliding the papers and tickets back into the envelope. "That's a great gift. How nice were you, exactly?"

"Not that nice." He laughs, managing to still look serious.

"You're not going to accept it, are you?"

"Why wouldn't I?" His stern expression offers no leeway. "This opportunity may never come around again. For once, your ignorance about baseball is paying off for me."

I'd roll my eyes if I didn't think he'd flick me. "Have fun. I'm glad you finally get to go to the new Renegades stadium."

"We're all going."

"I'm not." I'm off the barstool again, only this time, I'm leaving. "I'm going to the game, but I'm going with Toolbag, and I'm sitting in normal people seats and partying at a dive bar. None of that fancy manipulative stuff for me."

"Carl has already been told you can't go. Bristol has been informed too, and that's that."

"You had no right to do that." He probably has more right than anyone, but at this moment, it's an overstep.

"What did he do that was so terrible?" Uncle Rodney asks as I get to the door.

"He lied," I reply with one hand on the door handle.

"He omitted," my mother corrects, earning another sneer from me. "And technically his name *is* Vance. It's just shortened for superstardom."

"A lie by omission is still a lie. And he doesn't go by Vance. Therefore, it's a lie." Why am I the only one adulting in a room with old people?

"Did you tell him everything about you?"

"I'm not Jock Star of the Year!" I yell louder than either of us expected, and I have to lower my voice for the next part. "He's a liar, and a ticket to one of his games isn't going to change that. He's just trying to buy a better perception of himself."

"I think it's only your perception he cares about." Uncle Rodney rounds the bar, coming to stand beside my mom, both staring at me like I've been given a bad diagnosis. "Haven't you researched him?"

I shake my head. I haven't searched him at all. I'm a girl who likes clean breaks.

"You should," Uncle Rodney professes. "That kid doesn't give two shits about what people think of him. It's your mind and yours alone he cares about changing. Google him. You'll see that's a first. So, I wouldn't be so quick to judge. There is no perfection in you."

"Maybe not. But I never lied about my imperfections. I accessorized them with Crocs and flowered shorts."

LOSING THE BATTLE I WAGED WITH MYSELF AFTER LEAVING THE SEAM, I sit on my bed with my laptop, legs folded beneath my yellow blanket, and stare at the wall. I've been sitting here for an hour now, contemplating my mom's and Uncle Rodney's take on things. I want so badly not to give a shit. I want to wrap this chapter up and call it a night, but something nags at me. No one in my twenty-plus years has ever made me want more than I already have.

Deciding I can't sleep without knowing more, I type "Van Hatfield" into the search engine and wait as Google populates. I first scan the images and waffle between being appalled and impressed.

He dates models, none lasting longer than a picture or two. The most recent is a picture of him and a stripper named Amber Dietrich. This is a guy who likes plastic and beauty and was dating both a week before I met him. On one hand, I can see why I might be an embarrassment. On the other, why would he waste his time on me when there is no lack of willing, beautiful women?

I groan, confused, and click on my next option.

The most recent article I can find is about his "recommended leave of absence," imposed by the manager of the San Jose Renegades following an altercation with a photographer at a Ballers Against Bullying event in Las Vegas a week or so before I met him. In a video clip, he is apologetic but staunch: "Shoving someone at an event against bullying isn't a true representation of who I am, nor do I want it to reflect poorly on the Renegades franchise. With that being said, no man has the right to say the things Mr. Howard said to the woman beside me, and I will defend that no matter the fallout from my actions." The woman beside him, disrespected by the paparazzo Abel Howard, was Amber Dietrich, the stripper. I don't know if I should be upset or impressed. I'm an underdog, and few outside of my family have ever stood up for me. I think I'd appreciate the brutality if I was Amber.

The plethora of information about Vance online, which I know isn't all true, is overwhelmingly harsh and critical. More than one site called him "The Bad Boy of Baseball." Others called him "hotheaded and brooding." After viewing a bench-clearing fight that resulted in his ejection from a game along with another player and a manager, I can understand the criticism. Nevertheless, his teammates speak highly of him, and few comments are from Vance himself in any of the articles I read. The one I can find corroborates Uncle Rodney's opinion that Vance doesn't give two shits about what people think of him. At least three of the words were printed as expletives when he was asked about an article listing his brother, Eric, as a source.

According to his Wikipedia page, he was born Vance Dayton

Hatfield, but a little league coach shortened his name to "Van" after Vance pitched his first perfect game, calling him, "Van the Man." I feel a slight pang of guilt. It's just a twinge and could be ignored as gas if I didn't feel so much of it in my chest. He didn't lie about his name; in fact, he gave me the less famous one used only by those closest to him.

Dammit!

The rest of the page focuses more on his life prior to being drafted and his accomplishments on the field. There are statistics galore, which I skim over to get to the meat. It mentions his estranged brother, Eric, and speculates the estrangement to be over Eric's drug addiction and his penchant for speaking to the tabloids and selling memorabilia from Vance's childhood. There are less noteworthy comments about a younger sister, a grandfather he credits for his drive and his love of the game, and his parents, who never missed a game during his youth. He went to the Renegades right out of his Portland, Oregon high school with the help of his manager, Chip Pervis, and agent, Alex Swift. He hasn't had a moment's peace since. At twenty-five, he's lived his whole adult life in the tabloids.

The article his brother was a source for didn't paint Vance in a good light and made it look like he'd ditched all of them, family and friends, for fame and money. No wonder Vance basked in anonymity with me. He's never shown me an ounce of what's been said about him.

I'm confused.

Maybe I cut him off too soon. I contemplate using the number Tori gave me and decide, after typing out several texts and erasing them, that I'm not ready to overlook anything yet.

CHAPTER TEN

You would think we were born in a cave by the way Uncle Rodney touches and smells everything in the limousine. He runs his hand along the leather seat between him and my mom and looks at his fingers like maybe part of it rubbed off. He takes another deep breath in through his nose and blows it out, shaking his head reverently. "This is nice," he says to no one in particular.

Bristol, irritated we're indulging Vance in the slightest, is dressed for the runway at Fashion Week. She picks at her nails while humming a Disney tune, and her foot, shoved inside a wedge-heeled sandal, taps out the beat.

My mom, more nervous than when she's uploading her picture to a dating site, keeps checking her purse for our tickets despite being told a hundred times Uncle Rodney has them. He didn't trust her for exactly this reason, and they sit safely inside the envelope on his lap.

At the stadium, the limo pulls up, and our driver opens the door for us and assists me out first, then Bristol. The parking lot is virtually empty, and as Uncle Rodney steps out, he stares at his surroundings and sucks the heat right into his lungs. "What a beauty."

As much as I hate being here, I wouldn't want to miss him getting to do this.

"I still can't believe you let them talk you into coming." Bristol is pissed I didn't stick to my convictions.

My mom turns away, not wanting to be involved in our squabble. Her tendency to coddle Bristol because of all she's been through would make her a hypocrite anyway, considering she's the one who pressed me to come. Slightly paranoid, I check the unreliable zipper of my jean shorts. "I'm doing this for Uncle Rodney."

She sighs, softens, and grabs my hand. "Fair enough. But he's going to try and win you over."

I choose to let the insinuation I'll cave drop because I may, and instead, I thank her for being here with me, which draws an unexpected smile.

We're escorted to the dugout where we join about twenty other people in matching Goal Tender shirts. Holy damn! Are we taking some sick kid's spot? I realize we have mental issues, but nothing we might potentially die from and certainly nothing that warrants a charity spot at the meet and greet.

"Oh my God," I whisper to Bristol, who hasn't stopped looking for athletic man candy, "Those kids are wearing Goal Tender shirts. I'm pretty sure that's a wish-granting charity for sick children. We're not charity cases."

She cocks an eyebrow and speaks out of the side of her mouth. "I'm not, but you could be." She laughs, shoving me in the arm playfully. I would laugh, but a handler of some kind rounds us all up and gives us our instructions. He looks at the four of us and takes a second look at me, and I silently wonder if he thinks I'm the one with the disability.

The nerves I've been fighting all day really show themselves as three players enter the dugout. My hands shake, my heart batters my ribs, and I can't look away. I recognize Vance immediately, even behind the brim of his red Renegades ball cap. He's wearing a Renegades game shirt with jeans, and I would have to be dead not to look twice. He's hard to ignore.

He glances at me before turning his attention to a little boy who's about seven years old and shiny bald. He squats down to the boy's level and talks to him, getting him to laugh mid-way through the conversation. It's a different side of Vance, one not reported in the media.

The other two players, to Bristol's delight, are the Renegades' first baseman, Corky Alvarez, and their catcher, Ben Halsey. I know this because Tracy made me and Bristol sit through an hour's worth of detailed info about the team so we would be prepared.

Vance, after talking to each one of the children and their parents, wanders over to us. He claps Uncle Rodney on the shoulder and thanks him for coming. His eyes track to mine, and a reluctant grin settles on his lips. I wonder how many women he's ensnared with those lips and the occasional smile he lets slip.

"Hi," he says holding out a hand to me. "I'm Van Hatfield." His grin widens on the left side.

I look first at his hand and then at him, but do not take his hand. "You're being an idiot."

"Most people take the hand and offer their name."

"I'm not most people."

"I've noticed. But could you play nice for five minutes?" He holds out his hand one more time, and this time I take it because of his audience.

"Brenna Sloan," I offer with a small smirk I try to hide with my resting bitch face.

"Brenna Sloan." He says my name slow and deliberate, and hell if it doesn't make my sex clench. "Thank you for coming."

"I didn't have a choice," I say, glancing at a little boy. "But you set it up that way."

He shrugs. "I'm not someone who gives up."

"You have a fan." I nod to the little boy, who is tossing a baseball between his two hands. "I won't be the reason he doesn't get his autograph." I step back and wave the boy over. He looks up at me with wide brown eyes and smiles his appreciation.

"We're not done, Brenna Sloan."

My family, no longer at my side, have entangled themselves in the melee of excitement and are participating in a group picture with Corky, Halsey, and other team members I don't recognize.

The guys stay longer than their scheduled forty-five minutes and I successfully dodge Vance, though he hasn't really tried to get close despite occasionally glancing in my direction. When I'm about to leave with my group, though, he grabs me by the elbow.

"See you later?"

I look up at him, offering a nod as my response.

INLAND HEAT IS DIFFERENT THAN COASTAL HEAT, AND RIGHT NOW THE inland heat is getting the better of me. My eye makeup, applied generously between the meet and greet and the game, has smeared toward my temple and bogged down my tear duct. Meanwhile, my underwear has gone from comfortable cotton to wet, absorbent chamois.

We arrive at our seats extremely early for the game against the Padres so Uncle Rodney can have the full experience and Bristol can maximize her opportunity to see more players. Why she thinks she wants to be whisked off her feet smelling like ass and onion rings is beyond me, but I let her have her hour and forty-five minutes before game time without a verbal complaint.

The seats are phenomenal and no doubt come at a premium price. Home plate is visible without binoculars, and Uncle Rodney is in heaven. He uploads his first picture from Renegades Stadium to his Facebook with the caption, "Eat Me."

"I didn't know hell had stadium seating," my mom says, fanning herself with a heavy hand.

"Stadium seating, but apparently no baseball players. I'm a little surprised by that." Bristol's sense of humor, to my surprise, has been kept intact through today's heatwave.

I'm more upset about the Everglades between my thighs than the lack of hot guys in hell, but I remain silent and let the two of them troll for standouts.

After an hour of nothing, we are treated to a handful of players taking the field. A few crude exchanges between Bristol and number twenty-eight, Robbins, are the best part of warm-ups so far, but I'm pretty sure illegal in a handful of states. The sex education the rest of us get is priceless, and the little Oompa Loompa in front of us, who's the ripe old age of maybe twelve, now knows anal means more than attention to detail.

Music blares through the stadium, jazzing up the crowd, and the seats have filled in around us, making it even hotter. Body heat is not your friend when it's already eighty-something degrees and some people didn't see fit to wear deodorant. I fan myself with a souvenir program and thank the gods I'm not sitting beside the three-hundred-pound ball of sweating man-meat sitting one section up.

"Excuse me?" In unison, we look up at a stadium employee. I am instantly fearful we are being kicked out after Bristol's sexually-charged oral exchange with number twenty-eight. I have endured two hours in the blistering heat, and I am being escorted off the premises on my twenty-first birthday.

"Oh my God, are we being kicked out?" I ask, mortified and a little bit terrified of his stern expression. Is this going to be the next Sloan scandal?

The man with the authoritative demeanor and zero social warmth, actually smiles. "No. I'm here to provide you with your wristbands for Red Hooligans this evening. Mr. Hatfield offers his apologies for the oversight. He wasn't aware of the requirement."

Properly banded and relieved that we don't have to suffer through the humiliation of being tossed out, I settle in with the recently rare but enjoyable feeling of not being the center of attention for once.

Player announcements begin shortly after, and I focus on the names I know. "And on the mound, your returning starting pitcher, Van Hatfield . . ." The crowd cheers, and I watch as the girl in front of me, wearing his jersey, screams like a raving lunatic. It's funny when others appear that way, but not when they come from my own bloodline.

The game finally starts, and I watch as Van Hatfield, after a nine-day absence for "unrelated altercations on and off the field" according to the red-eared guy in front of us, strikes out the first three batters. The crowd is loud and obnoxious, but it helps to drown out my wavering thoughts.

While organ music plays, the Renegades head in, and as the teams switch, Robbins looks for Bristol. From the way he grabs his balls as he runs past us, he's found her. I, in sharp contrast to Bristol's engagement with the team, keep my eyes from straying to Vance—Van.

In a sweaty finish, the Renegades come out on top with a seven to zero shutout due in large part to Van Hatfield's return to the mound with his blazing fastball and their flawless execution at bat against San Diego's less-than-stellar relief squad. I get all this from the announcer, because all I know about baseball is it takes forever and little happens when one team or another doesn't hit the ball.

After the game, in front of the Renegades fountain, we meet up with Toolbag, his meathead friends, and Tracy and Tori, whom I've been texting with since arriving.

"Holy shit, Bristol." Carl's face is a mixture of pain and adoration as he runs a thumb over Bristol's bracelet. "Red Hooligans is damn near impossible to get into unless you get in line at nine a.m. or know someone. It's like the team bar. THE TEAM!" His eyes bulge, and he drops her hand with a nice helpful shove. "Who'd you screw for these?"

Bristol shrugs her shoulders. "Didn't have to lift a finger. Brenna did all the screwing."

Toolbag Carl looks at me, brows pinched in so they practically touch the bridge of his nose. "Brenna?"

Obviously, Tori and Tracy haven't broken the news or he'd know about Vance. I honestly hadn't expected them to keep it quiet, but I'm humbled by their loyalty.

I roll my eyes as Bristol responds with what she's been dying to reveal since Sunday. "Yeah, apparently Brenna has been dating Van Hatfield and didn't know it."

The entirety of the group looks at me, some bug-eyed, others, like Tori and Tracy, hold their breath. Bristol stands smug, gloating silently at my gullibility that is so much like our mother's.

"You and Van Hatfield?" Toolbag Carl sounds wounded. He must think I withheld it from him on purpose instead of to spare myself more drama and hurt.

"Oh, relax. I didn't know. And we're not dating. I bought him a beer. That's it."

"Well, that's not exactly true," Bristol adds. "She practically arm-wrestled me for him, and he had a front-row seat to her camel toe. Didn't you show him your ass too?"

Toolbag barks out a laugh that rattles the water. "So, it's your ass and not your boobs that gets the guy, huh?"

I glare at Bristol, not for sharing the Vance story, but for Toolbag's mention of the boob pic Bristol sent to Eli Perkins, my tenth-grade crush. I never told anyone that they were Bristol's boobs and not mine, sent by her on my unknowing behalf in the hopes Eli would finally notice me. And notice me he did, as did half the school who also saw the picture. I never came clean because Bristol was already handling her own scandal, and I couldn't throw her further under the bus.

The buried memory adds yet another black mark to this day, and my tolerance for unwanted bombshells is waning. I want memorable for my birthday, but not like this.

Seeing my disgruntled face, Bristol changes the subject fast, also taking the opportunity to rub our good fortune in Toolbag's face. "Wish you could celebrate with us at Red Houlihan's too."

"It's Hooligans," he snaps. "Jesus, you can't even say it right. Does Van know you can't pronounce that? How do two girls with zero interest in baseball, outside of getting laid by Van, get that lucky?"

"We're cute." If gloating had a color, Bristol would be radiating it.

"Hook a fan up, Brenna." He sounds sadly pathetic right now.

Bristol's flair for rubbing things into an open wound is state-of-the-art and occasionally hits below the belt. "If you'll excuse us, we have a club to get ready for." She taps the watch on Carl's wrist. "Best get in line. I heard it's long."

I hug him. "Do you want my wristband?" I'm dead serious. I want nothing more than to bag it now that I know what the hell Red Hooligans is. Toolbag would enjoy it more. The last thing I want to do is spend my birthday avoiding Vance at a club he frequents. Toolbag is too good to take my bait and declines, leaving me with plans I never asked for in an environment probably better suited for models with size F boobs.

CHAPTER ELEVEN

A
t nine p.m., a black stretch limo and its well-groomed driver arrive at the hotel to take us to Red Hooligans. It's a fairly short ride, all things considered for San Jose, and we pull up in front of the club, where a long line of hopefuls has formed just like Toolbag described.

The driver says something to one of four thick bouncers, and another one lifts a section of the velvet rope for us to pass through. I look briefly for Toolbag and his friends but don't have long before I'm pushed through like branded cattle.

The bouncer, dark-skinned and bald, guides us to a concierge-type booth and tells us to enjoy our night. It's at this booth that I get to show my I.D. for the first time since turning twenty-one. The attendant, a girl in a skin-tight black micro-mini, tells us the team should be arriving soon and to feel free to dance before heading up the staircase with our VIP passes.

In the club, loud music and lights assault the majority of my senses, leaving only my sense of smell, which is currently being consumed by my mom's perfume, sprayed way too heavily for a woman with a day job.

Dressed in a mid-thigh, two-toned, olive green and black mini-dress with long bell sleeves and peek-a-boo shoulders, I feel pretty, even as my nerves scream to run and my inner thighs wince at further abrasion. Next to Bristol, I usually feel like a pet rock, but tonight, I feel like I stand out on my own, and I don't know if it gives me confidence or the early rumblings of diarrhea.

Security is thick throughout the club but more so, it appears, on the upper deck where boobs the size of Kansas won't get you past the guard at the bottom step unless you have a VIP pass like the ones Uncle Rodney carries in his pocket.

I do my best to put on a happy face for Bristol and the celebration of our twenty-first birthday, but smiling is difficult, and I pray that every step I take is toward an exit. At the bar, the four of us toast Bristol's and my milestone birthday with a shot of Jameson that only serves to heat my skin and float my thoughts. After, Uncle Rodney and my mom head towards a corner table littered with glasses but unoccupied, and Bristol and I take to the dance floor, neither of us in a hurry to join Vance.

Someone comes up behind me and grinds up against my backside. I scoot forward and he follows like I'm wearing Velcro, his junk smashed against my ass. I turn to face the guy. "I think that's close enough." I raise my voice so he doesn't mistake my communication for acceptance. "Any closer and you'll need a condom."

He twirls his index finger at me to get me to turn around. "Too much talking," he yells over the sounds of Maroon Five. Before I can respond, I'm plucked from the dance floor, and Mr. "Too Much Talking" is saved from a junk-punch when he is shoved backward and away from me by the strong arm of someone much taller than me.

I look up into beautiful blue eyes, serious and intently plastered to my face. "Let's go." He gestures with his chin to the outside of the dance floor or an exit to his right, but I remain fixed, undeterred by his bossiness.

My heart sinks, remembering his deception, and I jerk my arm out of his grasp. One hour of civility at the meet and greet does not make up for his lies. "I'm here for Uncle Rodney."

He sets his jaw, looks up into the pulsing lights, and then lands a hard stare I want to shrink beneath. "I get that. Can we talk for two minutes?"

I shake my head and turn to find Bristol or a comfortable space I can submerge myself in, but he grabs my hand and pulls me toward a back door lit above with an "Exit" sign. Seeing no choice, I follow, hoping my ankles don't give out in my heels and my stomach rumbles don't forewarn of an impending blowout.

Vance walks past more security who nod at him as he pushes through the exit door, dragging me behind him. Out in the warm air of a late San Jose evening, he stops short of a parking lot filled with expensive cars bathed in the amber glow of streetlights. He drops his hand and pivots to look at me.

He pitchforks his fingers through his hair. "What do I have to do to make this up to you?"

I hold eye contact with him, noticing the distress in his expression. "You can't."

"It got away from me. I kind of hoped the VIP treatment would take care of some of my blunders. I didn't know how else to make it up to you after I left." His expression looks pained, like one I'd have after admitting something stupid to my mother.

"You thought better seats would make up for lying?"

He releases a heavy breath and drops his head back on his shoulders. "I know that sounds bad. Fuck. Let me start over." He squares a look right on me. In any other circumstance, I'd probably melt. Not tonight, though he continues without realizing that. "I didn't know the girl I introduced myself to. Not like I know her now, anyway. I bought a house in Milagro Beach six months ago to disengage from the spotlight. I was there to lay low and disconnect for a bit. The last thing I planned was finding you." He looks down, fixing his black tie with two fingers he runs down its length. "I should have told you or stayed away altogether. I know that now. I couldn't get the words out once they needed to be said."

"I looked like an ass the entire time."

"Not at all. I loved your confidence. Why do you think I came up with excuse after excuse to have a beer? In normal life, I have a beer like, once a week, if that."

That explains why he needed a damn nipple and a napkin, but I don't buy the rest. Why would a guy like him find anything about the Brenna I introduced him to remotely worth binge drinking for?

"So, you got entertainment, a chance to see how the other half lives, a few unwanted beers, and I got . . . lied to."

His body stiffens.

"I feel stupid."

"Dammit, Brenna, the fact you don't read *Candid* magazine or have TMZ notifications on your phone is fucking rare. I ate it up. And that's the truth. Don't feel stupid. I promise you, I don't see you that way."

The knot in my throat becomes an unbearable swallow. I believe him, but I'm not ready to make him my weakness. "I don't know, Vance. It's going to take time."

He sighs, relief seeming to relax his features. "I can work with that. Give me another shot to do this right, and if I can't, then walk."

I look away, gathering my thoughts, which center around wanting to get to know Van Hatfield, and I nod once. "Okay."

Inside, with Vance behind me, I look for Bristol, Uncle Rodney, and my mom but can't find them in the crowd or at the table where they were last. Vance touches my wrist and shouts above the music, "I'll have someone get them. We need to get upstairs."

I shake my head, yelling back at him, "I can't leave them. They only stayed down here because I wasn't ready to go up yet."

"Look!" A girl screams. "It's Van Hatfield!" She shrieks even louder, and as she bounces up and down, her boobs lob heavily. She slams against Vance, pressing her entire body to the front of his, and he tries to push her away with one hand while his other hand grapples for mine.

More and more hands rake over him, taking privileges they should be slapped for. "Van!" A chorus of girls shrieks in orchestral unity. "Van!" They scream in one final unified chant before he's ripped away and I'm left alone in a floundering crowd that's crawling over me and each other to get to him.

I am absorbed into the raucous crowd as they gather around us. Girls shriek, scream, and try to get a piece of Vance in any way they can. I'm lost, and not just within the crowd, but mentally. As I'm looking for an exit, I'm suddenly met in all directions with chests, broad shoulders, and forearm clotheslines that nearly behead me, and it's still less offensive than the airbags from girl number one.

By the dozen, security arrives using their massive bodies to thin the crowd and surround Vance. "Get to her!" he shouts at one of them. They both look in my direction. "Get to her!" he shouts again.

Chants for Van are intermixed with the occasional squeal when one manages to get a chunk of him, and obscene offers I'm not altogether certain aren't coming from Bristol. I realize the music has stopped, which explains why I can hear Vance and the sound of my erratic heartbeat. An arm encircles my waist and hitches me to a muscular body that carries me out of the crowd with the ease of an elephant clomping through a horde of chipmunks.

Away from the fray, the security guard sets me on my feet, making sure I'm balanced before letting me go. "Hang here for a minute, okay?" He looks into my eyes for understanding. "Just until we get the crowd under control," he adds upon seeing my expression.

Swallowing hard, I nod, my eyes not on him but on Vance, who has a security detail to rival the president's. Vance, tall by anyone's standards, is barely tall enough to look over their heads, and I can see him trying to talk his way out of their protection. One of the big guys plants a firm hand on his shoulder, keeping him in place. I can see arms and lips moving but hear nothing of their words.

"Okay, ma'am, I can escort you to Mr. Hatfield now if you'd like?" Anticipating my cooperation, he rests a light hand on the small of my back.

I shake my head. "I'm good. Thank you."

"Ma'am?"

"I'm leaving. I won't be a problem, I swear." He looks surprised, and I'm sure he is. I mean, what girl in her right mind wouldn't go to Van Hatfield? Based upon the screaming girls clawing and offering up things their mothers would be shocked over, I'm betting it's only me.

He pushes a finger into his right ear, presumably listening to Vance's security team, and questions me again. "Are you sure?"

I nod.

No longer needing my bravado, tears line my lashes. The fight to hold them off has been lost, and they run hot and heavy down my cheeks. I swipe at them with my fingertips, but more replace the smeared wreckage of the previous ones. How am I supposed to do this?

Before I can find the exit, Vance finds me, security all around him, pissing and moaning about his actions. "Brenna!"

I look at him, unsure.

"Please go upstairs?"

I shake my head. "I'm not ready for this."

"This is why you're rare. This is why I wasn't in a hurry to be Van with you. Do you get that now?"

I nod, realizing how wrong I've been, realizing I'm in no position to judge him. This is unlike anything I've ever experienced, just like being with me is unlike anything he's used to. I've stewed for days on end over Colette judging me and Bristol for our dad's mistakes and for believing her mom's opinion that any Sloan is a bad Sloan. I'm not what people say any more than Vance is.

Slipping my hand into the one Vance is offering, I look up at him. "I'll try."

CHAPTER TWELVE

t the top of the staircase to the VIP level of Red Hooligan's, black steps lit with red lights meet sleek black tiles and an expansive space that is upscale but inviting. I pause to take it in. At first, it's surreal and a bit intimidating to be in a room full of people you don't know intimately but have seen in magazines and television. As my surroundings sink in, I zero in on my family who were brought up here just before me. Uncle Rodney can hardly contain his glee, and if I were beside him, I'd tell him to close his mouth while he looks around. Mom, in a slightly different manner, scans the room like she's going to rob it later, and Bristol, pissed I ditched her again for Vance, heads right for us.

Hoping to avoid the conflict her expression suggests is coming, I leave Vance with the excuse of going to find a table for all of us while he tends to a man in a suit waving him over.

"Let's find a seat." Like the born peacekeeper I am, I grab Bristol before she can get within breathing distance of Vance. We sit at one of several tables fronting an empty bar. Along with us, there are other family members and friends joining the players and staff, and the room teems with reunions we're not a part of.

Corky Alvarez, Tracy's crush, stands feet away from us. He is quite the social butterfly and appears to have the personality of someone who would be voted Prom King. His gorgeous Latin looks have probably snared him a few pairs of panties without the girls even knowing he was taking them off.

"Hello, ladies." A guy, cute but not stand-out, sets a chair he's carried over between us.

"Hello." Bristol answers for the two of us and shifts her body to look at him.

"Twins?" he asks, looking at us one at a time.

"Our identical looks give us away every time," I tease, laughing as I deliver my irritation delicately.

He laughs. "You're a smartass—I like it. I was just trying to make conversation. I saw you from across the room." Bristol beams. There is nothing she likes more than being noticed.

"Hey." Another guy weasels his way between me and the first guy, making himself comfortable inside my bubble while Bristol and the other guy take off for the bar.

"Are you someone's sister? I can't say as I've ever seen you before. I'd definitely remember you if I had." He's a close talker, the kind that has no space issues of his own and doesn't give a shit about yours. His breath is nice, minty, and hasn't been tainted with alcohol yet.

"No. I'm a friend."

"Oh, whose?"

"Mine!" Vance, standing tall behind the second guy's chair, glares openly. Neither of us saw him coming, and the guy practically rockets backward to get out of the way.

I look up, my heart hammering with Vance's proximity and the still-fresh emotions of all that's transpired in the last weeks and hours.

Close Talker's departure is swift, and Vance takes his vacated seat.

"He wasn't bothering me," I say, looking straight into Vance's blue eyes.

"He was bothering me," he states, leaning forward in his chair. "Sorry, I hope you weren't uncomfortable."

Vance's lightly applied cologne temporarily distracts me from my nerves. I could inhale him for days. I don't know what it is about him and his scent, but God help me, I may be addicted.

"No more so than at any other time today."

"I'm sorry for what happened downstairs." His eyes grin, and his teeth are white between his parted lips.

"You couldn't help it."

"Doesn't matter. I feel bad." He nods up at someone who passes by our table and then returns his attention back to me.

I haven't had the wherewithal to find a smile. With so many conflicting emotions to process, I can't keep anything but my heartbeat in check.

"You look beautiful." His eyes roam over the leg crossed over my knee, and then up to my chest, where they dally but do not stop. My dress is short, coming only to mid-thigh, and since I'm sitting, it rises a little higher. His gaze doesn't rattle me like it probably should, and I handle it like it's routine.

He offers me a drink, which I decline, and he asks for a bottle of water from the busty waitress he hasn't even glanced at, though she feels the need to linger.

"Great game, by the way," I say, and a smile appears on my face of its own accord, and not with the forced sincerity I feared I'd have to muster.

"Thank you." His appreciation is spoken with a humbleness I didn't think someone like him possessed. "Shit!" Vance blasts, replying to some thought in his head, I'm guessing. He leans toward me putting his mouth close to my ear. "I need to make some introductions. Are you okay with that?"

I smile, waving him away with my hand. "Go," I say with indifference. "I won't be alone long."

His expression stiffens, but I wave him away and smile again. "I'm kidding. Take your time."

After about ten minutes pass and Vance still hasn't returned from his introductions, I get up and nudge my way through small groups of people. I stand next to the balcony railing and look out over the dance floor below. There are a lot of people down there seemingly oblivious to the party above them.

From up here, you can see the meat market for what it is. You can pick out the desperate women hoping to be noticed and the guys that notice them. There are no wallflowers here.

I feel a body press against me from behind and see hands grip the railing in front of me before I hear the voice that takes my breath. "Are you looking for an exit?"

I smile despite myself. "Maybe."

"Stop." His breath brushes against my cheek. I feel his jaw tick on the side of my head, right behind my ear.

"How did you know it was me and not Bristol you were grabbing down there?" I nod to the dance floor.

"Trust me. I can tell." His voice is hot and deep.

I spin within the cave of his arms and lean against the railing, putting an additional inch between us. He doesn't move, leaving his hands on the railing and his elbows straight.

I look him square in the eyes, faltering only a second when his eyes drop and flicker between my lips and my eyes. Parts of me want him like I've never wanted another human being, while others still revolt at the thought of letting my guard down. "You're not going to give up, are you?"

His eyes stop wandering, and his parted lips come together as he bites the lower one, shaking his head with a resounding, unspoken, *No.*

"Even if I tell you I'm not interested?"

Again, he shakes his head, his brows lifting a fraction to give him that devilish look that has probably sparked a lot of panties into a raging inferno. "Your body says something different."

"It does?"

"I bet if I checked, foreplay wouldn't be needed. Of course, I'd still insist upon it, but it would be strictly for my pleasure and not your necessity."

If he wasn't right before, he is now. My body pulses and aches for a kind of release it's never had, and anything other than him, I realize, would be a disappointment. I swallow, digging deep for my composure so I can play the game instead of getting lost in it.

"And if I told you I don't think you're interested but rather fixated because you're trying to prove me wrong, would you have an answer for that too?"

"I could let you feel for yourself how wrong you are." A flat-out wicked gleam sparks in his eyes.

I look down involuntarily at the part of his body he is referring to and back up to his eyes. "That could be for anyone. It's not like we aren't surrounded by goddesses." I look over his shoulder and can pinpoint at least two overly-endowed women that fit the description.

"I haven't looked at anyone else." His eyes remain trained on mine.

"Why me? Normally you wouldn't touch me with someone else's dick."

He winces, scrunching an eye. "You're the one hung up on quote-unquote normal. I wouldn't normally take this much time on a girl, but I'm doing it."

He has a point. He's put in a lot of effort when there are so many sure things out there for him.

"Hey, Hatfield?" I welcome the interruption by one of his team-mates and use it to put a little more distance between us when Vance stands up straight to talk to him.

"I'm out. I just wanted to congratulate you on a good game, man." Vance's teammate, older by a few years and ruggedly handsome, claps Vance on the shoulder and smiles. He then turns his attention to me. "Greg," he offers, extending a huge hand toward me, and if the theory about hand size is true, he's left no shortage of loose women in his wake.

I accept it without question, liking him instantly. "Brenna."

He exchanges a look with Vance that I question but will never ask about. "Nice to meet you, Brenna. Don't keep him out too late. We need him rested."

"I don't think you have to worry about that."

A small smirk transforms his kind face, making him look like a mischievous boy. "If you say so," he says, turning his attention solely to Vance. "Later, Hatfield."

Vance turns back to me. "You can keep me out late if you want. Middleton's not really the boss."

Taking inventory of my family, I spot Uncle Rodney looking like he's died and gone to heaven. Bristol, looking happier and holding her own with Robbins at the far side of the bar, gets the award for most improved attitude. It is my mom, who sits with an older gentleman, not to be confused with old, because he is beautifully handsome and austere, that surprises me. She seems to have absolutely captivated him, because he looks at no one but her. It could also be he thinks she's crazy when she throws her head back to laugh and her cackle breaks the sound barrier, but I don't think so. Saying she has had too much to drink might be exaggerating, because she hasn't stripped to her underwear and hula danced yet, but we're close.

"Thank you," I croak out like I ate a spoonful of sand. I clear it and try again. "I know you didn't do all this just for him, but you made Uncle Rodney happy today." It's delivered eloquently and without an ounce of scratch to my voice.

"I actually did do it for him," he says, his brows drawing together. "You were a perk, though."

I believe him, and things start easing up in my chest. "Regardless, I appreciate it. I didn't like taking the spot of a sick child, though. Thanks for that, by the way." I shove his arm.

Vance exhales. "I added you four to the lineup. You didn't take anyone's 'spot.' I promise." He studies me.

"What?" I ask, nervous about the track of his thoughts.

"I'm wondering what I have to do to see you again."

My stomach flips. "I think I was too quick to judge you. I'm used to really shitty people with ulterior motives, but you didn't deserve to be lumped in with them so quickly. I'm sorry."

He raises a shoulder and reaches for a tendril of my hair that he twirls lightly around his finger. "You don't have to apologize. I can't say my motives will always be on the upside of good. But they'll never be dishonest. You still haven't answered the question."

"I don't know, but you've got a game tomorrow, and I've got to get my drunk mother to bed."

"I don't have a game until tomorrow afternoon, and she looks fine to me." He hasn't looked away from me to know this.

"To the untrained eye, yes, but to the expert, her cackle precedes poor choices."

He concedes with a waffle of his head. "I guess you'd know. Things will be winding down here shortly anyway. I'll walk you out."

I gather the drunk crew, a forgotten purse on a chair, and a number from Mom's suitor, and we exit the club close to where we came into it. Cameras flash the second we hit fresh air, and I catch a small glimpse of the other aspect of Vance's life. I halt, turn around, and push Vance back inside the door while the others, oblivious, walk ahead mumbling and giggling on their way to the limo.

"No offense," I preface, feeling the weight of what I'm about to say next before it's even out there, "but I'm not quite ready to be on the cover of *Candid* with you." I draw in a breath and check my current state of indecision. I've lived my life explaining my actions, denying Bristol's, and defending my mom's. I don't know if I'm ready for the much broader spotlight his life will cast over mine. And what happens to me when he's done doing "normal?" Things were so much easier when I was feeling out my heart's curiosities and not wondering whether I could weather a global rumor storm or meet the expectations of a baseball god.

"I'm not ready for that either," he admits. From inside the doorway, I can't tell where the camera flashes are coming from, but I'm sure he's well versed. "But this isn't how I wanted to say goodnight to you."

"I'm sorry."

"I'm the one who should apologize." He looks out, seeming to think of another option before dragging me deeper inside the entryway, where security hovers close. "Will you stay for the game tomorrow?"

"I can't." I'm disappointed, but it will be a good test for his tenacity.

"Can't or won't?"

"Wow! You're cynical."

"You're hard to read lately." His tone is softer, a regretful edge to its sincerity.

I sigh. "I can't. My ride leaves at eight, and my beautiful room expires at eleven."

"Should I be worried about you changing into a pumpkin?"

"I think that's her chariot."

He's so close to a smile, I wait. "Chariot. Right." His smile hits his eyes, not his lips. "I can cover the chariot and all the other accommodations if you'll stay."

"I can't ask you to do that. Maybe we could meet up for dinner another day you're in town?"

"You're not asking. I'm offering."

"You know I'm not sleeping with you, right?"

"I'll be a perfect gentleman, I swear."

I nod slowly. "I'll take the chariot, but I'll pay for my own room."

"I'll have a car come for you at eleven, and there will be a ticket at Will Call. Just give them your name."

I'm not sure how to end this night with him any more than he knows how to end it with me. So I take the initiative and rise on my tiptoes, leaning toward him. I kiss him on the cheek, far, far away from his lips, where a small amount of stubble has risen. "Goodnight, and thank you for everything."

His hands encircle my arms, and at first I wonder if he is going to push me back. But he holds me steady and looks me in the eyes before he brushes his lips against mine. They are soft at first, tentative and testing, and when I don't hesitate, they become the pleasure-producers I knew they'd be. His hands lift to my face, cupping it while his tongue tests the waters to find me accepting. My breath catches as our tongues meet, and with each swirl and taste he takes, my knees weaken. The kisses I've had before him pale in comparison.

Pulling away before he gets too far, he looks at me. "I'll see you tomorrow."

CHAPTER THIRTEEN

S leep after a night like last night is near impossible. Throw in worrying whether or not Bristol will ever speak to me again after telling her about today's plans, and it's nonexistent.

I text Vance at the number Tori gave me when I finally got the nerve to ask for it.

Me: *Good morning.*

Vance's reply doesn't come right away and so, with the time I have, I tackle Bristol, and while laying on top of her remind her how awesome I am. "You can't stay mad at me," I tell her, lightly teasing but with more sincerity than she'll ever appreciate. "I've never been on an actual date I didn't get because I was your wing girl. You should actually be pushing me out the door."

She snorts, "You smoked crack for breakfast, didn't you?"

I press my palm into her forehead and press her head into the mattress, playful like we used to be when we were little and fighting over stickers. "I know how to handle my crack. I'm being serious." I let her head go after she squirms enough that I'm about to fall off of her. "I need you to at least pretend you're happy for me, so I can do this."

Breathing heavily after trying to dislodge my weight, Bristol exhales, her body a bit more compliant. "I'm happy for you. I am. I just worry about you becoming Mom and overlooking everything that's wrong because he's hot and says the right things. Not to mention, this family would be skewered in the tabloids, and we've got a lot of dirt to publish."

"You have dirt. I have dust. I'm not overlooking anything."

"You are! He lied, Brenna."

"He didn't *lie* lie."

"Oh, okay, Mom. See? It's already started and you haven't even slept with him. Please tell me you're not going to sleep with him. Of the two of us, you're the good one. Don't lose that for sweet talk and kick-ass abs."

"I know what I'm doing," I say, rolling off her and onto my back beside her. "Besides, I can't compete with the women he has access too. I'll be a footnote quickly."

My phone chimes a text notification, and I barely refrain from jumping on it. I roll sideways, kiss her cheek, and recite our motto: "Me and you against the world."

"Me and you," she says softly.

I gradually sit up, acting like it's a choice I don't want to make, and when I'm off the bed and she's returned to packing her bag, I check my phone.

Vance: *Who is this?*

I smile.

Me: *Guess.*

Vance: *No.*

He is so grouchy when he's not flirting with me.

Me: *I don't kiss and tell. I thought you'd know.*

Vance: *Brenna????*

I nod as if he can see me, and I must giggle out loud because Bristol snarks out something about my annoying happiness so early in the morning. But Vance obviously hasn't kissed anyone more recent than me, or he would have called me Betty or Bambi or Svetlanka.

"Who are you texting?" Bristol asks.

I look at her but don't answer and tap out my reply to Vance.

Me: *Yeah, it's me. In case you need my # to back out.*

Vance: *Not a chance.*

I practically squeal.

My phone sings Imagine Dragons' "Radioactive," and Bristol stops what she's doing to look at me.

"Who's calling you?"

I shrug, smile, and answer my phone as I walk out of the room and into the hall.

"Hey," Vance says softly. "How's your morning going?"

"Good. Quiet. They're all getting ready to leave, which might take a bit longer than normal since my mom is just now discovering why she doesn't go hard anymore, and Uncle Rodney thinks he needs to soak in the big bathtub. Are you sure you still want to do this?"

"Beyond sure. I added an extra night to your room, so don't check out."

"I told you I would get it." I'd never speak it, but I'm sort of glad I don't have to choose between paying off a room I can't afford and buying textbooks for Bristol when they cancel her scholarship due to her lack of attendance.

"I must have missed that. Sorry. Anyway, are you cool with keeping it low key tonight, after the game I mean? I don't think either of us is ready for the circus."

"Sounds perfect."

"I don't want to cut this short, but I've got a morning workout."

"You're fine. I just wanted you to have my number."

"Thank you. Oh, and Brenna?"

"Yeah?"

"I can't wait to see you."

I smile. "Me either."

AFTER SEEING UNCLE RODNEY, MOM, AND AN INCREASINGLY POUTY Bristol off after a mostly silent pre-paid room service brunch in Mom's room, the car arrives to take me to the ballpark. Will Call is surprisingly easy, and within fifteen minutes, I slip into my seat. Sitting beside a girl wearing a ball cap, sunglasses, and a number twelve Hatfield shirt, I wish I'd glammed up a bit. My nominal jealous side rears its ugly head, and I tamp down the inner monologue criticizing her beauty as I stand for the national anthem.

Sitting down at the end of the anthem, I stuff a chip into my mouth and chomp loudly. I don't know if it's the best way to get her attention or to make me look like I was raised by wolverines, but it works, and pretty girl with "Hatfield" on her T-shirt looks at me.

"I didn't think anyone was sitting there."

Not sure if she's being rude or making conversation, I'm careful with my expression. "Only for part of it." It's the sarcastic truth. I fully intend to be on my feet for most of it and not sitting beside her.

She shrugs. "I just meant it's usually empty. You're free to sit for the whole game." She smiles, yells as they put Vance's picture on the

Jumbotron, and returns to her seat. I'm hoping she's just rabid and not a stalking fangirl like Tracy.

Vance pitches for the first six innings, allowing few hits, which, if I'm being honest, makes for a boring game. I don't know all the rules, but I know it's more exciting if both teams hit the ball, and with a score of three to zero, excitement has been limited. Pretty brunette girl wearing number twelve chats away with me about how much she wishes she lived closer so she could attend more games and how she likes Van's new walk-up song and hated the one he had his rookie year. She knows a lot about him, but I can't get a word in through all her info and statistics, so I nod, grunt a few times, and yell when Robbins and Corky take a turn at bat. She leaves before the end of the ninth with a wave and a "nice to meet you," though I don't think we exchanged names.

After the game I wait in the tunnel, where security is tight and reporters are prevalent, along with what I guess are fans, who either have some sort of pass like me or sneaked in. It's calm chaos with thunderous acoustics as the team files past to the locker rooms. I watch for Vance, who passes by with a look and nothing more.

My name is announced, and though not through any equipment, it's loud and plenty clear. I walk up as far as I can without pissing people off, and it's announced again, so I wave my hand over my head, and security immediately clears a path and directs me to the front.

"Brenna Sloan?"

I nod, nervous as fuck and sweating bullets. The security guard, thick but short and rather underwhelming as far as security guards go, checks my I.D. and a laminated pass Vance left at Will Call. "You can wait in the press room."

"I'm not press."

Toneless, he responds, "I wouldn't claim it either. Right in there." He points to a red door that reads "Authorized Personnel Only," and I aim in its direction with him close behind me. He swipes his badge, and the door pops open to a nice air-conditioned room with a water cooler and a television playing highlights of Renegades practices, games, and charity events. It's all very propaganda-ish.

After I've watched propaganda on loop for about an hour, Vance enters the room. He's freshly showered, hair still damp, wearing an impeccably pressed black suit. While I'm checking him out, he's probably looked me over twice and is now questioning his taste in women. I didn't pack to stay an extra day, so I'm in recycled clothes and bathed in perfume.

"I'm sorry that took so long. I had press." He keeps a fair amount of distance between us, but he came and still remains, so I take that as a good sign he's not going to dump me here. "Are you okay with going back to my place?"

I CLIMB INTO VANCE'S SILVER AUDI SPYDER. THE SEAT FITS ME LIKE IT checked my body type before I climbed in and adjusted itself accordingly. I'm in awe and distressed all at the same time. I don't live around things this nice, and I feel like I'm in an all-white room with grease on my fingers. The thing is exquisite and fast as fuck as he flies down the highway at racetrack speeds.

Vance's home, where he primarily lives during the season, is located within a gated community fronted by a guard shack and cameras. The street, lined with pristine lawns and mature trees, is wide and unencumbered by vehicles parked along the curbing. Not a single motorhome, kayak trailer, or rusted-out nineteen seventy-six station wagon exists as far as the eye can see. His stamped concrete driveway is long and curves to his three-car garage which, by the standards around here, is small. The rest of his property, including the house and grounds, is well-lit, blooming up and out like a grand chandelier, making it a beautiful focal point against a painted sky.

Inside is magnificent yet somehow understated for the wealth. Beyond a grand foyer is a sitting room, and family pictures adorn a portion of one wall like a shrine to his All-American upbringing.

I point at a white frame stamped with colorful dinosaurs surrounding a smiling little brown-haired boy. "Yours?"

"My nephew, Jacoby. He loves his T-Rex." His face softens, exchanging the broad, happy smile for one of thoughtful remembrance. "That's my grandfather." He points to a wooden frame inscribed with the quote, "Pitchers, like poets, are born, not made. – Cy Young" The picture is of an older man crouched and squatting in front of a young dark-haired boy, presumably Vance at maybe five or six. They're exchanging a baseball from one slightly aged hand to a hand that hasn't yet discovered its destiny. I smile, looking up at Vance who has a faraway look in his eyes.

"Is he the reason you're a pitcher?"

He nods, lips tight, eyes linked to mine. "He knew. He got me." I get the feeling there is more to that story than I'm going to get out of him on our first date. I return my eyes to the pictures of Vance's life and career, finding them all very meaningful.

"Who is that?" It's a dark-haired guy in his early thirties with his arm around a teen-aged Vance.

"My manager, Chip. That's the day I signed with the Renegades." Grabbing my hand, he doesn't let me look long and drags me back through the foyer and into a much larger media room with all the comforts of home. The television is huge and hangs on a wall in front of a brown leather sofa and two recliners. Everything in here is rich tans and deep browns, neutral but masculine.

"I wasn't sure what you wanted to eat so I ordered sushi, and as a backup, I also have macaroni and cheese. Everyone likes macaroni and cheese, right?"

I giggle. "Sushi is fine."

Before dinner arrives, Vance takes a call from his manager who, based upon Vance's side of the conversation, isn't happy with him. Vance, mid eye-roll, dismisses his concerns with a curt, "My life, Chip. Mine," and hangs up, slightly more agitated than he was before.

"Everything okay?" I ask, curious, because I feel like the chill factor just went up.

He nods. "My manager, the one you saw in the picture, thinks he's my guardian, and sometimes I have to put him in his place. I'm good. What about you?"

I hesitate before parting with my honesty. "Are you sure you're really okay with this?"

"With what?"

"This." I gesture to the table, making a broad sweep over it with my hand. "Staying in and not having the advantage of a wait staff."

He sighs heavily, burdened by something I have a feeling he's about ready to unload. "This, Brenna, is what I was afraid of."

"What?"

"You didn't find anything wrong with watching a sunset or sitting on a barstool beside me saying nothing at all when I was just the guy beside you. Those things weren't too simple for him, but they are for Van Hatfield."

Shit. He's right. I swallow loud enough for it to be heard and sit forward. "I just don't want—"

"Stop." Eyes intense, he leans forward and runs his index finger along my jawline. "This, right here, is what I want."

I didn't know something so far removed from foreplay could be so seductive, but when he does it, it's sexy as hell. I stare at his beautiful hands and marvel at their wicked accuracy when he throws a ball. They've probably pleasured as many women as they've hurt, and I'm still not sure I want to be part of the statistics.

"What about me being interested in you bothers you so much?"

"Really? You date strippers, models, sometimes two or three at a time. I'm nobody."

His eyes shut momentarily, and long black lashes tickle his cheeks. "You are somebody. And honestly, you're somebody I like a lot. I'm actually a lot pickier than the tabloids make me out to be. I'm seen with a lot of women in Hollywood because it's a mutual convenience. I don't worry about them running their mouths to the tabloids, and they don't worry about me exploiting them. Loyalty in this world is hard to come by. I value it, so I surround myself with like-minded people, if that makes sense."

I nod. "It does. I've been burned too. Maybe not on the same scale as you, but betrayal is still betrayal."

"Agreed. What else bothers you?"

"We don't have that kinda time."

His eyebrows climb, and he leans back. "There's that much that bothers you?"

"Enough to fill at least an hour. But you're charming."

"And a gentleman. How'm I doing?"

"Not bad. I'm impressed."

"It's a fluke. I assure you."

"Oh, how so?"

"I'm dying to kiss you. I've been in turmoil all day."

"Gentlemen kiss. Bad boys ravage."

Vance is up and out of his chair in half a second. His hands, with those long beautiful fingers, are tangled in my hair and tilting my head back to kiss me. I grasp his shoulders, feeling the flex of the taut muscles beneath his dress shirt.

He pulls back, ending the kiss with slow cruelty. I open my eyes to find him still close and studying me. He pulls me up to my feet and wraps me in his arms, groaning softly into my hair. "Let's go for a swim."

"What? Why?" I say into his solid chest.

"If we keep doing this, Brenna, we're gonna fuck."

CHAPTER FOURTEEN

Did I hear him right?

I'm a fan of being forthright and have never been one to skirt the realities of life, but Vance takes being blunt to a whole other level. I stare stunned, my mouth a motionless oval, too paralyzed to utter a counteroffer or an agreement. And as astonishing as they are, his words are also a real panty-burner, and I suddenly don't want to be all that respectable. I know I said numerous times I wasn't going to sleep with him, but that was before, before . . . Jesus, before he said that.

"I—"

"You can wear my shirt or something, or we can sit by the pool if that's more comfortable, but we gotta do something else. I'm not a saint."

"Do you want me to go?" I bite the inside of my bottom lip as my nerves threaten to blow my thin cover of confidence.

"No!" he says grabbing hold of my shoulders. "I want you to make it hell on me." He kisses me hard, his lips demanding, and the small nip on my bottom lip he leaves behind as he pulls away weakens my dwindling dedication. "Just show me a little mercy every now and then."

I nod and follow him, with the guidance of his hand and a pace that feels far too rushed to be retrieving only a T-shirt. We climb the stairs, and I'm pretty sure if he wasn't having to drag me, he'd be taking them two at a time.

Vance's bedroom is a creamy ivory color with dark wood furniture and brushed bronze-colored accents. It's not at all the pleasure palace I would've expected if I'd envisioned it beforehand, which, oddly enough, I hadn't. Regardless, it's lackluster for a man of his reputation. I expected love swings and handcuffs, but you'd have to split a person in half to handcuff them to the bed unless they had the wingspan of a pterodactyl.

He lets go of my hand at the doorway and proceeds to his closet, where he grabs the first T-shirt he comes to, and without looking at it, he tosses it to me. "Here," he says. "It's going to dwarf you, but at least you won't have to get your clothes wet. Naked tonight wouldn't be good, so don't go that route."

He's awfully bossy. "Let's swim so we don't fuck." "Wear this." "Don't be naked." What if I want exactly the opposite of all that? He must sense my need for some discipline to offset my impulses. Maybe I'm mistaking his restraint for bossiness. After all, you don't become one of the best in your business without some discipline.

I wait poolside, looking stupid. The T-shirt he gave me hangs mid-thigh, and if I didn't have an ass, I'd be the equivalent of a coat rack. Khalid plays through the sound system at a volume I don't think he's quite determined by the way it keeps adjusting. Waiting on him, I skim my foot over the top of the water as purple lights come on, illuminating the waterfall situated on the far side where it slopes between the shallow and deep ends.

Pulling my foot back, I turn, and Vance is standing in the doorway between house and patio looking every bit a sexy cover model of *Jock* magazine. He looks a lot like he did the day I met him

—tattoos in full view, body a huge distraction, face contemplative. My eyes gravitate to his chest where a black and gray tattoo of two baseball bats crisscrossed over home plate sits square over his heart. The baseball, boasting the number twelve between the red seams, the only color in the tattoo, sits above the cross in the bats. The tattoos and the man are both magnificent.

I clear my thoughts to try to act normal. "I don't know if I can wear this." I tug on the shirt. "Would it be weird if I went in my bra and underwear? I mean, you've seen my ass." Between my dress being up around my neck and my camel toe, I really don't think I'm in danger of him seeing something new.

"I saw your ass when we weren't . . ." he pauses, thinking twice about what he was going to say. "I'm good with whatever you're comfortable with." He drops a few towels onto a chair and dives into the deep end, surfacing by the waterfall that's cascading from terraced rocks protruding from an upper-level pond.

I strip the shirt off over my head, toss it onto the chair with the towels, and dive in, hoping I won't have to see his critical gaze. My body isn't perfect, but it's far from frumpy. I shouldn't care what he thinks since I've never cared before, but for some godforsaken reason, his opinion matters to me now.

He swims past the waterfall to the deep end, avoiding me so entirely, the water he glides through doesn't even ripple around me. I swish the water around me, using my arms like wings to skim the top of the water and then, seeing a small basketball tucked in a corner of the yard beside a utility closet, I perk up. "Do you want to play some ball?"

Swiping his hands over his hair and blowing some water off his lips, he replies, "Sure."

I take the steps out of the pool slowly, feet uncertain beneath me, and retrieve the ball, hearing Vance's not-so-subtle growl.

"What?"

"Nothing," he growls out.

The ball is small enough I can palm it, and squeezing it to test its deflation, I call him out, "Dude, you've gotta chill, you're making me—"

My words just stop as blue eyes run over my body, making no attempt to hide their destination or the track they travel. My first instinct is to cover myself with the towel hanging over a chair, but I've been so forward, it seems ludicrous to be shy now. "Brenna." He points at me and then runs his finger up and down in the air. "That right there isn't showing me mercy."

My makeshift bathing suit is a hodgepodge of Walmart black boy shorts and an off-brand emerald green bra. It doesn't get more merciful than that without throwing in a pair of Spanx.

I jump in aiming the ball at his head and see him bat it away before my head sinks beneath the water. He dunks me as I surface, and I laugh, taking in water as I submerge. I come up cough-laughing, and he pats my back, apologizing.

"I'm good," I laugh, clutching my chest. "You're a bully."

"And you're a brat." He swims for the ball, which is being driven away by the bubbles of the waterfall, and when he gets to it, he tosses it to me. "The first one to ten, wins."

I toss and miss. I'm not too upset because the hoop in the center of a floating ring is a moving target. It's hard. Apparently, only for me though. One-handed and over his head, he tosses the ball in effortlessly.

I roll my eyes as he swims after it. "You got this," he says tossing it to me, and I wait for him to move away from the basket before making another attempt.

I yelp, celebrating a point it took me two turns to achieve. Back and forth we toss the ball, scooting back further each time and sometimes challenging ourselves with a left-handed toss, that in my case misses and lands on the surrounding concrete. "Shit!" I groan and swim to the edge.

"Oh, no you don't." Vance grabs my foot and pulls me backwards through the water until we're almost side by side. "We've talked about this."

I laugh, shoving him in the arm as he starts to swim past me. "No, you've talked about this."

He turns, pinning me with a look that makes my heart race. I swallow as his hand comes up to move a strand of wet hair from my cheek. He leans down and kisses me, lips soft and cool against mine as he cups my face, tilting my head back. "I want you so fucking bad." Confessions like that need warnings, maybe a huge neon billboard, so a girl, slow on the uptake, can prepare properly. "But not tonight."

He drops his hands and turns away, I assume to retrieve the ball, and I grab for his arm, reaching it before he gets too far. He looks at me over his shoulder, jaw clenched and ticking beside his ear, eyes intense and piercing. He looks me over, up and then down, stopping on my eyes before he grabs me, hands cupping my head, fingers buried in my wet hair, lips aiming for mine. They land and he kisses me hard, breaths rushed, hands moving restlessly down my shoulders to my hips and ass. He hefts me up, and I wrap my legs around him. "Is this what you want?" His voice is throaty, harsh.

He stills for a second, looking me in the eyes so intently my stomach churns with anticipation and something far more visceral than I've ever felt before. Nodding, sheepishly, I grip the back of his neck, my fingers splayed, touching the tops of his shoulders, too.

Carrying me with his lips on my jaw, then my neck and shoulder, he moves toward the waterfall and presses me up against the side out of the cascading water but still within its spray. It rumbles beside us, drowning out the music in the background. His lips never leave my skin but taste a different part of me each time they move.

A hand that hasn't touched anything more on me than my hair today cups my breast and kneads it over my bra. My barely contained composure splinters, and I moan into his mouth. His other hand, at the small of my back, presses me harder against him.

My grip on his hair is so tight you'd think he'd complain, but if he minds, he's not saying. I arch my back, needing that nagging pulse between my legs to be soothed. I have no conscious knowledge of him removing my bra until I see it floating in the water beside us.

Vance pulls his head away, stares down at what he's exposed, and pulls in a deep breath, holding it. "You are so beautiful," he whispers more to himself than to me.

I clasp my hands around the back of his neck, and he lifts his eyes and stares briefly into mine. He then lowers his head, and I arch deeper, head back, pelvis pressed against his abdomen. His warm breath fans out over my skin as he takes one of my nipples into his mouth. So much of me hums, it's exquisitely overwhelming. Nick Stevenson had no idea what he was doing in the back seat of his Volvo if this is what it was supposed to be like.

"Vance . . ." I hesitate. "Van . . ." I drop my head back, exhaling, not at all amused at my new train of thought. I was perfectly content with body parts competing for my focus, but this new path tamps down some of the heat.

"I won't go any further than this, I promise. I want to taste, but I won't . . . I promise I won't . . ."

"No. It's not that. I—I don't know what to call you. Van? Or Vance?"

His sigh is heavy, and he rests his forehead against mine. "I like Vance. Call me Vance." He pulls his hips back from me and my legs unlock, dropping down his thighs until I stand on tiptoes.

I kiss his chest, and he growls low and deep, which confuses me because I've only ever heard that from guys when I fell short of the rumors about me.

He scoops up my bra, trapped beneath the waterfall, and fists it.

"I wasn't going to ask you to stop."

Vance's devil grin emerges, giving me a bit of hope he'll pick up where he left off. He runs the pad of his thumb over my nipple and watches as it springs back up. "I know." He kisses the top of my shoulder. "But it's not your call tonight." His abs tense where I touch him, muddling my confusion with everything else his restrained behavior has spawned. I shiver as his nose trails back up to my throat.

With my bra still clasped in his fist, he lifts me up by the hips. "Put your legs around me." I do as instructed, and he carries me out of the pool to the waiting towels. He sets me on my feet, and I cover my chest with a two-armed hug.

His thumb brushes my cheek. "You shouldn't hide." His eyes roam over me again, and it feels like a gentle caress instead of a critical evaluation.

Well, now I am just confused. "I thought you wanted me to."

Slipping the towel over my shoulders, he pinches it closed over my chest with his fingers and drops my bra on the chair. "Want is a strong word."

"So you're just bossy."

He leaves me to hold my own towel and grabs one for himself and dries off. "Bossy? I thought I was being a gentleman."

"A bossy gentleman."

"How so?"

"I can't track what's happening here. I don't know if I'm supposed to want you or listen to you."

He dries his hair with one swipe of the towel. A slow, almost imperceptible grin spreads across his face as his amusement grows over my confusion. "You asked for a gentleman, Brenna."

"No. I said I wasn't sleeping with you. You offered the gentleman."

"Anything else from me would negate the first. I can't risk it. I promised." He kisses my cheek and heads toward the door. "And if I wasn't bossy, you'd cave the second I let you." Gesturing to my bra dripping water onto the floor from the chair, he adds, "Put that on, and let's go upstairs and take a shower."

Shower? Really? Is it a cold one? Because anything less than arctic probably isn't going to put out the fire between my legs.

Like everything else in his house, Vance's master bath is spacious, but I don't take time to memorize its opulence. Shivering, I step beneath the spray of one of four showerheads and wait for the heat to penetrate my skin before turning to face a doting Vance who's holding a palmful of shampoo.

Looking a tad sheepish, he shows me his hand. "I didn't know how much to use for your hair length."

I laugh. "We can use what's left to clean the shower when we're done."

"That bad?" His boyish look is endearing, a sharp contrast to his aloof behavior at the beach the first day I met him.

"It's okay," I say softly, still a little taken aback by his thoughtfulness.

Tentatively, and with less confidence than I've seen from him yet, he proceeds to wash my hair, gathering it up and taking a lot of care to make sure it's gentle and thorough. He's covered in suds, fingers to elbow, elbow to chest when he begins to rinse my hair, and when it's all said and done, we're standing in a foam pit of shampoo.

His hands grip my hips and, looking down into my eyes for a second in which neither of us speaks, he studies me before covering my mouth with his. His tongue teases my lips, parting them with an unspoken request that I don't hesitate to grant. I'm ready to end this delicious torture he thinks he needs to maintain because of something I said to sound respectable.

My hands fumble miserably at the ties of his swim shorts, an embarrassing display of my nerves and inexperience. How am I supposed to live up to a reputation I truly haven't earned? And then it dawns on me: with Vance, I'm not a reputation. I'm not a rumor he's trying to prove or discredit. I'm just Brenna.

Vance grabs my hand, stilling my efforts and undoing my progress with his firm grip. With his lips pressed to mine, he says, "Not yet. We're going to do this the right way."

I try to ask what could be more right than this, but he kisses me again and all thought, all reason, loses any value it had a moment ago.

When he comes up for breath, I'm tempted to try my hand at his shorts again, but he takes my chin between his thumb and forefinger, forcing my attention to his gaze. "Someday," his eyes lift and lower, looking from my eyes to my lips, "you'll thank me."

CHAPTER FIFTEEN

Early the next morning, my house and Bristol's third degree loom outside of the Spyder's passenger window. I'm already dreading the twenty questions I know I'll be bombarded with the second I step through the front door.

"What time is your flight?" I ask, worried about his two-and-a-half-hour drive back to San Jose. I offered to make other arrangements, but he wouldn't hear of it or even discuss it beyond my initial offering.

"Two," he replies, touching my cheek. "Stop worrying. They won't leave without me."

"I don't want to be—"

He kisses my lips, silencing my protest in the best way possible. "You won't be. I'll call you tonight."

I kiss him, taking the lead, and perhaps a presumptive foot forward, but when his hand presses on the back of my head and his tongue passes my lips, I don't question my confidence a second longer.

B<small>RISTOL, LOOKING LIKE SHE HASN'T SLEPT IN A DAY, IS ANTSY TO HEAR</small> all the details of my time with Vance. I don't know what I expected, but her cheerful curiosity isn't it. She's amped on something. Caffeine? I don't know, but she's cleaned the house so thoroughly the kitchen tile sparkles, and it's only nine a.m. Normally, I would think my mom trying to stave off a breakdown was responsible for the glowing house, but Bristol, still wearing rubber gloves to her elbows, kind of nixes that theory.

"Are you okay?" I ask, because Bristol only cleans when it's a punishment or she wants something that requires money or approval.

"Yeah, why?" She wipes her brow with the inside of her shoulder and takes a deep breath.

I look around the house, so clean, it smells new, "Uh—"

"Oh! The cleaning." She chuckles. "I was alone and feeling like a flat tire instead of a third wheel." She shrugs the shoulder she wiped her brow with and smiles a sad smile that tears at my heart, spawns some guilt, and triggers a knee-jerk thought to spill everything and promise never to see Vance or any guy ever again.

I open my mouth to promise her the moon if she'll let me, but she holds up a hand and I snap my mouth shut, thankful for the chance to rethink things.

She strips off her gloves, tosses them in the sink, and wipes her sweating hands on her butt. "You've stalled long enough. I need details."

I smile, thankful to see the Bristol I know and love again. I think she'll be relieved when I tell her I slept alone in my hotel room after a goodnight kiss in the parking lot. That thought hasn't even fully evolved yet when she drops her first question.

"Did you sleep with him?" With her hand buried to her forearm in a tube of Pringles, Bristol stares at me with lifted eyebrows and pinched lips. Her hair is pulled up into a messy bun, and it doesn't look like she took off her makeup last night before going to bed.

Sitting down, I grab the blanket off the back of the couch and fling it over me, gesturing for her to join me. I'm exhausted and mentally spent. Between worrying about Vance's intentions or lack thereof, and Bristol's feelings and how she'll act upon them, I'm drained, but I owe her some couch time.

"I don't kiss and tell."

My answer draws a dirty look and a tongue full of Pringles crumbs. I giggle, dropping my head as she opens her mouth to call me out on my lie. "Like hell. If you can blowjob and tell, you can kiss and tell." She chomps another chip, and I can hear its demolition as she sits across from me. "You gotta tell me, Brenna. You didn't text me or anything last night. You owe me."

As much as I want to tell her everything, she's not ready to hear it. She's still pissed I spent the night without her. If I tell her I had the best night of my life without her, she'll plot my death. "It was fun and he was incredible. Well, incredibly considerate and not at all like I expected." I tell her what I think will appease her without feeding her jealousy.

"Had he gotten into your panties yet, or was that a way to slip them off of you?" The Pringles container, with probably only a few chips left, is discarded onto the floor, and she tucks the blanket in around her legs.

I burrow in and intertwine our legs. I've missed Bristol. Even though she's been physically around, she hasn't been emotionally present since Vance entered the picture.

"He would have gotten them off without the consideration, but he never even tried." I hope the confession will help her to see him as something more than the douchebag she thinks he is.

"What?!" It's a solid shriek, delivered as she sits up straight and shoves my leg with the heel of her foot. "He didn't try? Like, not at all? What the hell? Is he gay?"

I laugh, chuckling over her response. "I don't think so." I fill her in on the hot and spicy and the mixed signals, and she looks as perplexed as I feel.

Bouncing our legs softly, she asks, "Are you going to see him again?"

"I don't know. He said he'd call, but if he'd wanted me last night, he could have had me. I could, right now, at this very second, be a notch on his bedpost, but I'm not."

"How old are you? Who says that?"

"Uncle Rodney. Notch on his belt?"

"That's only slightly better. How about a hump and dump? A fuck and chuck? A come and done? A do and shoo—"

"Alright," I yell, pushing her with my entire leg to get her to shut up, "I get the point." I bite my lip, surprised at the wealth of emotion her teasing disturbs.

"See, that's why you shouldn't have sex with him. You're too emotional about it." She nudges me. "You need to stick to being a fake girlfriend. Like you were with Dawson." She laughs, but I'm pretty sure she's being serious.

Trying to be a good friend to Dawson Crane, who was on the verge of being outed for being gay, I pretended to be his girlfriend. We had to fake kiss and everything. Sadly, it was probably my most influential relationship to date. Best part was no broken hearts, and Dawson got another few years of sexual anonymity. I learned how to kiss and handle shitty rumors of my own, so we were both winners.

"So, did you get him out of your system?" Bristol asks, pulling me out of my benevolent past. "Are you done forsaking me for some guy?"

"You do know that eventually we're both going to fall in love and have separate lives, right?"

"Only if I approve of him. And you have to approve of mine. I'm not going to let you date a douchebag, and I sure hope you wouldn't let me date one either." Her expression questions me. "The pact, Brenna. Guys aren't supposed to come between us."

"We're not supposed to fight over the same guy, asshole. We can love one, just not the same one. I agreed to approval if the guy was a douchebag like mom's boyfriends. You can't disapprove just because

I don't spend all my time with you. There has to be a reason." I point my finger at her, knowing she'll find a loophole if I don't close them all. "And it has to be a good one, like he's abusive or cheating or something." I can't believe we have to discuss this at twenty-one years of age. She interpreted the pact way differently than I did. Who wants to live with their sister their entire life? I know I don't. I love her, but she isn't going to meet all my needs, and I've discovered over the last week since meeting Vance, that my vagina has needs beyond a good scrubbing and a brand name tampon. I'd like to know what having those needs met is like. I may not find out from Vance, but someday, hopefully, I will with someone.

"I'm tired." I didn't sleep at all last night, and Vance picked me up at six this morning to drive me home.

She unwraps our legs, scoots to the edge of the couch, and grabs the TV remote off of the table. "Do you want to fall asleep to some mindless movie before you have to be at work?"

I nod, roll to my side and draw my legs in, tucking my hands beneath my cheek. Mindless anything sounds exquisite.

The television sparks to life, and Bristol files through half a dozen movies on Netflix before picking a comedy. She sinks back into the couch, curling up much the same as me, and sighs.

"Brenna?"

"Mm hmm?"

"I'm glad you're home."

"I'm still not staying forever."

"We'll see."

I lie awake, sleep tempting me at every turn, but my thoughts are stronger than the desire to sleep, and I lay there, eyes open, staring at the screen, worrying about stuff that's out of my control. Will Vance really call? Have I fallen too fast? Is he falling at all?

The front door opens, and a wide stream of sunlight precedes the last leg of my mother's walk of shame. Wearing a red tank top without the sheer blouse she usually wears over it, her bra strap droops off her shoulder and wraps around her bicep. Her hair, ringed in golden sunlight, looks like it was finger-combed or contained by a pillow. The aforementioned sheer blouse is gripped in her hand and caught on her keys that she's trying to yank free of the doorknob. She cusses before giving up and leaving them both hanging off the knob.

"Oh, hey, girls." She summons a fake smile that looks like she ate a tart lemon. "I thought you'd still be in bed."

Bristol groans. "It's almost ten. Don't they usually chase you out by eight?"

I kick her beneath the blanket and she kicks me back, face turned up in disapproval, sneering like she's daring me to kick her again.

My mom dismisses Bristol's dig with a flippant hand-wave. After kissing us both on the tops of our heads, she leaves a scented wake of men's cologne and stale cigarettes all the way to her bedroom. My chest falls. Yet another walk of shame. I feel a strengthening disappointment despite the familiarity, which strikes me as odd because I should be numb to it.

I think about it while Bristol snores at my feet. I think it's bugging me because I've never allowed myself to think about a future beyond my mom and Bristol before. It seemed pointless with our history, but now I want to think about it. I want to dream about it. I'm starting to think I want a different outcome than my parents have had, than the one they've led me to believe I'm destined for. I want to feel again what I've felt with Vance the past couple of days. Not to mention, now that my vagina is awake, it's not going to settle for ten second car sex and hurried flicks of the bean.

The chances of it going anywhere with him beyond today are unlikely, I know that. I'm not the Hollywood girls he's used to, and I don't even know if I can measure up in bed. I'm sure they're into everything—whips, chains, the whole sexy fun bank—and I don't even know if I can orgasm with anything but my own hand.

Unfortunately, after a non-nap, I have all day long to think about just that and more, and a four-hour, painfully slow shift at Stray Charlie's doesn't monopolize enough of my thoughts to stop any of it. I'm a magnet for every worry and doubt there is, and when no texts or calls come in from Vance, I'm stuck beneath a cloud of gloom exacerbated by the call I did get, from Tori telling me I'm in the "Rumor Has It" section of *Candid* magazine, or at least she thinks it's me.

"It could be anyone. The pictures aren't that good. But I know it's you."

It doesn't get better at home after work either.

Gathered around the television with my mom and Bristol, one hand on my chest, the other near my mouth so I can chew steadily on my fingernails, I make my first appearance ever on the tabloid news show *The Hook* labeled as "New Girl?" The pictures are terrible. Whoever took them caught my face at a poor angle and they're slightly blurry.

"Oh. My. God." My mom makes the words into three distinct sentences and squeals behind spread fingers, one of which is unpolished. "You're on TV, and not just any TV," she squeals again, prompting Bristol to plug her ears. "National TV!"

"Shh!" Bristol shushes her testily, bathing us in spit.

My mom snaps her mouth shut, and beaming behind tightly clenched lips, grabs hold of my upper arm, squeezing affectionately. "You're on *The Hook*." Her whispered enthusiasm almost makes up for the shitty picture they're using in the upper right corner of the television. It's hard to tell it's me. But we know.

Still berating us, Bristol turns up the television as Amy Melon adds her two cents to the shaky video of me, albeit mostly the back of me, caught between the best-looking guy in baseball and the cow shoving her udders into Vance's stomach.

"Security at Red Hooligans, typically tight on a night when Major League Baseball's resident Renegades are present, dropped the ball Saturday night as fans rushed Renegades starting pitcher, Van Hatfield." The video plays, taking over the screen as Amy's voice continues to narrate over the shitty recording. "Hatfield, best known for his fastball and bench-clearing fights, is keeping us on our toes with his love life. Within the last several months he's been seen with actress/model Nikki Kline, Las Vegas stripper Amber Dietrich, actress Juniper Jones, and Penny Sylvester of the new hit show *Street Wise*. And now it appears he's picking up strays at Red Hooligans."

"Did she just call you a stray?" The derogatory description draws my mom's claws. "Turn that shit off," she demands of Bristol, who has a death lock on the remote while looking poised and ready to spoil any of my mom's attempts to shut it off manually. There is no fear of that. My mom couldn't find the manual switch if it was 6'4", tanned, blond, and horny. I once watched her run her hand down the side of the TV for a half-hour, only to give up and go to bed with it still on.

"Shh!" Bristol spits again. "Let's hear what else Amy Melon can flatter Brenna with."

"One eyewitness says the two were intimately close as security escorted the couple out of the club," Amy continues, as a picture of Vance and me outside of Red Hooligans is displayed in a small frame beside her ear. "Other sources say Van and the unidentified young woman were in a heated conversation over what had transpired inside of Red Hooligans. The two left separately, the young woman in a limousine, and Van was later seen leaving in a truck driven by teammate Ben Halsey." She switches gears, and behind her a new screen displays the pictures of the previously mentioned women in Vance's life. One at a time they drop from their position into an animated virtual pile, with the last picture, of a question mark, remaining up for viewing. "Ladies, I don't think she's the one. I personally wouldn't count yourself out if you're still trying to land *Jock* magazine's Jock Star of the Year. I'm pretty sure he's still very much on the market, and if he's not today, he will be tomorrow. That's my two cents. Whaddya say? Do we let him off The Hook?"

What the fuck? We weren't fighting. We were planning a date. Assholes. And off the hook for what?

My mom rubs my back and then adjusts her halter top so her

boob doesn't fall out of the ancient cotton. "He looked absolutely smitten with you. Amy Melon is an idiot."

Bristol laughs at my mom's consolation speech and then chucks a couch pillow at her. "Van Hatfield is smitten with anything that doesn't tell him no."

My mom sets the pillow on the couch behind us like it wasn't meant to shut her up. "Not the Van Hatfield I met."

"You saw what he let you see."

"I don't think so." Her declaration sounds wishy-washy, and Bristol latches onto the uncertainty like a rabid dog.

"Oh please! You could be sweet-talked by that religious creeper who turned half his female congregation into sex slaves. What was his name?" Our response isn't necessary; she doesn't care about the answer. "Doesn't matter. Brenna barely survived being Backseat Brenna. How do you think she'll survive being 'Van Hatfield's Stray?'" She uses her fingers as quotes and her smug expression as an exclamation point. "You two are way too emotionally connected to sex. It should be a release or an enjoyment, but not an attachment."

"And you're an unemotional dick, Bristol."

"Whoa!" My mom pipes in, where, as usual, it's unwarranted and misdirected. "That's a little harsh, Brenna. You haven't had the same experiences as her." Bristol's loss of virginity will always be known as "an experience" to my mother.

I harden my eyes, eyeballing my mom, and open my mouth to speak when I should take a deep breath instead. "No, harsh is telling you you're incompetent at reading people and not giving me the credit I deserve for shouldering the brunt of her reputation. 'Experiences' don't give you license to be an asshole."

I storm out. The chatter about me being sensitive falls short and broken as I head out back, fuming, and dare I say it, a bit "sensitive."

CHAPTER SIXTEEN

Getting through another day without being reminded that Vance still hasn't called or that my life is now public fodder whether people recognize me or not is impossible.

Mr. Jones, my neighbor, is utterly amused by mine and Bristol's resemblance to the girl in the photographs when he stops by to show us the 'uncanny lookalikes' in his store-bought copy of *Candid* magazine.

The "Rumor Has It" section of the weekly tabloid features the same pictures *The Hook* was so proud of. Headline: *Lil' Miss Right Now*. The featured article talks about my plain looks and my uphill battle to hold onto baseball's most eligible bachelor. I stopped reading last night when they started discussing his conquests and my lack of anything worth pursuing.

I sigh at Mr. Jones's copy in my hand. What can you say to an eighty-year-old man who, despite being nosy, truly does have a soft spot for you? As my next-door neighbor for more than half my life, he's spent more time with me in one year than my dad has in eleven. My hope is if he can't recognize me, no one else can either.

"I thought you'd get a kick out of it," he says in that quivering voice he's acquired over the last year. Taking the folded copy back from me with a shaking right hand he can no longer garden with, he adds, "It's a shame they have to be so cruel. I'm glad it isn't you."

"Yeah, poor girl. I would hate to have my life on blast like that. It's going to get a lot worse for her if they ever discover who she is." Bristol, with a free opportunity to get under my skin and drive her point home, jumps in with both feet. "Pretty stupid if you ask me. So not worth it."

I glare a wicked side-eye at her and descend the front steps of our house, refusing to let her bully me. We've fought over it for nearly two days. "I'll see you later Mr. Jones. I have to pick up fliers from the printer."

"Fliers for what?" His interest makes me smile. I've spent a shit-load of time making those fliers worthy of Mrs. Dixon's faith in me.

"Miracle Days," I reply, walking backward toward the street, thankful for any distraction not related to Bristol's opinions.

FREE OF BRISTOL'S NOT-SO-SUBTLE HINTS THAT I'M WAY OUT OF MY small-town league, I stop in at The Seam after picking up the fliers and dropping them off at the Chamber of Commerce for distribution just before they closed. I timed it right so I could watch a portion of Vance's game against Colorado and grab a sip of water. Uncle Rodney, as expected, is behind the bar holding a beer mug, eyes on the TV, ears acutely aware of what's around him.

"Hi, doll." He hasn't looked away from the television in the corner above the bar, and still he knows it's me. The man is scary good. If he had kids, they'd get away with absolutely nothing. I always thought it was sad he never had a family of his own, but when I questioned him about it after I interviewed him for a history project, his answer was simple. "My life isn't conducive to little ones and a wife. I'm here all the time and don't want to be anywhere else."

"Who's winning?" The score is posted in the bottom left corner of the screen, but asking Uncle Rodney is my preference.

"It's on the screen. Bottom left."

I laugh, thinking I should have known better. "How's Vance doing?"

He looks away from the television, and he doesn't just look at me, he plants his green eyes on mine. "All these years, I've tried everything to get you interested in baseball. I sat through baseball tea so you'd be happy and I'd be halfway happy. I would have settled for mildly interested, and all I got for that hope was, 'Why do they grab their balls all the time, Uncle Rodney?' Van Hatfield shows up for a couple of beers, treats ME to a game, and now all of a sudden you give a shit how the game is going?"

I laugh, recalling the tea party and my inquiry into the male fascination with their junk. "Maybe you should have put beer in the teacups."

"Jesus, maybe." He grins, taps my hand and returns his eyes to the game. "Colorado has a goose egg. I can't ask for more than that," he says to me with a side-eye glance. "Would you like a beer?"

A big nod accompanies a smile, and Uncle Rodney, giddy at my acceptance, is probably also a bit fearful if he doesn't move fast enough, I'll change my mind.

Vance looks sexy as sin, and when they show a closeup of his face I can see his jaw tick and the intensity in the set of his eyes. He's all business, seeing nothing but his catcher and the line he wants his pitch to take. I'm mesmerized by him when he lifts his knee and lets that ball fly at ninety-five miles an hour, and by the time he's rolling the ball in his hand for the next pitch, I'm throat deep in butterflies and breathless when he licks his fingers.

I don't know what the stats are for Vance's six innings, and I don't particularly care because it's foreign to me, but I do know by the time Vance is relieved in the top of the seventh inning, I'm already buzzed.

"You're a lightweight," Uncle Rodney says to me as I climb off the barstool a little shaky.

"I'm also a cheap date, which bodes well for wallets, which bodes well for . . . I don't know. I've never made it to a second date." I laugh, grabbing the seat of the stool before the whole thing topples.

Uncle Rodney's smile falls, and his thick salt and pepper eyebrows pinch together. "He hasn't called?"

I shrug. "I didn't expect him to."

"Maybe that's your problem."

"What's that?"

"You don't have high enough expectations."

"They're always met that way though." I really should have left well enough alone, because when Uncle Rodney rounds the bar, he's on a parental mission. He wraps a tight arm around me, squeezes my shoulder and kisses the side of my head.

"Sit down."

I groan, huff, and take my spot back on the stool with as much trouble as I had getting off of it.

"Now face me."

Lips pinched and cockeyed, I turn to face him, placing my feet on the top rung of the barstool.

"Listen, doll, your mom has lived her life lowering her expectations so someone, anyone, will meet them. Does she look happy to you? If you expect nothing, Brenna, nothing is what you'll get every damn time." He tufts my chin with his index finger. "Aim high, love, and someone will jump to reach it."

I stare with a numb distance, trying to keep my tears behind my lashes and my lips from saying something stupid. On a normal day that is a full-time job; hopped up on alcohol, it's damn near impossible. I've only had the two beers, but it may as well be six. "I don't know if I'm destined for all of that, Uncle Rodney. If my family history has anything to say, I'm guessing I have one good relationship in me. I don't know if I want it this early in my twenties. Besides, I'm tougher than I look. I can withstand a lot."

"Horse shit!" he barks loudly, and half the bar, which at this time of the evening is around five people, looks at us. "Don't buy into that hogwash Bristol force-feeds you. I've never talked badly about your dad in front of you out of respect for who he is to you, but he was a piece of shit. While I don't believe a man should have to pay for his sins for a lifetime, your father certainly deserves to carry that cross for a good long way. Not only did he ruin your mother, but he left two little girls without a good male role model and a third without an identity. A man who fathers little girls has a responsibility, a duty, to show them what a good man looks and sounds like. They should know by how he treats their mother what kind of treatment they should expect from their partner. But you're not an idiot, Brenna. You know. You know that cheating is wrong. You know that your word is your bond. You know. Stop using your mother as a scapegoat for your lack of expectations. That's on you. You can turn this shit around. Your destiny is only crippled by your effort, not by your bloodline." He tosses a beer towel at me, and I catch it despite the blur of tears.

I wipe my eyes, lick my dry lips, and jump off the stool to stand toe-to-toe with him. "You sell yourself short," I tell him. "I couldn't ask for a better role model if one came packaged with Astronaut Barbie."

"Oh, hell. You need your head checked. There's a reason I don't have children."

"I hope that reason is sterility, because I think you'd have been a great dad."

His brow furrows, and he snaps me with the towel he swipes directly out of my hand. "Go home. Find something to do. Text Van and tell him you watched the game. Do something, Brenna."

On tiptoes, I kiss his cheek. "You are a great dad." The smells of cotton, beer, and Irish Spring make up Uncle Rodney, the only man who's ever really been a dad to me.

Let's face it, two beers does not a long buzz make, and after a sandwich and a tall glass of water at the Beachstro Café next door to

The Seam, I'm good to go. I'm only thirty minutes late when Tracy's mom answers the door in her straight-out-of-the-eighties blue leotard and a pink sweatband around her peanut-shaped head.

"Brenna!" she sings. "Come, come." She ushers me in and closes the front door. "The fliers turned out amazing. You, my dear, are amaziiiiing. Sooo beautiful! Is it too early to start working on next year's?" she sings again, double air kissing my cheeks. "Tracy and Bristol are in her room." She lifts an arm and fans a hand over her armpit. "They have big new-ooze." If she sang any higher, she'd shatter the porcelain duck on the table, all while maintaining the fan she's made out of her hand to cool her armpit.

Quietly wondering if I've been hired for next year's flier design or if I'm being toyed with, I head up the curved staircase, too afraid to ask. When I get to the top, I look over the banister and watch Mrs. Dixon, stuck in 1985, dance her way back into the den.

Tracy's room is two doors down from the "love pad," which is more than I ever wanted to know about her parents' kink, but Tracy can't keep anything to herself. I can hear *Project Runway* spilling out into the hallway from her bedroom a good ten steps before I get to it.

"Brenna!" Tracy screeches before I enter her sanctuary, highlighted by a smirking Bristol standing beside the window seat littered with Tracy's fifth-grade Beanie Babies collection. "Thank God you're here." She touches my shoulders, one hand on each so she can look me directly in the eyes.

"What's going on?" I question not only Tracy's enthusiasm but also Bristol's too-smug expression.

"Bristol got Van to donate a signed baseball for our auction." She squeals, jumps once, and siphons in another lung full of air. "Isn't that great?"

"You did what?!" I ignore Tracy and lock eyes on Bristol, who despite seeing my reaction, is still smirking.

Concerned I might see this as a Judas move, she begins to build her case. "It's so much better than Tiffany Langley's stupid signed golden ticket. Hers is a fucking replica anyway. Do you honestly think she's going to part with real *American Idol* memorabilia?

My mouth hangs open, paused between shock and the breath it's going to take to get out all the curse words I want to say.

"Oh, for shit's sake, Brenna, take a breath. He was okay with it."

"I'm not!" I yell. "How did you get his number anyway?"

"Same as you. Tori."

I open my mouth to yell at her, but I'm stopped by Tracy who interjects herself, trying to diffuse the situation. "Tori didn't want to. Don't be mad at her. And Van was truly fine with it." She nods her affirmation repeatedly.

My nostrils flare, I can hear my heartbeat in my ears, and my teeth, ground so tight they ache, clench deeper. I'm the last to know and yet the only one of us who has anything to lose.

"You don't own him, Brenna. I figured we may as well get what we could out of him while he still remembered our names."

"You are such a bitch," I spit out, unconcerned with Tracy's presence. I've been waiting two days for him to contact me, and Bristol's been texting him for favors. No wonder I haven't heard from him.

"It's a ball, Brenna."

"It's not just a ball, Bristol. Now he's going to think I want what everyone else wants from him."

Tracy grabs us both, one hand on my shoulder, another on Bristol's, and she pulls us in for a group hug. "Girls," she says, draping her arms over our shoulders, tightening our huddle, "let's take a break from this. No need to fight."

I try to shrug off a well-intentioned Tracy, but she's more invested in keeping the peace than I counted on, and I'm stuck beneath her heavy arm. I have nowhere to go to escape my own thoughts which are traveling to unwanted places that shake my faith in Bristol. I've questioned a lot of things about her actions over the years, but never her intentions toward me.

"I'm sorry," Bristol says in our small huddle. "I'll text him and tell him to forget it."

"It's done," I say too harshly to sound even remotely close to forgiveness. "You can't take it back now." I can't see her because Tracy is forcing our heads down and all I can see is our feet, but I know Bristol is smirking at her win. A win she probably knew she had when she called him. One-upping Tiffany was strictly a bonus.

Bristol breaks out the waterworks, and Tracy takes a step back, breaking our stupid friendship huddle so she can either repair or minimize the damage. "Don't!" It's meant for both of them. "Just . . . don't."

I sit down on twelve layers of plush, pink bedding, and sink in, wishing it would swallow me whole. I look up, finding a wide-eyed Tracy looking uncertain about her options and a teary-eyed Bristol making a good show of her remorse. As much as I want to continue being pissed off at her, she makes it hard. "At least now I know why he hasn't called." I'm bitter, but we aren't supposed to let boys come between us, and I'm supposed to choose her no matter what. Life, as usual, has made its intentions for me clear. I'm just tired of always coming up on the underside of what's fair. Me and Bristol against the world. But what if that world stops revolving around her? What then?

AT HOME AFTER SPENDING A TEN-MINUTE CAR RIDE TRYING TO convince Bristol I'm fine and she doesn't have to fear my retribution over the ball, we go to bed. Bristol, weightless and absolved from her dirty deeds, falls asleep quickly, leaving me to write and erase ten texts to Vance before deciding I'm not that girl. Despite Uncle Rodney's advice to do something, I will not chase him.

From a dead sleep I didn't know I'd succumbed to, my phone sings me awake. I roll to my side and grasp blindly for my phone on the nightstand, and after a few F-bombs, covers thrashed around me, I end up finding it on the floor.

In disbelief, I disentangle from my sheets and talk myself out of squealing. I stare at Vance's text for minutes on end, stomach churning.

Vance: *You still awake?*

My heart skips about six beats more than it did when I thought I might be dreaming. I look at the clock in the upper right corner of my phone. Eleven twenty-five p.m., which means the game I watched with Uncle Rodney has been over for about four hours now.

Waiting an embarrassingly small amount of time to type out a reply, I send it before I can think about it.

Me: *Yeah.*

Vance: *Sorry it's so late.*

Me: *It's okay. What are you up to?*

Vance: *Thinking about you.*

Me: *Really?*

Vance: *Yes, really. How've you been?*

I sit on my reply, but within a few minutes I decide to remain true to myself, and if he doesn't like it, what am I truly out?

Me: *Other than second-guessing everything, I'm fine.*

Vance: *What are you second-guessing?*

Me: *I know about the signed ball. I'm sorry.*

Vance's reply isn't as quick as the last several, but I remind myself it's nearly one o'clock in the morning where he is. I'm sure he's tired and in the middle of getting ready for bed after partying or something. While I wait, I listen to Bristol's breathing, and the familiar sound puts things into perspective. Bristol, though feeling threatened, isn't going anywhere. She's just trying to see how far I'll venture.

Vance: *Don't be sorry. Why is that what you're thinking about?*

A second after the last text, another text comes in before I've typed out my reply.

Vance: *Can I call?*

I erase my reply, walk out of my bedroom so I don't accidentally wake Bristol, and alone in the hall, I hit the phone icon to call him. He picks up on the second ring, and his voice, deep and sexy, makes me smile and eases the tightness I've been carrying in my chest because I hadn't heard from him.

"Hey." It's one word. One simple word, and I feel like half of the weight I'm carrying is being lifted.

I sit on the sofa, easing into it slowly as I respond, smiling like a lovestruck idiot. "Hi."

"There's that voice I've missed."

I can hear the smile in his tone, and I think I absorb it too long and forget to reply.

"Brenna?"

"Oh, sorry. How are you?"

"What's wrong?"

"You know, I guess I just worried that when I didn't hear from you—you know, it doesn't matter. Great game tonight."

"Brenna?" His tone changes, and I'm acutely aware of the shift as I kick myself for not just enjoying the relief of his call. I pull a blanket from the back of the sofa and flop it on top of me. "I'm sorry it took so long to call. I forgot my charger at home and I didn't realize it until my phone was too dead to call out. I didn't get time until tonight to get another charger and just got enough juice to call you now." I hear his exchange of breath, his contrition heavy. "I wanted to call sooner. I really did."

"It's okay." I am quick to forgive, an instant offering I will want to analyze later for signs of my mother, but for right now, it feels right. "I thought after Bristol asked for the ball—"

"The ball is nothing, Brenna. She texted the afternoon I flew out. I said yes. End of story."

"But I don't want you to think—"

"I think she needed an auction item, and I have the means to provide one. That's it."

"Really?"

"Really. Now can we talk about us?"

I cozy up to the corner of the sofa, draw my knees in and cinch the blanket tighter around my legs. "Us?" I didn't know there was an "us," but I'm willing to discuss the possibility.

"Can I come see you on Tuesday?"

I reply softly, "I'd like that."

CHAPTER SEVENTEEN

The week between my phone call with Vance and today, when I'll finally get to see him, has been a blur of Miracle Days preparations and giddy anticipation. I can't concentrate or pony up the energy needed to make Miracle Days any better. The festival is still four days away, but seeing as it's the town's biggest event of the year, there is a lot to be done, and Tracy's mom, organizer and chief dictator of Miracle Days, is too keyed up to allow any kind of downtime.

Today, I'm using my Stray Charlie's shift as a reprieve from Mrs. Dixon's relentless whip-cracking. Bristol, however, got stuck organizing the auction items all morning with Tracy, and while I've received several texts from her bitching about how long it's taking, she's surprisingly silent about my date with Vance tonight. I don't know if she's using Miracle Days prep as a distraction or if she's actually not preoccupied with it. The mystery is solved when Bristol shows up to start her shift at Stray Charlie's just as mine is ending. She's in a mood.

"So," she begins, signing in for her shift with a flourish of cuss words as she drops the clipboard. "While you're out tonight acting like Vance didn't lie to you, ignore you for two days, and hasn't blown you off night after night to party, I'm going out with Tracy and her rich, snobby friends. I hope that makes you feel like shit."

I roll my eyes, shoulder my messenger bag, and open the door aggressively enough to rattle the bell and clink it off the glass. "Nope. Nothing."

"Why are you doing this? We both know you're not the easy one. You try to hang with the slutty crowd, but you just aren't a member. That's where your similarity with Mom ends. He's going to find out, you know?"

Standing in the doorway, I prop the door open with my foot. "I hope so."

After producing a believable smile, she rushes to the other side of the counter to hug me. She throws her arms around me and squeezes me so tight I can't breathe. "For your sake, I hope so too." She kisses my cheek. "I know I've been a horrible bitch about all of this, but I want to protect you. I hope it goes well. Not so well you fall madly in love, but well enough you can clear out the dust bunnies in your vagina." She holds a finger up, runs back in the shop and digs through her purse before coming back to me with a sample size Mary Kay perfume in her hand. "You smell like hand sanitizer. You're not getting any action smelling like rubbing alcohol. And what if there are scratch n' sniff tabloids? You'll be a smelly stray with less staying power than Tiffany's chlamydia."

She's all over the place. Mood swings left and right, and I don't know which way to turn half the time. Is she or isn't she? Will she or won't she? I'm thankful that, for the moment, I can relax and maybe enjoy my date with Vance without having to worry about whether or not Bristol is planning our demise.

I nod and try to sneak a word of thanks in, but she shoves me and waves over my head with the other. "He's here. I want graphic texts. Oh, and take this." She hands me the perfume and makes me palm it tight. "You never know. It could smell musty down there." I leave her to head towards Vance, and she hollers after me, "Remember, release not attachment."

Bristol's impromptu sex advice and mood-whiplash leave me smiling as I meet Vance outside of Stray Charlie's. He's wearing his mirrored aviators and a ball cap that sits low. The tattoos on his arms show beneath a short-sleeved white T-shirt with some sort of black logo on his right pec. Damn, he's gorgeous.

I don't know how to greet him. He's Van Hatfield, cautious of his exposure, and we haven't established the lines. So, I approach with casual confidence and a smile discernible from any distance.

I'm met with what Vance would call a smile and a softly spoken, "Hey, you."

We walk a foot apart in silence until we reach his car parked across the street in front of Stricker Bait and Tackle Shop. Vance, utilizing his recently acquired chivalry skills, opens my door, and I climb into the Spyder wondering what the rest of the day is going to hold if he's already starting out like a gentleman. He climbs into the driver's seat and immediately grabs my hand and squeezes before shifting into reverse.

Once he hits the street, he places his hand back on my bare thigh. "You okay with another lowkey night at my place? It's not far from here."

I place my hand over his. "Sounds great."

The house Vance purchased before meeting me is located past Grundy Beach in an area the locals dubbed Honey Hill as upper-class homes were being built. Vance's house sits on the ocean side of the street at the top of Honey Hill. Shielded by flowering shrubs, tall, bushy trees, and a white solid gate that spans his driveway, it's about as secluded as you can get on a public beach. He pulls in, and the gate slides closed behind us before we've pulled into the one-car garage stall where he parks and shuts the engine off.

The hand on my thigh moves to my chin, and Vance leans in for a kiss, wrapping up any insecurities I may have been harboring about his intentions.

"God, I've wanted to do that for a week."

"Why'd you wait?"

"Privacy. Not knowing how you'd respond. I don't know, lots of reservations, I guess." He strokes my cheek with his thumb, eyes searching for something he's not seeing. "I'll figure it out, I promise. In the meantime, tell me what's wrong."

I shake my head. "I'm fine."

"No, you're not. Is it the ball?"

"Vance, I . . ." I don't know how to ask. We're not exclusive or even really dating. Do I have a right to ask if what the tabloids report is true? Is he dating the other girls the tabloids mentioned? "In *Candid*—"

He sits back in his seat, tilts his head back against it, and lets out a breath. "Chip mentioned it. I haven't read it, though."

"Are you dating them?"

He jerks his head to look at me, face pinched. "Who this time?"

"Nikki Kline, and I can't remember her name, but she's a stripper."

He growls but doesn't answer.

"Don't take this wrong. I'm not judging you, and I'm not asking for something from you, but I don't want to be that girl. If you're seeing them, I shouldn't be here."

His look softens. "Nikki is a friend. Occasionally we hit events together because we don't want the complication of asking anyone else. It's easy. We dated briefly a year ago, but there wasn't anything there for either of us. And the stripper," he pauses, releasing a breath before taking another, "is my sister."

I come off the seat and pin him with a wide-eyed look, mouth fully open, waiting for something to land in it other than a string of curse words. "You're dating your sister?"

He laughs, shaking his head. "No. I just didn't correct the press. Tabloids don't research. They got her stripper name and never dug deeper. Had they, they'd have discovered that Amber Dietrich is also my sister, Camille Hatfield. Me being with a stripper was the story. End of story. Truth doesn't matter."

My mouth bobs like it's on strings attached to someone else's hands. I don't know what to say and wish that damn puppeteer would speak for me instead of just working the hinges of my mouth.

"It's not common knowledge outside my family, so I'd appreciate it, for her sake, if you'd keep it between us. I'm telling you because I don't want that to be a source of contention for us."

I wouldn't deny him for a lesser reason. "Your secret is safe with me. But why wouldn't you correct it?"

He contemplates for a moment before speaking. "Her four-year-old son, Jacoby. My life doesn't provide a lot of anonymity for those around me."

"Is she pretty private about what she does for a living?"

"Camille doesn't really care. She just wants to dance. Retail wasn't cutting it, and she won't take my money. Not to sound arrogant, but if it weren't for me, no one would care that she strips to provide for her kid. But because expectations are high for me, they're high for my family too. I don't want Jacoby hurt by a witch hunt because of me and people's intense need to know everything about me. Everyone has an opinion, and trust me, there will be fallout if they find out Camille is raising her son on stripping money. It's perfectly legal, but some morally superior bitch will want to look into his custody, and because of the far-reaching media, it will become a debated topic."

I nod, understanding that gossip and rumors can destroy a life, or at the very least, make its path very rocky. I know the fallout well, having lived through it my entire life either through my own mistakes or through another's. "It makes me sick to think someone who doesn't know you or them would even have a say."

"People feel like they know me because I'm on their televisions every Saturday night. I'm on the tabloid in the doctor's office. I'm an alert on their TMZ app. And when you know someone intimately enough to know who they're sleeping with, they think they have a say in your life. It sucks, but I chose it. Camille and Jacoby didn't. I don't need some religious lawyer trying to make a name for himself using Camille's life choices as a platform to get elected Attorney General or some shit. I shouldn't have taken her to the event. We're usually cautious, but she wanted to see J Trudy's dance performance, and I relented because that's her idol."

Hearing all this humanizes him for me yet again. "Jeez, I barely survived the rumor mill of a small town. How do you survive it at your level?"

"I bought this house. Milagro Beach isn't exactly a tabloid mecca."

"Yeah, until me, that is."

"I don't think so. Chip said they hadn't gotten ahold of your name yet. Shitty pictures, I guess. So for your sake, I figured lowkey today would be for the best."

"Lowkey, boring, uneventful. Call it what you like, I need a day with no crazy in it. Can you manage that?"

"I'll see what I can arrange."

CHAPTER EIGHTEEN

Normal begins with a change of clothes, and while Vance changes into his swimming trunks, I peek around the second level of his three-story beach house. It's quaint for a three-story, or at least this level is, with the kitchen and living room in one open space. Decorated in whites, blues, and varying shades of grays and blacks, it's crisp, neat, and sleek.

Hearing him moving around upstairs, I bag the self-guided tour and peel my top layer of clothes off to get down to my red bikini, the suit my mom considers too risky for the ocean because the ties can loosen in the surf.

Vance descends the stairs, and I turn around to look at him as he steps into the living room wearing blue and white trunks. "You know how to make a guy work for his composure."

He looks good, every inch of him tight, tanned, and toned. "I could say the same."

Using the stairs off his back deck, we head down to the beach, me wrapped in a towel and him wearing sunglasses and his hat that I'm beginning to think he wears for anonymity. After our earlier talk, I realize how little privacy he has, so once we get onto the sand, I increase the space between us and lower my sunglasses from the top of my head to my face.

A few yards from the wet part of the sand, we lay our towels out and sit on them facing the ocean. A few approaching beachcombers have put Vance on edge, and his demeanor shifts accordingly. "I know this isn't ideal," he says, facing away from me to say it. "Out here, I can at least tell who's carrying camera equipment or looks out of place enough to be worrisome."

"It's perfect." I dig my toes in the sand and listen for the constant roll and crash of the ocean in the hopes it will ease my nerves.

He looks at me, and I can see myself propped on my elbows in his sunglasses. It's a rare glimpse of how he sees me, and other than the usual insecurities, I feel okay in my skin.

Vance, unable to relax, heads out to the ocean, and I watch him as he stands alone in the surf. I'm not one to pee on my possessions, but I could be after listening to three girls discussing him as they walk past me. He's not mine, but I'll be damned if he'll be theirs today.

I head out, tramping through the dry sand on a mission to join him in the surf. Keeping a respectable distance to preserve his efforts, I dive beneath the water to get my entire body used to the cold.

We play in the ocean, riding waves for a while like two kids with boundless energy and no interest in each other whatsoever. His hand hasn't so much as grazed my arm by accident, though not for a lack of trying on my part.

Vance shrugs his right shoulder, rolling it forward, backward, and up and down repeatedly. I watch as he tries numerous times to work something out of it, but he never seems to succeed. Giving up on the shoulder, he dives into a wave, dodging its crest, but it grabs hold of me, tosses me in the middle of its chaos, and before I know it, I'm floundering around in a gritty, brown funnel. Disoriented, I open my eyes trying to find the surface as the churning water subsides and then rebounds, slamming me into something hard. It gives me a point of reference, and as I try to climb up it, I am plucked from the water and held above it.

"Are you okay?"

Gasping for air, I sputter, coughing up enough seawater to float an ark. My eyes sting, and the gritty sand overlay makes blinking painful. Waves continue their assault as I struggle with air intake and subsequent release. "Hold on!" Vance shouts over the noise of the water, and I latch on like a monkey.

Vance's hands slide down my arms and grip my hips as he moves us closer to shore and out of the big swells. He trudges through the water with me attached, a man on a mission. The waves crash near his hips and then his knees until they lap harmlessly at his ankles.

I find my legs as he sets me down and runs for our towels, probably wondering about my ocean fitness. If I thought it would help, I'd tell him I had my eyes on him and not the wave, but somehow admitting that seems almost worse than drowning in three feet of raging water.

After a slow trek back up to Vance's house, during which I tripped repeatedly on the steps and nearly coughed my lungs out my ass, I sit in a lounger on the deck.

"Here." He hands me a chilled bottle of water, and I take it gratefully.

Once I appear recovered, Vance squats in front of me and places his hands on my knees, craning and crooking his neck so he can see my downturned eyes. "You good?"

I nod, laughing. "Perfect. Good thing I skipped breakfast. There's no way I would have been able to take in that much water if I hadn't."

He kisses me innocently on the cheek. "Sucked for you, not so much for me," he says next to my ear in the voice that makes my sex tighten. He stands up to his full height of six-foot-two, according to his stats online, stretches, rolls his shoulder again, and pops his neck.

"So," he says like he didn't just make my entire day, "what's Bristol doing after she gets off work?" He walks through the doors into the house and reappears again in the kitchen window. He slides the window open and proceeds to do whatever he went in there to do, while I lie back on my lounger to hide the disappointment on my face.

"She's hanging out with the snooty crew," I offer. "Why?"

"I thought maybe you'd want to include her tonight. I'm not used to dating a twin. I wasn't sure if I was crossing some sort of line by keeping you two apart."

I relax a little, relief settling my jealous hackles, and his choice of the word "dating" makes my heart race. I could swoon openly over the sweetness of him even thinking about including Bristol, but I refrain because I'm not ready to share him. "She may have mentioned missing me a time or two. But it's good for her—us, actually. I think you're good."

"You'll let me know if I'm not, right?"

"If I don't, Bristol will."

Vance returns with an elaborate icepack and two drinks that he sets on a table between two loungers. He then proceeds to move the lounger I'm not occupying across from me, so that the feet of each meet.

He adjusts the backrest, eases into it with a small wince, and plops the ice pack over his shoulder so that it drapes over both sides, front and back, sort of like a saddle pouch. His legs, long, whiter than his arms and chest, and thinly covered in dark hairs, stretch out in front of him, toes slightly pointed out. He places another ice pack on his elbow, this one smaller, but it wraps around fully.

The sun, thinly veiled behind a gauzy layer of clouds, bathes his skin in muted gold. I have wanted to examine the tattoos on his arms, chest, and back, but haven't had the opportunity without making it obvious what I'm doing. Not that I've ever been casual about checking him out. I'm pretty sure I'm as obvious as an armed, hooded guy in a bank. His eyes are shielded behind a pair of aviators, but I know he's looking at me, so, I use his apparent pain to my advantage.

"What's wrong with your shoulder?" I ask, sitting forward.

"It's nothing," he responds. "Just part of the job."

"Have you ever had it massaged? By a professional I mean, not like from one of your girls."

"Never by one of 'my girls.'" "My girls" is spoken with a different inflection that's executed to make sure I don't miss his dislike for my insinuation that he has many. "But, yes, we keep one on staff, but I didn't want to go in today."

"I could, you know, uh . . . massage it for you." I don't know why that sounds so dirty, because I truly mean what I've offered. But I blush and swallow loudly.

One eyebrow pops up high from under his sunglasses.

"Slow down, it's not what you think. I used to rub my mom's shoulders when she worked as a painter. I got pretty good at it."

"Is that so?"

I make a move to get up, setting my glass on the table beside me, and Vance, moving to stop me, accidentally drops both icepacks onto the deck.

"You're not here to serve me. Relax," he says, gesturing for me to sit back down.

I get up anyway, careful not to expose the goods as I swing my leg over the chair and get to my feet. "On your stomach," I command rather authoritatively and not unlike how I would talk to Bristol. I adjust my suit pulling it out of my butt and back over my ample cheeks. I toss him my beach towel. "Put this under your stomach to support your lower back."

He tosses me a look. "And you think I'm bossy?"

Ignoring him, I gesture in a swirling motion with my finger to turn over. He flattens the back of the lounger and rolls over, towel beneath his belly, arms at his sides. "Do you have any baby oil?"

"No, fresh out." He sounds amused, and I silently muse about him having lube in some drawer beside his bed he doesn't want to volunteer.

I settle for some lotion I find beneath the kitchen sink. It's not ideal, but it will lessen the friction. I straddle his back, sitting on his ass, and lean forward to smooth my hands up his back. I knead his knotted muscles, working my way up to his shoulder where he seems to be in the most pain. He moans into the cushion, his forehead pressed into the fabric of the lounger. His skin is warm, smooth and pliable beneath my touch. I press my thumbs into his muscle and knead with pointed pressure and feel it loosen ever so slightly. I work it another fifteen minutes, listening to his moans and an uttered curse of what I hope is more pleasure than pain.

My body tingles, aware of the intimacy and the lack of separation between us as my hands glide over his glistening skin and my ass skims over him with my movements. Seeing my hands on him is erotic by any standards, but watching my fingers glide over his tattooed arms would make for an embarrassing situation if I could get wood. I don't know if it would be Forrest Gump embarrassing or boner in front of the class embarrassing, but I'm glad I'm not a dude. Fortunately for me, every bit of my arousal is hidden beneath a triangle scrap of material. As I press forward so I can use some of my weight to push deeper into his muscle tissue, he flips over, taking advantage of my weight being off him.

I now straddle his front. That narrow scrap of material concealing my girl is now spread thin and on the verge of exposing far more than my arousal. He holds onto my wrists, restraining me, but I, being on top, still have the power if I choose to assert it, which I make no move to do, curiosity winning out over control. My self-esteem is high but isn't without its dings, and I quietly obsess over what he may or may not be thinking about me.

"If I let go, you have to stay put," he says, loosening his grip on my wrists while he waits for my response. With no forthcoming words, I nod slowly. He sits up, raises the reclined backrest, and moves his hips, shimmying us both up the lounger. "As nice as that was, this is better." He leans back, his eyes intent on mine as he lays his hands on my thighs and rubs his fingers into my flesh.

I smile. A thousand thoughts scurry through my head, none of which are talking me out of staying right where I am. I should be terrified, but no warning bells ring. Not that I would listen to them anyway. Common sense is not a dominant gene in the Sloan pool. If it were, I'd run now and spare myself being just one more of Van Hatfield's one-night stands.

My fear isn't enough to keep my hands to myself any more than I can keep my mouth shut when I should. I trail my fingers down the center of his chest between the hard, curved edges of his pecs and over his tattoo. My fingers, light, uncertain, and shaking, trace the outside of the home plate tattoo on his chest. "It's beautiful," I offer honestly. His arousal, while no longer beneath me, thickens under his shorts, lifting the blue fabric enough to draw my eyes downward. I've had only a few experiences with penises, one of which was in the back seat of Nick's Volvo. The other was a semi-failed attempt at a blowjob that left us both wondering if I wasn't better suited for bulimia.

He breathes in, his chest lifting with the deep intake, and I look up at him, my inexperience for once not in question.

Hands, larger and far more assured than mine run up my outer thighs. He has long, beautiful fingers like a pianist, and he knows how to play my keys when he runs a few fingers up my spine. "Thank you. Out of all of my tattoos, it means the most."

"And this one?" I point to the words "Hold the Count" written in a simple black font below his left collarbone. "What does that mean?"

He smiles. "When I was learning to pitch, I'd let the ball fly way too early, and my grandfather would yell, 'Hold the count, Vance.' Later, as my temper would get the better of me, he'd whisper it in my ear, 'Hold the count, Son,' asking me to count to ten before opening my mouth."

That makes me smile. I can see it. "Are the others sentimental?" He has full sleeves that would take hours to examine to see each detail, but if given the opportunity to do so, I will, gladly. The word "LOYALTY," written in script, runs down his right side from armpit to hip bone, and I'm guessing there is a story behind it as well.

This time he shakes his head. "Not really. Just life and lessons." His touch is feather-light, and nails, trimmed to the edge of his skin, tickle my humming flesh and elicit a shiver I'm too inexperienced to hide. One firm tug on the string of my top loosens the bind, freeing it from me before it lands on the deck beside the chair.

European sirens blast off in my head. Not the familiar ones of the cops in America, but those distinct ones that blare through the streets of Paris in the movies. I cover my peach-sized boobs with an arm and fret about the exposure,

He grins and drops his hands to my thighs. "I should have asked. I got carried away."

"No. It's not that." I bite my lip, closing my eyes as I search for the exact excuse I want to offer. "It's just that . . ." I look around, feeling too childish to say it.

"No one can see you unless they're flying overhead, which I won't say is unheard of, but I think we'd notice. And I'm not The Rock. No one cares enough to send a drone." He's right, the walls are high and our only exposure comes from above, or at least that's what I tell myself, because I'm starting to realize I may not want to be talked out of this. His eyes lighten a fraction. "But it's up to you."

"Am I going to be the only one exposed?"

Vance's grin is subtle. Blink and you'd miss it. "I hope not."

I slowly drop my arms, aware he is watching me, them—the boobs I've had an issue with since they grew in small—and I want to shrink. He doesn't lift his eyes for a long time, and while it's unnerving, his smile offers some solace and eases that niggling voice of doubt.

My breath hitches in between my throat and chest as he reaches up to touch them, and running the pad of his thumb over my nipple, he asks softly, "Are you okay with this?"

I nod, eyes keeping contact with his because it's the only way to know what he may be thinking.

"You're beautiful, Brenna." It's whispered adoringly, like he means it, not like he's trying to get me to bend to his will.

His eyes stray from mine, lowering as he shifts the material of my suit bottoms aside, exposing the most private part of me. I suck in half the earth's air supply as he runs his thumb, while he watches, over the wet center of my sex. He applies more pressure with the pad of his thumb, parting me with the pressure, before he pushes one long finger inside me.

In a mind usually so filled with useless crap it spills out of my mouth on a regular basis, nothing is in there now. Blank. Empty. Had I known pleasure came like this, I would have straddled a few fingers instead of Nick Stevenson's dick.

"Breathe, Brenna." Vance's voice is deep, soft, and so assured of what he's commanding me to do, I open my lungs and take air in, which in turn funds movement in my hips.

To my horror as much as my pleasure, he watches me ride his fingers, eyes turned down to watch them move in and out of me while the pad of his thumb circles my clit. Sitting up with no noticeable change in his rhythm, he leans forward and, sucking one of my nipples into his mouth, growls softly.

That small seed of pleasure has grown, blooming into something I've never felt other than by my own hand, and it's incomparable and utterly inconceivable that I would try to duplicate it on my own. I know my body, and I'm still not as good at pleasuring it as he is.

He whispers something heavily into my breast while he nips my nipple between his teeth. "Fucking beautiful."

His strokes are shorter and faster while his thumb rubs in a circle. I'm so close, but the edge scares the shit out of me, and I just want him to stop and fuck me like a normal person would. It feels almost like an audition, and my body is on display for his intimate inspection. This one-sided orgasm isn't for the faint of heart, and I'm realizing that way too late.

I arch my back, my breath hisses on the intake, and the whimper that escapes on my exhale makes me blush. I collapse, my body shuddering at my climax. Vance wraps his arms around me, and I press my forehead into his shoulder while the rest of me collapses in his arms.

His lips caress my shoulder, then he kisses my neck, his tongue slipping across my flesh. "That was hot as fuck," he whispers into my neck. "Jesus!"

With my arm across my little goods, I sit up straight and meet his gaze even though all I want to do is cover up and cower. His blue eyes assess me, and I wonder how I'm not supposed to over-think things when he looks at me like that.

With a finger, he tips my chin up, giving me no choice but to meet his gaze. "How 'bout we take this inside?"

CHAPTER NINETEEN

In the shower, we wash off the ocean and sweat from our skin. I rinse the last of the lather from my body and find myself pressed against the wall, Vance's hard body holding me there while his hands hold mine in place above my head. Heat, and not just from the water, circulates around us. My chest heaves with my breaths as I anticipate his next move.

His kiss is deep, hard, and filled with pent-up passion that he has denied himself since offering me a gentleman. His knee parts my legs, and he drops one of my hands so he can touch me in that spot that has craved him since I met him.

With his mouth against my ear, he whispers heavily into it, "I would fuck you right here if I didn't think you deserved a better experience than your first."

"I'm okay with right here." Breathless from his kiss and uncertain where my next breath is going to come from, I don't care if I sound desperate. I want him.

"You deserve better." He grins, scraping his teeth over my lip before lowering his head to lick my nipple.

I moan loudly, arching into him, wanting more from his mouth than a few nips and tugs. "This is already a big improvement over that."

His fingers pleasure me while his mouth devours me. His words rumble against my chest. "Trust me, it gets better."

I realize, as I'm growing frustrated with the R-rated shower he's insisting upon, that I haven't contributed much to creating the X-rated version I want. I've memorized every hard muscle of his body except the one between his legs.

I don't want this to be one-sided yet again, but I'm also terrified I'll do it wrong. I'm not a complete stranger to the male anatomy, but Vance is a definite upgrade from Volvo Nick, so I can't help but wonder if different sizes require different things.

I am not shy, most likely never will be, so I take the bull by the horns, if you will, and reach between us to grab a hold of him. Stroking slowly at first to get a feel for what's required, I gather momentum based on his sounds and his movements. He thrusts his hips forward, pressing himself into my hand, and I move faster, cupping him, stroking him, until he stills my hand with one of his own.

"You're going to be the death of me," he pants into my neck.

"I don't have to be."

"Not here, Brenna. I mean it." Naked, wet, and so sexed up we can't stand another second of torturous denial, he lifts me off my feet and I wrap my legs around him. I don't miss the moment he takes to stare down between us at what most certainly is one hell of a sex shot.

Unconcerned about our wet bodies, he lays me on his bed and climbs above me, hovering out of reach of my mouth but not my hands. Water from his hair, chest, face, and every other rippled section of his body drips down onto mine.

I've only just begun to navigate around his body when he stills my hand once more.

"I love your touch, baby, but, Jesus, you're going to make me come."

While I'm wrapped up in my glory and contemplating making him call me 'baby' all the time, he apologizes and leaves me to hunt for his wallet where he keeps his provisions. He has two nightstands, a foot thingy at the end of his bed, and he has to find his wallet for his condoms? Where does he do his fucking?

He spends a few extra minutes kissing me and priming what's been primed since meeting him. "Brenna, if I drag this out a second longer, we'll both be disappointed."

"So don't."

Resting on his forearms and elbows he thrusts slowly inside me, giving me only half of what I expect. It's a tight fit, and it hurts slightly, but the pleasure far exceeds the pain. He's gentle, considerate, as he presses forward slowly.

"Ahh," I breathe out as he fills me.

"You okay?" he asks, slowing again and brushing my hair away with his fingers.

"Uh-huh." Proper words aren't at the forefront of my thoughts, and therefore none are ready. Needing to feel him, I run my hands up his sides, along his ribcage, and along his back, pressing my fingertips into him.

He pushes forward, thrusting harder, moving me up the bed, but I am so lost in the feeling, little else registers. We both pant, our breathlessness the only sound I hear over our moving bodies. I move my hips to meet him, and dig my fingertips into his flesh, needing another release as I feel an overwhelming upsurge of pleasure. Knowing what I need, he assists my climax with his thumb and pumps harder.

"Please tell me you're close?" His voice rasps into my ear, but his body keeps its momentum, no backslide, only commitment to my pleasure as he fights off his own.

Utter delirium ensures I am unable to measure my distance from the finish line, but not long after his inquiry and without the courtesy of a warning, I am liquid beneath him, my release a silent surprise based on the inner porn star I channeled earlier. He still chases his, and I tighten around him, finally sending him over the edge.

He rolls off of me and onto his back beside me, his stomach rising and falling in sync with his chest. It takes him a few moments to catch his breath before he is up and taking care of the condom. Upon his return, he throws a blanket over me and slides in next to me, snuggling me up to his chest.

"I didn't hurt you, did I?"

I shake my head, ready to go again if I were forward enough to ask. Who am I kidding? I'm pretty damn forward, but years of trying to prove I'm not just made of slutty rumors and Sloan indiscretions have left me a bit gun-shy. There is so much more to me, and my hope is he gains an appreciation for those things too.

He kisses my forehead, and even though it's a sisterly location, it feels tender and intimate. I want to believe he's falling for me like I'm falling for him, but do guys like Van Hatfield fall? I know if I read too much into it, I'll spoil the moment, and if all I'm going to get is one moment, I'm damn well going to savor it. Deciding words aren't necessary to get my point across, I reach between us and cup him. Even soft or semi-hard, he is impressive, and I try to gently coax him out to his full potential.

Vance laughs. "You're an optimist, that's for sure." Again, he kisses my head and pumps once into my hand. "Thankfully for us both, I know how to pass the time until I'm ready again." He flips me on my back and straddles me, pinning my hands against the bed above my head. He kisses me hard, biting my lip, inciting a little bit of sting. He rotates his hips against me, rubbing himself up against my clit while he watches.

He kisses his way down between my breasts, taking a detour to tend to each one before heading further south. His hands let go of mine to skim down my arms, sides, and hips, until he is directly over that pulse aching for him. He looks up through his dark lashes, and that devil grin, easily the sexiest part of him, grows wide. "You can thank me later."

His tongue skims over my slit, and I grip the bedding and hiss in a breath. Rocked by the intense intimacy, I instinctively close my legs. Not having it, he presses his palms against my inner thighs and pushes them back open, looking up at me while he flicks his tongue over that white-hot spot.

A few minutes of that, and I am writhing and moaning, finding once again my inner porn star. Another orgasm lifts my ass off the bed and makes my legs quake. Vance is relentless and drags it out long past my tolerance, and I become a puddle of skin beneath his tongue and touch. I can't even lift my head when he allows my surrender, and I silently wonder if I'll ever be able to reciprocate, or if a quivering mass of contentment is all I'll ever be.

Recovered and a little nervous, but oddly excited to taste him, I take him in my mouth, eliciting a slow groan from deep in his chest. I utilize the techniques that Bristol has shared with me because she can't keep anything to herself, and hope her narrative is enough to see me through.

Vance holds my head but doesn't drive. He seems content to let me work at my own pace and manage the depth. I am more than happy to experiment on him.

"Brenna, I'm gonna come." His warning says a lot about him, and I pull back—my inner porn star showing its limits—and use my hand to finish him off.

"STAY." VANCE, TONE SERIOUS, STRIPS ME OF THE BAG I'VE JUST shoved my swimsuit into and wraps me up in his arms, his chest pressed against my back, his lips near my ear.

"Stay. I'll take you to work in the morning."

"I don't have clothes." My excuse is weak, but I can't give him the real one. I'm scared shitless. I can't fucking want this. I can't.

"Then I'll take you home first. Stay."

My inner battle for self-preservation loses some ground, and I lean back against him, torn between staying and knowing the sooner I walk away, the easier it will be to take my heart with me. As much as I pride myself on being independent and not being a girly-girl, I have the emotions of one, and I know the longer I stay, the more I'll want.

He kisses my neck, dragging his teeth along my skin. "Say you'll stay," he whispers. I shiver, and my eyes involuntarily close as my skin explodes with a rush of new goose bumps beneath his breath.

I shove all my reservations aside and give in to the consuming and sometimes frightening craving I have for all things Vance. Knowing there's no way I can walk away now, I turn around in his arms. "Only if we can take a shower and finish what we started in there earlier." I may as well enjoy the time I have with him today instead of worrying about what I'll be left with tomorrow. There is something to be said for living in the moment.

He presses me harder against him. "You ask a lot of a guy. Now I'm going to ask something of you."

I look up, eyes hopeful, heart hammering. "My answer is yes."

"I haven't asked yet."

"Doesn't matter. I'd still say yes."

He takes my lips in another kiss that leaves me barely able to stand. "I'll see you Saturday after my game for another date."

Okay, wasn't what I was expecting, but not altogether worse or better than the triple-X scene I'd anticipated him asking for. Somehow, I figured we'd part ways after tonight. I'm not sure if it's relief or a mild case of uncertainty expanding the spaces between my ribs. "It's Miracle Days."

"You can't take back your yes. I'll see you at Miracle Days."

CHAPTER TWENTY

I f it wasn't for Miracle Days and the prep work for the auction, the four days in between my last date with Vance and our next would have been fraught with nervous anticipation. As it was, I barely had time to take on a side job designing a new brochure for a local surf instructor, let alone worrying about what another date might imply. But now that Bristol won't stop chatting about it, my insecurities flare.

"He's supposed to be here after his game," I snap my answer at Bristol. I'm tired of the fifty-question interrogation she's been putting me through since I told her Vance was hoping to be here in time to for the auction.

Using her shoulder, she slides a skimboard into the holding rack and nearly topples over when it doesn't give her the typical resistance. "I thought you said you were done with Hollywood after *Candid* called you 'the equivalent of a gas station egg salad sandwich.'"

I fume, checking the skimboard in but trying my damnedest not to give her too much rope. "I was pissed, Bristol. They don't even know me, and who wants to be compared to a sandwich that could potentially give you explosive diarrhea? I survived the shit people said about me when you sucked off half the school. I think I can survive one lousy article."

"That was a rumor, Brenna. I didn't blow half the school."

"Exactly my point. I'm not an egg salad sandwich, either."

"My point is, if this blows up, it won't just be you they talk about. They could talk about Dad and Colette and any other offspring we may not be aware of, Mom's bus terminal of ex-boyfriends, and our slut-shaming. Are you ready for that? If you thought last year was bad with the kegger at Kale's house, wait until *Candid* gets ahold of your name and it goes global."

"I don't know what I'm ready for, Bristol, which is why I'm nervous. We're still getting to know each other." I grab the broom to sweep up the mound of sand forming beneath the racks.

"You should know everything you need to by now. You spent, what, like two hours on the phone with him last night?"

I roll my eyes for the hundredth time over her petty arguments, but I don't engage her. I've spent hours over a few days getting to know him on the phone. And those few hours were in between work, auction preparation, and side jobs I have to pick up because Bristol can't attend classes like a normal college student on scholarship. "We're feeling it out. Nothing more."

She's given up returning the boards to their slots and stands there looking at me. "It's Miracle Days, Brenna. Your 'feeling it out' won't be with just the town drunks at The Seam this time. He's Van Hatfield, womanizing man-whore and Jock Star of the Year. The tabloids are going to follow him here eventually."

"It's Milagro Beach, not Hollywood. I think we're fine." I groan, not really confident in that statement but standing behind it just the same as I shove a surfboard into the rack with more force than is required. I'm typically not this motivated to put something away that will be out again in five minutes due to the heavier Miracle Days traffic. It's our busiest day of the year next to the Fourth of July, and inventory doesn't sit long.

Bristol stretches, moving her arms like they're sore, and they probably are. She's moved a lot of product today, but I'm more concerned it's from the shit she's shoveling my way. "Suit yourself. Just remember, it's me you're dragging down with you."

"Welcome to my show. I've had a supporting role in yours for years. And news flash, you dragged us down years ago."

Bristol's glare is deadly. "Go ahead, rewrite history. You weren't fixing your skirt in Nick's back seat." A few bikes arrive, and she's forced to table her argument.

By the end of our shift, Bristol and I have fought and made up half a dozen times. I'm pretty sure we're in a stable truce as we wander the boardwalk, sampling the food from one end to the other with the occasional stop to check out the vendors selling everything from watercolor paintings to jewelry.

We pick up fish tacos for my mom and Uncle Rodney, who will be too busy working at the bar to get anything for themselves, and make our way back toward The Seam, detouring occasionally to snap pictures of tourists who didn't bother looking in a mirror this morning.

The Seam, where Uncle Rodney will be announcing the silent auction winners in less than an hour, is bursting at the seams, which Bristol doesn't find as funny as I do when I say it to her. She elbows me in the side instead of laughing as we cross in front of the barricade blocking off one section of Ocean Avenue's traffic.

Motorcycles galore are parked along the next city block not cordoned off with orange barricades, and it looks like Milagro Beach has been taken over by motorcycle gangs. Bristol and I approach cautiously and slowly weave our way through leather pants and patched vests. It's intimidating at first, but when we realize most are with their women or are old enough to be our dad, we relax and cut through them like we would anyone else.

Inside The Seam, Uncle Rodney has an entire staff working and wearing buttons for Remington General's Cardiac Wing, which is this year's beneficiary of the silent auction and near and dear to

Uncle Rodney since he had a mild heart attack in his late forties. It was "nothing" according to him, but it must have been a little something, because he's never volunteered to host anything community-oriented at The Seam before, much less the biggest event of the year.

"Did you see Vance?" Uncle Rodney shouts over a classic rock song playing through the overhead speaker.

Bristol beams brightly, though I'm not sure why she looks so happy after bitching the last several days about me continuing to see him. "He's here?" She looks around, eyes scanning a crowd she'll never find him in.

"He's out back," Uncle Rodney yells, "helping your mom with something."

I hand Uncle Rodney the fish tacos, receiving in return a grateful sigh and a mouthed "thank you." Bristol disappears somewhere between me catching her beaming and Uncle Rodney's directions, and I find myself looking for her instead of Vance.

Feeling a little exposed in my white Stray Charlie's tank top, I hoist the curved neckline up for the tenth time since I left work so I look more disheveled and less like I'm for sale. I turn and make it no further than a face plant into a hard chest.

Hands grip my shoulders. "Going somewhere?"

I look up, rub my nose where it collided with sternum, and see the one face that's kept my mind occupied during the quiet moments between sleep and work. If I allowed him to, he could destroy my world, but the potential for something real and honest with someone who doesn't care about my family history is a tempting lure. I already feel the calm of his presence, and despite the unknown, I lean toward it.

Vance blends in wearing a new ball cap that sits low on his forehead, shielding blue eyes that are usually blocked by his sunglasses. "Where do you think you're going?"

I smile wide, my squashed nose forgotten as the world once again feels level. "You came!"

"I said I would." He tips his head toward me to hear what the crowd and music stifle.

"I know, but it's so public and, well . . ." I don't have to say it. I don't have to spell out what he already knows.

"I'll be cautious. Why is your shirt like that?" With two fingers he fixes my bunched scoop-neck tank top, and I once again look like Stray Charlie's call girl.

I ignore his clothing assist and prattle on without losing my focus. "Cautious would be waiting until dark." He cups his ear like he can't hear me, so I drag him toward the storage room but stop short of entering and stand at the closed door.

"I wanted to see you." He bends to kiss my cheek. "Can you blame a guy?"

I close my eyes, relishing the compliment before I have to respond. In all of our phone conversations, we've never talked about the next step, both seemingly content behind closed doors, with no real desire to take it public or ask for a label. He has a piece of my heart whether we call it anything or not. If I could have Vance without the publicity, that would make Bristol happier—me happier too—but that's not reality, and to pretend that it is won't serve anyone.

The music stops, saving me from a reply, and Uncle Rodney with a microphone to his lips calls the crowd to order. We move back into the fray, and Vance slips his hand around mine in a brief but open display of affection. I felt it much longer than it lasted and knowing it would cost him if anyone noticed, made it mean that much more.

"The silent bids have been counted by our Miracle Days committee, and our winners will be posted beside each item's bid sheet. If you bid on anything, folks, you'll want to check the table to see if you have won," Uncle Rodney continues, despite the lingering conversations and offshoots of rowdy hoots. "All items can be picked up this evening at the Rec Center or tomorrow morning if you'd prefer. Milagro Beach, we raised a whopping sixteen thousand dollars this year. Sixteen!" he shouts, lifting an arm in the air like he's celebrating. "Thank you all for your participation."

"How much did the Hatfield ball go for?" I hear the question from the crowd but can't pinpoint the body it comes from.

Uncle Rodney hesitates, struggling briefly between his fierce protection of Vance's privacy inside his bar and his hometown's curiosity about their baseball hero. It's still a sore subject with me, and I find myself once again irritated with Bristol. "As much as I'd like to say my bid took it, I'm afraid the ten-thousand-dollar bid was too rich for my blood."

The crowd hoots, appeased it at least went for a good price and one they couldn't afford. I look away from the melee to see Vance shifting uncomfortably beside me, too modest to peacock over his involvement. I would still be peacocking over my kindergarten noodle sculpture if my dad hadn't slammed it against a wall two weeks after its blue-ribbon win.

I scoot closer to him and he grabs my hand, leaning down into my ear to talk to me. "We don't have to go, but I could use a second—"

Pops of bright light precede a commotion I'm too startled to follow. The crowd in front of me clears, replaced by a hungrier one that wants, it seems, a piece of me. I'm not claustrophobic in the slightest. I once hid in the dryer for two hours while Bristol hunted for me, but this is nothing like that, and a heaviness akin to fear blankets me. I hold out a defensive hand in front of me while my other tangles with Vance's. The warm grip around my right hand is pulling me in one direction while an unfamiliar hand reaches, snares, and pulls me from above the elbow in the opposite. More flashes of light flare and then diminish, leaving the bar in a sea of melting orbs like you see when you've rubbed your eyes too hard or looked too long at the sun.

Voices of all levels and tones vie for Vance's undivided attention as I realize it's his name repeatedly being called out while they paw me. I stand between Vance and the photographers, who I'm pretty sure aren't all that reputable by the parts of me they grab.

"Get the fuck back!" Vance yells, pushing one of the guys with a chunk of my Stray Charlie's tank top in his fist. The guy, who looks a little bit like Shrek, falls against the woman behind him, and her camera hits the ground, shedding a piece that hits my foot.

With Uncle Rodney's booming voice on the microphone, his friend John acting as a bouncer, and Vance using his body as a barrier between me and the photographers, I feel a tinge of relief as the crowd thins. Despite Vance's aggression and my retreat, the occasional flashbulb still pops, and the bastards still fling their questions at Vance faster than he can possibly answer.

"Does this mean you and Amber Dietrich are done? What about Nikki Kline? Is she in the picture?"

"Are you ever going to set the record straight about your leave of absence? Was it due to the fight with McEntire or your fight with Able Howard?"

"After the fight with McEntire, are the Renegades looking to trade you?"

"What's her name? How did you meet her? Give us your name, sweetheart."

"How long before..."

It's nonstop. The questions, like debris in a funnel cloud, shoot out randomly. There is no rhyme or reason, or maybe there is and I'm not grasping the ins and outs. I don't usually like to mix my gossip with the six o'clock news, but these people don't care. It's like *People* magazine up in here, and by the way they're firing questions at him, I'm not really sure they give a shit whether Vance answers or not.

"Back off!" I've heard Vance say more than once, but they don't listen and seem to close in tighter. I've seen him strong-arm and shove them only to be provoked into more. I've seen his anger, understood his frustration, and sensed his fear with the uncontrolled escalations and outright disrespect displayed by the relentless reporters.

When the police arrive like they're busting an underage house party, Vance gets the distraction he needs to gain the upper hand. He's still wound tight, and if his grip on my hand is any indication of where we're at on the Richter scale, we're barely avoiding complete destruction.

"Are you hurt?" he asks, concern overriding his other emotions.

I shake my head, looking up at him, eyes wide, mind reeling.

"I'm sorry, Brenna. Dammit, I'm sorry."

"Excuse me." Deputy Solomon, a somewhat lanky man with a trash 'stache and a God complex, obviously can't tell that Vance and I are in the middle of something or are about to be. He's awfully arrogant for a guy who gets from point A to point B on his bicycle. "Mr. Hatfield, we're going to have to take a statement from you."

Vance groans, runs his fingers through his hair, and growls out, "Why?"

"The gentleman you shoved is filing a complaint."

CHAPTER TWENTY-ONE

I'm still reeling from my first experience with paparazzi when my fifth experience with Milagro Beach's Finest pulls the rug out from under me with talk of arresting Vance for assault and battery. Now I'm locked in the storage room because Uncle Rodney doesn't think I'm capable of keeping my mouth shut long enough for them to figure out there is no merit to Shrek's claim. I can't say he's wrong, but frantically pacing between a wall of shelves and a door Uncle Rodney is guarding isn't helping my mood any.

My pacing comes to an abrupt halt when Bristol flies in, yelling, "What are you going to do, Solomon, peck me to death with your nose? You're a security guard. You can't arrest me." Her hair is a blonde halo of mass discord, and she looks like she may have fought her way out of a burlap sack. I don't know what she had to do to get in here, but whoever is on the outside wants her to stay, and the door slams shut behind her.

When Bristol finally calms down enough to notice me, she plows into me, hugging me tightly. "You're okay." Her smile, slow to form, brightens.

"Solomon *is* a cop," I say through strained breaths as she squeezes me to death.

I feel her shrug, but her arms around me don't loosen. "Then why is he always in the beach parking lot?"

"He's a bike cop. He patrols the beach, but he has the same authority."

She laughs, pulls back to let me reclaim some old, dusty, storage room air, but questions me further, face scrunched up in confusion. "What's he going to do with me after he arrests me? WE can't both fit on that bike."

Good question. Never thought of it, and don't care. "Wait. Why is he going to arrest you?" I stop her with a hand up to her face. "Never mind, I don't care. Are they arresting Vance?"

She shifts her feet, lowers her eyes, and bites her lip, which incidentally has a red blotchy mark beneath it. That she won't make eye contact with me worries me. "I don't think so. I heard Uncle Rodney threaten to charge the camera guy with trespassing if he tried, and he even mentioned assault for grabbing you. Did they really grab you?" She looks me over for signs of a struggle, but still hesitates with her eye contact.

"I'm fine." I'm worse than fine, but because I know next to nothing about what's going on out there, not because some asshole grabbed me.

Bristol shifts her feet again, as red blotches appear on her chest, and her expressive eyes deteriorate from curious to worried. The last time she had red, blotchy skin, she was guilty of something.

The door opens and Uncle Rodney, using a sweeping, impatient hand motion, ushers us out. "Brenna, they'll need your statement before you can leave, but other than that, we're done here. Bristol." He places a veined hand on her shoulder, and it's a heavy one, because Bristol's height shrinks an inch beneath it. "You pull shit like that again and you're on your own. Niece or no, I will disown you for that shit. Do I make myself clear?"

She swallows hard, nods, and accidentally makes eye contact with me, which she breaks the moment she realizes her mistake. I hesitate between the old habit of defending and protecting Bristol regardless of what she's done, and my expanding heart that now sometimes beats independently from hers. I grab her by the elbow as she tries to lose herself in the crowded bar.

"What did you do? Why would Uncle Rodney say that?" My eyes skirt between her eyes and her blotches—the red flags I knew better than to ignore.

Her eyes plead with Uncle Rodney's, and I know that if I'm going to get any answers, I'll need to watch him and not Bristol. His lips are tight, eyes stern, and when he gives one single firm nod, I know it's not a nod of permission but one of command, and she's not getting out of here without confessing something.

"Bristol?" I now look to her.

"I—" she hesitates, wrings her fingers, thumbs the belt loop of her shorts, scrapes the ribbing of her Stray Charlie's tank top with her thumbnail, and swallows like she has a giant hairball in her throat she can't cough up or pass.

"Spit it out," I say between clenched teeth and depleted patience. I've still got to give a statement to bike cop Solomon, hunt down Vance, and find the time to pray that my face isn't plastered all over the tabloids with my shirt up around my neck. For once, there is something more important to me than getting Bristol out of a jam, and she can't even tell me what the hell that jam is.

"Can't you see that this is hard for me? I'm trying."

A few breaths calm me long enough to wait another second for her to spit it out, but by the way she's doing everything possible to stall, my patience isn't going to outlast her procrastination. "Bristol —" I yell, but she cuts me off before I can scream my frazzled ultimatum.

"I called the photographers." Her eyes fill with tears, her regret evident, but way too late. "They're here because I tipped them off."

I wish now I'd been more patient—allowed myself more time to live in my crappy moment of ignorance before she obliterated said shitty moment with one even worse. I soak up her confession, feel it in every fiber and pore until it consumes even the smallest part of me that knows she would never have done that had she known the outcome.

Bristol has knee-jerk responses. That's how she works. She never thinks of what comes after. She lives in today and I clean up tomorrow. We've always lived that way, and up until this second, it's worked. It's always worked, but like all things that run on collected parts pieced together by necessity and not design, something will eventually break, malfunction, or require tweaking. I don't know which this is, but our pieced-together parts have stopped working together.

She reaches out, thinks twice, and pulls her hand back. "Say something."

"Why?" It's all I can get out.

"Oh my God, Brenna, you wouldn't listen to me. I had to do something."

I seethe, lacking even the smallest amount of understanding.

"Someone has to save you. You sure in the hell aren't going to do it."

I point a stern finger right to the middle of her chest. "I am not Mom. Stop treating me like I am."

"You're a lot more like her than you think."

I shake my head, scowling like a bitter bitch. Needing air and space to breathe, I head outdoors, but bike cop Solomon catches me at the door.

"Ms. Sloan, you can't leave yet." Fat tears form in my eyes like they had been there all along and just swelled to perfection. Like most guys, he clearly doesn't like tears or any emotion that he can't tamp down with sheer will and/or a shot of whiskey. "Uh, go ahead, take a second." He grabs hold of the handle on the door and holds it open so I can suck in some much-needed air.

I look both ways down Ocean Avenue, seeing bikers, bleached-blonde natives, a few lingering police officers, and the horde of photographers they've pushed across the street to the boardwalk. I don't see Vance. He's tall, so he stands out in most crowds, but I can't find him. I wipe away the last of the moisture from my cheeks and press my fingers into my eyes until the tears dry.

"Hey! There she is!" The isolated paparazzi buzz, coming to life like a swatted wasp nest. "Give us your name, sweetheart. You may as well soak up your fifteen minutes. It's about all you're going to last," one shouts through an open mouth I want to punch her in.

"Give us something, and we'll leave you alone." It's a promise they won't keep and more than likely don't have the power to offer.

"Brenna!" One amongst the wasp nest shouts for me, and I turn my head with a jerk that rattles some curse words loose. "Brenna Sloan!"

"Fuck!" I say beneath my breath, torn between being impressed and utter astonishment. I've had guys stumble over my name on a date, and these people have it within ten minutes of actually seeing my face.

I head back into The Seam, and Uncle Rodney, expecting me back, is waiting by the door talking to bike cop Solomon with his hands as much as his vocabulary.

His eyes land on mine, sympathetic but impatient, and he excuses himself from Solomon to retrieve me before I've gotten too far inside. "He's gone home, love."

It doesn't register right away, but when it does, it's another information body blow. "Home? Why?"

He slides an arm over my shoulders and squeezes me into his side. "He thinks it's what's best for you."

"Me?"

"His life is public and it's always going to be. I don't think he wants that for you."

"This is Bristol's doing. Not his. Oh God! Does he know it was Bristol?"

"He knows," he says softly, eyes maddeningly sympathetic. "I couldn't have protected her if I'd wanted to."

I'm done spiraling and then rallying for Bristol. I'll deal with her later. Waiting is the least she deserves. "Home, as in his house here, or home, as in he's driving back to San Jose?"

If he's surprised I'm not cussing up a storm and hightailing it after Bristol, he doesn't show it. "He didn't say." His eyes are kind and hold a wealth of love I've always taken for granted. He's always been a strength I've relied on to see us through anything, but how is he going to see me through this? Feeling like I'm on the brink of losing everything I thought I'd have forever, and the one thing I thought I'd never have, I want him to fix this.

He grabs hold of my face, palms my head between his hands and kisses my forehead. "Whatever you do, love, make sure it's not out of spite. And desperation rarely results in the outcome you hope for. Think with this," he points at my chest. "It always has good intentions. This," he taps my forehead, "this will talk you out of the right thing if you let it, and often overthinks the simple things your heart already knows."

"What happened?" My mom, out of breath and late to the party as usual, inserts herself between me and Uncle Rodney, grabs hold of me, and throws a quick set of eyes over me like she's looking for imperfections on the surface of an apple. "Are you okay?"

I nod, kiss her on the cheek and extricate myself from her grasp. "I have to talk to bike cop Solomon."

"What? Why? Oh dear God, Brenna, don't call him that to his face, honey."

I'm about to open my mouth to say something sarcastic, when I spot Joe, my mom's piece of shit ex-boyfriend, blocking the entrance and exit into The Seam. I look at my mom, whose repentant look is enough to pass for contrite but not apologetic. I open my mouth, clamp it shut, and walk away, because for once, she's not going to stop me from going after what I want.

After I've spoken to bike cop Solomon, I find Bristol in the storage room rummaging behind the shelves for our hidden bottle of Jameson. It's got to be at least four years old, dusty, and harboring the dead shells of critters behind its peeling label. "Give me the keys."

Oblivious to my presence, she jumps at my command, hits her head against the wall, and rattles the shelf. "Not funny, Brenna." Standing up empty-handed, she dusts off her arm and shoulder with a heavy hand, filling the air with gray flour. "I could have broken the bottle."

"I'm going to break more than that if you don't give me the car keys." She knows how I fight. I'm not a contender, but the threat alone raises her hackles.

"I did you a favor. You may not see it now, but I did."

"Keys!"

"No. I won't let you go after him. With everything we've been through in this town, I can't believe you want to date a guy who can't kiss a girl without it making the cover of *Candid*. You'll regret it."

"You don't get to decide what I do. I stuck by you. You can stick by me."

"No! Totally different scale. This, Brenna, will be global. And for what? A guy who likes the chase but not the commitment? He'll never stay."

"I'm not Mom." I thrust my hand out, palm up. "I'm not going to ask you again. Give me the keys!"

"No." She doesn't even balk at my aggression. "It's me or him."

I'm powered by anger, and what I might ordinarily refrain from saying spills out with venom. "This isn't the night you want to make me choose."

Bristol's blotchy red spots find new life. "I'm your ride or die. Are you saying you'd choose him?"

"I'm saying a break from you sounds pretty damn good right now. So, ask me again to choose."

"Fine!" She struggles to pull the keys out of her shorts pocket, and for a second I think they may be permanently trapped, but a few grunts and tugs later, she slaps the keys into my hand with a disgruntled smack. "You need to reassess your priorities."

"You're right. Maybe I should move your betrayal to the top of the list.

Her blotches flare red, but to my astonishment, she snaps her mouth shut and hardens her features. "Have it your way."

CHAPTER TWENTY-TWO

Vance has ignored my texts, calls, and the Silver Stallion's wimpy horn blasts that sound more like timid hello's than confident holler's. I check out the white paneled gate to see if it's something I can climb over, but there are no footholds high enough to boost me anywhere near the top, and I don't have enough arm strength to pull myself up from the ground. There is public parking down at the bottom of the hill. I could park there, walk around, and get to his house from the back steps, but that seems desperate, and Uncle Rodney warned me about the repercussions of desperation, so I compromise, and shoot him another text.

Me: *I'm at your gate. Will you let me in?*

Minutes later, my phone sings a text, and I about nosedive into the hood of the Silver Stallion.

Vance: *I'm not home.*

Me: *Will you be soon?*

Five eternal minutes pass, and I'm ashamed to say I have that down to within a half-second, give or take, before response dots appear on my phone.

Vance: *No.*

Me: *Then answer your phone.*

Vance: *Busy.*

Me: *Avoiding me doesn't make you busy. It makes you an asshole.*

Endless seconds, minutes . . .

Vance: *Not avoiding. Busy!!*

Me: *I'm not leaving until we talk.*

I've always been the product of someone else's decisions, and just once I want to hold the cards. I want to be the one who wins or fails based on my choices and input. He hasn't known me long enough to be my voice, and if he's walking away, it had better be because he doesn't want me and not because he thinks it's "best for me." Besides, I walked out on Bristol after always vowing to choose her, and I'll be damned if it's going to be for nothing.

Vance: *It could be a while. I'll call you when I'm done.*

Me: *I'll wait.*

×

I'M SITTING ON THE HOOD, FACE DOWN IN MY PHONE, WAITING FOR contact and feeling more and more like the desperate woman who raised me than the woman I thought I'd eventually grow to be, when the gate slides open. The roar of a motorcycle behind me gives my heart an exhilarated beat. I look up as Vance pulls up beside me and stops.

"Pull in," he says, and gives the bike enough throttle to proceed through the gate and into the opening garage stall where his Spyder is parked.

I pull in, park behind the Spyder, and take a breath before hopping out. Vance clears the garage door as it starts to lower and stands within a foot of me and the front of my car. He's perfect except for the eyes that hold something a little darker than the last time they landed on me.

I follow him inside the house without the anticipation of the last time I was here. He's distant and I'm pretty sure resigned to whatever decision he's made without me. At the top of the stairs where the living room and kitchen intersect, he asks if I want anything.

If by anything he means him, then yes, but I think he means a drink or trip to the bathroom. "I'm fine," I reply, feeling anything but fine as I feel him slipping away and me slipping away from Bristol. Dear God, how does one person handle this alone?

"I'm sorry," I blurt out. "If I had known they'd be there, I never would have asked you to come." My fingers ache from being tangled around one another, and I have to flex them to loosen the settling pain.

"I'm not mad at you, Brenna."

"How could you—the paparazzi—the cameras—I—you—" Even speech class didn't make me stutter this badly, and I was the worst.

"I'm not mad, Brenna, I just don't want that for you. It's not fair for me to come into your life and uproot it like that. I knew better, and I still pursued you. That's my fault, not yours."

"Don't I get a say?"

I see him stiffen, and his fist down at his side tightens. "No. My life isn't going to change."

"It's not your fault, it's—"

"If it's not her, it'll be someone else," he barks, interrupting my explanation. If he only knew Bristol better, he'd understand, or perhaps not, since understanding Bristol requires a degree and he chose baseball. "That's what you're not getting."

"I get it. I'm here, aren't I? I could have just as easily chosen Bristol." I make it sound like it's some heroic feat not choosing Bristol, but even as I say it, I know I'm returning to her regardless of the outcome here.

Exasperated, he runs a hand through his hair, looks up and blows out a breath. "I don't want you to choose me."

"Like, at all?" That's something my mom would ask, and I cringe, wishing I could take the bullet out of the chamber. I will not beg him. I will not tell him my worth if he cannot see it for himself. Not in this lifetime and certainly not in this moment.

"You shouldn't have to choose." It's a form of retreat I recognize for what it is— his way out.

Mentally distancing myself, I harden my tone. "Can I ask you a question?"

He nods.

"If none of this were an issue, would you let me walk out this door?"

He doesn't flinch, his reply quick. "I don't know, Brenna, because that's not our situation."

"You do know," I say flatly. It's more obvious now than ever that he never intended for me to be more than a diversion from his public life. "You've always known." I turn to leave the way he led me in. He grabs my elbow before I can hit the first step.

His eyes dance, circling my features before dropping to my lips and back up to my eyes where they hold briefly. For a moment my heart feels hope, and then he drops my arm without a word exchanged.

I've never been more confused, but now I'm hell-bent on making this hard on him too. I've got nothing to lose, so I grip his shirt, pull him toward me, and on tiptoes, I kiss him one last time. With no protest, I slip in a little tongue, conscious of my breath, which I freshened with a broken cherry Lifesaver I found in the cup holder of my car. He kisses me back, but before he can find his restraint and reject me, I pull away, dropping down onto flat feet. "If this is good-bye, I'm not going to regret what I didn't do."

With every ounce of strength and pride I have, I pivot on feet that want to stay planted and walk out.

CHAPTER TWENTY-THREE

Ignoring Bristol's questions, hopeful looks, and well-timed sniffles, I pull the Silver Stallion into an empty spot in a lot two blocks farther away from work than normal. I'm an emotional, sleepless wreck, and I haven't planned for this shit. So, between the five minutes of circling the block looking for a spot to park and having to walk an extra two blocks, we're going to be late for work.

Rubbing my stinging eyes, I grab my coffee out of the cup holder, my messenger bag from the back seat, and shut the door, which requires an extra hip nudge to close. I'd normally yell at Bristol for taking too long to get out of the car, but she's waiting on me this time with no shortage of sad, pathetic sighs.

I feel bad, sick in fact, but I don't know how to forgive her this time. Being mad at Bristol isn't something new. I've gone an entire day without speaking to her or her to me, and it's never made me feel physically ill, until now.

We run the two blocks, coffee sloshing, bags jostling, asses bouncing until we're forced to stop for traffic on Ocean Avenue. "What's with all the cars?" Bristol asks, both of us looking from side to side at the cars, trucks, and an outrageous number of serial killer vans parked along the boardwalk. Even the day after Miracle Days shouldn't be this congested.

Bristol's casual question isn't enough to get me to end the silent treatment, so I let the question hang. We cross in the middle of the street between two lights and skirt between a parked serial killer van and a black SUV. We continue to jog for the last block of our jaunt, and when Stray Charlie's should be coming into view, all I can see is a crowd.

"What the fuck?" Bristol's mouth responds to my thoughts, and as one, we shield our eyes with a hand above our sunglasses. It may block a bit of the sun, but it doesn't make the scene we're approaching any clearer.

"Is that her?" It comes from the Stray Charlie's crowd, and as it does, the middle thins as the people on the ends fan out to look in our direction.

"Which one's Brenna? There's two? Are there two? There's two . . ."

"Bren-nah . . ." Bristol looks at me, a question in there somewhere. I'm at a loss—stone-cold immobile and speechless. "Should we run? We should totally run."

Six or seven of the hundred-plus crowd break away and begin running toward us, questions spilling from open mouths like squawking seagulls fighting over a French fry. "Brenna! Are you and Van Hatfield exclusive? How'd you meet? Brenna! When are you going to see him again? Brenna! Which one of you is he dating? Is he dating you both?"

They're on us, cigarette smoke preceding at least one of them, video cameras bringing up the rear. At the moment, the only thing I can think is I'm going to die without a shower and please, let me get out of this without being molested by the guy with his belly hanging out of his unbuttoned plaid shirt.

"Throw your coffee, then run!" I yell at Bristol, and for once today, we're in sync. We lob our coffee grenades. One hits a pair of shins and the other splatters off the shoes of the guy in plaid. It would be mass casualties if it wasn't lukewarm coffee shrapnel. The harmless beverage buys us a little time, and Bristol and I, channeling our twin powers, retreat at the same time.

Running with a few of the more agile ones on our tails, Bristol and I take off down the boardwalk. We cross the street at Stricker Bait, narrowly missing a collision with a guy on a bicycle. He yells at us, but after what we've faced, he's not at all scary in his aerodynamic helmet, spandex shorts, and reflector socks. We run up Thurston Street for a block, and then turn right onto San Bari, where we can access a back entrance into Ace Hardware if we need it, but looking behind me for a status check, it's unnecessary.

"I think we lost 'em," I shout out to Bristol, who is a little bit ahead of me. Slowing, she cranes her neck and looks over her shoulder before coming to a stop beside a dumpster full of black trash bags and cardboard boxes.

"Holy shit," Bristol barely gets out between breaths.

"That was insane," I say through heavy breaths of my own.

She flings herself at me and bear hugs me to her. "You're talking to me again!"

I try to peel her sweaty body off of me, but she's stronger than she looks. "No, I'm not," I say, trying to wedge my arms in between us to see if that will work to pry us apart.

"See," she chirps right next to my ear, "you did it again." She bounces us from side to side, far too excited for a girl who just ran four blocks from stalking paparazzi.

"It won't happen again."

"Okay," she says loosening her hold. "I'll continue to talk to you, and you can continue not to talk back to me just like you have the last three times. I'll learn to live with it." She pulls back, looks me in the eyes, and she smack-kisses me on my forehead. "Ew, if kissing your sweat doesn't say I love you, I don't know what does." She spits and wipes her mouth on the back of her hand.

I fight a chuckle, the first since Bristol betrayed me and Vance decided he didn't want me. Eating my sweat feels like small penance for what she did.

"So, how do you think they figured out who you were?"

If there was ever a question to end my silent treatment, she dished it on a silver platter. "Well," I start without the biting tone I'm building toward, "my guess would be *you.*"

"Me?" She points to herself for emphasis, sweaty forehead crinkled, eyes squinting at the sun. "I didn't give them your name. I told them Van Hatfield was spotted at The Seam."

"I was with him, dipshit, wearing a Stray Charlie's tank top. Did you honestly think they wouldn't put two and two together?"

Her expression changes, comprehension dawning. "Oh shit, Brenna." She chomps down on her bottom lip, eyes still squinting but showing regret. "I didn't even think about that. I . . ." Dropping her head, she doesn't finish her sentence and covers her face with her hands. Two seconds later I hear her sniffle, tears sparking a tremor in her body.

Watching her cry adds to my heartbreak. Our fights have always been petty. Not talking to her was usually just to prove a point, but this time around, our differences are a little more difficult to wade through. I want to hurt her for hurting me, but retaliation will only hurt us both. Last night and today, I truly had to live without her, in my heart at least, and I found out I like it less than I like what she did. She's my other half. I can't stay mad at her and function.

"Stop," I say softly, before wrapping my arms around her. "For now, we'll look at the bright side. We ran four blocks with paparazzi on our asses. How many people can say that?"

Bristol looks up, tears glistening in her eyes and on her cheeks. "I screwed up."

I nod, agreeing. "Yes. Yes, you did. But that shit was fun."

She laughs through her tears, wiping her upper lip and nose on her wrist. "That was a blast." We laugh, Bristol with a few hiccups in hers, and in mine, a bit more joy than I would have found an hour ago.

"What are we going to do now?"

"About the paparazzi?"

She nods.

"I don't know. I've never had to deal with them before. But we should probably call Charlie and tell him we can't come to work."

PER CHARLIE, OUR DAY AT WORK IS CANCELED AND OUR RETURN DATE is, "Who the hell knows? I can't have that kind of crap going on. Stay away. I'll call you." He's crabby on a good day. Throw in not taking in money on Miracle Days weekend, and we have a whole other level of crabby Charlie. He'll get over it, but whether or not he gets over it in time to save our jobs before the end of the summer depends on whether or not the media tires of us.

As we walk back to the Silver Stallion, I throw Bristol a bone and fill her in on what I withheld from her last night. I should feel better about finally having her to talk to about my heartbreak, but I find myself judging her reaction instead of finding comfort in our bond.

"Brenna, we have a pact." Her voice is whisper-soft as we reach the car.

"Vance isn't coming between us, Bristol."

"I'm not talking about that. I mean, I am, but not really. I'm talking about our pact to live with each other forever."

"You can't be serious." We made that pact after witnessing Mom's serial short-term relationships, dealing with Uncle Rodney's heart attack, and finding out our loser dad had another kid. We learned early on that our relationship was the only thing we could count on and control. We were, and are, the only thing solid and accountable each of us has ever had. I think I'm finally understanding that maybe it's not Vance Bristol is afraid of. I think she's afraid to end up alone.

"We've lost so much. My world can't sustain losing you too." Achingly vulnerable, she looks at me, eyes begging me to reassure her, and I'm reminded of how much I love this side of her.

I come around the front of the car to meet her on the passenger side. "I'm not going anywhere, but you can't chase off everyone I date to maintain a pact we made when we were kids. I want to have a full life, Bristol, whether that's what you want or not. I'm not going to shove a guy into your life, and you can't shove them out of mine."

She nods several times, stopping only when I pull her into a hug. "I'll try to work with that."

Without prompting, we recite our motto together. "Me and you against the world."

CHAPTER TWENTY-FOUR

Before heading over to The Seam with Tori, Bristol and I drop off our work keys to Charlie, since he officially let us go today. He tried giving us a "temporary leave of absence," but now that it's mid-July and the media still hasn't found a more interesting story to obsess over, he has to hire people who don't draw the unwanted crowds. I get it, but I don't like it. The lingering paparazzi are a nuisance, but their presence is dwindling, and in a few days they'll probably be gone altogether. I wish he'd give us more time. Besides, it's only feeding Bristol's argument about Vance not being good for me. He's gone. What more does she want? I'm not harping on her about having to take on side jobs because she can't make it to class on time or even at all on some days. That seems like a much bigger deal than me and Vance, even after you factor in the paparazzi and my emotional connection to sex that she loathes so much. Never have the differences in our personalities been more prominent than they have in the last month.

I pull into a spot out front of The Seam, and the three of us jump out. Tori, looking like a pumpkin in her orange dress, sighs heavily, her annoyance no doubt brought on by Bristol continuously bitching about the scholarship review committee. "As long as my GPA remains above the cutoff, who cares?" she repeats in case we missed the last two times she said it. "Oh," she presses us with a hard glare as she puts her hand on the door to The Seam, "and don't say a word. I'm not ready to tell Uncle Rodney."

Confident her secret is safe with us, Bristol ushers us in ahead of her.

"What the hell did you do to that kid?" Uncle Rodney looks and sounds like I killed his pet hamster the second I walk through the door of the bar. His face bears none of the telltale signs of his teasing, and I don't know exactly how to respond. I usually follow through with something mildly inappropriate, but this time I feel like maybe I shouldn't.

"Whose kid did I ruin now?" I ask.

"Not you. Her!" He directs a pointed look at Bristol, jaw hard-set in his business-only greeting. "He hasn't been the same since you called the paps." Uncle Rodney using the word "paps" for paparazzi draws genuine laughter from me.

We all look up at the game on the television above the bar. I feel my heart trip over a beat and plop my ass on the barstool beside Mr. Davidson, who is watching the fifth inning of the Renegades/Diamondbacks game with Uncle Rodney. Vance is pitching, and based upon Uncle Rodney's tone of voice, he's not doing very well and, with a three to zero spread in favor of the Diamondbacks, it's safe to say he's given up a few runs.

"Is he sucking?" Bristol asks with a tad too much hope in her voice for a girl trying to get back on my good side.

I watch the television hesitantly, unsure if I really want to see him. Avoiding him has suited me well, and I'm not sure I want to change things up yet. Even as I think it, though, I wait for the camera to pan away from the batter scraping the dirt with his shoe like Ferdinand the Bull. By the time I get a glimpse of Vance, the ball is flying out of his hand and into the batter's left knee, or it would have if Ferdinand hadn't dodged it in the nick of time. He throws his helmet and charges toward Vance, who's already dropped his glove and is ready to duke it out midway between home plate and the pitching mound.

"That damn hot head of his is going to get him ejected, and if that doesn't do it, his lack of focus will. How many players is he going to walk tonight?" Up in arms, hands flying in all manner of direction, Uncle Rodney testifies bitterly, "I blame you!"

Openly enjoying Bristol's verbal beatdown, I smile until she glares at me and my lips fall along with my shoulders as I try to look more supportive.

Bristol, opening her mouth to defend herself, is stopped by Uncle Rodney's hand abruptly thrust out to stop her as the TV commentary continues about Vance's wild pitch and "questionable focus."

There is a mob scene between home plate and the pitching mound, with everyone coming out of the woodwork to fight over a stray fastball to the knee. Ferdinand is red-faced and still flinging insults at Vance who is being held back by a handful of guys who are yelling at the both of them.

I feel sick.

"Thanks, Bristol. He's been ejected." Uncle Rodney drops his flat-palm stop sign after unleashing his bitter indignation and grumbles beneath a few puffs of released breath.

"What I did was weeks ago. I don't think his lack of focus tonight is because of me." Bristol's whine draws another dirty look from Uncle Rodney. "Just sayin'."

His eyes briefly dart to mine, and Bristol's face hardens, resolute in her belief she's been misjudged. She's right. I'm pretty sure Vance hasn't sucked for weeks because of paparazzi, but Uncle Rodney needs his reasons, and tonight, his reason is Bristol, who continues to offer helpful comments.

"Did it ever occur to you maybe he sucks or he's a one-hit wonder?"

"One-hit wonder?" Uncle Rodney's eyebrows settle near his hair-line. "Bobby Day was a one-hit wonder. You, if you don't stop meddling, will be a one-hit wonder. Van Hatfield is no one-hit wonder."

"You're as bad as her," Bristol says, pointing to me.

I tune them out, focusing on the game instead of their fight.

The camera, nosy little shit that it is, focuses in on Vance as he heads to the dugout for what I'm assuming is an ass-chewing based on the spit flying from the guy yelling at him. As he enters the dugout, the camera gets a good shot of his face, and for a split second, my heart beats a little faster for him, which it hasn't had a reason to do since I left his house feeling like a fool.

Between being let go from work, Bristol and her verbal opinions, and trying to stay out of my mom's relationship with Joe now that she doesn't consider wandering hands as cheating, I haven't had time to figure out my feelings for Vance. Not that it matters. I could pine all day long for him and it wouldn't change where we are right now. He doesn't want me.

"Excuse me?"

Everything, including Uncle Rodney's and Bristol's argument, ceases as the five of us turn to find the source of the soft voice asking for our attention.

She's a cute brunette, petite and narrow-hipped with a huge smile to balance her out. She looks familiar, but I don't know how or where from, and while I'm trying to figure it out, Uncle Rodney addresses her.

"You can take a seat anywhere, and we don't bite if you want to sit at the bar and watch the game. The Renegades could use a cheering section if you're about that."

Clearly as enamored as I am with his bushy black-and-white eyebrows and the small paunch that precedes him, she smiles. "I'm actually looking for Brenna Sloan." She looks at both me and Bristol, curiosity written but not expressed.

She'd be cute if she wasn't a reporter, or some other vulture, preying on what's left of my decaying flesh since the last time someone came in looking for me. She obviously knows what I look like, so I can't deny anything. I should throw Bristol under the bus for this one since she owes me, but I don't think she'd serve me well. I'd come out looking like a redneck wind chime—noisy and simple.

I jump off the barstool and extend a hand toward her, far more polite than she deserves, but what I do now, she may print later. I'd like to avoid a repeat of the headline "White Trash After His Cash." Instead of taking my hand, though, she embraces me in a hug that is way too familiar for our two-second courtship.

"Ohh-kay," I say taking a step back. "What brings you by The Seam? The story is over. The baseball player has moved on, and I'm a nobody. I highly doubt anyone wants to read about my irritable bowels."

She's grinning from ear to ear, blue eyes sparkling like she has a secret she's dying to share. "He said you were a spitfire."

"Who's 'he'?" Bristol asks, appearing from behind me in total defense mode. She should come to my aid; she's the reason people know how to find me.

"Van." Her smile broadens, but her eyes don't leave mine, not even for Bristol. "I'm Camille Hatfield."

CHAPTER TWENTY-FIVE

F rozen, I stand a bit stunned, sucking my bloated stomach in like some self-conscious pubescent girl. I miss half of what she says before she has to ask me if I'm okay.

"I'm fine," I manage, before Bristol pipes in with her unnecessary checks and balances.

"If you're here to make trouble," Bristol says, pointing a finger at Camille, "you can leave now. For us, this is over." Bristol looks at me to corroborate, but I can't. Maybe for her it's over, but I'm still feeling the effects of heartbreak and sister betrayal.

"No. Gosh, no. I just wanted to have a word with you if you're available? I won't take up much of your time."

I nod. "We can step outside."

Bristol makes a move to come with us, but I shoot her a look and she reluctantly backs off.

Outside, I direct Camille to one of a few open tables. I'm leery of being in public with her because I've been stalked for weeks by reporters trying to get a feel for me and my lifestyle, which they quickly surmised was well-beneath Vance's. It's just one of many adjustments I've had to make since meeting Vance and pissing off

Bristol. And now that things are getting back to normal, Camille Hatfield shows up on my community doorstep.

She sets an oversized purse down on the ground beside her feet and adjusts her body for comfort, laying her forearms on the black iron table as a final adjustment. "You're exactly how I pictured you."

I can't relax, and my feet bounce nervously. I'm sweating in places I can't wipe without encouraging or offending someone. She's not at all what I expected. She looks nothing like her Amber Dietrich persona in the tabloids. She's wearing baggy white Capris with a loose-fitting shirt that hangs off of one shoulder, and the only thing sparkling on her is a band of gems on her sandals. Curiosity about her motives wins out over decorum, and I blurt out, "Why are you here? As usual, the tabloids exaggerated Vance's relationship with me. We're friends, nothing more, and I can't really even say that we're still that."

She frowns. "Vance doesn't know I'm here. He'd be mortified, no, back up—he'd be murderous." She smiles, tilting her head to the side like she's studying me, a quirky habit she shares with her brother. "May I be upfront with you?"

I trace the diamond pattern in the table with my index finger and pointedly look at her. "I'd prefer that."

"Vance doesn't usually do what's best for him unless it's for his career. He's notorious for shutting people out, and I think maybe he's done that with you."

"What would you know about that?"

She smiles. "When we spoke about you the other night, he sounded like maybe things were unfinished. I thought maybe I could see if you felt the same way?"

The diamond pattern I'm tracing is now two fingers wide and repetitive. "I was never given a choice, and he sure didn't take long to make his." I get to my feet, fully intending to have the last word, but she stands up too.

"Brenna, did Van tell you about Amber Dietrich?"

I nod.

"Did he tell you that we haven't seen each other since they reported us to be dating?"

I shake my head, surprised.

"As soon as *Candid* ran the stripper story, Van cut himself off from everyone. I had to communicate with him through Chip, and if you know Chip Pervis, you know it sucked. He probably had a hard-on from so much power."

"I didn't know, but Vance did tell me that he felt responsible for protecting you and Jacoby," I offer, in hopes that whatever residual hurt she may have from his handling of things might be eased a bit by his concern for them.

"I know," she says, rolling her eyes and smiling at the same time. "He doesn't half-ass anything, and this time maybe he should have. The photographer for *Candid* recognized me from my show in Vegas, not as Van's little sister. He didn't care about my real name. I was a stripper with Van Hatfield, for God's sake. What else did he need?"

"So, why cut you out then?" Without the diamond pattern to trace, I twirl my hair around my finger.

An exaggerated eye-roll precedes her reply. "I'd like to say it was Chip. He doesn't let anything, not even family, get between Van and his career, but Van makes up his own mind, and once Jacoby was at risk, bam! Decision made. I think that's what he's done with you too." She clears her throat and speaks deeply, mimicking Vance's tone with a nice added head shimmy, "You know, 'just to be safe.'"

"Uh, I don't think our situations are the same. I have a lot less to lose, and he and I don't have a history."

Camille shrugs, and the boobs I wish I'd been born with follow with her shoulders, tempting my eyes to stray to her chest. "I know my brother, and I don't think he wants it to be this way. I know he misses me and Jacoby. I know if things were different, he'd be a part of our lives every second he could. But I need you to know that too. Vance didn't let you go because he doesn't want you, Brenna. He let you go because he doesn't want to be the one who upsets your world."

My eyes briefly stray to the traffic behind her. "I think that's an awful lot to assume." I look back at her, noticing for the first time that she's no longer smiling.

Camille's relaxed demeanor shifts. "Is it?"

"I asked him if he'd let me go if things were different. He couldn't say no."

Camille takes a deep breath. "Vance isn't always the best with communication, in case you haven't noticed. Well, unless he's pissed, and then he has no trouble expressing himself. He hasn't talked to our brother, Eric, in a year. Can't say as I blame him, but it's Eric. If Vance didn't care about you, he'd take what he wanted. I don't think he'd sacrifice his wants for your needs."

Vance's motive to end things with me could have been anything, the least of which is sacrifice. "Camille, Vance made his choice—twice. And after the past weeks I've been through with the tabloids, I can't say that he was wrong."

"Do you really think that? Is what people print about you so much more important than what someone feels for you? You don't strike me as someone who caves under pressure."

I open my mouth to protest, to give her the almighty Sloan speech about how she doesn't know me and she isn't in my shoes, blah, blah, blah, but she holds up a hand to stop me before I can rant, and I clamp down my lips, curious.

"I have two tickets for tomorrow's home game. Come with me? See for yourself what he's like. I think you'll see what I'm failing miserably to express."

Seeing Vance again in living, breathing, inked-up color, would not be good for my heart. It barely withstood seeing him on television tonight. "I can't." Again, I wish my answer were different. I wish I had balls like I have camel toe, but I'm taking my lumps and calling it a day. I'm not chasing a guy who doesn't want me just to prove his sister wrong.

"Can't or won't?"

Holy shit, are they the cynical siblings or what? Vance said that the last time he invited me to a game too. "Won't," I say this time, feeling no shame in the confession.

Camille reaches for her purse and pulls it up by its straps. The damn thing is big enough to place in an overhead bin on a plane. She reaches in, grabs something small, and though part of me expects a Mary Poppins coat rack, instead it's a ticket. "Here." She shoves it at me, holding it between us like it's worth fighting over. "In case you change your mind."

I look at it but don't reach for it. My mind wars with the wants of my heart, but my head knows that for all of us, distance is better. "I won't."

She inhales and pulls her hand back to place the ticket on the tabletop. Apparently, she has plans to leave her date up to fate, because if I don't take the ticket, someone is bound to, and she might end up sitting next to Toothless Tony, the guy who smokes cigarette butts out of boardwalk planters. "My number is on the back. Come with me, Brenna. At least you'll know one way or another."

My throat involuntarily swallows. "It was nice to meet you," I say, ignoring the ticket but tossing around the possibilities in my head. "I mean that."

She smiles. "You too." Camille walks away, and six or so spaces down, she gets into a black Mercedes.

I'm not a total shitbag, and I pick up the ticket so that Toothless Tony doesn't happen across it when he's stumbling home later. I thumb the corner of the ticket until it has a nice floppy edge. I don't even make it into the bar before I'm accosted by a team of two, led by Bristol barreling her way outside, with Tori tripping over herself to keep up.

The warpath Bristol's on pinks her cheeks and narrows her stare. She's all business when she opens her mouth, which should have an explicit language warning slapped over it. "That cu—uh . . ." she catches herself, chomping down on the second half of the cuss word like Uncle Rodney is protesting from her shoulder. He thinks the C-word should only be used on Colette's mom and the person who invented colonoscopies, so we don't use it—ever. "If that C-word harmed a hair on your head, I'm going to kick her ass. Her beef should be with Van. He's the one who cheated on her, NOT you!" She scans the sidewalk and Ocean Avenue with her eyes, her head doing most of the work. "Where'd she go? She and I are going to have a little chat, and by chat, I mean a fist fight."

Confused, I blink several times. What does she mean by "he cheated on her"? Never mind, I don't want to address any of it out here. We're probably on TMZ already. "You're not going to fight anyone."

I shove past them, hoping to avoid a conversation, but Bristol grabs a hold of my upper arm and pulls me back. "That wasn't Camille Hatfield, Brenna. That was Amber Deerdick."

"Dietrich." Tori corrects Bristol's butchering of Amber's last name, and though she gets a brief side-eye glare from Bristol to tell her she's not helping, she shrugs unapologetically and shows me her phone with a Google photo of Amber on the screen.

Bristol's cheating comment makes sense now, but I'm still not discussing it with her in public, or ever.

"Dietrich, whatever. Doesn't matter. Did she threaten you?" Bristol asks.

"No," I grumble out and try once again to get past them.

"Brenna, she wasn't here to make friends. You get that, right?"

"I get that it's none of your business."

"None of my business?" she shouts, drawing looks from patio dwellers. "Like hell it's none of my business. She walked in here and tried to pass herself off as Van's sister. She's his fucking girlfriend, Brenna, and if she's a girlfriend like mom is a girlfriend, she's going to eat your eyeballs right from their sockets."

"Maybe we should do this somewhere else." Tori's suggestion and unwelcome grasp on Bristol's arm draws a death glare and an exaggerated shrug-off, to which Tori responds by letting go and taking a precautionary step back. "Maybe I should leave the two of you to work it out."

When neither of us disagrees, Tori takes her leave, forsaking her beloved gossip for safety inside The Seam. Bristol doesn't see Tori go because she's studying me.

"Wait. You're not surprised, are you? You knew? You knew when you went outside with her that she was Amber. Are you fucking cracked? Strippers are scrappy. And Van isn't worth losing your eyes over. Hell, he's not worth losing an eyelash over. Why in the hell would you do that?"

"Let it go, Bristol." I once again try for the bar's entrance, but Bristol, in fighting mode, is quick and reaches a hand out to grab me. Her grip is tight, her eyes tighter as she narrows them on me.

"NO! What the hell are you hiding? I will make a skin suit out of her before she or Van hurt you."

"Stop it. No one is hurting me."

"Fine. Lie to me. I'll find out for myself. One way or another, someone is going to pay for her showing up here uninvited." She pulls her phone from her back pocket and stabs her finger into the screen, pulling up a number with two stabs of her pissed-off finger.

"Who are you calling?"

She puts the phone to her ear, her determination not changing to respond to my question. I grab the phone, scratching her hand in the process, and for my persistence and unplanned brutality, I get a curse and the explanation I asked for.

"If you won't let me control his girlfriends, Van damn sure better."

"NO!" I grab again for the phone, but she dodges me, and before I can stop them, words are tumbling out of my mouth with the consistency of baby oil. "Amber Dietrich and Camille Hatfield are the same person. She's not his girlfriend. She's his sister." It's out as swiftly as my regret. The phone falls away from her ear, her bottom lip drops from her top lip, and she stares at me while Vance's phone still rings on the other side of hers. "Hang up!" I screech, even though the damage is done with the registered missed call he'll have.

Bristol fumbles, trying with anxious fingers to end the call, and when his voice on his voicemail comes to an abrupt end, I relax a fraction, but not enough to stave off the stress sweats.

Marginally recovered from my bombshell, Bristol thrusts herself toward me, gripping my hand with a strong one of her own. "Get the fuck out. You've got to spill the tea now." Bristol beams, her eyes alight with info that a week ago she would have sold her soul for.

"You have to promise me you won't say a word. I wasn't supposed to say anything."

"I won't say a word. I promise." She exudes joy, the outrageousness still tickling her thoughts, but something in there suddenly shifts and she becomes softer. "This. This is what I've missed, Brenna. We used to talk shit out. We used to plan. It used to be me and you against the world. I've missed knowing everything about you."

I didn't think my guilt could deepen, but somehow Bristol manages the impossible. I have obligations to her and Vance that directly contradict each other. It was all so easy before I had someone else's secrets to keep. Neither of them seems to understand how small the space between the rock and the hard place truly is. I groan, feeling the space tighten even further as I'm now relieved she's happy, but also feeling forced into damage control.

"After the shit you pulled with the baseball and the paparazzi, it was hard to want to share anything of importance with you. You seriously can't tell anyone, Bristol. Not Toolbag, not Tracy or Tori. Not the tabloids. NO ONE."

Her shoulders drop, caving her whole body to a much more relaxed pose. A deep breath she exhales forcefully precedes her acceptance like I knew it would, but in true Bristol fashion, it comes with a price of its own. "Forgive me for Miracle Days and I'll do anything you want."

A sigh too brittle to hide escapes. I'm trying. I truly am. Staying mad at Bristol isn't in my DNA. She's in the marrow of my bones. We've been through hell and back, and always together. She's my one constant, and no matter how angry at her I might get or how many times she pulls shit I don't agree with, I suck it up because that's what we do.

"I'm trying. You haven't done anything as rotten as the paparazzi thing before. I need breathing room, and now I need a promise from you."

"I did promise."

"The whole thing, Bristol."

She sighs like I've asked her to recite the Declaration of Independence and holds up her pinky to give me the kind of promise I require. We kiss our own pinkies, hook them together, and she recites the vow made up forever ago. "My word is my bond, your trust is key, no matter what, you can count on me." We kiss the knot our pinkies make to seal her oath. It's so juvenile, but I can't remember a time when it wasn't required for serious things like the loss of virginity or now, because of my desperation, a secret that never should have left my mouth.

CHAPTER TWENTY-SIX

"Have fun today," I call to Bristol as I head out the door. "Tell Toolbag I'm sorry for bailing."

She scoffs from the bathroom, "He'll be fine. He knows we need the money. Good luck with the consultation."

Guilt at having lied to her about what I'm actually doing today seeps into my voice, and I wonder if she can sense my inner turmoil. I'm desperately holding back the urge to purge. The Silver Stallion's keys are in my hand before I can reconsider spilling my guts, and I'm in the driver's seat before I can do anything about it once I have.

In the two-and-a-half-hour drive to San Jose, my guilt is chased away by my nerves, and in the additional half-hour bonus traffic out front of the stadium, I'm all but oozing them both. What the hell was I thinking? I am not a liar, and I sure in the hell shouldn't be lying over some guy who dumped me.

I'm waved into the lot by a flashlight-wielding, safety vest-wearing teenager and directed to the most southern end of the parking lot, where I park in the farthest spot possible right as Bristol answers her phone.

"So," I start pathetically, nearly hitting the bumper of the

Hummer in the space in front of me before slamming on my breaks, "I lied. I don't have a side job today. I'm not making any money. I went to see Vance, so if Toolbag offers to buy lunch, take him up on it. You can be mad, but you can't hold it against me, because I know you took the car a week ago." I think about hanging up, but that's a dick move, so I hold out for the lecture as I get out of the car.

"You're what?" The shriek is eardrum penetrable. "Are you in San Jose?"

"Yes." I fast-walk through the lot with others arriving on the tail end of fashionably late. "I'm sorry I spun the truth—"

"You lied!"

"I came clean, which is something you should understand having to do quite well. And now that I have, I have to go. Just wanted to get that off my chest. Love you, bye."

I shove my phone into my back pocket as it vibrates with Bristol's return call, and speed-walk a little faster. At security, I adjust my Renegades ball cap, fully aware my anonymity is no longer guaranteed, and proceed without incident to my middle-of-the-pack, second-deck seat.

Camille, barely recognizable in her floppy hat and sunglasses, stares at me slack-jawed as I take the seat beside her. "Brenna!" she squeals, grabbing me by the shoulders to negotiate a hug made awkward by our hats. "I'm not even going to ask why you changed your mind. I'm just going to appreciate that you did."

The crowd cheers Halsey's base hit, and whatever she says next gets lost in the noise. Like her brother, Camille is flawless, and even in disguise, she is probably the prettiest person in the working-class section of the stadium. We're behind third base, still close enough to hear the bat crack off the ball but not close enough to see nose hairs. It's refreshing and a lot less likely we'll be recognized by anyone on the team, much less the media. I start to relax until I'm reminded why I'm here.

"He's going to be so happy." She touches my arm and gives me a smile she's thinking will ease the worry on my face.

I nod, not because I agree, but because it leads me to my nagging question. "And how can you be so sure?"

"Trust me," she says before cheering a perfectly placed line drive by Robbins that lands him on first base and pushes Halsey to second. "If I didn't know my brother so well, he would have gotten away with this. Truth is, he's miserable, and you're the reason why."

My eyebrows touch, but before I can choke out a sarcastic, "Thanks," Camille grabs my arm.

"Miserable in a good way." She grins, squeezing my forearm, the brim of her hat flopping with her enthusiasm.

"Why does his misery have to be because of me. Maybe it's over you or Nikki Kline?"

She grows serious, her smile replaced by pinched, flesh-toned lips. "Eww," she says with about as much distaste as Bristol has when she talks about Tiffany. "I can't believe people are still talking about us dating." She shudders. "I can't speak about Nikki. He's never mentioned her, but he has mentioned you. Kind of telling, don't you think?"

"I don't know. Does he talk about all his friends with you?"

"No," she says adamantly, leaning in closer to whisper, "until you." A smug grin tops off her perceived mic drop.

"I talk about my vagina a lot with my sister. It doesn't mean I want to date it."

She laughs. "God, I wish I had a sister. Van never wants to talk about my vagina."

"That's not what the media is reporting."

"Touché," she laughs. "I threw up a bit in my mouth, but it at least cancels out some of the calories in the hot dog I ate." She smiles, pats my hand, and groans with the end of another scoreless inning for the Renegades. "Look, Brenna. Van and I don't talk about his conquests. I asked about you after I saw you online, and when he didn't give me the standard 'don't believe everything you read' answer, I knew he'd fallen."

I don't know what to say to that, so I watch Vance return to the pitcher's mound, heart in my throat, regret in my bones. I admire the bold confidence of the guy who exudes irreverence everywhere but on the field. He is mesmerizing to watch. Nowhere is his intensity more prevalent than it is on the mound. From the roll of the ball in his grasp to the way his body adjusts its form to the unique batter in front of him, it's all by design. He does nothing by mistake. I've called him bossy half a dozen times since meeting him, but I've since learned it's his innate drive and not necessarily a need for dominance. But that proves my point: Vance doesn't make mistakes, so if he let me go, there is a reason.

I've never had an even balance of discipline and drive. For me, it's been balls to the wall chaos my entire life, and I don't know how to live any other way than on the edge of disaster. Hesitate and you become a gossip topic or teary-eyed in a courtroom when you discover you have a half-sister who isn't allowed to be around you because you're a Sloan. Hesitate and you never see the top side of the rumor pile, so, driven is all I've ever been. With Vance, I can hesitate. I can think. I can breathe. Or at least I thought I could until the media tipped the scales.

I look again at Camille, who I think has been watching me the whole time I've been watching Vance. "Why me?"

"Why not you?" She shifts in her seat, body facing me, eyes free of her sunglasses, "Van doesn't lose himself in people like he used to. I think you should know that everything he does now is calculated. It may not always be what's best for him, but it's usually what's best for his heart and his career."

The game is a minor inconvenience as I listen to her, my thoughts running rampant. "Why is that?"

Camille sighs, takes a deep breath and resigns herself to opening up to me, a virtual stranger she's got no choice but to place her faith in if she wants to keep me in the picture. "I thought he was going to end up marrying his high school sweetheart right after they graduated. But she sold his baseball glove for five thousand dollars two days after he signed with the Renegades." Another pause for effect.

"That was his last serious relationship. So when I tell you he doesn't fall often, I mean it. He cut her out cold turkey when she proved to be useless baggage that didn't have his best interests at heart. Same with Eric, our brother. He cut him out the second he sold a story to the media for drug money. Both broke his heart, but he didn't hesitate. He's calculated, Brenna, but he's not always right."

"I would have cut them off too," I say, switching my gaze to Vance on the pitching mound, feeling sorry for his hard choices, but understanding them.

She nods knowingly. "He thought maybe your sister had the same motives as Eric, and that's all he saw until I pointed out that she may have called the press for publicity on your event, not to make money or to do irreparable damage. That helped for all of a second, then he blamed himself for ruining the event with his presence. He's so egotistical, it's maddening. I think in some crazy way, he thought that by breaking up with you, he'd be saving you from what he endured with Eric and Cassie. He didn't want you to lose your sister." She pauses, a sad turn to her expression. "But if he wants you, he's going to have to get over it. And if you want him, you're going to have to get used to it."

I drop my eyes and look at my feet, noticing that my toenails are in desperate need of attention. She talks a good game. She even makes this realist girl want to believe in fairy tales. "I hope you're right."

CHAPTER TWENTY-SEVEN

The Renegades' loss to the Braves by one run leaves a hungry Renegades crowd bitter and disappointed. Middle finger salutes, cuss words, and a few unnecessary fights break out as San Jose protects its own with thuggery and intimidation. They're known as hooligans for a reason, and I'm starting to understand why we had to cross through metal detectors to get within shouting distance of the team's tunnel.

Camille breezes through the rabid fans like a pro who has braved these halls a thousand times. "Don't mind them," she says over her shoulder, hair tucked up under her hat. "They're harmless. They'll be buying each other drinks in an hour."

In the tunnel that leads to the locker room, press room, and rooms with purposes I can only guess at, Camille and I wait. The team has yet to pour through the entrance, and I look at the wide opening lit by slivers of remaining summer daylight and the lights of the stadium. It feels a bit surreal to be standing here. Not knowing what I may encounter, I sweat stress from every pore.

"Relax," Camille says, sneakily peeking around the corner to see if she can see signs of them. Fans have already started to fill in around the entrance, and a few brazen ones have trickled in without passes. "He's going to be happy."

Despite her reassurances, I can't help but think this is a mistake. What will I do if he publicly shuns me? Then I think even if he hated me, he wouldn't be rude, not like Eli Perkins was years back after my boob pic. While I'm throat deep in my private worries, the tunnel takes on a hum, a resounding vibration that alerts me to change and triggers my pulse. I'm on edge, heart hammering, as the team, one by one, appears in the mouth of the tunnel, each somber face mirroring another as they pass by me.

It's hard to look a single one of them in the eyes, fearing the next set will be a pair of blues I won't be able to look away from. And then I see him, head bowed, glove in hand, a wholly dejected slump to his shoulders.

"Hey!" Camille yells, sunglasses in hand, and a couple of them along with Vance look in her direction. I think she's a staple and most know her by face if not by introduction, but no one seems to recognize her in her Kentucky Derby disguise, and everyone but Vance continues on. He detours to her, and she nods her head in my direction.

It takes a second, but when recognition hits, it's solid, fierce, and absolutely soul-crushing. The even plain of his lips tightens, shoring up his detachment, bearing a wealth of information he's unaware of. Unsure of what I should do next, I stay put, wringing my hands while Camille speaks to him. Keeping an obvious distance from her, he nods once and walks toward me.

My butterflies somersault. "Hi." I'm about as creative as a sloth in a hammock, but what do you say after what was said the last time? "I'm probably the last person you expected to see."

"You could say that."

"I hope you don't mind that I came."

"Mind?" He fidgets with his glove and then tucks it beneath his arm.

"Camille thought that—" cutting myself off, I hang my head. I need to own this. For the first time in my life, I've chosen myself over Bristol, and I better damn well fight for why I'm here or it will all be for nothing. I lift my head and square my shoulders, looking him in the eyes. "I wanted to see you. I know you said—"

Eyes pinched, he interrupts me. "I said a lot of things, and most of them I regret."

Hope rising, I swallow hard enough to crackle my ears, but when his expression doesn't change, I waffle. "Regret enough that you don't mind me being here? Or . . .?"

"I'm so far from minding, Brenna. I'm struggling to maintain a respectable distance."

Relieved, I smile, eyes intent, hands itching to get a piece of his red and white shirt to tug him toward me.

"Hatfield!" someone half-dressed yells from the far side of the tunnel.

Vance deflates, blowing out an exasperated breath. "Yeah, be there in a minute."

"It's okay," I say, shooing him with my hand. "Go."

He lowers his head and then lifts it to look at me. "We have to watch game tape tonight." Filled with something other than his initial reservations, his tone is softer and, if I'm not reading it wrong, tinted with disappointment.

"We can do this another time," I say softly, nearly choking on my accommodating response when all I want is to be selfish.

"Give me a few. I'll find a way out of it."

"Oh, geez, go." Camille shoves his arm, maneuvering between us. "I'm on stage tonight at the Wicked Lantern. It's downtown across from San Jose Improv on South Second. Brenna can come with me and you can pick her up there." She looks at me. "Assuming you can stay?"

I weigh my options and, deciding not to waste the opportunity I came here for, I nod.

She grins. "It's settled. You'll talk later. Now go, before you get fined."

Surprising me, he grabs hold of my elbow, eyes searching for something. "It'll be late, but I'll see you later." Dropping my arm, he backs away, walking backward toward the door he was being summoned from, and then after a few steps, he turns to walk the remainder of the way facing away from me.

PLAGUED BY NERVES, I CLIMB INTO VANCE'S CAR A LITTLE AFTER TEN, but when he guides my head toward his the second my door closes, my insecurity seems stupid. The kiss, full of rekindled fire and weeks of reservations, takes my breath. He growls as he lets me go, holding my face long past the kiss. "I know that was probably out of line, but it will never be one of my regrets."

"It's okay," I say softly, smiling, "I'm not objecting."

With his hand still cupping the side of my head, he leans into me, stalling briefly before his lips and tongue take full possession. It's hot and leaves us both breathless. When he pulls back to look at me, I'm dizzy, wondering why we both wasted so much time.

"I don't want to do this in the Wicked Lantern parking lot," he says, "and I don't want to assume there is someplace else to take it, so you tell me what you want."

"I wasn't sure what was going to happen . . . I—I didn't know what you wanted."

I can't read the expression that crosses his face. At first, it looks like frustration or maybe regret, and then he recovers with a slow, almost sad smile. "I want you with me if you want to stay. We can take it slow if that's what you want or if that's what the rest of the night dictates, but I want you with me."

I nod once. "I want that too."

He smiles, rubs my bottom lip with his thumb and nods several times, his thoughts left unspoken. "Ready?"

I nod and pull my seat belt across me as he starts the car.

"Did you suffer long in there?" he asks, clearing his throat and throwing the Spyder into gear. He zips through the parking lot, slowing for a few cars without the good sense to stay out of his way.

I grin, turning halfway in my seat to look at him. "No. It was amazing." My enthusiastic response might be too much for just having left a strip club. It was not at all how I envisioned Camille when he said she 'stripped.' "You should go."

He hisses a breath in, looking in his rearview as he switches lanes. "I'd rather dig glass out of my eye."

"It's not what you think. When she gets on that pole, holy shit, she has talent." I rave about her while he silently cringes. "She can move, Vance. It's not seedy at all. She's not performing for dollar bills. They don't even do that. What strip club doesn't have dollar bills?"

"Brenna, we're still talking about my sister." He swerves into the far lane on the freeway and stomps on the gas, whizzing us past a convoy of muscle cars and an old cop car.

"Sorry," I offer, turning to look forward. "I thought you'd want to know that your sister isn't the kind of stripper you see in the movies. I also thought you should know that I make my own decisions, and I'm not going to let you make any more for me."

He stomps harder on the gas. "Is that so?" He tries to hide his grin, but even in the dark, I can see it.

"I'm not afraid of a little paparazzi. For me, you're worth it."

I have to hold on as he suddenly jerks the car across three lanes of traffic to pull off the freeway. He barrels down the ramp and pulls into the nearest parking lot, bringing the car to a stop in front of a closed Home Depot.

He leans across the car and cups the side of my head with his hand, his fingers pressing into the back of my neck to urge me toward him. My heart beats so fast it pounds in my ears, drowning out my second thoughts and also my thoughts of coming clean about telling Bristol Camille's secret.

His lips crash into mine, relentless in their possession and certain of their message. "The past few weeks have killed me."

"Vance?" I drag out his name, tilting my head slightly, my body questioning him as well.

"Screw it all, Brenna. I'll find a way to live with it—all of it. I want you."

"What are you saying? Sometimes you're all over the place. This time, I need you to say it."

"I want only you, Brenna. I want . . ." he runs his hand down my arm and over the top part of my hip where it stays. "I want this—you —all the time. Just me and you."

I open my mouth and a rough impersonation of a frog tumbles out. Any eye contact I had before falls away, and I'm looking down between us at the center console.

Using two fingers, he pulls my chin up and waits for me to look him in the eyes again. "What do you say we try this?" His eyes search mine for a response I'm not quick to give. "I want this, Brenna. I want you."

I stare at him, eyes unseeing. After seconds that seem like minutes that feel like hours, I finally speak. "You're going to break my heart, aren't you?"

He drops my chin and brushes a thumb across my cheek, and I close my eyes. "Not intentionally," he says softly. "Never intentional-ly." I feel his lips on mine, and at this moment, I can honestly say I understand why my mother has searched all these years for this feeling.

I slip out of my seatbelt without breaking our kiss and climb into his lap. The maneuver isn't easy, as the car is cramped and I'm not skip-a-meal thin, graceful, or double-jointed. Add to that his long legs, and this could be my next disaster. I straddle him, holding his face in between my hands while my hip pretty much pops out of its socket. I have no doubt the discomfort will be worth it.

"Brenna?" He could say my name that way all day, but the wailing horn drowns out the intoxication of it. I laugh into his neck and lift my ass up to silence it.

"It was meant to be sexier than this, I promise."

"It's sexy," he reassures me as he places a kiss on my neck and maneuvers the seat back as far as it will go. I pivot my hips, trying for a different position, and he grips my hips with his hands, pulling me into his abdomen. "God, I want you." He runs his hands down my thighs and then up under my dress, growling when he finds my sweet spot.

By the heat my cheeks are suddenly putting out, I'm probably blushing. "I want you too."

Vance abandons his self-restraint, and almost instantaneously my panties are torn and on the floorboard of the car, along with my shoes, purse, and Vance's ringing cell phone, which he tossed without thought to pull his cock free of his pants. It's probably his manager, who used to call him every day when he was in Milagro Beach.

"Leave it!" Vance barks breathlessly when I break stride to look over my shoulder at it. He brings my face back to his. "It can wait," he whispers.

Bracing myself against his chest, I lift and lower myself onto him, regaining the lost momentum. I bounce and writhe, desperately needing him to quench the ache of not having him for weeks.

"Damn, you feel good." He groans loudly, helping lift and raise my body with his hands on my hips as I falter, growing tired. "I'm close, I promise baby. Don't stop." It's more encouragement than command, and I push on, weakening but not spent.

I lay over his chest, practically smothering him as I grab hold of his shoulders for leverage. His grip on my hips tightens, holding me steady as his upward thrusts increase to take us both higher. I tighten around him, not wanting it to end but needing relief. "Ah, Jesus, Brenna. Fuuuck." Hot doesn't explain the fire burning within us. It's been too long, and neither of us wants to quit, but I can't keep this pace. I can barely breathe, let alone move. Thank God Vance is an athlete, or we'd both have to finish each other off with a hand job.

"Vance, I—I . . ." My release comes, my body slows, but I swivel my hips until his last thrust ends with a curse and he presses my hips down, holding me down over him until his climax ebbs.

Vance rubs my back soothing me to slower breaths. "Brenna," he whispers, kissing where his breath fans over my shoulder. "I will never let you go again."

CHAPTER TWENTY-EIGHT

A week and a half after my reconciliation with Vance, I'm buzzed, overly friendly, and wondering what the hell has gotten into Uncle Rodney.

Uncle Rodney's idea of a party is ordering nachos and having his television on split-screen to watch the Renegades and his favorite hockey team, the L.A. Burn, play simultaneously. So the fact he has a beer pong table set up in the back half of The Seam, a dance floor in the middle, and Shawn Mendes on the sound system pretty much confirms he's been possessed.

"I'm not possessed!" he bellows, swatting me with a bar towel after I accuse him of it. "I just want to send you two off to college next week with a bang." He replaces his friend John, who is playing part-time bartender, behind the bar. "And for the record, I'm not holding your hair back or bailing you out of your loose lips. That's your mom's job, and she's not here."

I sip from my red Solo cup. "Uncle Rodney, you have no faith."

"You don't need faith when you can see the disaster coming."

I giggle, a clear sign he's probably not wrong, and swing around with loose, unencumbered limbs. Everyone I love, semi-love, or can tolerate is here tonight. Summer has burned its way through another calendar year, and for most of us, a good chunk of our savings, so we're kissing another summer together goodbye. With only a few social summers ahead of us, it's easy to want to cling to this one.

Just shy of my alcohol tolerance, I look for Bristol, who, since deciding I'm public enemy number one for running off to San Jose to get Vance back, has started hanging out with Toolbag a lot more. Other than a stern warning that Vance will break my heart, she's all but ignored me. So when she asked me for a Vance-free night tonight, I couldn't tell her no. It's easier to oblige her since he's playing in New York, but that doesn't mean I don't want to tune in to the game or video chat him after it.

I spot Bristol and Toolbag dancing in an area Uncle Rodney cleared of tables and chairs for that purpose. Tori and Tracy are out there too, but my eyes are on my sister and Toolbag and the limited space between their bodies. With her dressed for Hollywood and him in gym shorts and a T-shirt that reads "Got Balls?", it's baffling to most of us how they remain attracted to one another.

After ten minutes of mingling and carrying on meaningless conversations with people who want to know the scoop on Vance, I find myself looking for an exit, but Eli Perkins finds me first. Eli, two years older, recent college graduate, and the only guy to think he has my boob pic, eyes me with mistaken familiarity.

I stop, ignoring the hand he places on my hip and the look that says he thinks it belongs there. "Bristol."

"Brenna!" My correction is sharp—rude even, and he grins, shrugging one lazy, uninterested shoulder. He's had years to figure out our differences but never quite cared enough to do so.

"Sorry. Maybe if I'd run into your tits, I'd have recognized you." He laughs, gaining a glare and a sharp slap to his wrist. He pulls his hand back but doesn't look at all offended or deterred.

His reference to the boob pic Bristol sent him on my unknowing behalf pisses me off. If I wasn't already irritated by him, this would do it. "You're an ass. And I don't recall inviting you."

"Did I need an invite? I thought you had a thing for me." He oozes arrogance.

"If by 'thing' you mean a fear of herpes, then yeah, but otherwise, not even in your dreams."

"Come on, let me taste Van Hatfield's flavor of the month." He grabs my hand and pulls me toward him.

I twist my hand out of his and take a step back, looking up at him with complete disdain. People who believe our reputation seem to think it's okay to touch us. We're like a pregnant belly. "Hard pass. I haven't heard good things about your tongue, and I'm pretty sure you're no better with it than you are with your dick."

"I didn't hear any complaints from Bristol the other night."

"You may not recognize it, but barfing is a complaint."

Growing defensive, he chuckles bitterly. "Funny." He leans in sort of close and whispers like he has a secret. "I wonder what the media would say about our local celebrity having a tit pic."

"I think they'd tell you to check Pornhub because those tits belong to Misty Steele."

He looks confused, and he should because the boobs are Bristol's. But if I can get him to believe they're Misty Steele's, a name I pulled out of my ass, then I can hopefully avoid Bristol's boobs showing up on the front of *Candid* magazine tomorrow with my name attached to them.

"Who's Misty Steele?"

"I don't know. I found her boobs on the internet and sent them to you."

"Seriously?"

"Look at these things." I point at my chest, rethinking it only after it's done. Unable to take back the command, I power through, convincingly cavalier. "Why on earth would I send anyone a picture of these? And to you of all people?"

"Why on earth would you say they were yours, then?"

I roll my eyes. "Would you have believed me if I'd said they were Misty's?"

I've stumped him. Scratching his head, he curls his lips in. "I don't know that I believe it now. I find it hard to believe those tits were famous."

I should be insulted, but it's Eli. "Look it up. Misty Steele. Trust me, she's not famous for her tits."

He starts to say something, but I skirt on past him leaving his two cents behind me. I shimmy onto the dance floor with Tori, awkwardly thumb some pre-goodbye tears off of her cheeks, and move on through until I find Uncle Rodney pouring a shot for Dawson Crane, my one-time fake boyfriend.

"Make that two." I hold up two fingers, ignore Uncle Rodney's wide, judgmental owl-eyes, and bump hips with Dawson. "I heard you were in town."

He grins, pulling his shot in close to him and scooting mine closer to me. I hold it with two fingers and a thumb and lift it up as Dawson prompts a toast.

"To my favorite ex."

"And mine." I tap my glass against his before downing the clear liquid. I cough, nearly choking. "Tequila?" I eye Uncle Rodney with one eye because I think my other is permanently seized.

"You said make it two." He shakes his head, figuring his wide owl-eye warning was enough for me to have known better.

I glare at him and then return my focus back to Dawson before the tequila really blurs his features and corrupts mine.

"What's up with you these days?" He grins, waiting on my version of events from the summer scandal.

"Don't believe what you read."

"I never do." Dawson's forehead crinkles beneath a tuft of brown bangs. "But is the Van Hatfield thing true?"

Sighing, I reply, "Yes. But it was Bristol who put it on the media's radar. I didn't want the world to know."

His smile falters, empathy pulling his lips downward. "You always did get the short end of that stick."

Uncommitted, I shrug. "The hazards of being a set, I guess."

He's equally evasive, knowing better than to degrade Bristol, though he's made his opinion known a time or two in the past. "I hope it works out for you. Maybe if it does you can kiss this town goodbye and finally separate yourself from all the shit."

He means the Sloan reputation that hasn't yet lost its grip despite our moving away for college, our community involvement, and the lack of a major scandal in several years. Dawson knows the mouths of a small town all too well. When he looks at me, his boyish grin makes me smile back at him. He's come a long way since his football days, and I like his new confidence. He pats my shoulder. "I gotta hit up Carl for a bit. I'll talk to you later."

The night wears on with more shots than I can handle and friendships that suddenly become more important to me the more I have to drink. It also makes me miss my nightly conversation with Vance a bit more.

It's after nine when I sneak out to call him, midnight on the east coast. His game ended two hours ago, so he's either back in his room or at the hotel bar. He answers on the third ring, and when his face takes over my screen, my emotions take over me.

"Hey, you!" He's propped against the headboard of his hotel bed, tattoos in full view, hair tousled, eyes on me.

"Hey." My voice is at an octave I don't think I've used this year, or any year for that matter, and I clear my throat. "How'd it go t'night?"

"We won because they played worse than us, not because we were on fire. How's the party?"

I smile wide, my face bright and happy in the upper right corner of the screen, with the Captain Morgan and Bud Light neon signs in The Seam's front window as my backdrop. "Iss been fun."

"That's good." He grins, sitting up straighter in the bed, abs, for a short time, in clear view. "Did you see everyone you hoped to?"

Nodding more times than is necessary to answer him, my smile falters as I think about the reminders from Eli and Dawson that I haven't quite beat Milagro Beach's opinion of me—us. "Too many." I take a deep breath. "I don' wanna make thingss worse fer you. I kind of have baggage." I lower my chin, hanging my head.

If he's noticed my slurring, he doesn't let on, but he does quirk an eyebrow. "I'm not sure what's bringing this up, but your baggage can't be any worse than mine."

"The Sloans aren't saints."

"Neither are the Hatfields. What happened, Brenna? What's driving this?"

"Nuthin' really. Someone just reminded me that people have loooong memories, and I wasn't always as perfect as I am now." I grin sheepishly, teasing.

He's laughing as he answers, "I can't imagine a day you weren't perfect."

"Ask anyone here. They'll tell you."

"Those aren't friends, then."

"Most aren't." It's true. I have a few good friends; the rest would sell me out in a heartbeat. "What if I ruin your career? I couldn't live with myself."

He chuckles his reply. "Don't sell me out, and we'll be good. If I haven't ruined my career by now, you can't. If you're worried, we'll keep us private. I don't want you hurt. Can you handle the scrutiny you'll be under by dating me?"

"I was born under scrutiny. I'm used to it. Mush shmaller audience, of course. What about yer image?"

"Fuck my image. They're going to print what they want anyway, Brenna. Don't give 'em anything you don't have to, and we'll weather the rest."

"So, you don't care at all about my family's dirt?"

"Not even a little." He adjusts himself on the bed, his phone shaking as he fluffs the pillow beneath him.

"You're beautiful." My eyes land on his chest. "I want to kiss home plate." The truth escapes my lips unapologetically.

"You're drunk."

"A lil', but the truth isss the truth."

"Okay, lush." He chuckles, shaking his head like I'm crazy, and averts the conversation away from himself and completely clear of my skeletons.

The front door to The Seam opens, and Bristol's voice, heightened by irritation, filters out, startling a jump out of me.

"I asked for one fucking night. One . . ." The rest of her sentence is cut short by the closing of the door.

"Everything okay?" Vance asks.

I nod, looking back at him, pulse pumping in my neck from being caught. "I haf to go. Bristol's s'on a warpath."

Vance's chest rises with a deep inhale. "Be good. Call me in the morning."

I nod, but I don't know if my finger on the "end call" button beat the response.

I slowly open the door to The Seam, entering with caution and the inadequate sleuthing of a drunk. For once, a Sloan is stumbling into a bar without causing a scene since everyone is preoccupied with themselves and unconcerned with me. I stop short, seeing Uncle Rodney with a finger in Bristol's face, his expression grave.

"Maybe if you spent a little more time on that guy over there," he points to the back of the bar where Toolbag is hanging out with Dawson, "you'd have less time to spend meddling out there."

Bristol's spine straightens. "Without a job, I have a lot of time these days. I can do both. And I'm not meddling. She owes me a night."

I hunker, cowering inside the entrance to spy on a conversation neither wants me to hear.

He grabs her by both shoulders, his touch affectionate but controlling. "Maybe you owe her this time. You have to let it run its course, whatever that course may be. He's a good kid, Bristol, and they deserve to see where this goes without your interference, even if they can't have your blessing."

"Someone has to look out for her. You're obviously only in it for him, and Mom's too busy trying to get Joe to put a ring on it, evident by her no-show tonight. While you've been fawning all over your new baseball toy, I've been trying to figure out how to pay for college without a job. Like you, Brenna's too caught up in *him* to give a shit about the little things like money."

"Oh, for the love of God, you have a job you're starting in less than a week. Stop being so dramatic. You sound like one of those Kardashian housewives."

If I wasn't so rapt with their conversation, I'd laugh at Uncle Rodney for ever thinking a Kardashian could be as mundane as a housewife.

"That wasn't dramatic. Dramatic would be telling you 'our job' in L.A. let us go because they don't think Brenna's recent foray into the media spotlight would be good for their business. And as of two days ago, it's official; I lost my scholarship, Uncle Rodney. I'm going to have to sell myself on some street corner to afford first semester. So, sorry to burst your bubble, but it *can* get more dramatic."

Uncle Rodney's surprised reaction is drowned out by music and laughter, so I miss it, and hearing only the last part doesn't help me. "It's a sinkhole, Bristol. What you're doing is wrong."

"I haven't done anything yet."

"What are you planning?" I blurt out, tripping over my own feet and stumbling over air to wobble upright in front of her. Bristol collects her guilty look too late, and I pounce. "What did you do?"

"Nothing."

She tries to storm off, but Uncle Rodney catches her arm, delaying her dramatic exit. "Tell her."

Bristol's teeth clamp together as she huffs out her confession. "*Candid* offered me five thousand for an exclusive interview."

"No." The one word I can manage is tacky on my tongue, and with my buzz now completely gone, I can't even slur a stupid response.

"I didn't. Thanks for the faith."

"You haven't exactly—"

"Haven't exactly what? Said I wouldn't? Told you a hundred times that I was sorry? Oh, wait, I have said all that."

"Don't put this on me. I'm not wrong. I heard Uncle Rodney tell you not to."

"Because, like you, he doesn't think I'm capable of doing the right thing either."

She's right. I was quick to think the worst of her after hearing only part of a conversation, but lately, she's left no room for me to think anything else. For the sake of the party and to save a fight I'm not in any condition to win, I cave, with questions unasked. "I shouldn't have assumed. But it's hard not to worry, Bristol."

Bristol offers no reply or facial expression I can legitimately count as forgiveness before integrating herself back into the party.

Uncle Rodney draws me into him, holding me tight against his side, kissing the side of my head with the love of a father. "For what it's worth, I don't think she would have done it even without our input." Uncle Rodney's faith in Bristol sounds a lot like mine used to. I wonder if I'll ever get it back. I miss it.

CHAPTER TWENTY-NINE

Two weeks after starting my third year of college, I'm making my debut at Red Hooligans as Van Hatfield's girlfriend in a dress I borrowed from Tracy. As I step out of the car, I am immediately accosted by camera-wielding vultures hell-bent on picking my flesh to get their next meal. They swarm me, making it difficult to maneuver past the damn curb or to see anything beyond my toes.

Looking around, I don't know that they are as thick as they are relentless, but I can't get through them without being thwarted at every opening I try. They shout question after question, some of which are cruel and bear no substance whatsoever. "Are you after his money or your fifteen minutes of fame? The Renegades struggled tonight. Do you think that has anything to do with you? Are you exclusive?" I don't know if I'll ever be able to get used to this, no matter what lies I tell myself to convince me otherwise.

Blooms of bright lights make the late evening sky seem like late afternoon. It's a bit overwhelming for a girl whose only fame came from a bathroom wall that didn't even get her cell number right. This is the biggest pool of photographers I've faced since Stray

Charlie's, and they shout at me from all directions. "What is Van Hatfield going to do with a virgin?"

Where the hell do they get this shit from? Have they not consulted Milagro Beach's archives? I'm sure the date and time of my cherry popping are listed there.

"Just one question?" The guy blocking my path presses, but I keep my head down and welcome the entrance ahead of me.

Once inside, I feel the relief of safety and the letdown of adrenaline that has me glistening in sweat. I want to catch my breath before becoming the object of curiosity at the top of the stairs. The last time I was here, I was of mild interest and probably viewed as a groupie. This time, based on the questions being flung, they'll know I'm more than a story.

The hypervelocity of my pulse keeps me at the foot of the stairs longer than security would like, but I keep holding up a finger for one more minute. I take a deep breath that feels like I inhaled nails, and head up the curved staircase, not quite ready to face Vance's peers.

I've entered harsher places wearing worse, so I pop my shoulders back and lift my chin, ready for harsh critique and instant disapproval. To my relief as much as my horror, my fears don't even come close to being met. I don't make a dent in the conversations or even warrant an interested glance that lasts longer than a few seconds. I may as well be dirt dragged in on a shoe for all the notice I receive until the friendly grin of Greg Middleton, the only teammate of Vance's that he's officially introduced me to, catches my eye. His grin expands to a smile between the thick brown hairs of his goatee as he offers a quick wave, even though he is otherwise occupied by one of the tallest women I've ever seen.

I stop at the bar and order a Jameson whiskey, something familiar. Glass in hand, I feel the small presence of home, and with that friendly reminder, I can do anything.

"What do you think you're doing?" Vance has my glass in his hand and is sniffing it before I can protest. His grin is wicked behind the clear glass, and as he pulls the glass away, it broadens further. "Whiskey?"

I don't see the need to respond, and I wait for him to say something that might spark a conversation between us. Instead, he leans in for a kiss and I forget what the hell I'm doing because this is a first. Vance, while affectionate, doesn't put it on display often.

"You good?" he asks, setting the glass down on the bar behind me.

I slump in the shoulders and pull on his tie. "You just took me by surprise."

He leans in closer and I breathe him in, making no effort to hide it. "Too much too soon? Want me to ease up on the PDA?"

"No," I say softly. "I want more of that . . . much more." I lift my eyebrows, teasing him with my meaning.

"Let's go," he says, grabbing my hand.

I shake my head. "You have schmoozing to do. I can wait."

"I can't." He sucks on my earlobe making it nice and wet like another part of me. "I've missed you . . . a lot," he whispers, and his face crashes into mine as Halsey, catcher for the Renegades, claps him on the back.

"She really does exist."

Ben Halsey is hot. One lone dimple on his right cheek could spark a conversation from nothing. His brown hair is straight, one length, and comes to his shoulders. In his pictures, it's pulled back into a ponytail so that it looks uniformly short. Tonight, it hangs loose and glows healthy beneath the low lighting. He's jovial, and even if he were ass-ugly, his personality would draw women to him in flocks of naked flesh. He brushes Vance to the side, and I grin, enjoying the attention.

I reach out a hand to introduce myself and he takes it, completing the introductions. "Brenna, right?" He allows me a nod to confirm and then continues. "You're way prettier than Van described."

I look at Vance. All sorts of possible retorts are flooding my mouth, but before I can spit one out, Ben is taking it back with both a grin and a wave of his hand. "Kidding. Totally kidding. He says great things about you, which is why I thought you were made up. Well, that, and who would be with this ugly mug?" He pinches Vance's cheeks together like a fat aunt, and Vance slaps his hand away with none of the nephew affection.

Chip, Vance's overbearing manager whom I've had the displeasure of meeting only once and briefly at that, squeezes in between Ben and Vance, his demeanor brusque. He's dark-haired and light-eyed, always moving too fast for the environment but never fast enough to keep Vance in a good mood. "And here she is." Chip looks at me, his smirk a tad too condescending for my liking. "Where's your entourage?" He looks around, for what or whom I'm not sure.

"And what entourage would that be?"

"The family usually attached to your hip. Didn't they come with you the last time?"

"Once." My tone is guarded, uncertainty keeping it on the cordial side of defensive.

"Yeah, yeah, of course, just the one time." He waves off any reservations his question may have incited and brightens his smirk into a lovely smile. I wouldn't buy if it came with Cheetos and a drink.

"Yeah, where's the fam bam?" Ben asks, grinning, and that winning dimple deepens. "I heard there was a twin."

"Both of you, go bother someone else." Vance presents them with his back then worms his way in front of me and places both hands on the bar behind me, caging me in and shutting the other two out. I look up at him and grin. His tie hangs away from his body and dangles like a pendulum between us. I grab it and tug him down to me.

"That's not schmoozing."

"I don't have to schmooze those two."

Ben buckles Vance's knee with a toe tap to the back of it and laughs as he walks away. "Nice meeting you, Brenna," he shouts over his shoulder. "Glad to know you're not inflatable latex." He treks off for parts unknown, leaving a wake of quivering flesh at a table of groupies as he passes.

Chip isn't so quick to depart. "Van, I'm not done. We need to discuss some business." Vance turns to face him, giving Chip the attention he's learned over the years to produce. "You have a photoshoot with *Jock* magazine tomorrow. We'll meet downtown at VOA Studios at noon. Don't be late."

Vance groans. "I don't do photoshoots."

"You don't have that option. It's not just you. It's the team too. The top dog set it up. And if they ask, make yourself available for an interview."

"No fucking way."

"I'm not asking." His brusque demeanor flows to his tone, and Vance's body stiffens beside mine.

"Brenna is only in town for one day. I'm not spending it at a photoshoot. Reschedule it."

Backing up and out of the conversation with Vance, Chip's expression hardens and his gaze briefly strays to mine before tightening on Vance. "I'm not rescheduling shit. Don't be late, Van."

Vance, looking irritated, returns his attention to me, though his thoughts are still likely on Chip and the photoshoot. He groans, getting really close and personal with his body against mine. "Where were we?"

"You were supposed to schmooze."

He tilts his head down, kissing my neck. "How'm I doing?"

"I'm not complaining, but if this is how you schmooze everyone, we're going to have a problem."

He pulls back a fraction, looking at me like I'm a tabloid and he doesn't know how much of it to believe. "Really? Do you need me to show you just how exclusive you are?" He runs a finger up my inner thigh and everything between my ears and ankles tingles.

I grab his hand, pulling it away before he can coax me into a hands-on demonstration. "What you have in mind will convince more than me, and I'm okay with the tabloids not knowing everything. They think I'm a virgin. I kind of like that." I kiss his chin, looking up at him, expression playful.

"I'm changing that later. Don't expect to be a virgin long."

ABSOLUTELY NO ONE OTHER THAN BRISTOL HAS EVER HAD THE POWER to sweet talk me into doing something I'm not comfortable doing. Even with her, I'm usually pretty headstrong before I cave. But then along came Vance, who only had to ask me twice and kiss me once to convince me to go to his photoshoot. I gave him a million-and-one reasons why I didn't think it was a good idea, but he only had to give me one: time. We just don't have enough of it together, and in his words, "a stupid photoshoot shouldn't rob us of more." Well, that and he said he wouldn't go unless I came along. I heard the warnings from Chip, even if Vance didn't. So here I wait alongside Vance and the others at VOA Studios.

A rep from *Jock* finally greets us thirty minutes past the scheduled time. She's at least apologetic and looking guiltily frantic as she tries to make up for her tardiness with an awkward smile and rushed wrangling. Vance expresses his irritation as she separates us from the pack of fifteen. Having probably dealt with much worse than Van Hatfield and his asshole manager, she doesn't validate their irritability with another apology and continues guiding us to another area.

"Why do you find this funny?" Vance directs his question to me.

"You're a diva. I've spent longer waiting for a parking spot."

"If Van isn't working on his art, he should be selling it. In the time you take to circle the parking lot, Vance could be losing a million-dollar endorsement. You need to understand that." Chip, walking a few steps behind us chimes in, uninvited and irritatingly dickish because he's not happy I'm here. If not for the plain-looking woman who greets us while extending a hand to Vance, I'd have retorted with something equally dickish, and I like to think mine is bigger than his.

"Mr. Hatfield, I'm Lena Liu. I'll be photographing you today."

He accepts her hand and shakes it. "Van, and this is my girlfriend, Brenna—"

Talking over Vance, Chip introduces himself, his job title preceding his four-letter name and the hand he juts out at her. Arrogant prick.

She smiles at all of us, revealing straight teeth, stained by nothing more than a long life. Her black, shiny hair is thin, straight, and hangs in a natural sheet over both shoulders. She has an odd sense of style, but it's not altogether unpleasing, just . . . different. Definitely eclectic, as none of her clothing matches, but somehow on her it's the right blend of mismatch and swank. In a world dominated by busty blondes and arrogant men, this woman who is so exceptionally herself is a welcome sight.

She leads us to a back room where she directs Vance to a chair in front of a mirror flanked by a stylist who doesn't have a personable bone in her body. Chip, on his cell phone, follows Vance, and I wait with Lena while they prep Vance for his shoot. Since it's about sports, I've never really paid much attention to *Jock* magazine, but Uncle Rodney always has it lying around The Seam. All I really know about it is that it's a sports magazine that uses the name in every cover title. For instance, the one that stands out the most in my mind is the one they used for quarterback Matt Marrow of the Cincinnati Bengals, which read: Captain Jock Marrow. The play on the popular *Pirates of the Caribbean* character was brilliant. It's a clever marketing strategy because even though I'm not a sports fan, I always look to see what the cover says.

I talk shop for a bit with Lena, asking her questions about the business in hopes of learning whether I would want to use my graphic design degree in this capacity rather than for the freelance plans I have. While not discouraging me from freelancing, she isn't fully supportive either and says I should at least wait until I've established a name for myself.

"You could always start someplace like *Jock* or a publishing company that does their own book covers and marketing materials, and then, once you have some experience there, you can test the waters and your supporters for freelance work. Remind me to give you my card after this, and if you'd like to talk some more, we can set up a time. There are a lot of opportunities out there. You just have to know the right people." She smiles and winks, adjusting the vintage silver cuff around her wrist. "I know the right people."

Vance joins us, and Lena is instantly on her feet and prepping him for his first frame. Fifteen minutes after the shoot begins, I can tell how this is going to go if something doesn't change. Vance is on edge, still pissed about his time being wasted and irritated that he's here at all. Lena tries to put him at ease and direct him, but Vance either isn't listening or is flat out being obstinate.

He's sexier than he is portraying, funnier than he comes across, and as of this moment, he's wasting more of his own time than anyone else has been up to this point. I close my eyes and stare down into my lap, gripping the edge of the chair in frustration as Lena tells him one more time to relax, and Chip gripes at him about needing a good shot.

"Could you give us a minute?" I pop out of my chair hoping she'll oblige, but I wait in case I have no right to ask. This is her show, and by the way Chip is barking orders, it's his too, so I hesitate out of respect.

She nods once, taking a reluctant Chip with her as she and her camera step aside and take my vacated spot over by the desk. Vance paces in short strides, running his hand through his recently styled hair.

As I reach him, I grab his wrist and pull his hand out of his mussed hair.

"What?" His impatience is tangible.

"Relax," I say softly, drawing him into me with my hand still on his wrist. "Let them see what I see."

"I hate this," he admits, but I can feel him loosening as he wraps both hands around my waist.

"Think about it differently then. Quit looking at it as a tax on your time and see it as a step to your future. This article could lead to endorsements." His lips drop the scowl and tighten into a thin line. "With this little bit of scruff," I run my hand along his cheek where a day's worth of growth blooms black, "you could get a razor commercial." I run my hands down his arms, touching the taut muscles and tattoos that adorn them. "Or a Giorgio Armani ad." I lift his shirt with two fingers on the hem and expose his abs, running my index finger up to his navel. "I wouldn't mind seeing this in a cologne ad, or with the caption 'what's beneath your jeans' on a Calvin's billboard."

Vance groans and grabs both my wrists, restraining them behind my back while he lowers his lips to my neck. "You've made your point. And if you don't stop, they're going to get more than just photographs and Chip's going to have a coronary."

I grin and kiss his chest, and he rests his chin on top of my head.

"Thank you," he says softly.

I move to let him have the stage and Lena to get her shots, but she stops us, placing a hand on my arm to keep me beside him. "I'd like to try something different," she says, positioning my body to face hers. "But first I'd like you to see this." She shows us the viewing window of her camera and pulses through several pictures, first of Vance alone, and then of us, in our pep-talk embrace. "See the difference?"

I don't think either of us knows what we're looking for, so Lena goes back to the first picture of Vance, posing with his ball and glove. "Look," and then she scrolls forward to one of us facing each other, his hands on my hips, and his chin on the top of my head. "Now, look at this one. What do you see?"

"She looks a hell of a lot better than the props," Vance replies.

Lena smiles, nodding with vigorous agreement, while I still look a little lost. "There is no denying that. But look at you. Look at your reaction to her. You're relaxed. We could spend all day here and I wouldn't be able to coax that out of you. Three minutes and she had you."

"No!" He pulls away from both of us.

"Hear me out?" Lena begs.

"Hear you out about what?" I ask, confused by his reaction.

Vance's hand is through his hair again and he paces behind us, coming to a stop a few feet from me. "She wants to photograph you," he says bitterly. "There isn't a chance in hell I'm going to let you exploit her. Not a fucking chance." There doesn't seem to be any room for negotiation as far as I can tell, but Lena doesn't shrink.

"Don't you think that's already happened? Each time you two step out in public, or even at times when you think you're in private, they're snapping pictures of her. With me at least, you control what they see. You can't deny the chemistry. What I just shot is magic, and you weren't even trying."

"No!" he barks.

"I concur," Chip adds. His face, a few shades short of crimson, is tight and his dark hair, touched with silver, is mussed by an impatient hand. He's beginning to sweat, and I question why concern about a few lousy pictures has him sweating out of his business attire.

Tearing my eyes from his sweat-soaked pits, I look between the artist and her subject, wondering when any one of them is going to consult me. "I'll do it," I chime in, but no one notices and they continue to fight it out. "I'll do it," I repeat louder.

They simultaneously stop and look at me with varying expressions. Vance is the first to speak, not because he's quicker, but because Lena defers to him when she sees his expression.

"Hell no!"

"Why?" she asks.

"Because it'll be a permanent fucking record. That's why!" Chip's outburst draws everyone's attention. "Van, you do this and you may as well put a ring on it. You've worked hard to establish an image. Don't fuck it up now by adding permanence to something that is passing."

Vance asks Lena for another moment, and promising us ten

minutes, she walks out. Vance follows her with his eyes until she is out the door and out of sight. He then directs his attention to Chip, who has sweated through his blue dress shirt. "Watch it. You're walking a thin line."

"Sorry. It came out wrong. I meant the tabloids think she's a passing thing, not that she actually is. Posing for a picture is quite different from being captured in one. It's giving them an unspoken response, and we don't respond, remember?"

I should be bothered by his opinion of me, but it's shared by everyone Vance comes in contact with. Anyone who pulls his attention away from baseball and endorsements isn't going to get a favorable review from Chip.

"You've advised me. Consider your job done. I'll call you when we're through."

He waits around like Vance might change his mind, and I shift on my feet nervously, looking down to witness Chip's fist furiously opening and closing at his side. "Van, now isn't the time to be impulsive."

Cords of taught tendons tighten further in Vance's neck. "Impulsive would be firing you for that comment. My restraint is limited, so I suggest you wait in the hall or leave altogether."

One dutiful nod and a passing look of disdain in my direction and Chip takes his leave.

"I'm sorry. I didn't mean to start anything," I offer, not sure why I'm so willing to take the blame.

"You didn't. That's Chip. He's as obsessed with the media as he is with my career. It has nothing to do with you. He hates it when I go off script, and with good reason. I'm not the best at making myself look good."

"It's okay, Vance. You don't have to do this if you don't want to. I was agreeing to do the shoot just to stop the disagreement."

"It's not a matter of want, Brenna. I don't care what the tabloids print about me. I care what they print about you."

I look up at him, pulling him closer to me with a pinch of his shirt. "You make the call. I'm okay either way."

A confident Lena enters carrying her camera and a fistful of papers she sets on the desk. "I'll need these releases signed."

On a mission, Vance stalks across the room. "If we do this, we get full say in what's published, and we take what you don't use."

Lena's face falls. "That's not how this works."

"It is today. We have a lot more to lose than you do." He slams back. "My way or no way."

Hoping for an ally she looks at me, but I don't speak for Vance. After a spell of silence, she counters, "You give me creative freedom, regardless of whether you think it's appropriate, and I'll give you the power to okay the shots we use, and you take what's vetoed. *But* I keep all the rights to the ones we select, used for this issue or not, for future use at our discretion."

It takes a few seconds for Vance to toss around his options, and then he nods once with extreme curtness. "I want it in writing."

CHAPTER THIRTY

The apartment Bristol and I share with four other girls is a pigsty. It smells like leftovers and mildew, and I think it may have been seen in an episode of *Hoarders*. Six girls shouldn't have this much shit.

I hold the phone so Vance can see me and a drywall patch but not the crayon drawing of a stick figure family with purple penises. This is where I'm going to hang one of those photos Lena took of us a few weeks ago. If I ever get my hands on one, that is.

"Are you coming to San Francisco?" Vance's irritable tone rubs me the wrong way. It's the first week of October, exactly one month and ten days since I parked my ass in Mr. Chang's Animation and Digital Imaging class, among others, and he still hasn't adjusted to my school schedule. I've known children better suited to change. The distance is hard on me too, but I don't expect him to drop everything to come see me. We knew it would be hard. I just don't think either of us knew how hard.

"I can't. I'm working. I told you that the last time you asked." I have a surprise planned for him, and to make it work out, I've taken every graphic design job I can find, including making a brochure for a lady who walks cats. I babysat for parents who thought their kids were bratty enough to warrant a thousand dollars for two days—they weren't wrong. All to surprise him, and I'm not going to let him bully me into confessing my plans.

He grumbles, releasing a heavy breath. "I thought maybe you had time to change that. I get not missing school for the other games, especially since Bristol lost her scholarship for missing too much, but..."

I get his irritability at my dismissal. Only two of the five National League Division Series games are being played on the weekend, both in San Francisco, and I'm planning on going, but as a damn surprise and not on command. "Oh, I'm sorry I have to work in order to eat or buy socks." Using my financial status hits a little below the belt, but I need him to drop it, or by the end of this conversation he'll have my confession and my firstborn. Since losing my job at Stray Charlie's and moving back to L.A., where a job wasn't waiting for me for the first time in three years, it's a solid argument, just cruel. Being infamous takes a toll on a girl's bank account, but I've planned for this, I've busted my ass for this, and I'm not caving.

"Damn it, Brenna. You're taking this all wrong. I'm not demeaning you. But it's important to me, and I want to share some of it with you, even if it is just game three."

Game three of the series isn't small like he makes out. I know it's important to him, and since they fell short last year, I know he wants this win more than anything. Between school, work, lack of money, and his schedule, we haven't seen each other outside of video chats in weeks. It's been hell and he's losing his patience with the distance, but I can't give him big gifts, so I have to give him inexpensive surprises. And making it to his game after making him believe I can't is my surprise. "I'll try, but no promises. I'll still have to convince Bristol I need the car for the next few days, and she just started a full-time job since she can't attend classes this semester."

"Bring her too. I don't care. I'll have two tickets at Will Call. They're not giving us time with family after, so you'll have to meet me at the room. It's room 1310 at the Palace Hotel on New Montgomery."

"What about Halsey? You two usually share."

"He won't mind."

"Vance, I don't know—"

"Then I'll get us our own room."

"It's not that . . ."

"If it's not that, it'll be something else. You know what? Forget it. Do your thing. I'll do mine." Temper surging, his tightly reigned composure takes a nosedive and his face disappears from my phone.

I don't let his reaction bother me, knowing he'll forget all about it when he sees me in the flesh. I grab my overnight bag and the keys from Bristol's nightstand.

Bristol is sitting in the front seat when I get to the car, and I stop, my mouth gaped open like an imbecile. I feel an instant sting of animosity at her presence, ready to do battle if she presses me. I won the right to have the car, and she doesn't have a say in where I take it.

She smirks, reading my thoughts perfectly. "Relax. I filled it with gas." She slips past the steering wheel and out of the car.

I narrow my eyes and wait for the price tag. "What do you want?"

"Nothing," she says far too innocently. She shoves me toward the car. "Don't run him too hard, he's old." I drop my jaw, and she laughs. "Not Vance, stupid. The Silver Stallion."

I laugh, hugging her before I toss my suitcase into the back seat because the trunk is full of stuff we haven't moved into the apartment. "He set aside a ticket for you too, if you want to come?" With my head tilted at a questioning slant, I plead with my eyes. "It could be fun."

AN INCESSANT DRIZZLE PUTS A DAMPER ON THE DRIVE NORTH, AND THE one good windshield wiper we have squeaks across the glass lamenting the lack of water while the other one skates across without touching a drop.

Despite the traffic obstacles and the brief stop at The Seam to make ourselves feel better about driving through town on our way to San Francisco, Bristol and I make the game with four innings to spare.

We pick up our tickets, take our seats next to a couple wearing bride and groom T-shirts, and hunker down beneath the drizzle for six more innings in which the Renegades finally squeak out a win in the eleventh, scoring two more runs on the Giants. It's a pro-Giant crowd, but we're not the only ones excessively celebrating the hard-fought win. We hang with the stragglers as the crowd thins and the team attends to their press obligations and private celebrations.

Since Vance told me he has to spend time with the press and the team, Bristol and I decide to spend our time being tourists, and after a long and unnerving construction detour through neighborhoods on the ATF watch lists, we end up at Fisherman's Wharf. For future reference, riding a carousel in the rain isn't as fun as it sounds when you're planning it in traffic. It's cold, slick, and believe it or not, dirty. Every speck of dirt, vomit, and spilled sugary treat from the last decade is now on the seat of my pants. When I do finally get to see Vance, and I will whether he answers his damn phone or not, I'm going to look and smell like a wet dog.

After numerous calls to Vance go unanswered, we arrive in the parking lot of the Palace Hotel hours after the game's end, soggy but upbeat despite Vance's radio silence.

The media is heavy at the entrance but are being kept back beyond the covered valet reception, and I get past them unnoticed. The drowned rat look obviously isn't attention-getting. I wander into the lobby with Bristol singing out of tune behind me. The lobby is large and outfitted with red and gold furnishings. A large crystal chandelier draws my attention up into a domed ceiling with the dark, starless sky peering through its glass panels.

My twentieth attempt to call Vance goes right to voicemail. I hang up before his voice kicks in and plop down into a high-backed red and gold throne chair to sulk.

"Oh, for Christ's sake, go up."

"He shares a room with Halsey," I bark, irritated with her and Vance.

"That's the stupidest thing I've ever heard. He gave you his room number for a reason." Bristol doesn't get the inconvenience to Halsey because she's never the one put out.

"Look at this." Bristol nods toward a group of four girls walking past the lobby. "Should I direct them to Hollywood and Vine, or do you think they're branching out here in San Fran?"

Sitting in the uncomfortable throne seat, I twist my body and crane my neck over my shoulder to look at the group of girls. I agree with Bristol; I'm pretty sure they bypassed their street corner altogether and went straight to the hotel for groupie transgressions.

Bristol sighs, "I can't spend another second looking like I'm recovering from a toilet swirly when you got girls workin' it like that. We're going up. Halsey can blame me."

Vance's room is about four doors down from the bank of elevators, and Bristol, in far more of a hurry than I am, arrives first. "It's open," she states, just before I arrive to see the partially opened door with visible light in its one-inch gap.

Staring at the crack with a groaning conscience, I grumble out, "Knock anyway."

She knocks, rapping hard enough to gain another inch of unsealed entry. Greeted by silence, she pushes the door in.

A blast of cool air, too cool for the wet San Francisco evening, pebbles my skin with goose bumps. The room is nice, with a common area situated between two bedrooms. It has a bar, television, and a view of the city through a large, dark picture window. Bristol plops her ass in one of the chairs and sighs, "I'll wait here." Draped over the entirety of the chair, she looks exhausted.

I drop my purse on the love seat, eenie-meenie-miney-mo a room, and head to the left. One lamp beside the bed lights the room, and I can see the bathroom counter is littered with Halsey's hair product, razor, and cocoa butter lotion. I groan, spin, and head toward the room with a partially opened door on the other side.

I push it in, but instead of walking in on an empty bed or a surprised Vance, I almost stumble into pussy. It takes me a minute to register what I'm seeing, but it's hard not to recognize the pink of a vagina or the gaping hole that says Vance wasn't her first.

Once her bald vagina is hidden behind a pair of long legs drawn up defensively, she manages a smile. Black stilettos nearly poke a hole in the mattress.

"Who the hell are you?" she asks in a raspy voice. "I'm not into threesomes with other girls."

I will my mind to connect to the other organs and tissues of my body. I'm immobile, air-starved, and speechless. This is why I can't fight. This is why I can't throw a punch when one is so richly deserved. My mind will not work with my body. It's as if its power source is unplugged and nothing runs sensibly.

Her tits bounce as she scoots off the bed. They're real but have the perkiness of youth. She is super tall when she gets to her feet, and the heels give her an extra few inches. Long, dark hair damaged by over-treatment hangs over one shoulder. She is everything I am not and nothing I ever thought he'd want me to be.

The shower shuts off in the bathroom to my right, and for whatever reason, it's then my body becomes one with my mind and I am able to move, think, and function as one nearly-cohesive unit.

Stiletto Girl smiles. "Wait! I know who you are." Her lips curve up, teeth bared between them in a satisfied smile. "You're the chick from *Candid*." She drops her hands to her side. "They weren't kidding when they said you were homely. Kind of hard to keep a guy when you have that face?" She looks me over, eyes taking a distasteful course that ends in a smug pinched-lipped smirk.

Really? *Candid*? That's what she's going to quote? I pretend her observations don't hurt. "Is that Vance in there?" Still trembling and on the verge of a face-plant, I try to stiffen my spine.

"Look, I was here first." She places her hand on her bony hip, and her eyes, under heavy-handed makeup, narrow as she looks over her competition. She could totally take me if we were indeed competing. I've been traveling for hours and didn't know when I started the trip I would have to wear stilettos to vie for my place in my boyfriend's bed. "And three's a crowd." Biting the inside of her bottom lip, she plays with a strand of her hair, looking at it as if she's looking for split ends.

"What the fuck?" Vance, in a white towel draped around his hips, emerges from the bathroom, toothbrush sticking out of the corner of his mouth. His short, dark hair is wet and mussed from an attempt at towel drying it. His abs are striking above the knot in the towel, and I wish I could focus there instead of on the bitch in his bed.

"I was just informed three's a crowd," I say, fighting back tears. I try for cool, calm, and collected in a moment that is anything but deserving of it, and fail miserably.

Vance at least has the decency to look surprised and maybe even a little shocked. "Brenna." He says my name like a question, but I don't think it is. "Oh fuck, this isn't what it looks like." He turns his attention to the naked girl who just climbed out of his bed and whose pink stink he just washed off his body. Toothbrush discarded, his head shifts back and forth between her and me, but his eyes settle on her. "Tell her!" he yells, snapping at her like she's deaf.

Caked beneath a layer of concealer, her forehead wrinkles in a questioning expression. "Tell her what?" Her attempt at covering her chest with her skinny arms belies the nasty attitude.

"Tell her we didn't fuck." Vance advances toward her, and grabbing her by the arm yells, "Tell her!"

Tears, weighted with a thousand questions, spill down my cheeks no matter the fight to keep them back. I back out of the room, chest heaving as the full weight of what I've witnessed hits me full force. My shock, fully gone now, has left me open for the gut-wrenching ache that eluded me ten seconds earlier.

"Brenna! Holy shit, this isn't what it looks like." He lunges for me, his towel hanging precariously off his hips, but the potential for full-frontal doesn't deter him from advancing into the room's common area.

I slap madly at him, connecting with his hands, wrists, and forearms. "Get away from me," I scream, my voice hoarse with emotion. I hear Bristol cussing but can't make out more than the four-letter words.

"No, no, no, no, no," Vance protests hysterically. "Brenna, you gotta hear me out."

Bristol appears between us, hands defensively out in front of her as she backs herself and me toward the door to the hallway. "Stay away from her!" she yells, reaching a hand behind her to grab a hold of me. She grasps for my hand but connects with my shirt and holds on tightly. "Brenna, go!"

Hearing her panic, I blindly pat my way backward out of the room, and Bristol, attached to my shirt, follows.

"Brenna. This isn't what you think. I swear to God, it's not."

"I knew you'd hurt her," Bristol screams, shoving him in the chest as he draws closer to us. "You don't deserve her, and I will make you pay for thinking you do."

Vance shoves her hand away. "Stay out of this." He tries to maneuver around her protectiveness.

The towel around his waist drops around his feet. Standing in the hall, he's solidly naked. Stiletto Girl, right behind him in the doorway, smirks her appreciation, oblivious to the wrecked lives around her. Vance, dick out and ass bared to the world, doesn't even flinch and skirts around Bristol while her attention is directed to the naked bean pole posed in the door frame.

"Brenna?" Vance manages to cinch a piece of me into his hand. "Please?"

I look down at our contact point. Fast food flavored vomit flows toward my lips and I swallow it back, much like I would have to do with my pride to listen to a word he has to say. I've spent too many nights with my mom to ever want to do this for myself.

Bristol's temporary lapse of focus evaporates, and she's back to separating us with a few choice words, tugs, and pulls that Vance doesn't budge through. She scoffs, narrows her eyes, and pushes his shoulder. "Let her go! You made your choice. Now let her make hers."

"Why?" I croak out, managing for the moment to keep my stomach contents. "Why bother with me if you were going to fuck other people anyway?" A new revelation dawns, a bit too late to be of use, but dawns, nonetheless. "Shit, am I the side chick?"

"God, no. It's only you." His hold on my wrist tightens, and I yank it free, nearly falling on my ass.

"What the fuck?" I hear Halsey's voice come from behind me, and something similar in Spanish from Corky.

Vance continues despite their arrival. "I know it looks bad—"

"Bad?" I scream. "You still smell like pussy."

"Ah, shit." Someone from behind me spits, and more cursing from assorted voices fills the hall.

I feel a hand on my elbow and I shake it off, shifting away from the gesture to feel the full hatred for the girl wearing nothing but her black stilettos. Her smirk as the situation suddenly becomes retrievable for her with the arrival of the other players pisses me off.

"Come on, Brenna," Greg says, draping an arm around my shoulders. "Let me get you out of here."

Vance advances, his dick moving with his strides. "Brenna, I have no idea who she is. She wasn't here when I got in the shower."

I laugh, but it's bitter and full of malice. "I'm not stupid," I say softly.

"Come on," Halsey says, pushing Vance backward with his hand in the center of his chest, "Let's take this inside before you get arrested."

Vance won't budge. "I'm not leaving unless she comes with."

"She's not going anywhere with you!" Bristol screams, squeezing herself in between Halsey and Vance. "She's done with you!"

"You'd fucking like that wouldn't you?" Vance, advancing on her, yells in her face, and Halsey, no match for Vance's distaste for my sister, can't contain him. "Is she yours, Bristol? Did you set this shit up?"

"You wish. This shit-show is all yours, buddy."

I find myself leaning against Greg, thankful for the prop as my body trembles.

Halsey, more serious than I've ever seen him, gains the upper hand and manages to separate Bristol and Vance. "I don't care what any of you do, but you can't do it out here. Who do you want gone?" Halsey raises his voice toward Vance, who jerks his head, and my attention is once again redirected to Stiletto Girl. "Cork, get her some damn clothes and get her out of here. Van wants her gone."

The skank doesn't budge from the doorway. Her smirk riles my temper, and even knowing I can't fight worth a damn, I swing at her face. I watch as my hand connects with her cheek and her head cranks to the side. I swing again, but I'm pulled up short and my fist stops mid-stride as my feet lift off the ground.

"Get her out of here!" Greg, holding me off the ground, yells over her crying yelps and my huffing and puffing.

"How's that for homely, bitch?" I scream, kicking my legs like a swimming puppy.

Corky, there in seconds, is shoving clothes into her arms and wrapping a sheet around her. "Let's go, sweetheart." He all but shoves her out of the room. "I think you've done enough damage for one night."

"She hit me," she whines through thick tears. "I'm pressing charges," she screams over her shoulder, holding her cheek in the palm of her hand.

Anger like I've never felt races like a damn inferno through my blood, and I take off at a dead sprint, but instead of connecting with my target, I fold in half over Greg's stiff and unforgiving arm, shocking us both. He grumbles beneath the strength it takes to keep an adrenaline-fueled body at bay, and I groan with unexpected rib pain.

Greg holds me in place, cursing loudly, "Fuck me!" he bellows, grunting as he sidelines my efforts. "Easy there, Mayweather," he says, pulling me back so my ass is pressed against his groin. I groan, coughing, and we pant together.

I refuse to go into the room, but Halsey manages to get Vance to agree to, leaving me, Greg, and Bristol standing in the hallway.

"If you'll get my purse," I pause for a breath, "I—I'll—I c-can go." I scrub at my tears.

"Brenna?" Greg's voice is calm but super uncertain as to which Brenna he might get. "I really don't think you have the full picture. I mean, I get what you saw, but I don't believe it."

I stare at him, unconvinced and pissed. "Are you kidding me right now?"

He laughs, but not with amusement, more nervous than anything. "I don't think you should be so hasty."

"Hasty?" I walk away from him and pace in a tight circle. "I saw her snatch." He chuckles a little. "Her. Snatch!" I reiterate loudly for effect, to which I get another chuckle and two hands up in the air as if in surrender.

"I get it," he says. "I do."

The door to the hotel room opens, and Halsey sticks his head out. "You coming in?" He looks pointedly at Greg and then to me.

"I need my purse," I say, and they both look at me, waiting for a decision I'm not about to make. "What?" I ask icily. "I saw snatch."

Halsey, uncharacteristically serious, speaks directly to me. "Van doesn't usually go for cleat-chaser snatch. Hear him out?" He holds out his hand to me.

Bristol, abnormally silent for most of the hallway antics, screams at Halsey, "Go to hell."

CHAPTER THIRTY-ONE

I wake up in Greg's room with my cheek on Bristol's thigh and my legs hanging off the sofa. I must have fallen asleep at some point while faking it. With Greg's and Bristol's vastly different approaches to Stiletto Girl, there was no other way to find quiet but to fake sleep.

I tiptoe to the bathroom, travel attire finally dry, cheeks a bit chapped. I wish instantly that I had peed in the dark, because seeing my green eyes with makeup cried off and sleep lines that mirror Bristol's jeans across one cheek is too much too soon.

Swishing a capful of Greg's mouthwash, I wash my face with cold water and shaking hands, but the attempt at retrieving some of my mediocre looks is laughable.

When I leave the bathroom with better breath and a cool face, Greg is sitting on the edge of his bed wearing a pair of shorts and a tired expression. His hair is tousled like some midnight goblin messed with it in his sleep and made sure it wouldn't lie back down.

"Do you need anything?"

"My purse," I say in passing as I walk out of the bedroom and into the sitting area where thankfully, with her head in the corner of the

245

sofa, Bristol is still sleeping. I sit down pinning my hands between my knees, unsure what to do while my phone, inside my purse, is being held hostage by a cheater.

Greg, typically quiet but itching to say something, scratches his chest and runs his fingers through thick, matted, brown hair. "He's called my phone a hundred times. What do you want me to tell him?"

"Tell him I want my stuff."

He growls and heads back to his room only to return with his phone out so I can see the screen with Vance's response.

Van: *She can come get it.*

I grab his phone, anger seizing the last emotion I have for him, and I tap out a response.

Greg grabs the phone back and looks at the text I sent. "Really? *Fuck off.* That's what you wanted to say?"

The knock on the door interrupts whatever wisdom he was about to spout, and he stalks to the door, opening it with a mighty pull and a grumbled, "What?"

Someone other than Greg speaks, but it's not clear enough to hear who it is.

"That had better not be him. So help me God, if it is, Brenna, I may kill him," Bristol says, waking from her fitful beauty sleep.

"She's upset. How 'bout you give it a rest?" I hear Greg say.

"If she wants her stuff, she can talk to me."

Hiding won't get me home, and I must face him at some point. It would be preferable if I were stronger, not still attracted to him, and in a space with minimal input from Bristol, but that's not my reality.

"Fine," I hear Greg say, and I squeeze my eyes tight, pissed I'm trapped in this room belonging to a person loyal to Vance and not me. "Work it out or don't, I don't give a shit, just wrap it up."

I walk toward the window that looks out over the city and the street that fronts the hotel. Traffic, despite the early hour, is thick. It's still drizzling, and I find it ironic that the drought in California chooses the two days I'm mentally unstable to find some relief.

"Can we talk?" He doesn't sound like the cocky asshole I've grown to love. I choke on a sob as that registers. I loved him. I still love him.

I can see a vague reflection of him in the glass, but I don't focus on it. I just stare at the traffic, allowing Bristol to speak for me.

"No." Bristol snaps. "Give us our shit, and get the fuck out."

Vance blatantly ignores her and speaks directly to me. "Please?"

I look up from the traffic and stare at his reflection. "You have nothing to say that I want to hear." Tears choke off my throat. "I just want my stuff so I can go."

"Brenna, please?" Sedate as he asks, it's not the Vance I know.

I bawl, hanging my head, sick over the loss and hurting over the knowledge that this can't be fixed. "I want to go," I say through my tears, turning to face him finally. "Please, just let me go." I hate the cower in my voice, but it remains. "If you wanted me, you wouldn't have slept with her."

Unshaven and sleepless, he's still the best-looking man I've ever seen, and when he speaks, it chills me. "I didn't sleep with her." The exasperation in his voice strengthens. Last night he sounded defensive, today, he sounds desperate. "If you hear nothing else, hear that."

"Oh, my God! You were caught. She had Van Hatfield all over her."

"I'm not doing this with you, Bristol."

"Oh, yes—"

He cuts her off and points a dark glare at her. "If you want your shit back, you'll stay the fuck out of it. And before you open your trap to argue, it's not open for negotiation. Take a walk."

She wants to blast him, but she looks at me instead, thankfully knowing her cooperation is integral to us not having to catch a Greyhound with an IOU. I nod, giving her permission to leave me alone. These have got to be the hardest steps she's ever taken, because I know if it were me, my shoes would feel like lead as I walked away from her.

"You're such a dick," she spits as she storms out of the room and into the hall, screaming one last insult as she disappears down it.

He growls, gathers his temper, and softens his gaze as his eyes find mine. "I—"

Nipping his next excuse at its origin, I interrupt him. "I know what I saw. You can't explain that away no matter how many times you try."

"I know what you saw," he says, inching closer, "but it's not—"

"Don't come near me," I warn, holding my hand out to stop him from coming any closer. I know I couldn't stop him if he really wanted to get near me, but he stops. "I saw enough of her to know I want none of you now."

He rolls his eyes up to the ceiling, sighing heavily. He locks his hands behind his head and presses his head back into them. "She was a groupie, Brenna." More exasperation pours out of him on a heavy breath exhaled with force.

My disdain is heavy, laden with a disgust I couldn't have fathomed before last night. "I don't really care if she was a regular or a first. It's all the same to me."

"She wasn't there when I got into the shower."

In a visual betrayal of my despair, tears fall heavily against my cheeks and I wipe them away with my fingertips. I laugh with no amusement, my tears and laughter at bitter odds. "Let me guess, she came with the room as a perk? Pussy on a pillow."

"No." He doesn't acknowledge my sarcasm, skips right over my attempt at humorous indignation.

"Do you honestly expect me to believe that some random girl climbed into your bed uninvited? Go fuck yourself, Vance. I'm—"

"Let me talk." He cuts me off in the middle of my outburst, further angering me. "It happens, Brenna." There is no tenderness in that statement, and for the first time this morning, conviction mixes with his desperation. He presses in, closing off a few more inches separating us. "They have a friend on staff, or they are the staff, I don't fucking know. But it happens more than you think. Trust me, it's not a turn-on. Not one of them has ever gotten laid because of it, at least not in my room." He pauses and lowers his head, releasing another heavy breath and then, almost as an afterthought, adds, "We usually lock the deadbolt when we're in our rooms, but we can't really do anything to prevent it when we're not."

I stare at him, absorbing the new information but not swallowing it. "So, why didn't you lock the deadbolt?"

He lifts his head. Eyes fraught with distress, lack of sleep, and maybe defeat meet mine. "Halsey left while I was in the bathroom. He can't lock it from the outside." Still holding my stare, he draws in a breath. "I swear to God, I didn't know she was there until I walked out and saw her." Another sigh. "Just consider the possibility, that's all I'm asking."

My head swims. I believe it could happen. But he could just be well-versed in lying his way out of relationship indiscretions. He may think I'm young and naïve, but I've lived a long life through my mom.

"I need you to believe me, Brenna." He pleads with me, eyes so desperate I almost cave, but I can't dismiss the niggling bitch in the back of my head calling me a fool.

Nostrils the size of canyons widen as I draw in air. It takes several swallows to unload the Sahara Desert in my throat, but I manage to come within a few sandy grains of its entire depletion. "Why should I believe you over my own eyes?"

Tortured eyes hold mine. "Because I'm in love with you," he says softly.

If I hadn't just found a slut in his bed, I would be the happiest girl alive. Instead, it feels like a manipulative move to win me back. More tears pass my eyelashes. These ones aren't fueled by my anger or my hurt but have the distinguished mark of regret for not having heard those words sooner.

"I love you, Brenna." Before I know it, he is standing directly in front of me, able to touch me if he wants to. "I need you to know that."

Endless tears stream down my cheeks. Confusion rocks me to my core. I'm at a crossroads and have no idea which direction to go.

"I didn't sleep with her. I haven't wanted to sleep with anyone since meeting you. That's the God's honest truth. I know what I'm asking of you is a lot. And I'll be honest, I don't know that I could do it if you asked me to believe that you hadn't slept with the naked guy in your bed." He cups my face in his palms, tilting my head back so I have to look at him, and for the first time, I allow him to touch me without shirking it off. I want desperately to lean into his hand, close my eyes, and wait for his lips to touch mine, but I can't. Instead, I blink several times, dislodging more tears. "I'm begging you, Brenna, to take a leap of faith. Jump in feet first. Please believe me and not your eyes. Please?"

I hold his gaze, mine blurred but unwavering. I want to believe, but what fool discounts her own eyes for the word of a known player? I can think of only one. Two if Bristol is right. My mother. And me.

"Jump, Brenna," he whispers. "Please, jump." He's no longer disguising his pleas behind sentiment or smooth talk. It's blatantly desperate. With my eyes, I follow his Adam's apple as it bobbles in his throat. I can physically see his fear, distress, and that diminishing seed of hope in his eyes.

His thumbs slowly caress my cheeks, wiping away tears. I close my eyes and take in several breaths. "I—I . . . I need a few minutes."

He nods and takes a step back, giving me the space I desperately crave but no longer think I want. I hide a sob behind my trembling hands and run for the door. In the hallway, I take my first breath and then another and another, until my chest is heaving.

Straight from the elevator, through the hotel's turnstile glass front door and past the valet and bellhop, I bolt out into the drizzling rain. Somewhere out front, but away from the clamor of arriving guests and departing tourists, I lean forward, clutching my knees, exhausted by my emotions and worn thin by indecision.

This decision is likely to kill me, especially when I think back to how many times I've criticized my mother for her incredible weakness. In the dark of night and in the quiet of my room, it was easy to judge her when it wasn't my heart being crushed. To believe Vance means I have to swallow my pride and live with the regret and the shame if I'm wrong. To believe my eyes means I have to have wholehearted faith in myself not to have made a bad judgment call without all the facts. Being so focused on the bared snatch in front of me, did I miss other signs? I mean, the bitch still had her shoes on, and now that I look back on it, didn't look like she'd recently been satisfied. And by the way she was talking, she was still waiting for him and wasn't happy I might be joining in.

Holy shit!

My legs won't hold me, and I sit down on the concrete walkway, as ungraceful as I am haggard-looking. I have a nasty habit of rushing to judgment where Vance is concerned, and I don't know if I'm capable of being impartial and loving him too. Holding him accountable for what's been said about him in the press has been unfair to him, but I don't know how to separate rumor from fact or past from the present.

I have no idea how much time passes, but it's not enough for him to come looking for me yet, and my clothes aren't so wet that hypothermia has set in. In the last twelve hours, I have sobbed until I couldn't breathe, seethed until I couldn't feel, and loved like I've loved no other, but at this moment, I wish I were empty. This mass of emotion, heightened by my indecision, drains the last of my strength, and this time I cry for my weakness instead of my loss.

At the threshold of Greg's room, I take one last deep breath, push the heavy door in, and step inside. I'm dripping wet, hair stringy and stuck to my face. My clothes cling to my curves, and my shirt, as I saw with horror in the glass of the turnstile doors, is see-through.

After informing me that Bristol is "contained in Corky's room," Greg excuses himself to the bedroom, leaving Vance and me alone. "Are you okay?" Vance asks without moving toward me. He looks tired, and for the first time, now that I can see past my own ache, I notice his fear.

I nod then shake my head, confused. Is there a way to answer that? Fresh tears roll down my cheeks, and I'm beginning to wonder when the well will run dry. I take in a breath to clear my throat of the remaining Sahara. "I think I want to jump."

CHAPTER THIRTY-TWO

Even though Vance is adamant he didn't cheat on me and I've decided I really do believe him, returning to our chaotic normal isn't automatic. In the two weeks since Stiletto Girl waved her snatch in my face, I've barely seen Vance. My school schedule is heavy, and Vance, understandably preoccupied with winning the National League Championship Series against Chicago, hasn't had the luxury of free time either. We've had to improvise what normal couples take for granted after a major event, but makeup sex on FaceTime isn't perfect when one of us can't take dirty commands without laughing. As much as I wanted to, I wasn't even able to attend any of the LCS games before last night, but that was the most important one—a home game that decided the series. Being there for the win was amazing. Seeing Vance lose himself in the celebration with his teammates when he struck out the final batter, off-the-charts amazing. Not having the ghost of Stiletto Girl in the middle of every fucking thing we do, did, or are about to do, triple amazing. The few chances we've had at makeup sex have been fantastic, but I'm ready to move on to mind-blowing I-haven't-seen-you-in-two-weeks sex. That's the sex I want to have today, and that's the sex I'm forced to rush my prep for because he's home early from his team meeting.

I strip off my cropped sweats and panties, hopping on one leg like a jackhammer because my heel is stuck and I'm in too much of a hurry to find another way. Finally free, I kick them beneath the table and start peeling off the rest of my clothing, which I accomplish with the approximate gracefulness of an ungainly rhino.

Finally naked, I frantically position myself backward on one of the kitchen chairs, straddling the seat. I look over the top rung and place my arms across it. Thankfully, I already have makeup and hair done for this little sex surprise that is now as much of a surprise for me as it's going to be for him. I feel sexy, except that I'm out of breath from hopping on one foot, and my girl is sore from last night's combination celebration and makeup sex.

Vance drops his gym bag onto the floor as his eyes land on me, and the only noise I hear is the hissing of his breath as he draws it in. I smile, feeling the slightest bit of red creep up my neck and into my cheeks.

"Damn, Brenna." He doesn't know whether to come and get me or stare at me. His movements are staggered—inch forward, stop, stare, inch forward, stop, stare. It's the dance of a man at war with his needs.

When he gets to me, he tucks a finger beneath my chin and lifts upward so I look up at him. He leans down, kisses me hard and growls into my mouth. I am wrecked heat when he slides a finger up my sex and hisses. "Is this for me?" he whispers, feeling the evidence of my arousal.

I flush to my eyelashes.

"We have an hour, Brenna. With you like this, I can't promise gentle. You sure you're ready for that kind of intensity?" Vance's voice is deep and tinged with a lusty rasp, but despite all the pleasure that tone promises, I hear nothing but the screeching sound of everything coming to an abrupt halt in my brain.

"Wait! What? Why do we only have an hour?" I try to stand, but he puts a heavy hand on my shoulder bending down to kiss my neck.

"We're supposed to be at Coi's at eight. The team party? I texted you." He licks my earlobe, temporarily shifting my focus back to my throbbing girl parts. Eyes closed, I let myself fall back into the moment, pushing my disappointment aside.

Reading me, and knowing what we both need, he asks, "Wanna show up late?"

Lip pinned between my teeth, I nod.

VANCE, DRESSED IN A BLACK SUIT, STOPS OUTSIDE OF THE RESTAURANT to speak to the press gathered at the entrance. With his hand protectively tight around mine, he's courteous but brief in his answer when they ask him if he's leaving the Renegades after the postseason.

"We've still got one more team to beat. That's my focus," he says politely.

One of the reporters, a bald guy wearing wire-rimmed glasses and a smile that at first seems genuine but comes with reservations, raises a hand, and Vance leads us toward him. Vance stops, leans in, and takes his quiet question. "How do you feel about your performance tonight? You had a great run until Stanger got that hit off of you."

I feel his hand twitch around mine, but it's the only sign that he's uncomfortable. "I think we had a great game," he replies. "We're headed to Texas, aren't we?" He grins, taps the reporter on the side of the shoulder and moves us along, avoiding any further questions as the doors to the restaurant open for us.

Inside, the restaurant teems with laughter and loud conversations that carry over the soft instrumental music playing through the sound system. I recognize Halsey standing at the bar, hand wrapped around a half-empty glass. He smiles and waves, heading toward us.

They do some sort of handshake that seems ridiculous for two guys who probably showered together today. He turns his attention to me, hugging me in a way only Halsey can. "You look beautiful," he says, taking an open look at me. "I like the red."

I take the compliment and shake off a blush, especially since I had fifteen minutes to figure out what to wear and touch up my post-sex hair and makeup. "You look pretty sharp too."

He lifts a shoulder, flashes a dimple, and waves at someone beyond me. "I think there's someone here to see you."

I turn my head in the direction he waved, and after looking between bodies, I spot the one person missing from this perfect day.

Bristol, cheeks glistening in pink neon tears, stands within the glow of a dangling lamp emitting pink light in a blue-hued room. She is stunning, and would be even if we were on speaking terms. We haven't spoken any more than necessary since I chose to believe Vance, so seeing her now, looking happy to see me, makes my hands tremble. Wearing a body-hugging dress that absorbs the pink tint of the lamp, she makes her way toward me.

I can't wait for her to reach me, and despite the height of my heels, I run toward her. We hug in the middle of a crowd that moved for our embrace, and I cry into her neck as she cries into mine. She smells like flowers and feels like home as my heart finds its missing beat.

"I love you," she whispers into my ear. "I will always love you."

I nod against her face, smile-crying, happier than I've been since San Francisco over a week ago. "I love you too. Thank you for coming."

She pulls away, still close and hands still on me. "It was douche canoe. He did it. Otherwise, I'd still be at home wearing jammies and eating peanut butter with my finger."

I look over my shoulder at Vance standing beside Halsey, who beams and toasts me in the air with a glass of ice. Vance looks solemn but appeased, and I mouth the words, "Thank you." Certainly not enough gratitude for the gift he's given me on what is really his night, but suitable for the mixed company. He offers one simple nod and a brief grin before turning toward the bar.

"I can't believe you're here," I say, turning back to Bristol.

"Sorry I couldn't make it for the game last night. I wanted to, but I had to work. Damn. Who knew they'd win it? Oh, and I'm still pissed off at you," she says, loud enough to be overheard.

"I don't care," I say, grabbing hold of her face to look her in the eyes. "Be mad. Just love me. That's all I ask."

She hugs me to her, squeezing tight, and for Bristol, that's the equivalent of a full-mouth kiss. "We'll talk later. We're here to celebrate, not hash things out. I guess even cheaters can be thoughtful."

I groan, choosing for the sake of our reunion and Vance's night to accept her temporary truce. She touches her head to mine and puts her arm around me, steering us both toward the bar where Vance and Halsey have been joined by Corky.

As I head toward Vance, Bristol aims right for Halsey, the king of flirtation himself, and a reserved Corky who has yet to determine whether Bristol is crazy or just over-protective.

Spotting me, Vance reaches a hand out and draws me in when I take it, kissing my forehead.

I look up, eyelashes struggling to maintain the well of tears behind them. "I can't believe you did this."

A small smile forms, sad mostly, but progressing. "We may not see eye to eye on your sister, but she's still your sister. I won't ever be the reason you don't see her." He tilts my chin up with the back of his finger. "No tears."

"I love you." I smile and turn to the conversation between Halsey, Corky, and Bristol.

Seeing that she has my attention again, Bristol announces, "Uncle Rodney sent me with money for a celebratory round of shots. But he said it had to be Jameson, or he wouldn't buy."

Halsey claps a hand on the bar. "Irish whiskey it is."

With Corky, Halsey, and Vance flanking Bristol and me, and Uncle Rodney on video smiling from my phone, we toast to the championship win, Uncle Rodney, and beautiful women, before taking our shots of Jameson. Bristol and I are used to Jameson—I'm pretty sure it's still what's in the bottle behind the bookcase in the storage room—so it's an easy shot to kill for me, Bristol, and Halsey, who takes the shot like it's water, but Corky and Vance are not as well-primed. They take a chaser as we all say goodbye and thank you to Uncle Rodney.

Normally, Bristol would be all over that, teasing her way into another shot and a flirtatious battle, and Vance would fall for it, buying another round to prove he can handle the shot as well as we can—but before he has a chance, Bristol signals the bartender for two more. She hands him a twenty and pushes one of the shots toward Vance. I stare, completely out of my comfort zone but inclined to let it play out since I have no clue where it's heading. Only after Bristol signals with a head nod does Vance pick up his shot, looking just as uncertain as me. "To winning," she toasts, eyes intent on his.

"Why do I get the feeling that means something different to you than it does to me?" he asks.

Bristol shrugs and just keeps smiling.

After returning her look for a few seconds, he touches his glass to hers. "To winning."

That they both love me enough to put their differences aside, if only for one night, means the world, even if the underlying tone is unmistakably adversarial. Somehow, though, as happy as I am right now, the rift has never felt more prominent.

CHAPTER THIRTY-THREE

J OCK THE GIANT SLAYER. I read the headline as Vance drops the November issue of *Jock* magazine right next to my half-empty bowl of sugar and Wheaties.

Vance, on a backdrop of Renegade red, is front and center on the cover dressed in his uniform and holding a baseball in his right hand.

Lena nailed it.

I fly into his arms, the barstool wobbling beneath me. "Oh my God," I shriek. "You got the cover!"

"It's not a big deal."

I sneer at his dismissal and hop back up on the stool to finish looking at the magazine. It's only been two days since the Renegades beat the Houston Astros in game seven of the World Series, but it's been close to a month since they beat the Giants.

"How long have you had this?" I ask.

Vance, standing beside me leaning over the counter, flips impatiently to the back third of the magazine where, in several of the photographs, I am featured with him. "It just came out."

Too shocked to do much else, I stare at one picture in particular until he snaps me out of it.

"Gorgeous, huh?" he says softly, before kissing the tip of my nose.

I recall it like it was yesterday, including the hissy fit he threw when Lena asked me to take off my shirt and bra. I thought he was going to come unglued and tear the place apart. But Lena merely stuck her pointer finger in the air to quiet him and uttered a simple four words: "My vision, your veto." And with that, this picture was born.

The picture is intimate with both of us topless, but it's also playful, and I stare at it, completely in awe. We're chest to chest, me facing away from the camera with my cheek against his pec. I'm palming a baseball behind my back while my other hand is looped around his neck. His hand is on my hip below the waist of my jeans, and he's looking at the camera with a serious face that can only be described as breathtaking. He looks vulnerable and achingly handsome. My heart melts.

Looking at myself as anything other than Bristol's twin sister is still foreign, but I'm starting to see myself in my own ray of light instead of in the shadow of hers. On that emotional thought, I switch my gaze to Vance to see if I can gather what his thoughts are based on his expression. The pictures they selected for the article allow us to keep our privacy while allowing Vance's fans into his private world. It couldn't be more perfect. I respect Lena even more than I already did.

"Okay, that's enough." Vance tries to close the magazine, and I slap his hand away.

"I want to read it."

"It's boring shit," he says, and swipes the magazine from me.

"What are you hiding?" I'm suddenly worried about the content.

"Nothing. I don't want to make a big deal out of it. I just wanted you to see the pictures of us."

"And I love them. I'm having them framed."

He grins. "Working on it. Should have them back Tuesday."

"Are you for real right now?" My elated squeal draws a wince from him and his sensitive ears.

He snakes an arm around me and draws me in, growling into my ear. "I wanted to get laid."

"As if that's ever been a problem for you." I slip out of his grasp to reach around him for the magazine he thinks he's distracted me from.

He stops me with a sidestep, expression contemplative, immersed in something private that reflects in his eyes but hasn't yet escaped his mouth.

Vance seldom, if ever, talks about his feelings or shares what's bugging him. I usually have to dig, and unless I'm persuasively naked, he doesn't budge. I know better than to quiz him now, but damn it if I don't want to.

I press my body against him and his arm winds around me, his hand grabbing my ass affectionately. I touch his cheek like I'm touching a delicate painting. "I'm going to read that article here or at a viewing party with Bristol. It's up to you."

He hangs his head. "Can we drop it for now?"

"What? Did you share intimate details about me? Is the world going to know I sound like a dolphin when I have an orgasm?"

He chuckles. "You don't sound like a dolphin."

"That's not really an answer."

"No. I didn't kiss and tell."

"Did you break up with me?"

This draws an irritated look from him that matches the exhale of air and he tries to pull away from me, but I'm persistent with a grip on his waistband. I look up at him, my eyes expressive enough that words aren't necessary.

"I didn't break up with you." He uses his hands to push me away, and I stand there feeling a bit dejected. I watch curiously as he heads toward the staircase that leads to his bedroom, but he stops short and picks up the magazine. Making no real show, he hands it to me, jaw clenched. "Here." He waits until I take it fully then walks away. "I was a bit more open than I normally am, and I don't really care for the outcome." Halfway up the staircase, he utters, "Cancel the viewing party."

When I get upstairs after reading the article, he is fresh out of the shower and standing in front of the mirror, body on full display as he reaches for his toothbrush. After all this time, I'm still mesmerized by his body and its capabilities. I think when God created man, this is the image he had in mind. Not the bloated, too-indulgent, human form most of us have.

In the mirror, he catches me staring at him. Instead of offering an excuse, I slip behind him and wrap him up in my arms, my cheek against his damp back, my hands splayed across his pecs. He lowers his head and covers one of my hands with his. Muscles, without prompting, swell and stretch, elongating into beautiful strands of perfection as he reaches and puts an arm around me.

Beneath my touch, he's hard muscle and erratic heartbeat. I can feel his irritation escape as I press my lips to his bare back, sneaking in a kiss before I speak. "I liked it. I don't know what you're so upset about."

He turns slowly in my embrace and wraps my hair up in his fingers, tilting my head back with a slight tug. "I'm a 'no comment' kind of guy, but because of the pictures in the magazine and our very public outings, I can't clam up and not answer questions about you. I invited their curiosity, but I also want to protect your privacy," he says, lowering his mouth to my neck. He places a kiss on my throat, and the heat of it blossoms all over me. If he wanted my attention, he's got it. Pulling his mouth away, he adds, "I don't want to make you feel slighted by something I've said to shut them up. And I don't want them to have all the answers because I don't want to slight you. I'm not very good at walking that fine line just yet."

I nod, entranced by both his eyes and his heart. "I love you," I whisper, pressing my body into his. "I know none of this is easy for you."

He wraps his arms around me, smothering me against his chest where the fresh scent of his body wash clings. "I love you too, and I'll get better with this, I promise."

My phone, sitting in my bag in Vance's bedroom, sings Bristol's ringtone, and as with any sign of Bristol, Vance tenses. He drops his arms and grips the counter behind him. I remain clinging, reluctant to part with his tenderness for fear that Bristol will once again hijack his mood.

"Get it," he says, pushing off the counter. "She won't stop until you do."

The ringtone dies before I can get to it but bursts back to life within a few seconds as Vance predicted. "Hello?"

"I'm here," she says without an ounce of warmth.

"You can come in. I've got to finish getting dressed and grab my stuff."

"I'll wait out here," she says, deadpan.

I toss my phone in the bag after she hangs up. I hustle through my tasks, sniff Vance's T-shirt—because who knows how long it will be before I see him again—and grab the last of my things from his room. He's waiting downstairs for me when I emerge with my bag in hand, my hair still tousled, and without a stitch of makeup on.

He should be more relaxed than ever now that his season is behind him and only mandatory press and obligatory celebrations are ahead of him, but instead he looks like his asshole is burning. I drop my bag at my feet and step toward him without it.

He grabs hold of me, a rough edge to the well-intentioned gesture. With one hand laced in my hair and the other pressed into my lower back, he presses me into him, and I look up, meeting his intense gaze.

"Is it okay if I come see you for the weekend? I have a charity game in Anaheim on Saturday, but . . ." he trails off, kissing my temple, "I'd be happy to make up the time later." Pulling away, he grins. "I promise I won't disappoint."

"You've never disappointed." I say it softly, realizing Uncle

263

Rodney is the only other person I can say that about. "I won't turn you down, though."

The Silver Stallion's horn wails, and I snap my jaw closed to grind my teeth.

"Best not keep her waiting," he whispers against my mouth before taking a firm hold of my lips. He kisses me hard, tongue dominating, hand on the back of my head keeping pressure.

I never want to open my eyes. I want this kiss to extend long into my future, but it can't, and we're both reminded of that by another blaring horn call.

"I love you," I say, lips still pressed to his.

"Me too." He smacks my ass then picks up my bag, and together we walk out to meet an impatient Bristol, who despite my protests to the contrary, still believes Vance cheated on me.

"Morning, Bristol," Vance says, opening the car door to put my bag in the back seat. His tone is playful, knowing hers will be at best cordial but teetering toward sarcastic.

"Is it still morning?" It's cordial sarcasm with an irritable smirk accompaniment. Not openly hostile, but nowhere close to friendly.

"Yep. Still morning." He grabs my hand and kisses me. "Call me when you get to L.A. I'll see you Friday night."

Bristol's aloof demeanor ebbs slightly when it's just her and me, but in general, the distance between us has continued to grow as I spend more time with Vance. Before Stiletto Girl, I expected she would eventually adjust to a new normal that included Vance, but that fiasco has only given her something to hang her resentment on.

"Does he still taste like that girl in San Fran?" She doesn't look at me, but I can see her face plenty clear with her hair pulled back into a ponytail.

My nostrils suck in the heated air of the car and the icy stench of her demeanor now that she's fired the first shots. "Stop it! You're not being fair."

"Fair would be you honoring our pact not to let boys come between us."

I shift in my seat, pulling my knee up, and face her head-on while she side-eyes me. "A boy is coming between us because you don't want me to be with him. That's not a pact I agreed to. A boy is coming between us because you're being a judgmental bitch."

"He had a naked girl in his bed. HE was naked. If it kills me, Brenna, I will make you see him for what he is—a cheater—since you can't seem to see it for yourself. That's the pact I made, to always put you first."

I blow out an exasperated breath. "Vance didn't cheat on me."

"Then why are you always on edge when you're not with him? Worried he's cheating?"

"No."

"Bullshit."

"You want the truth?"

She nods.

"I'm worried he's going to get tired of all your shit and decide I'm not worth fighting you for."

Bristol slows her roll, her body relaxing, a sigh signaling a change. "If you weren't worth fighting for, I wouldn't still be harping on this and he wouldn't be making the efforts he is." She reaches over, grabbing my hand. "I'll try, but if you want me to accept this relationship, I'm going to need more than just your faith in him."

CHAPTER THIRTY-FOUR

"**Y**ou look tired."

It's the first thing Vance says to me when I answer his video call. "I am. But not too tired for you." I offer a pleasant smile despite the exhaustion I'm fighting having been up late all week finishing assignments.

Vance keeps the irritation out of his voice, but he can't keep it out of the creases in his forehead. "I don't like seeing you so tired. I'll be glad when this is all done."

The months of weekend commutes to L.A. for Vance are done, and I'll be home this weekend for winter break. It's a good thing, because he's starting to lose his patience for the college grind. Between homework, work, Bristol, my roommates, and me being drained, our weekends come down to a couple of hours where we get to enjoy each other alone. The distance is hard on both of us.

Video chats like the one we're having now are typically late at night when Bristol is out or asleep. Appeasing her and accommodating him has become a full-time job I can barely keep up with.

"What are your plans when you get home?" Vance asks me, like he's not sure where he'll fit into the picture.

"Depends on how long my test takes, but I planned on going home first to drop off my stuff and see my mom. Then I'll have someone drop me off at your house, if that's okay?"

"Okay? It's more than okay. I'll pick you up, though. I have a surprise if you haven't already made plans."

"You're my plans."

"Then I'll pick you up."

I grin. "I don't need a surprise. I just need you."

"You get both." He sighs heavily, rolling over to his side to prop on a mound of pillows. This is where we should transition to phone sex, but I always laugh, so it has no appeal, and we just end up talking about how our week has been. He's been playing a lot of golf with Halsey. My routine never changes, and I leave out the days I'm too tired to brush my teeth or take a shower. He doesn't need to know I have swamp girl tendencies when I've run out of steam.

"Babe, you're killin' me. I hate seeing you so tired. I don't want to be the reason you're exhausted when you get here. Get some sleep. I'll see you in a few days."

Smiling weakly, I blow him a kiss and close the call.

"WHERE ARE WE GOING?" I ASK WHEN I REALIZE WE'RE HEADING OUT of Milagro Beach.

Vance glances into the rear-view mirror, which I'm convinced is a stall tactic after I follow up my question with, "I'm not dressed for anything fancy." I didn't say it, but he isn't either, though he looks distractingly beautiful, dressed in a ball cap, jeans, and a long-sleeved, blue Henley pushed to his elbows. "Are you going to answer me?"

"It's a surprise."

A few hours later we check into some gorgeous hotel on a bluff overlooking the rough Pacific Ocean. It's cold. The wind whips my hair into a tangled frenzy and carries with it a salty-scented mist lifted right from the sea. I inhale deeply, loving the smell and the feeling of cool humidity on my cheeks and lips.

The pale, ginger kid tasked with seeing us to our room deposits Vance's bags inside the door. "Thank you," Vance says, slipping him a fifty. His face, full of freckles, bears the quickest hint of recognition when he looks at Vance, but he errs on the side of professionalism and bows out gracefully, closing the door quietly behind him.

I'm temporarily awestruck by the sheer size of the place as I step deeper into what I thought would be a hotel room and not a damn condo. The little girl in me wants to do cartwheels from wall to wall to measure its size.

It has all the amenities of a hotel room, just on a much larger scale. A white-washed four-poster canopied bed built out of some freak-of-nature-sized piece of driftwood looks directly at a gas fireplace topped by a mantel decorated with poinsettias, white glittered ribbon, and starfish. The view of the Pacific is visible from a wall of windows you have to climb up two steps to stand beside. A table for two also sits on the platform in front of the windows and boasts a tray of chocolate-covered strawberries, champagne, and an oblong box wrapped in red foil paper.

I look at Vance, who shrugs and offers a tentative smile before stepping in front of the fireplace to light it.

I follow him, stepping down off the platform to stand beside him. "Um." I stare straight at him, eyebrows lifted. "Did you forget to tell me something?"

He shoves his hands into his pockets like a chastised boy. "No. Surprises are usually a secret." Unlike me, he stares into the fire, finding something in it more interesting than my displeasure at being without a gift or even a lace underthing to make up for it.

Firelight dances across his face, highlighting his dark hair in an amber glow that makes it look like his head is ringed with fire, because he's too good in bed for it to be a halo. "I'm talking about that on the table, not the destination."

He grins, not even trying to hide his amusement. "It's all a surprise," he says, still not glancing at me. "The next two days are the surprise."

"Two days?" I drag the two words out, shocked. It's three days before Christmas. Bristol is going to have a conniption fit if I'm not there to go shopping for Mom's standard gift of See's Candy and whatever else we can find as we stroll the mall making fun of people in their Christmas sweaters.

He nods, still grinning. "I've had to share you with Bristol and your roommates for the last few months. I want you all to myself somewhere they can't pop in as they please or call you away."

"We stayed in hotels alone when you visited me, Vance. It's not like you had to sleep on a blowup mattress between mine and Bristol's beds."

"I've still had to share you, and for the next two days, I don't. What do you want to do first? Are you hungry?"

"Vance!" I shriek his name while simultaneously grabbing his arm. "I don't have clothes for two days. Hell, to be honest, I don't have good-enough clothes for this hotel."

Turning sideways, he looks at me, eyes alight with the flickering firelight. "You don't need clothes." His deep voice along with the heat in his gaze manages to do what the fire hasn't yet accomplished, and my body heats expectantly.

He steps toward me and tilts his head down to look at my chest, then flicks his mischievous blue eyes back up to mine. "I want you naked."

"Fuck," I say beneath my breath, earning his grin as he lifts my shirt over my head and unclasps my bra.

He brushes his lips against my ear, leaving a soft breath there when he whispers, "I love your dirty mouth." After sliding my bra straps down my shoulders, he tosses my bra to the side, and an even softer growl next to my ear rumbles my chest. "I love everything about you." His index finger runs up my bared stomach from the waistband of my pants to the bottom of my sternum. My skin tingles where he touches and hums when he palms my breast. His lips move

269

once again beside my ear. "I love your tits." I feel his hand sneak around me to cup an ass cheek. "God, I love your ass." My eyes are closed, savoring every blind second of his caresses. As I feel his hand come between us, every inch of my flesh responds like his touch is new. My anticipation builds the lower his hand goes, and when he finally stops to caress my girl over my jeans, my thighs quiver. "Mmm, I want this." He covers another one of my moaned curses with his mouth and quiets all further dialogue with his tongue.

Holy shit. That was hot. If I could melt any further into his body I would. I'm like uncontained liquid, and I feel like I'm spilling out everywhere making a mess on the plush carpet.

Eyes now open, and minutes from an embarrassing orgasm brought on by his words alone, I run my hands up underneath his shirt to feel his skin and the hard contours of his muscles. I manage to get his shirt up and over his head with only a minor mishap on his nose. I'll never manage his pants, so I focus on getting my pants down my thighs, shimmying back and forth like the hula dancer on Uncle Rodney's dashboard when he drives down pot-hole-ridden San Mateo Drive. Vance, way more aesthetically pleasing to watch while he undresses, is naked before I am and is unfortunately an amused witness to my undignified strip show.

Two feet from me, he pads across the open space to wrap an arm around my waist, eyes intent on mine. The tattoos along his arms look like one singular black piece in the odd lighting of the fire and waning outdoor light. Loving the ink covering his skin, I kiss the bottom of his shoulder right where it joins his bicep. He runs his other hand over my hip and down my thigh, making several lazy trips up and down it, drawing up patches of goose bumps.

"Are you cold?" he asks, pulling his head back to look at me.

"No." I am, but I don't want him to alter his path because of it. I kiss his chest, and his hand on my hip rises to the back of my neck and fists my hair.

He tugs, forcing me to look up at him, and taking my mouth hard, he leaves no question as to who is going to be in charge of my body tonight. I'm so completely lost in him, I don't know how many taps of his foot against my ankle it takes before I finally part my feet. With a light touch, he runs a finger over my slit, and I moan into his mouth, receiving from him in return a tiny groan and a nip on my bottom lip.

I climb onto my tiptoes, holding onto both of his biceps as one, then two of his fingers enter me, and his mouth latches onto my neck. Out of instinct, because lord knows I'm too immersed in my own pleasure to think of his, I stroke his erection. He groans against my neck, the deep noise rumbling my throat, shoulder, and chin.

He's rough when he spins me so that my back is against his chest, our bodies flush. I like this bold Vance whose sole focus isn't on my well-being, but so intent on my gratification he's willing to forgo his. Holding me firm with one arm across my chest and the other around my waist, I can feel his erection in the small of my back and at the top of my ass. As I'm on the verge of questioning him, he halts all coherent communication when he drops one hand to massage my clit with one finger while another two fingers on his other hand roll and pinch my nipple with near textbook-perfect pressure. I whimper between speechless parted lips, never happier to be without words.

"I want to hear more of that," he whispers against my cheek. "I love it when you own it, Brenna."

A moan, thick in my throat, escapes, and I squirm in his embrace, but he only tightens around me and ups the pressure in both places. "Feel it, Brenna." Both hands move in their own steady rhythm, evoking the same response but moving at different speeds, motions, and pressures. "I want you to come." He lowers his head and bites my neck, leaving the tiniest bit of sting behind. "And I want you to come a lot."

"GET DRESSED," HE SAYS, SITTING UP AND TAKING HIS ARM OUT FROM under my head. I need more than a few minutes to catch my breath after that love session, but he's acting like he didn't just take me three different ways. "Let's go to a nice restaurant." He rolls over, covering my side with his body. He plants a kiss on the side of my head. "And then we'll go on a real date. Like, to the movies or something."

"A nice restaurant?" I laugh and he sits up a little.

"What? Would you prefer McDonald's?"

"No, smartass." I roll onto my back, feeling infinitely better and with a bit more energy than I had two minutes ago. For someone who runs and surfs, I swear I have no stamina for sex with Vance. "The only clothes I have are barely good enough for takeout."

He pops up like it's nothing and gets to his feet. I gawk as he walks to where his jeans lie in a heap on the floor. He pulls them on, and I close my mouth as he covers his firm ass. Doing up the button, he turns to me, and I refocus my attention on his abs. "Your bag is right over there, next to mine." He gestures with a head jerk, and I look at the two bags sitting at the foot of the bed.

"How'd I get a bag?"

"Bristol packed it."

I grab up his shirt before he can and slip it over my head. "Bristol?!" I chirp her name loudly, hoping against hope that's not the name he said.

He grins, plops down on the bed, and leans back on his hands. "I got her Katy Perry tickets."

"No shit?" I ponder this. If she knew about the tickets, I may be good. If not, I'm screwed.

I hold my breath and stalk to the bags, Vance's shirt hanging like a shower curtain over me. I unzip the bag I probably should have recognized, and I start to pull out the items Bristol packed. Toolbag Carl's blue plaid boxer shorts top the heap, and below them a pair of fringed novelty socks and my comfy, sweat-stained, washed-twice-in-two-years bra. Cushioned between a homemade cropped tank top and high-waisted jean shorts from my mom's bottom drawer is a framed picture of Bristol. I can't wear any of this. Not a single fucking thing. And where in the hell are my fresh panties? I toss everything onto the bed except for the bra, which I hide beneath the huge package of Always super-absorbent maxi pads.

"What the hell is this?" Vance picks up the striped boxers that not all that long ago cupped Toolbag's sack, and I panic, snatching them back like a thief.

"I'm going to kill her."

CHAPTER THIRTY-FIVE

"I'm sorry," Vance says for the hundredth time. "I honestly thought she'd pack a few outfits and we'd be good."

I look at him from over the top of my champagne flute as I plop onto his lap and straddle him, wrapping my hands around his neck. "There are worse things than being stuck in this room with you all weekend," I say, kissing him softly. "I'm sorry Bristol ruined your plans, but I'm not at all upset about the alternate possibilities." I kiss him again, shimmying up his lap to get a little closer, isolating my girl right over his new erection.

He chuckles and wedges his hands beneath my ass, lifting me up a fraction. "I'm not as sorry as I sound," he admits, grinning.

I kiss him again, this time with tongue, and taste the lingering fizz of champagne. His hands squeeze my ass. "How 'bout you open that gift?" He nods toward the oblong box sitting beside the only strawberry left on the plate. "Then we can get to other things." He squeezes my ass again.

I shake my head like I used to do when Uncle Rodney would ask me if I ate the last Hershey's kiss out of his candy bowl. "I don't want a gift," I say softly.

"Open the gift." His blue eyes are stern, and I can feel his shoulders tense beneath my hands. He pulls the hand closest to the table out from underneath my ass and grabs the box, handing it to me.

I hold onto it for a long time looking between him and it before I slowly tear the foil paper away. It's a black velvet box, the kind that cushions jewelry, and I can't bring myself to open it.

"Just open it."

I stare at him for a few moments and then slowly open the black velvet box, its hinges creaking as I lift the lid. My mouth drops, and I stare like an imbecile at the key fob lying in the cushioned box. A key fob? A key fob only goes to one thing I know of. I close the lid and jump at the noise it makes when it snaps shut. "I can't accept this." I set the box on the table at the same time I climb off of his lap with an unladylike shot of my womanhood.

I don't know where to go or where to place the anxiety that is rising in my body. I leave Vance sitting beside the table and stalk down the steps of the raised platform just so I can walk aimlessly in a circle by myself.

I feel Vance's hands on my arms before I know he's even moved. He stills me before wrapping me in his arms, my back against his chest. "What's the matter?"

I stiffen and jerk out of his hold, turning to face him. "Who gives someone a car as a gift?"

He tries to close the space between us, but I put up my hand to halt him and take a few steps back, deepening the separation further. He concedes and remains where he is, though a heavy exhale contradicts his outward calm. "Someone who wants to see you more than once a fucking year. It's not like I can't afford it."

"Vance, this is a gift." I gesture around the room indicating the room but meaning the entire getaway. "Victoria's Secret panties are a gift. A DVD is a gift. Cars are not gifts."

"If you want gifts like that, date Cum Bag Carl." He stalks up the steps to the platform, grabs the velvet box off the table, and retrieves the key fob, tossing the empty box back down with a hard thwack that adds heat to the tension. "Get dressed!" The barked command offsets the funny in his butchering of Toolbag's name.

I stomp to my pants lying beside our love pallet and shove my legs inside them, curious as to why I'm obeying him. I button them with the dexterity of sausage fingers and practically rip my nail off.

Vance is shirtless and standing in the open doorway with his hand on the edge of the door when I find him a few minutes later. "It's about damn time. For someone who only has boxers in her bag, you sure took long enough."

"I don't think I want to go."

"I'm tired of hearing about what you don't want. Let's go." He opens the door and waits for me to proceed into the hallway ahead of him.

Reluctantly, I proceed through, talking as I wait on him to shut the door. "Where are we going?"

"To show you what you're turning down."

"It's *here*?" I screech, surprised. He just turns and walks down the hallway. In silence, we head down to the lobby, his expression stern, his body tight.

Arctic air blasts my face, and my bare toes curl the instant they hit the concrete. Vance either doesn't care or hasn't yet noticed we aren't dressed for Northern California's coastal winter weather and treks right on over to my so-called present.

With the press of a button, he unlocks a beautiful white BMW that probably cost more than I will make in ten years. He jerks the door open exposing the soft, gray leather interior. He turns a hardened gaze toward me, and I match it with a stubborn one of my own. "The least you can do is sit in it."

"I don't need to. I still can't accept it." I don't move, my feet, toes curled under, remain planted on the walkway fronting the hotel.

"That's it? You're still going to refuse it?"

I nod, eyes locked on my feet, wondering silently if my refusal is about more than just the price tag. I'm still horribly insecure about being left. Vance trying to bind our relationship with something tangible spikes my fears, and I realize I still struggle to have faith in the staying power of any relationship other than the one I share with Bristol.

"Un-fucking-believable." He slams the car door, stalks toward me until he's within a foot of me. "Why, Brenna?"

"It's too much. People already think I'm dating you for your money; I don't need a car to confirm it. My whole life I've been categorized as something I'm not. I don't need to add gold-digger to that list." I didn't even know I feared that until it slips out unfiltered. I have thicker skin than that, but suddenly I realize my thick skin also has scars.

I've never seen his eyebrows higher. "Who cares what people think? I know better. You know better. Your family knows better. Who else fucking matters?" He shoves his hand through his hair, turns away from me to take an angry breath, and then faces me again, agitated. "I want to see you, Brenna. I love you. This long-distance shit is killing me, and if a car of your own will make that easier for us, why wouldn't you take it? Unless we're a temporary thing. Is that it?"

My issues run deeper than I knew, and this car has shined a huge, glaring spotlight on all of them. I love him. It's about the only thing I'm certain of these days, and I don't want him thinking anything else. "Nothing about you is temporary. I love you. I just can't accept the car. Please don't read more into it than that."

Vance turns away from me, hands laced behind his head as he draws in a heavy breath. I've ruined everything, and he's still trying not to lose his patience with me. I reach out to him, touching his bare back, his skin cool to the touch even beneath my cool fingertips.

"Don't go!" Vance fills in the silence as I'm contemplating how to salvage this.

"Excuse me?"

"If you won't take the car, don't go," he says, and then turns to face me. "Don't go back to L.A. If anything is going to come between us, it's the distance and Bristol's influence, not your concern about gold-digging rumors. Don't go." His voice is low, drawing my attention, not for what was said, but for its ache. He can't be serious.

I'm stunned. I can't move or speak or do anything more than snap my jaw shut to prevent the escape of whatever unintelligible thing might come out of my mouth. A few deep breaths later, I feel confident enough to speak.

"I have to," I say, feeling the sadness clear to my soul.

"Why?"

"Because, Vance, I can't live off of ten dollars an hour for the rest of my life."

"Go to school in San Jose. I'll help you."

"I can't let you do that." I have no doubt he would, but it's not something I can rely on. "I love you for that, but what happens if you get traded to the Yankees or Mariners? Where do I go, then? I can't follow you around. Or, God forbid, what if you get tired of having me around all the time? We're dating, and dating people break up. What happens to me then?" Tears burn like acid in my throat and eyes.

He cups my face in his hands and his fingers lace in my hair. "I've told you I want you, only you. I need you, Brenna. What more do I have to do or say to prove that to you? I'm not going anywhere. I'm not Joe. I'm not your dad. I'm not the dude in the Volvo."

I touch his chest, my heart bleeding from our circumstances and what this night has turned into. "I have to go back, Vance," I whisper to thwart the crack in my voice. "It's always been the plan."

"Plans change."

"Not for me."

He backs away, separating us, then looks up into my eyes. "Marry me."

CHAPTER THIRTY-SIX

Marry him?

Everything on my face widens, and my heart pitter-patters to an obnoxious hammering we both can hear. Shocked doesn't begin to cover what I am. I'm not even certain if I've heard him correctly, and my flapping mouth without words isn't helping me find out.

"Marry me, Brenna."

He's fucking serious. Well as serious as someone who hadn't planned on proposing could be.

"Vance?" Losing my breath, I shake my head several times, doing next to nothing to get my jammed-up words out.

"You don't have to decide now—"

I cut him off, stopping him before he backs himself into a corner he can't walk out of. "You don't want to marry me," I say with resigned sadness.

"How do you know what I want?"

A pitiful smile forms. "It's only been six months. It's not what you want."

"I love you, Brenna. It doesn't take a lifetime to know that. I'm serious. If security is what you need, let's get married."

I take a step back, and he stares at me as I try and process. "If you really want to marry me, why aren't you on your knee with a ring?"

"I didn't come prepared, but that doesn't mean I don't want to. It means I wasn't expecting to propose this very second."

"You weren't expecting to propose at all." I lower my eyes and then bring them back to his, which haven't faltered. "It's okay. I don't think I'd want to tell our ten kids that proposal story anyway."

"Ten kids?"

"See? You didn't know that about me. That's something dating couples should know about each other before they get engaged."

To his credit, he doesn't skip a beat after my outlandish lie. "Alright, I'm good with ten."

I laugh softly, the amusement not there but the action natural. "Stop. I'm not going to marry you." I want to touch him, but I keep the necessary distance I think we both need. "Marriage isn't the answer."

"Then what is?"

"I don't know, Vance, but marriage still won't ease the separation when you're on the road and I'm in class. And if you think Bristol is a problem now..."

"I don't stand a chance with Bristol if I'm in your life three times a month. And I want you close, Brenna. Not because I can't go two days without sex, but because I genuinely look forward to seeing you. If a goddamned ring is what you need to prove that, then I'll go get one now and do it right."

"You're such a bastard." I skirt past him, running to the front doors once I'm clear of him. I run through the lobby ever mindful that I'm drawing unwanted attention, so I toss a sham smile at the desk clerk and drop a fake excuse. "It's freezing out there." She nods in agreement, and fearing the elevator will take its dear sweet time, I run up the stairs.

"Stop!" Vance grabs hold of my shirt, tugging on the bottom. "Stop! I'm sorry. I'm frustrated. That came out wrong."

Three stairs into my climb, I turn, harden my eyes, and look down at him, bound and determined not to let those soul-crushing blue eyes trap me into compliance. It's hard to dig in with conviction when every fiber in me is begging to be held by him.

"You didn't deserve that." He takes hold of my hand. "My desperation shouldn't cheat you out of a memorable proposal."

Tugging my hand out of his, I bring it to my face, wiping the tears that have fallen in the absence of my self-control. "You are truly fucking dense." I finish my climb, running up the stairs until I get to a room I don't have the key for and now have to wait until Vance arrives to let me in. It's embarrassing, but he doesn't say anything until we're inside and the door closes behind us.

He keeps his distance, his gaze the only thing connecting us. "If I'm so dense, explain it to me, because you're right, I don't get any of it."

I deepen the space between us. "This went all wrong." I cover my face with my hands and lower my head, feeling suddenly very vulnerable. "The car is too much. It really doesn't feel right accepting something that extravagant, and I wouldn't need a ring if I believed for a second you wanted to marry me, but you don't, or you would have had one. That's all I meant."

Looking defeated, he lifts his arms in a surrender-ish pose, like he's giving up. "So, tell me what to do here. I don't want to lose you, Brenna, and I'm going to if you stay in L.A."

Suddenly the room feels too big, and I can't get to him fast enough. I wrap my arms around his waist and he slowly reciprocates, stretching his arms around my shoulders and drawing me hard into his chest. He's cold from the arctic air I forced upon him with our argument, yet sparks between us ignite where my bare flesh touches his. "I don't want to do this. I don't want to fight. I love you. That's all I really know for sure. I'll handle Bristol. I don't know what tomorrow holds, but I have to prepare myself for it all. That means staying in L.A. and finishing what I started before you."

Drawing in a deep breath, he picks up my hand and places it against his chest. I can feel the pounding of his heart and the thrum that is wild at first, then restrained as it descends to an almost normal tempo.

He looks down at me. "Feel that?" he asks, not waiting for a response, and with his hand covering mine he presses harder, so my fingers are pinned tightly between his chest and his hand. "That's for you," he says, eyes pinned to mine. "Don't ever doubt you're enough. My heart doesn't beat like that for anyone else."

CHAPTER THIRTY-SEVEN

Rather than try to salvage what's left of our time away, we head for home early the next morning. The drive back to Milagro Beach is quiet. Vance hasn't said a word, but he's that quiet, introspective type that uses a filter. I, on the other hand, have to ask if he's mad at me, to which he calmly says, "No."

"Are we okay?" I ask, grabbing the hand he hasn't moved from my thigh since hitting the highway.

"We're fine." He looks briefly at me before returning his eyes and his thoughts back to the highway.

I swallow back the questions I really have and opt for the other topic putting weight on my shoulders. "I have to Christmas shop with Bristol tomorrow, but when I'm done, do you want to come over?"

His deep breath precedes doom. I can feel it. I can see that little indent by his ear tick like a heartbeat. We're not fine.

"To save any hassle, I think I'm going to fly home, see my parents for a bit, let you and Bristol have your time."

"For how long?"

"About a week. I'll fly back New Year's Day."

I let his hand go and turn my face toward the passing scenery, which is mostly cars now that we're out of the scenic part of the drive. "I don't have a lot of winter break left, and you want to be gone for a week of it? Nice." I shouldn't be pissed. I know that. He probably has those fun family traditions of opening presents in his pajamas while the Christmas quiche is baking in the oven. How can I be this selfish and still love so fiercely? "I thought you hated the distance, and now you're choosing it?"

"No, actually I thought it would be the easiest on you."

"Easy, how?" I face him, needing to see the explanation as much as hear it. "This is the only time of year when we don't have to share each other with school and baseball, and you want to give up a week. How is that easier?"

"I don't want you to have to choose between me and Bristol for Christmas. I know she doesn't want me there. I also know that if you come to me, she'll make you feel guilty about it."

"I can handle it."

"You don't think I see the fucking toll it takes on you, Brenna? You're stressed right now asking me about it. You're trying to please us both, and it's not working anymore. Take the out, just this once, and spend your holidays with your family like you always have. Concede once so that you can have some peace. You say you don't care about Christmas, but I know better."

Christmas for me isn't filled with usual traditions. It is an obligatory celebration with presents and a choked-down meal. It hasn't held much appeal since we were five and dad brought his girlfriend home to meet his wife. Mom has tried to erase the cruel memory with different tactics over the years, but in the end, the gift of Suzie was too big to forget, and Bristol and I found ourselves in the company of inattentive babysitters while mom found her own company for the holidays.

Vance is right, though. Those damn traditionless holidays eventually morphed into traditions I didn't recognize as such until Bristol was faced with them changing. The thought of Bristol upset over Vance's intrusion into our unconventional celebrations has been weighing on me, but so has the idea of Vance having to spend his holidays dealing with her and her blatantly low opinion of him. I thought I was hiding it well enough that he wouldn't have to do something drastic. I guess not.

"It's fine, Brenna, really," Vance says as I work through his keen observations and wiggle in his blind spot. No matter what he does, I'm going to feel guilt over something, whether it's his concessions to keep the peace between me and Bristol or mine to keep the peace between Bristol and him. He doesn't see that though. "I could use the time with my family anyway. It'll be good." He grabs my hand and kisses it, then uses them both to wipe a tear from my cheek, easing my guilt with his tenderness. "But when I get back, you're all mine. No interruptions. None of Bristol's bullshit. Just you and me. I want one day, that's it."

Two days after a tearful goodbye with Vance, I sneak out of The Seam, where I've spent the last few hours of our traditionless Christmas hanging out with the regulars and a few new stragglers needing a place to spend their holiday. It's a bit sad when you think about it, but then again, if you don't know any better, it's quite fun, and you learn you really don't have it as bad as some.

My mom may not have shown for our Christmas dinner of frozen pizza and hard cider with Uncle Rodney, but she showed for our gift exchange and cherry Pop-Tart breakfast without Joe. She's a lot savvier with her diplomacy than I am and managed to split her time without alienating anyone. If I knew how to do that, I wouldn't be sneaking out to call Vance while Bristol is distracted with Toolbag Carl.

Vance answers my video chat as I'm about to hang up. "Merry Christmas." His usually rare smile is toothy, and he looks like he's dressed for church.

"Merry Christmas!" I beam, hoping to appear like a seven-year-old girl showing off her Santa loot and not a twenty-one-year-old girl hiding her disappointment.

"Are you at The Seam?"

I nod, cursing myself for not finding a backdrop that didn't include a neon Bud Light sign. "Yeah, we're heading home soon." I don't know when exactly, but I've reached my tolerance for drunks and depressing family stories that make mine look like excerpts from the Brady Bunch family album. "How was your Christmas? How's your family?"

He leans forward over his lap, and I can see the warm glow of a house full of lights behind him. "All is good. How 'bout yours?"

I don't know where to start. Pop-Tarts or pizza? Joe or the absence of my mother at dinner? It's a tough one to call when he's probably stuffed to the gills with prime rib and Christmas carols around the family piano. "Well, we didn't kill each other, and my stomach is full."

"Tell me I'm not missing you for nothing. Is Bristol at least happy?"

"Define happy."

"Brenna?" He takes me with him as he steps outside. "Talk to me."

"She's happy. She's just not happy, happy. It's complicated." She's happy about spending time with me alone, but that's about it. She's not happy about being broke, which she mentioned ten times while we shopped for my mom and Uncle Rodney on Christmas Eve. She's still not happy about me and Vance or Mom and Joe or the pact she swears I'm not honoring, and if we're laying it all out there, she hates Uncle Rodney's relationship with Vance too. Bristol has diverse unhappiness, and no one, not even me, seems capable of changing that with any sort of permanence. "A lot has changed for her in a short time. She's still adjusting to not being number one all the time."

"What has honestly changed for her, Brenna? What of any major significance, anyway?"

It's an obvious answer to me, but to outsiders who don't know our tight bond and the family dynamics that forged it, it probably isn't so easy to spot. "It may not seem like much to you, but we made a pact when we were ten not to let boys come between us. You're a boy, in case you didn't know. It's never really been tested until now, and she's never had to share me before. I'm the one constant in her life. We live together, sleep together, work together, play together. The longest we've been apart was the fifteen minutes between our births, until you." The fifteen minutes is an exaggeration, the pact is not. I need him to understand that Bristol's seeming craziness maybe isn't crazy at all. "It's going to take time for her to get used to the idea of it not just being her and me against the world anymore."

Vance is obnoxiously silent. He's probably thinking he hasn't noticed a difference in her standing where I'm concerned. She still gets her way with me, today is a testament to that, so in his mind, the change to her life is probably negligible. I can't stand the dead air, so I continue trying to defend Bristol.

"We're at odds for the first time ever, and we're trying to get through it the best we can." I think he can hear how torn I am, and he finally has mercy on me.

"Look, I don't want to ruin our time talking about Bristol or making you feel worse. I love you, Brenna. I hate that I've made this hard for you."

"I'd rather it be you than someone else. I just have to get through New Year's, and then I have you all to myself."

"Actually, you have to get through tonight. I changed my flight and I'll be in tomorrow at seven. I don't want to be anywhere but with you."

After a traffic delay getting to Milagro Beach from the airport, Vance is mine by eleven the next night, and my body is marathon-fatigued by two. I haven't been this tired in a long time, and I see no end in sight as his breath fans over my cool skin sometime after five in the morning, light and then heavy, as he scrapes his teeth across my shoulder.

"It's still dark. What are you doing up?" I whisper. I can barely keep my eyes open, and the faint sound of waves outside his bedroom window lull me back toward sleep. Three hours of sleep isn't enough, but I have to take my time with him when I can get it.

Winter break ends shortly, and I think he's feeling the time crunch more than ever. Since his arrival from the airport, we've shut the world out, and too soon we'll be dealing with schedules and separations again. Right now, Vance is all mine and wanting me, but the pull of sleep seems the bigger temptation. I do my best to wake up, but my eyes flicker closed again.

Vance presses his erection against my hip bone and rolls me from my side to my back, hovering above me with a grin I can barely see through the crack in my lids. I touch his chest with a flat palm and then skim my nails down his skin, stopping when I get to his pelvis. "Again?" I may ask like it's a chore, but my body is already responding.

"Mm hmm," he moans into my neck, coating me with kisses and swipes of his tongue at the base of my throat. That tongue, most recently at my hot spot, now taunts and caresses me awake.

I wrap my legs around his hips, eyes still closed, mouth smiling. "You are going to kill me." I run my fingers up his side delicately to pull goose bumps from his skin.

A nip of his teeth on my bottom lip sparks something between my legs, and I can't imagine sleep any longer. "Are you complaining?" he asks against my mouth.

"Uh-uh." My response is uttered in conjunction with my hands reaching his ass. I squeeze, pushing him against me. He rubs his erection right where I need and soaks up my soft moan into his mouth. I roll my hips.

"If you won't marry me and you won't move in with me, I have to take care of you this way." Shifting his hips to stroke himself over my pulse, he sucks a nipple into his mouth, nipping enough to make me groan and buck beneath him.

I arch my back, pressing my chest toward him. "Then stop stalling."

He thrusts hard, entering me in one seamless motion and I groan, bucking to build off his momentum and my close proximity to orgasm. Too soon, I fall over the edge, panting but still aching. Groaning, Vance flips me over, enters me again, and moves until I can no longer tighten around him.

"Ah, fuck," he growls, picking up his pace. "One more. I want to hear you."

Not one to deny him, I lift my face as his fingers roll my sensitive clit. I arch my back, and his name escapes on the tail end of another plummet, seconds before I go limp. He grips my hips, the only thing in the air now, and he finally finds his own release. Spent, he collapses over me, taking me with him as he drops to his side to lay beside me. Spooning me, he kisses my shoulder, and I melt with ease into his sweat-slicked chest. Draped in his warmth, with a cool taste of fresh air trickling in through the window and a feeling of all-around contentment, I drift off.

"Brenna?"

"Hmm?" I mumble through a closed mouth that hasn't even begun to drool yet. There is no way I can keep up with him and function for my afternoon with my mother if he's going to wake me every fifteen minutes for extracurricular activities. How am I going to survive more than a week apart from him if this is how we come back together?

Vance hands me my phone as he climbs out of bed. "Answer your phone. Your mom is calling."

My eyes peel apart, and the sun blanketing the entire room makes me question the time of day. I can't sleep through wind chimes, but I've managed to sleep through my outdated ring tone and the rising sun? I bitch under my breath and answer my phone as Vance steps into the bathroom to shower.

"Hello."

"Brenna?"

"Yeah, it's me. What's up?"

"I was wondering if you could meet me for lunch a bit earlier. I have something I want to talk to you and Bristol about, and I think we're going to need more time."

CHAPTER THIRTY-EIGHT

I join Bristol at The Seam several hours after mom told us at lunch that she is thinking about moving Joe in and turning our bedroom into his man cave. Rough translation: "You girls are holding my relationship back, and this is the only way I can have what I really want."

It took us both by surprise, but Bristol perhaps a little more so. She sees it as abandonment, not evolution, and despite my mom's protests to the contrary, Bristol shut her down and stormed out. I should have followed her, but my mom wasn't the only one accused of abandoning her for "a pussy prowler."

Bristol is sitting at the bar, an untouched shot of liquor in front of her. Uncle Rodney is wearing one of his parental faces and trying to talk her off a ledge. This isn't how I wanted to spend one of my remaining days in town, but this is where her unhappiness has led me.

"Glad you're here," Uncle Rodney calls out before the door can close behind me. "I've called your mom, and she's on her way. We're resolving this shit today." Today is boldly spoken, like he's not kidding, in case we were wondering.

"There is nothing to resolve. Men have been chosen over me yet again. I know where I stand." The liquor is gone in one slug, and she slams the glass back down.

"I haven't chosen anyone over you." My voice is so firm, it sounds harsh.

"No?" She turns on the stool, facing me as I approach. "What would you call it then?"

"Bristol, we're not ten anymore. You had to know that change would inevitably come with age. What would you do if the roles were reversed and you fell in love? Would you leave him to make me happy? Would you sacrifice your own heart for one more day, a month, a year of appeasing mine?" Tears break past my bravado. "Because that's what you're asking me to do."

"I would," she says, infinitely sure, and I finally understand the impossible situation I'm in. It's been the two of us against the world since we were born, and now I'm asking her to take a step back so I can take on the world with someone else. She'll never see my growth as anything but a threat to her status quo. I don't know how to combat that, short of her having a true love of her own.

Uncle Rodney's sigh is the first indication of my mother's arrival. Bristol and I turn simultaneously, an air of dread already evident in our postures even before we see Mom's miscalculation. As usual, she has completely misread the situation and brought Joe along. She holds his hand as she tries to explain herself.

"I need you girls to see that we're happy. I'm not trying to push you out. I'm trying to move on."

I'm temporarily immobilized while her words penetrate my thick, heartless, sanctimonious ass. For the first time in years, I really look at her, and in this frame of mind, I see a grown woman trying to find the love of her life without taking the opinion of others as gospel. She just told us what I've been trying to say to Bristol about me and Vance. Are Bristol and I holding our mom back because we don't want change?

Holy shit! I'm my mom.

I'm speechless. Bristol, however, is not.

"Don't worry, Mother. I'll move my shit out tonight."

"Bristol!" my mom shouts, surprising us all, including the patrons who didn't know they were going to get three Sloans for the price of two. "I told you so you could prepare, not so you'd move out. We're not changing the room until you graduate. You have a place to live with me as long as you're in college. But sweetheart, you graduate in a little over a year. It'll be here before you know it."

"Got it," Bristol snarks bitterly. She's already turned around and is asking for another shot before I've even closed my mouth.

When I'm finally able to focus on the scene again, Joe stands modestly absolved of his sins at Mom's side, a transition I'm sure he's been hoping for since he grabbed the chick's ass at the beach. Maybe he deserves a second chance, maybe he doesn't, but I've learned today that it's not up to me. While I've been simultaneously criticizing and emulating her, I've missed their progression. Maybe Bristol is right. I've been too caught up in my life to recognize what's happening in anyone else's. Am I so far out of touch that I missed a working reconciliation?

The phone to The Seam rings, which it's done more times since the press found out about Vance than it has in the last five years. Uncle Rodney answers with a polite greeting despite the tension around him

"She is. May I tell her who's calling?" His face whitens as he lifts his eyes to mine. "Brenna, it's Grace something or other with *Candid* magazine. She's wanting a comment on Camille?"

"Camille?" I question what I think is his mistake until I grab the phone and it's made clear that Uncle Rodney didn't have a brain fart.

"Ms. Sloan, Grace Arlington with *Candid* magazine. I was wondering if you'd like to comment on the claim that Amber Dietrich, the stripper Van has been reported to be dating is actually his sister, Camille Hatfield?" The questions continue in a blur of vomited words, none computing, while my mind reels that they know about Camille. "Were you aware of this? How long have you known Amber Dietrich's true identity?"

The floor is threatening to meet my face as realization dawns, and I have to grab the lip of the bar to stay on my feet. "H-how did you find this out?"

"So, it's true? You did know? Do you have something you'd like to add?"

"How?" I ask again. "Who?"

"*Candid*'s sources are confidential, Ms. Sloan. Will you be adding a comment?"

I hang up without answering. The phone immediately rings again, prompting me to pick it up and slam it back down again. It rings another five times before Uncle Rodney pulls it from the wall.

And I thought my mom's news and Bristol's reaction would be the worst part of my day. I'm stunned, shaken to my core, and ready to accept any and all handouts for stability when Joe departs to smoke a cigarette he's already jammed into his mouth, and Bristol's phone rings, drawing everyone's attention away from me.

She looks at her phone and then at me before silencing it and putting it in her back pocket with a look of anguish I'm not sure is over the confrontation with me and my mom.

"Who was it?" I ask, because Bristol, like me, doesn't get a lot of calls from anyone other than the people in the room with us. I'm hoping it's a coincidence and not an answer to one of my questions.

"Telemarketer."

I release a breath, ready to explain so they don't find out about Camille the way the rest of world is about to.

With three sets of eyes back on me, I fight for composure so I can alleviate their curiosity and get to Vance. "*Candid* is about to—"

Bristol's phone rings again, and this time she silences it without looking and encourages me with a gesture of her hand to keep going. Yet another call follows that one, and her face loses some of its color.

"Who is it?" I ask again.

"Telemarketer."

"Bullshit," I accuse, advancing on her with shaking legs that make me look more like Bambi than a confident girl putting two and two together. "Give me your phone."

"No." She keeps a firm grip on her phone as I grab for it and fail to come away with it.

"Is it *Candid*? Are you their source?"

Uncle Rodney, beet red and sweating, steps between us, a hand on each of us. "Girls!" he admonishes, and usually it's enough to draw us back, but not this day. Not for me.

"Give me your phone or—"

"Or what?" she yells, stumbling off the stool and backward to get away from me.

"Or I'll assume it's *Candid* and cut you out of my life for good."

"Brenna! Don't threaten things like that." My mom's two cents would have been better spent after finding out who in this conversation is in the wrong.

"Unless you're picking sides, stay out of it!" I yell, with none of the reserved calm I typically use with her. I turn my attention back to Bristol. "It was you, wasn't it?" I don't want to believe it. I can't. "You pinky promised." The last sentence is more for me than her as the gravity of what she's done hits me.

"Brenna, those are serious allegations. Stop and think." Again, my mom's advice is unwelcome.

Bristol's phone, vulnerable in her shaking hand, hits the floor and I lunge, coming up with it after she practically tackles me on top of it. With one hand I keep her at an arm's length while the other fumbles with her phone.

"It's going to look bad," she says, pulling back with rare resignation after I slap at her. "I swear to God and on every oath, promise, and pinky swear we've ever had, it wasn't me."

With my jaw clenched, I enter her password and check her missed calls. The last several calls are from the same number. We both know whose it is before I call it back.

"Grace Arlington."

My world peels away. The foundation that has supported me for twenty-one-and-a-half years crumbles beneath me as Grace Arlington of *Candid* continues speaking as if my world weren't shattering.

"Are you there? Bristol?"

I throw the phone at my traitorous sister, who catches it in two hands against her chest while Grace is still chatting away. Tears have slowly begun to descend in thick streaks down her cheeks, and I can no longer see the other half of me.

"Did you even once think about your promise to me, or just about what was best for you?"

"It wasn't me! I kept my promise to you. Even though I wanted to break it a hundred times, I didn't." She's desperate, but red blotches on her skin have yet to bloom, leaving the smallest room for doubt.

I watch her closely knowing her body will give something away in time even if her answers won't. She's a die-before-you-break kind of person, but she's not infallible, and lying straight to my face isn't easy for her. "I don't believe you!" I scream, feeling every raw wound as my world breaks open.

"I don't know how to change that if my word isn't enough. I'll pinky swear it."

"After everything you've pulled, your promises don't mean shit anymore. Even if you were telling me the truth, I still wouldn't believe you." Tears stream down my cheeks, and I choke out a sob that sears my throat. "I'm done. This is where you finally pay for your choices, and I finally get to make my own." On one exhaled breath, I cement my decision and crush the only relationship I was certain I'd have through eternity. Headstrong, but fighting collapse, I look around at a room full of people and feel more alone than I have at any point in my life.

"We have a pact! No boys can come between us. You swore it!" Bristol screams at me in one last ditch effort to control me. "You fucking swore it!"

I feel every word as it builds in my chest, exaggerating every thump of my heartbeat. "A boy isn't coming between us. You are!"

"Brenna, step outside with me." Uncle Rodney grabs my arm, ushering me toward the door without my consent. I shake his grip loose, pinning him with a look he doesn't deserve.

"Don't." It's barely a decipherable whisper, and I feel guilt immediately. "You can't fix this."

He nods once, eyes glistening with unshed tears, and I gasp on a sob I catch in the side of my clenched fist. He'll never know the depth to which his tears are gutting me or just how much his support means to me.

Bristol sobs, squatting down to hold her head between both hands, crying her innocence into her chest. Anything I had left dissipates. I'm a shell. I'm a fucking wreck and ten seconds away from losing it when my mom grabs hold of my arm, her grip strong, hurtful.

"Not so fast, Missy."

My eyes full of tears meet the anger in hers.

"You don't get to walk out. You both made mistakes—her on the pinky swear, you on the pact. You were children. For God's sake let it go."

I yank my arm free, eyes cold, tears temporarily dried while I heave anger and hurt. "Congratulations! You just picked a side." I brush past her, our shoulders crashing, the heat of my anger showing no boundaries.

Outside I gasp for air, my entire torso heaving with my breaths as I hastily fill and empty my lungs.

"Calm down. Slow breaths." Uncle Rodney's soft voice soothes me enough to ward off hyperventilation.

When I can focus, I look up, finding more concern than judgment in his eyes. His authority, tender but commanding, doesn't lord over me, but I know it expects accountability.

"You have other options, Brenna. Are you sure you want to leave it like this?"

Tears resurface, but they can't drown out the bitterness in my voice. "She swore an oath, Uncle Rodney. She promised to keep his secret."

He sighs, tilts his head ever so gently to the sympathetic side of his right shoulder and speaks softly. "So did you, love."

I swallow hard as realization floods my brain like the mother of all tsunamis. Waves of guilt crash into me along with the debris of my own duplicity. She would never have had the ammo had I not given it to her. Had I kept my promise to Vance not to tell anyone, we wouldn't be here. Uncle Rodney's right. The blame lands on me and me alone. Bristol betrayed me, but I betrayed Vance.

"I don't think she would have done it without something very powerful driving her, and I think you need to know more before you do something you can't take back."

Nothing he says matters. There is no justifying what either of us has done. Another swallow knots in my throat and my stomach threatens eruption. I swallow again, and the next time I do, I'm racing to the planter beside Ocean Avenue to relieve my stomach of its contents. I heave, the action doing nothing to stop the reels of footage playing in my mind of all the reasons Bristol would have for betraying me. Without my blind faith in her, I have no insulation from her underhanded tactics. Unwavering confidence in her has protected me for many years, and now that it's gone, all I see is selfish Bristol concerned with what she might lose.

Uncle Rodney touches my back, offering me the bar towel from his shoulder to wipe my mouth. I look up at him with my eyes full of tears and my heart breaking for all that comes next. "I have to tell him."

CHAPTER THIRTY-NINE

I walk the blocks between The Seam and Vance's beach house on autopilot. After tripping over nothing twice, ignoring a dog walker who called me a bitch when I didn't respond to her hello, and pacing in front of Vance's gate for ten minutes, I finally punch in the code to open it.

Standing on the front step, I stare at the white door and the glass that borders both sides of it. What I wouldn't give to be in his bed right now debating sleep over sex again.

Taking a deep breath, laden with indecision and guilt, I knock, wait, and then knock again as the door jerks open and Vance is on the other side of the threshold, phone to his ear talking angrily as he waves me in.

"NO!" he barks. "I'm not going to let them say that about her and not defend her." Vance shoves the door closed, and it slams, rattling a picture hanging on the wall.

"Stop trying to manage me and find out who they have as a source. That's it. I'll handle me. You handle that." Together, we walk up the steps, him slightly ahead and continuing to rant into his phone. He stops at the top of the stairs where living room connects with kitchen, and I stop short of that, facing the glass doors to the deck. "I know what I pay you for. And now I'm paying you to find me a name, not manage my reactions. Chip, I need to know if it was Eric."

Hearing his brother's name, my heart drops into my stomach. Any thought of not saying a word about mine and Bristol's involvement just slipped away, not that it was ever really an option.

"It's him. He spoke to *Candid* just like he did the last two times . . . To express how certain I am, Chip, stop all payments going to his rent and therapy."

I grab Vance's forearm, shaking my head vehemently, and the look he gives me turns my blood cold.

Staring at me, he speaks into his phone. "I'm gonna have to call you back."

My body nearly collapses under the weight of my knowledge and what I now have to do to save his brother.

"Brenna?"

I look up to find Vance, head tilted to the side, staring at me through narrowed eyes. His brow, clenched into tight white lines, creases deeper. My stomach rolls with that sick, sinking feeling you get when you know you've done something wrong and you must now atone for it.

"It wasn't Eric," I say softly, shaking my head a few times for emphasis.

The tilt of Vance's head deepens. "How would you know?"

I stare straight ahead at him, but I can't speak. My words are trapped behind my ingrained loyalty to Bristol and the natural instinct to protect her. He is everything I've ever wanted, but she is everything I've ever needed. He is the balance I've longed for, and she is the air I breathe. How am I supposed to choose?

"Brenna?" His tone hovers on the edge of sharp. His eyes plead with me, and then I see the turn. I see the click of the switch when it hits him. I see the pain as it hits his eyes and bleeds his face of color. I see when realization strikes, and he no longer has a buffer. "You?"

My time has run out. I have to decide between my heart and my lungs. Vance or Bristol. One breath. Just one. That's all it takes to get a single nod out.

"No. Tell me it wasn't you."

I'm guilty. Maybe not for *Candid*, but I'm still guilty. I'm at a pivotal crossroads. I can do what I've always done and protect Bristol, taking the blame for it all in hopes that he'll forgive me, since I know he'll never forgive her. Tears blanket my cheeks, my heart breaking beneath them. And I realize that more than anything, Vance deserves the truth, and I would never be able to live with the weight of a lie.

"It was Bristol." It's the first time I've ever actively incriminated her. It's the first time I haven't taken the blame for her. My stomach lurches with my betrayal. None of this feels right. Not one damn thing. Not the truth. Not the lie I wish I could give. Not one damn thing. "But I'm the one who told her. I didn't know she'd . . . I didn't know she'd run to *Candid*."

He's red like Uncle Rodney, a sign I've always feared to mean Uncle Rodney was having another heart attack, but on Vance, it's pure anger, a sign of his blood boiling close to the surface. "How could you not fucking know?" he yells, pacing with no clear destination. "When has Bristol ever done anything that didn't benefit Bristol? Keeping that secret didn't fucking benefit her, Brenna. She has school to pay for. What pays more? Secrets or loyalty?"

"I didn't know. It wasn't—"

"How much?" he asks, an eerie calm in his delivery.

"How much?" I don't know what he's asking me.

Vance's phone connects with the wall, and I jump, cowering behind my raised shoulders as it shatters into parts and glass. "Yeah, how fucking much was she paid?"

"I—I—nothing, I don't think. I d-don't know."

"Oh, there was payment, Brenna. You're fucking naive if you think there wasn't. It all has a price, and school isn't cheap." His fingers dig into the back of his neck as he turns away from me, facing the kitchen.

Crying, I try to explain, but how do I explain what I don't know for sure? I never once considered why she did it, only that she had. "I didn't—"

He spins, a full-bodied twist driven by his anger. "*You* fucking did!"

"Vance, I—"

"Save it, Brenna. Save it for someone who gives a shit about your excuses. You knew when you told her that you were divulging something not yours to divulge. You put my family at risk for what? To maintain a bond only one of you fucking cares about? Some stupid fucking pact she only honors when it suits her?"

"Don't," I say, willing to take only so much of his angry observations. "That's not fair."

"You don't get to decide what's fair today."

My voice raised and fueled a bit by his animosity, I try and reason with him. "I walked in on you with a naked girl in your bed and still let you speak. The least you could do is hear me out."

"You walked in on a girl. Not me with her. I didn't do anything wrong. That's the difference here, Brenna. You may not have gone to *Candid* with the story, but you're every bit as responsible as Bristol for them having it."

"I swear to you, this isn't like Bristol. I don't know why—"

"Stop fucking defending her!" he yells, veins popping in his neck like roots beneath a tree. "Don't betray me twice by trying to justify it."

"Pl-Please don't say that. I made a mistake." Close to sobbing, my chest heaves, sputters, as I strive futilely for a seamless breath. This isn't how I pictured things going. This isn't how I worked things out in my head. "Va-ance . . ." I manage his name, but nothing comes after it except my hand that reaches for him. He shirks it, pulling away so callously, I feel his contempt like a cloak of thorns.

"Don't, Brenna," he says, eyes cold, my name spoken like a curse on his tongue.

"I—I . . ." I catch a breath, hold it for precious seconds and continue. "I—I didn't know she'd tell. I trusted her."

"And I trusted youuuuu!" he yells, extending the last word for emphasis.

"Y-you have to know I love-love you."

He laughs bitterly, his expression unchanged. "No, Brenna, love doesn't look like this." Spinning, he grabs his wallet from the top of the breakfast bar. He opens it, peers inside a pocket, and retrieves something. He turns, jaw set hard, body precise in its movement as he walks toward me. He lifts his hand, index finger pointed at me, and on the tip of it is a diamond ring. I stare at it, blurry-eyed and sobbing. "This is what love looks like." He flicks it into the air with the upward thrust of his thumb, and the ring flies over my head landing somewhere behind me. His tears fall and he wipes them away angrily, taking with them the last of my composure.

Seeing his pain is the last thing I can take, and the heaves in my chest collapse upon hiccups. I am wrecked, and not for what I've lost, but for what I've cost him with my betrayal.

"Sad. I would rather it had been my own fucking brother than you. What kind of fucked-up is that?" He walks past me toward the stairs we just came up, a purpose to his step, a stubborn set to his shoulders.

"Are—are you . . .? Please, don't!" Everything in me feels broken. I don't know if any of what I wanted to say translated, but he pauses before hitting the top step and I look over my shoulder at him, hopeful that his pause means something good for me. "Please, don't go." I hear my mom's voice in my plea. I hear all the times she ever begged a man to stay with her, and I hear the ghost of myself berating her weakness and judging her choices. It's now, as I'm about to lose Vance and a piece of me he'll own forever, that I finally get it. I finally understand her, and while I may have viewed it as weakness before, now I see it as self-preservation.

He doesn't move. He doesn't turn to look back at me. He stands there, shoulders rigid, head laid back on them, hands clenched at his sides. "If you're looking for resolution, Brenna, this is it. Don't be here when I get back." His voice cracks on the last word before I collapse over myself and he runs down the stairs.

I hear his exit as something else shatters against the wall. Pieces scatter and then settle with a finality I feel to the core. I'm on my knees, collapsed over my legs, sobbing into the cold tile. It's here, lying on the floor, that I realize my mistake. I know now what I didn't calculate correctly. Vance, having been betrayed by his brother before and a girlfriend before that, demands loyalty above all else. He lives in a world where it's required. The *LOYALTY* tattoo down his right side isn't just a word, it's a reminder. He was never going to forgive me no matter what I said. No matter my pleas, I failed him. For him, forgiveness was never an option.

CHAPTER FORTY

M y nerves kick in double-time the second I walk through the glass doors of *Jock* magazine's L.A. headquarters with an idea, a prayer, and a hope. I thought calling Camille to apologize and ask for permission to give a more enlightened rundown of her profession was hard. Entering here may be harder. Encased in tinted glass, the lobby is open and inviting. The scent of freshly brewed coffee is the second thing I notice, and off to the left, I see a barista. I am small-town U.S.A. if I think that's the coolest thing since online pizza orders.

Pausing between the front doors and the sleek, granite desk in front of me, I waver on my decision to move forward. I haven't committed to anything yet. I can bail and never look back, but if I do, *Candid* will have the final word on Camille.

Two days ago, Camille's story headlined *Candid* magazine, and their depiction of her was harsh, inaccurate, downright cruel, and not at all about the Camille I've come to know. I would never want her son to read that bullshit someday and ever question his mother's character.

I take a deep breath before checking in at the desk, and five minutes later the blonde behind it instructs me to head up to the eleventh floor via the bank of elevators to my left. When the doors on the eleventh-floor slide open, I'm greeted by another woman who leads me to an office down several corridors. I wait there another five minutes, sweaty palms pressed to my thighs, for Katherine Symons, head of *Jock* magazine's editorial staff.

"Good morning," she says, entering the room. Rather than sit in the high-backed chair behind her desk, she parks her ass on the edge of the desk itself. She is in her mid-forties but looks timeless with her red hair in a French twist that ends below the nape of her neck. I've heard she's shrewd and without compromise, so I wonder if I'm about to be eaten for lunch.

"Well, Miss Sloan." She looks at me, her deep green eyes roaming intimidatingly over my business attire. "I don't have a lot of time, and you're low on my priority list. You're only here because Lena thinks you have something with potential." She shimmies a little, parking more of her ass on the desk. "I've reviewed your pitch on Camille Hatfield's profession, and I've discussed it with a number of the staff here who, unlike me, don't think it's a terrible idea." She grabs a folder off her desk, opens it and reads from one of the papers inside. "They seem to think you're more than just a pretty face with an ax to grind." She lifts her eyes to mine. "That remains to be seen. Furthermore, I don't necessarily think stripping is a sport. Forgive me for still thinking it's trashy and just barely on the upside of prostitution. Convince me and we have a deal. Don't, and Miss Hatfield will have to be content with *Candid*'s trash piece."

Unsure how to respond, I shift uncomfortably and wait for her to continue.

"I will commit Nancy to the Hatfield piece, and if I'm not convinced there is more to stripping than a pole and glitter, I'm trashing it. Are we clear?"

I nod silently, knowing Camille's strict commitment to the gym, her diet, and her dance rehearsals are enough to convince anyone, even Katherine Symons, that Camille is indeed an athlete.

"I can't proceed without doing my due diligence in vetting this. I'm meeting with both Hatfields shortly. I don't suppose you'd want to stay for that?"

I shake my head. I'm sure that's the last thing they'd want, and I don't think they need any more reminders of my connection to the story. "Only if it's required."

Her lips pinch, and she stares at me for a second past comfortable and then shakes her head. "No, it's not required. How can I reach you? I'm sure there will be some questions, and I don't want to have to hunt you down."

I give her my cell number, which she writes on the outside of the file she's holding.

"What hours can you be reached? Lena said you're attending school."

I don't tell her I've taken a month-long leave of absence from school to get my shit together. I also leave out that I'm subsisting on some booked freelance work that's about to run out, sleeping on Tori's floor, and doing everything I can just to keep upright. A simple, "I'm flexible," appeases her perfectly, and I'm free of having to admit I'm a loser.

She pushes to her feet, walks past me, and opens the door. "Miss Sloan?"

I stand, taking her gesture as my clue to vacate.

"Have you thought of a cover title? It is, after all, our signature."

I smile on my way out, grinning like I've got the right answer. "Jockeying for Pole Position, or Jock, Lock, and Drop it." Profoundly certain she'll love them, I smile.

"Clever." She offers a ghost of a smile, and I watch her closely, looking for anything that might suggest warmth. "If you're not trying to destroy her, you may just save her."

I CLEAR THE LOBBY, FEELING CONFIDENT I'VE PAVED A PATH TO CLEAR Camille's name. It won't erase what Bristol and I did, but if the article comes out half as good as it is in my head, Camille will have her reputation back, and *Jock* will have its newest cover model.

The door to the lobby swings open and I see Chip Pervis, Vance's manager, holding it open for Camille. By the look on his face, he's as unhappy to see me as I am him. "Ohh!" He stops, eyeing me as I push open my side of the double doors without making eye contact. "Hey, Brenna. Makin' the rounds I see."

Camille backhands him in the gut at the same time I glare, mortified by his insinuation that I'm selling secrets to more than one magazine.

"Hi, Brenna." Camille's polite greeting is more than I deserve but short of friendly. Her gentle demeanor is like a salve on dry skin. Chip, on the other hand, is brittle, but I've never been in his good graces and now never will be. Not that I give a shit. I don't bother with a fake smile. He's not worth the sin of being two-faced, and Camille has already transitioned inside, choosing not to witness the spontaneous reunion between me and her brother, whom I now see approaching the door behind them. I shift my disgruntled gaze from Chip to Vance.

He's gorgeous in a pair of loose denim jeans, a casual T-shirt, and a pair of mirrored aviators that hide any reaction to seeing me he might have let slip. It's not his good looks that catch my attention, though, but rather the sight of his right hand hanging at his side with white medical tape wrapped around his ring and pinky fingers.

Stepping further out into the L.A. air, I let the door go without thought. "Wha-what happened?"

Vance opens his mouth, appears to think twice about whatever is on the tip of his tongue, and lifts his sunglasses to look at me. "Broke some drywall."

His response is so clipped, I almost flinch, but manage to keep my emotions in check, aside from the hammering of my heart. I haven't seen him since that awful day at his house, and my heart doesn't acknowledge the rift that has come between us. It beats like it did the night he sat beside me at the Lookout. It beats like it did with our first kiss and every intimate moment after. "Are you going to be okay? What about pitching?"

Beneath a knitted brow, cold blue eyes land on my despair. They used to look at me like I was human perfection, or so I'm coming to realize as I look into the harsh disconnect in them now. I never had enough faith in his words, and definitely not enough in myself to ever feel worthy of them. I was constantly looking for fault or an opening to be disappointed. I never once believed we'd get out of this together. No matter what he said or did to convince me other-wise, I always expected him to leave or that Bristol would push him away.

"I'll be fine." His reply, stripped of elaboration, is short and lacking what I need.

It's sixty degrees outside, but my armpits and underboobs sweat like I'm in a summer desert as I square my shoulders and ask again. "S-so you can still pitch?" I stumble through the question, terrified of the response and sinking by the second beneath the storm of emotion in his eyes.

By some miracle, his gaze softens, and for a flicker of a second, I feel hope, which for me is usually fleeting, because hope precedes disappointment. "I'm going to be out about five weeks. Should only affect the first few weeks of spring training."

My guilt at possibly being the catalyst for his injury lifts a frac-tion. "That's good."

He nods several times, a clear indicator he's got nothing to add, but Chip doesn't hesitate to fill our space with his authoritative presence.

"Thanks to Ms. Sloan here, we've got an appointment, Van. Let's go." Chip's interruption riles the tiny hairs on the back of my neck, and it's a fight to contain my irritation. In a world where I wasn't trying to get Vance to see a better me, I'd tell Chip where to stick his appointment, but I'm at the mercy of my mistakes.

"Be there in a minute." Vance's severe tone is punctuated by a side glance he only sets on Chip long enough to make his point clearer. Trepidation again blends with hope. Vance doesn't do anything he doesn't want to.

Chip's teeth grind behind his thin lips. He's not a bad looking man, if you like intense, high-energy assholes, but stir his wrath even a little, and he morphs into a troll. A silent exchange ensues between them, and Chip caves first, backing away with a single nod to wait a few paces to the left.

I'm not sure what to do with the space Chip's absence allows us, and Vance's stiff back and squared shoulders don't offer advice. Uncle Rodney used to tell me I'd be formidable if I allowed myself to soar beneath the power of my own wings and quit using Bristol's strength to get me off the ground. Even though I've started to use them, my wings are new. I'm not sure of their capabilities yet, and I'm definitely not sure if they'll carry me through a pleading session.

"I need to get going," he says, his voice softer with me than it was with Chip. He takes a step toward Chip, who is lurking beside a pillar, ear pressed into his cell phone.

"Can we meet later? For coffee? I'd even choke down a protein shake if you'd agree."

I don't quite get a smile, but the twitch of his upper lip strengthens my confidence. My newfound wings are itching to soar.

"Nothing has changed for me, Brenna."

"I don't want you to hate me."

He releases a sigh, looks up reluctantly at first, and then square at me. "I don't hate you."

I swallow back the tears starting to form. I didn't cut ties with all the people who matter to me just to beg someone I don't matter to. "But you don't love me anymore. Is that it?"

"Loving you isn't the problem. Trusting you is. I can't be with someone I don't trust."

"I told Bristol. I didn't tell *Candid*. Please don't punish me for putting my trust in someone I've trusted since birth."

"It's beyond that, Brenna. I need one hundred percent loyalty, and I'll never have that with you. Bristol will always come first, and I can't live with being second."

"You're not."

"I am!" His voice rises, and then, as if he's trying to maintain some business-like decorum, he clamps his mouth shut, looks away, and then returns his eyes to mine after control is achieved. "We're all here today because you had to spin what Bristol spewed. Where the fuck is she today? You'll always choose her, Brenna, and I'll never ask you not to. That's our problem."

I step closer to him, feeling my nerves in every pore as I reach for his shirt, and when he remains solid, I take one more step to stand toe to toe with him. Looking up, my tears spill over and I don't bother with stopping them. "Ask me."

With his teeth ground together, he replies, "Ask you what?"

"Ask me to stay, Vance. You did it once. Ask me again." His non-response and lowered eyes cast a shadow over the hope I relied upon to get me to this place. I've grown. I've matured over horrible circumstances, and that growth won't allow me to ask again. If I've learned anything observing my mom all these years, it's that you can't force something that isn't there. The end result will never be what you wanted anyway. I press my forehead into his chest, my hand still gripping his shirt, my nose grasping for his familiar scent. I feel his intake of breath and the release that reveals his decision.

"You can't, can you?" I squeeze my eyes shut, forcing tears out onto his shirt before he grabs hold of my upper arm to enforce some distance between us. Whatever I've felt over the last few weeks in the lingering silence between me and Bristol, the unreturned phone calls from my mother, and reading about my breakup with Vance in the tabloids, I never once thought any of it was permanent. Until now.

"I want to." His whisper cracks, emotion breaking the soft sound of his voice. "But I can't."

"Van?"

Chip's deep voice cancels out everything. The euphoria of hearing "I want to" and the crush of hearing "I can't" crumble together upon hearing him call for Vance. I look up, pulling away from Vance to wipe at my cheeks.

"We've got to get in there if you plan on them taking you seriously."

I hang my head, regret taking the place of my hope.

"I've got to go. I'm sorry," he says softly.

New tears sting, but I derail them at their source, focusing on all the things my mom did wrong so that I don't falter in the footprints she's left for me. "Don't be sorry. Just be sure."

"I'm not sure of anything anymore, Brenna."

"Van!" More forceful now, Chip's impatient call is a command and not a request.

He looks away from me, seeming to choke up as he's forced to make a permanent decision he wasn't prepared to make today. Seeing any flicker of emotion other than anger cross his features is encouraging. His jaw ticks beside his ear; a sigh precedes his reply. "Dammit, Brenna—"

On tiptoes and with a forceful tug of his shirt, I steal his next word with a kiss pressed hard against his unforgiving lips. With the one-sided show of affection, my embarrassment flares, but he needs more than words, and I need validation I'm not wrong. Finally, I feel his uninjured hand cup my cheek as he gives in and kisses me back.

Hope once again knocks.

Growling, he forces me away, a hand on my wrist to part us. "I want you, Brenna. I've never made that a secret. But your loyalties lie elsewhere, and my expectations haven't changed."

"You don't know anything about my loyalties. You have one shitty example. I trusted the wrong person, Vance. That doesn't make me disloyal. I didn't set out to hurt you or your family, and I certainly haven't gained anything by what happened. That's the difference between me and the others who've hurt you."

"I don't see a difference. Whether you set out to betray me or not is irrelevant. You did, and I can't see past that."

"What do I have to do, Vance? How can I prove to you that I made a bad call, not a calculated move?"

He sighs, body moving like he's itching to bolt. "You act like the difference between the two matters. The degree of malice isn't the problem." He looks around, exhales a breath, and points his softening blue eyes at me. "I can't do this, Brenna. I've got to get in there so I can see if there is anything left to salvage for Camille."

Finally, pride knees me in the balls, and I square my shoulders. If my past were different and I hadn't witnessed my mom beg too many men to stay in our lives, I'd give him more time, but it's not, so I don't. Spine rigid, I adopt a new stance, harden my features, and summon enough courage to walk away. There is no point in prolonging the inevitable, no matter how hard it is to accept, and I pivot on trembling ankles in shoes I can barely walk in on a confident day.

This is by far the hardest walk I've ever taken alone. I wish I'd seen this moment more clearly back when the option to choose him was still mine. There have been a lot of people in my world who've passed on being in my life, notably my Dad and Colette, but where they left bitterness, Vance leaves a lesson. Loving someone isn't always enough.

EPILOGUE

VANCE

Stay!

It's on the tip of my tongue moving right past all the bullshit I had to say to keep my head. I can taste the relief of the word on my tongue even as it dissipates and dies a slow, agonizing death to save me from an impetuous decision. There's a part of me that wishes she knew. There is an even bigger part of me that's grateful she doesn't. One more plea and she'd have me. She'll always fucking have me.

Sheltered beneath my fear and the stupid promise I made to Chip not to do something impulsive "like taking her back," I bite back the compulsion to stop her as I watch her walk away. I know she's only leaving because I've asked her to. I've never doubted her love. Sometimes her commitment, but never her love. What the fuck am I doing?

The lump I try to swallow before I turn back to Chip sits low in my throat and won't budge despite a number of attempts, so he hears my despair when I finally speak. "Let's go."

"Give it a day," Chip says reassuringly, keeping stride with me, "and you'll be thankful you took my advice."

How many fucking days has it been already? Twelve? Fifteen? All of fucking January? Chip should stick to giving career advice like "don't punch the guy at the bullying benefit" or "keep your mouth shut when they ask you what you think of the rookie pitcher." That's the advice I need from a guy paid to manage my career. Teeth grinding together, I hold the door open and wait on Chip to enter first before responding to him. "I'm not sure you're the right guy to be doling out relationship advice." I don't disguise my distaste for his interference.

He maneuvers past me, eyes expressive as he does so. "I'm the right guy for everything. Had you listened to me months ago, we wouldn't be here and you wouldn't be on the questionable roster. Now's not a good time to be anywhere but out in front. The team picked up Diego Silva, that kid out of Arizona playing for the Hellcats. He's been in the minors less than a year, Van. What's that tell you? Kid's good."

No, it says he wasn't good enough to be drafted straight to the majors, but saying that would incite a riot with Chip, so my opinion remains trapped behind a bigger need to keep the peace.

He continues despite my non-participation. "You can't afford to be injured or have distractions of any kind if you're going to stay on top, and that includes Brenna. Kids like him are gunning for you. And girls like her are going to ruin you."

He acts like I'm thirty-five and not twenty-five. I'm not exactly being fitted for orthotic shoes yet. In baseball, I'm a kid, but because he's been with me for eight years now, he's already trying to hold off my retirement and brand me a perpetual bachelor. "I'm not worried about Diego Silva," I say, too casually for his liking, skipping right over his Brenna insult.

Camille flanks me as the smell of coffee replaces the L.A. exhaust fumes and the entrance doors swoosh closed. She's anxiously awaiting an update she was decent enough not to eavesdrop on. Her soft spot for Brenna tends to be a source of contention when I'm trying so diligently to move on.

"Don't look at me like that," I warn her. Her questioning blue eyes aren't going to get her far today.

"Like I know you made a mistake and I think you're a dumbass? Is that the look I'm giving you?"

"We're late." I avoid her eyes and proceed toward the desk, hoping she'll take the hint and drop it. I don't need Brenna's fan club president barking at me any more than I need the petitioner for her execution telling me to "give it a day."

"It was her sister, Van. Not Brenna. You yourself have been guilty of trusting the wrong people. She's human and therefore prone to mistakes."

"Maybe you should focus on cleaning up your legacy and leave my relationships to me."

"Wow!" Angered, Camille drops off, leaving me to walk to the front desk alone.

At the desk, I speak to the receptionist with aloof indifference, my mood preceding me. While she looks for my appointment, I run a critical gaze over her. I'm not on the market, but I'm curious to know if she can even spark an ounce of my interest. Brenna has been every waking thought I've had for the better half of a year, and I'm wondering now if my dick knows how to respond accordingly to an attractive woman.

She smiles, her painted lips curving up and out in a pleasant enough smile to win just about anyone over—except me. I feel nothing except gratitude that she didn't turn me away for being late.

At the elevators, Camille is conspicuously quiet, her silent treatment annoying as hell but still preferable to Chip's arrogant verbal assault on Brenna's character. He is my Bristol.

"When we get in there, you need to distance yourself from Brenna and her spin doctoring."

"You don't know that it's spin doctoring." Camille departs from her silence to argue with Chip, a pastime she's enjoyed since meeting him. I don't respond, my focus on keeping myself from imploding.

"When you become a publicist, you can argue with me."

"When you become human, I'll take your opinion under advisement."

I scratch my forehead, eyes pinched shut to ward off the mounting headache their arguing feeds. At this point I'd take a fight with Brenna over this shit. At least with Brenna, my heart instead of my head would be challenged.

THE DRIVE FROM L.A. TO SAN JOSE IS FILLED WITH THOUGHTS OF Brenna, and the angry rap music is unable to drive any of them away. I'm tired. I'm angry. I'm so fucking lost, even my driveway is a surprise when I finally pull in a little past dark.

Donning the splint that wraps around everything on my hand but my middle and index finger, I curse its limitations and the pain that ensues as I tighten it. In public, I wear the tape to minimize the gossip. In private, this black contraption limits my movements for as many hours as I can stand it. Whether it's Brenna or my hand, nothing is particularly pleasant to think about these days, but in less than an hour I'll have a better idea of what I'm facing with my hand at least.

Inside the house, despite the efforts I've made to flush Brenna out of my life, she's everywhere, and no number of tossed pictures or broken knick-knacks has mattered in the end. She isn't just in the things I've accumulated, and there is no way to toss the quiet, still the memories, or bleed my heart of her presence. At first my anger ate up a huge portion of her absence, but now it only tides me over a few hours each day.

I toss my keys on the bar and struggle miserably to get my wallet out of my pocket, cussing the splint the entire fucking time it takes to do a menial task that a month ago could have been done without thought.

My phone rings, and dealing with it turns into a production of uncoordinated maneuvers with a hand not used to doing anything but holding a baseball glove. I finally answer with a disgruntled, "Yeah."

"Van, Doctor Klamath. Sorry to bother you so late." He's driving, his deep voice compromised by the inadequacy of hands-free calling.

I have to check my irritation to sound somewhat thankful when I reply. "You're okay. I appreciate you taking the time to review my x-rays on such short notice."

His sigh foretells what I already guessed, and I sit down, leaning forward over my thighs, eyes glued to the floor, exposed fingers on my splinted hand twitching.

"I can fix it, but you're going to be out for at least six weeks, twenty if I can convince you it's for the best and your longevity depends on it."

"Five months?" I question the timeframe, knowing full well my minimal medical expertise comes from the few episodes of *Grey's Anatomy* I watched with Brenna. I sit back against the sofa, slouching into the soft cushions with resigned exasperation. I don't see a lot of choice in his findings. I can't live half in, half out, wondering when the temporary fix will fail. For me, it's all or nothing.

"I can have you back pitching in six weeks. Can't tell you for how long, but your pain threshold will give you an indication. Give me five months, and your shoulder will give out before your hand does."

I've lived my entire life on a baseball field; I can't imagine not spending the rest of it there. I can't lose that and Brenna too. My grandfather would be kicking my ass right now for blowing it all having a temper tantrum over a girl. My thoughts are choppy as they flip through possibilities while I listen to Klamath.

"It's your decision, Van. Think about it tonight, give me an answer in the morning. We can schedule you as early as Friday and have you playing by June. You'll have half a season left, and you'll be able to play it."

I respond without hesitation. "Schedule it," I tell him, biting on my reservations in order to proceed with one of the top orthopedic surgeons in the country. He tells me I'll be hearing from his nurse by midday tomorrow and then ends the call.

A chest-clogging fear I have never in my life felt before overwhelms the confidence I had a minute ago when I made my split-second decision. I wish I had Brenna to bounce this off of. Who am I kidding? I just wish I had Brenna.

After a quick shower, which I used to separate myself from my phone and Brenna's cell number, I put on a pair of gray sweats and condemn myself to Chip's disapproval as I dial Brenna's number anyway.

"Vance?"

Brenna's voice triggers my emotions, and not all are sentimental. I've never loved someone as much as I've despised them, but right now with Brenna, it's pretty equal. To take the next step, I bury some of the animosity beneath the much larger blanket of familiarity. As much as I hate to admit it, I feel calmer. The edge I was walking on widens, and if I knew what the hell to say, I'd be golden.

The End

Read the conclusion to Vance and Brenna's story in *Truth Be Told*, Book 2 in the Jock Star series, **coming February 15, 2022**

Pre-order now: Truth Be Told: Jock Star Book 2

Truth Be Told

Together they sparked a media frenzy. Apart, they'll watch it all burn.

Van Hatfield's baseball empire is imploding.
The hot-headed San Jose Renegades starting pitcher has two choices:
Change his attitude or be traded.
The ultimatum comes on the heels of a scandal, born of a betrayal he can't forgive.
Until one look, one touch, and a chance encounter expose truths he didn't see coming.

Brenna Sloan has moved on but his heart hasn't.
She left a mark he can't erase and time has yet to heal.
Bad blood, broken hearts, and choices they can't take back stand between them.
But from the ashes comes opportunity and another chance to get things right . . .
Until one kiss, one night, and one promise threatens their fragile truce.

When past and present collide, will there be anything left to salvage?

ACKNOWLEDGMENTS

This book should probably be dedicated to Patron. There were a lot of tequila shots consumed during this process. If I counted them all up, I'd have a problem, so we'll just say it was A LOT. I never did any alone, though. It's been close to a ten-year process from conception to formatting. Self-doubt, indecision, and getting out of my comfort zone were my biggest obstacles, but I conquered them. However, I did not conquer them alone.

Many thanks to the following:

My Husband, Ron (aka, Soop), where do I start? Tequila or bourbon? They were equal opportunity stress relievers and milestone markers. Thanks for "cheering" me on, never losing faith, and holding down the fort when I was grumpy, on deadline, or just plain senseless. I couldn't have done it without you. My children, Tiana, Cameron, Chaney, and Brielle, you are incredible humans and my greatest joy. There were days you probably wanted to disown me. Thank you for sticking it out and for putting up with my freak-outs, occasional absences, forgetfulness, indecision, writing on road trips and vacations, and endless inquiries into photos and character names. I hope you know or at least could see I tried to find balance. This book would not be possible without a single one of you. You all sacrificed so much to give me this dream. You were all there when I needed you. Always. I love you.

Jaymes and Finley. You complete us. I love you like my own.

Mom, thank you for allowing me to read romance and always having the faith and belief that I could be a writer, not just a reader.

Thank you for giving me the gift of life and a sense of humor. I wish I had a quarter of your courage and strength. Dad, thank you for teaching me to work hard for the things I want, the true meaning of selflessness, integrity, and the power of God in my life. You are the kindest man I know. I had the best parents and childhood ever! I love you both.

My partners in crime since birth: Ross, Janet, Denise, Nichole, and Steven. Thanks for sharing in the best childhood ever. I am tougher, saner, happier, well-preserved with alcohol, and alive because of you. I wouldn't trade you or the memories for the world. I love you dearly.

Apryl, you thought I could, and I DID! Thank you for never doubting me. You believed in me long before I did. I cannot thank you enough for pushing me forward and having just the right words to keep me moving forward. I am beyond blessed. I Love you to pieces.

Brian and Keri, Samantha and Aaron, the only thing missing is DNA. You are every bit my family.

I Love you.

Grahame, without you, I would not have taken the first step toward publishing. Thank you for your guidance, support, and advice. I asked, and you answered. You are indispensable. Everyone should have their own Grahame.

Shanna, thank you for coming to my rescue, continuously checking on me, and always having that right amount of encouragement to get me through. I am blessed to call you, friend.

Beta Readers: Tiana Campbell, Kayla Zaldivar, Sara Firth, Grahame Claire, Miranda Grant, and Shanna Swenson. Your time, keen eyes, input, advice, and support meant everything. Thank you.

To my early readers, the ones who read when it was crap. Tiana, Apryl, Janet, Denise, Jastine, Shannon, and Kayla. You are saints. Thank you for not laughing at me.

Angela Houle: You made my clumsy words shine. Thank you for

not tossing the first, second, or third draft. You are a miracle worker. I can't imagine going through this process without you.

Rebecca Kimmell and Sarah Kil, thank you for the advice, check-ins and for doing all those little extras to make my first foray into publishing a success.

To all those that shaped, formed, helped, healed, and or bettered me. Thank you from the bottom of my heart.

And last but not least, to my readers, thank you for taking a chance on me. Without you, my words would have no home and my stories no escape. Thank you. Thank you. Thank you.

I hope I haven't forgotten anyone. Obviously, if I have, you know who you are. Please forgive me. Tequila, stress, sleep deprivation, and the beginning stages of lunacy have all played a factor in my disorganization. Numerous people touched this book in one way or another, and I wish I could thank you all properly. Please know that I am forever thankful for your support, input, and belief in me.

Xo, Caterina

ABOUT THE AUTHOR

As a self-proclaimed book nerd, opera singer, and drinking game champion, Caterina spends her time perfecting them all. Of those three things, only one of them is appreciated by her husband and four children, whom she credits for pushing her toward her dream of publishing. Thanks to her mother, who encouraged her love of writing, she has penned 7 full-length novels, one of which remains between the covers of 14 notebooks.

Rumor Has It took six months to write, but four years to get here, due in part to a full-time job, fear, and multiple obligations (some involving drinking games), but mostly life in general.

facebook.com/authorcaterinacampbell
twitter.com/ccampbellbooks
instagram.com/caterina_campbell
bookbub.com/authors/caterina-campbell
amazon.com/~/e/B09K6WJ8H4

Made in the USA
Las Vegas, NV
27 January 2022

42424854R00192